T0278703

SNAPSHOT

SNAPSHOT

KAY COVE

Page & Vine
An Imprint of Meredith Wild LLC

Paperback ISBN: 979-8-9895288-2-0

This one is for every single woman who was told to calm down, stop meddling, take up less space, and be a little quieter...

Here's a bullhorn.

Use it often.

PROLOGUE

Dottie

Three Years Earlier

Miami

The pen is barely in my hand before the arthritis in my wrist angrily protests. Perhaps handwritten letters are a young woman's game. But it's the only way I can keep him close.

My mother used to tell me true love transcends death. But how would she know? She didn't marry her true love. Then again, neither did I.

Anyway, this doesn't feel like love, just pain. The sharp stabbing in my wrist from writing letters he'll never read. The throbbing pressure in my head from trying to piece together broken memories. The constant gnawing ache in my chest, knowing my whole life has been spent regretting one foolish decision.

But the pain is necessary. It reminds me that it was real. So, I keep writing to cling tightly to the hazy memories.

Dear Jacob,

After fifty years, no matter how hard I fight, I find myself losing some of the little details.

That night at the gazebo, I can't remember if we saw stars in the sky or if it was too cloudy? Was my hair loose or braided? Was it cold? I remember you put your coat around me, likely because I was shivering. But it was probably just from the nerves.

Were you nervous, too? Did you have any idea we'd start our family that night?

I remember the bouquet of white daisies you had waiting for me.

Oftentimes, I picture the gazebo decorated in daisies like we planned. Daisies wrapped around all the pillars. Scattered all across the dock. Pinned in my hair. Woven into the bottom of my veil.

All the promises we made still dance in my mind. Along with all the ones we broke.

There were no daisies at my wedding. Harrison's mother suggested them, but I refused.

Daisies were ours. For us. For our daughter.

I still lay a thick bouquet of white daisies on her grave at least once a week. I know you're with her now. Can you ask her if she still likes them? Or if I should stop?

Do you still like them?

Because I picked out a dress for when they finally put me in that casket. It's handsewn lace in the shape of daisies. I know I missed my chance in this lifetime, but if there's any hope of a second chance for us...

I'll be there.

In a white dress.

Waiting for you at the gazebo.

I'm interrupted by a soft knock on my office door. I drop my pen, hastily fold my letter, then cover up the evidence of my tears.

"Come in." I push away from my ivory desk, glowing under the overhead lights I set to low. I like to see the Miami skyline at night. My city is always busy in the evening. The lit-up buildings look like frozen fireworks against the dark sky, reflecting off the still water. When I designed headquarters, I ensured all the executive offices and meeting rooms had this view.

The handle turns, and my grandson's handsome face appears through the crack of the door. "Grandma. Why are you still here? It's late."

Dex is such a worrier. I'm the CEO of Hessler Group. I'm no stranger to late nights at the office. "Come in, Dex. Sit down. I want to talk to you." I point to the sofa in the sitting area, and he begrudgingly obliges.

After grabbing two thick crystal lowballs and the matching decanter full of aged bourbon, I kick off my heels and join Dex in the sitting area of my much-too-large office.

"How did it go today with the settlement?"

I pour us both a generous drink before passing a glass to Dex. He takes it and mutters a soft, "Thank you," but sets it down on a coaster instead of drinking it.

He melts into the sofa, his shoulders slumping as he presses against his temples. "No surprises. It was exactly what we agreed upon."

"Look at me." One little command and his eyes snap to mine obediently. "How are you?"

He shrugs, looking confused, as if my question is unwarranted. "Fine."

"Dex." I hold his stare. "You don't need to placate me. I want your honesty."

He closes his eyes. "I just paid a woman six million dollars to not lie and publicly say I tried to drug and sexually assault her during a dinner date. How do you think I feel?" He lowers his voice to a whisper. "Grandma, after the investigation, they found out she had the waitress spike her champagne...and she actually drank it."

I'm aware of the theatrics women go to get my grandson's attention, but none of us anticipated this. "You have no fault or blame in this."

"I know that, but she roofied herself to try and frame me. Who goes that far? She could've seriously hurt herself, all for a payout. Briar was certain that my reputation is so fragile I would just give in to her demands... And I hate that she was right."

The latest scandal Dex was roped into was cruelty at its most extreme. The woman, Briar, didn't have a court case, not by far. Mainly because Dex was innocent. But also because there was no evidence outside of her baseless accusations. Jail wasn't what he was afraid of. It was the social media shitstorm. The scariest threat of this generation. You don't have to be guilty of anything to be punished by the internet.

"Oh, Dex. I'm sorry."

He exhales, and it comes out like a shudder. Pressing his lips together tightly, he recomposes himself. "Every time this stuff happens, I'm worried about what's coming next. It just keeps getting worse and worse. There's never a day I'm not looking over my shoulder. I'm going to need these women to sign a fucking contract of consent before I feel safe taking my pants off." He checks my expression and hangs his head. "Sorry. You didn't need to know all that."

I tilt my head and give him a smart-ass smile. "Goodness gracious. You're telling me you're not a virgin? Shocking."

"Hilarious," he mutters.

I set my drink down and reach for him across the coffee table. He holds my hands firmly in his, studying my wrinkles, blatant evidence of my age. The reminder wears on me; it means time is running out. Soon, he'll be alone, without me. Without a soul to trust. And I'm running out of time to keep him from making the same mistakes that I did.

I flinch when he turns my hand, the wrong angle making the pain in my wrist flare up. "Ow," I wince.

"Oh shit, Grandma." He loosens his grip. "I'm sorry."

I let out a warm hum as he tenderly squeezes my hand. "Pay it no mind."

"Sensitive today?" he asks. "Do you want me to grab your pain medication?"

I shake my head. "I was writing. I need to feel the pain so I know when I've pushed it too far."

He sets my hands back on the table so gingerly, the way you'd lower a wounded baby bird back into its nest. "Writing who?"

"An old friend."

Staring at my grandson, it's like Jacob's here. Cloudy, hazel eyes. Deep dimples carved against slim cheeks and a strong, square jaw. Thick, dark hair. A shocking likeness. It's good I only have one grandchild. It wouldn't have been fair. Dex would've outshone the rest. He was always destined to be my favorite.

He quirks a brow. "You guys can't call each other, instead? For the sake of your wrist?"

I look away from his face, tearing myself from the beautiful, haunting reminder of my broken heart. I was hurt when I lost my husband, Harrison. I did love him in a way. When my daughter died, she took half my heart. But when Jacob passed, my only true love, he took the rest. I'm not sure what's still feebly beating in my chest, keeping me alive each day. All I know is if I were to lose Dex, the world would go dark. I would have no more business here. My body isn't fighting to keep revenue up and gainshares high. I'm not here to earn more money and secure the Hessler legacy.

I'm only here for this boy in front of me. Right now, he's hurting, and it's my job to fix it.

"Writing letters is a lost art, honey."

"What's that thing you always told me? Anything worthwhile,

you should say it to their face. Right? Letters are for lost apologies."

Don't I know. It's why I write so many.

Ignoring my grandson using my own wisdom against me, I inform him, "I got you an early birthday present."

"We don't do presents," he says, scrunching his face. "Just dinner at Rooster's like usual. I already made the reservation. What's gotten into you?"

I raise my brow, daring him. "I wanted to get you a birthday present, so I did. Or are you in the business of telling your grandma *and boss* what she can and can't do?"

Dex smirks, then shuts his eyes and holds out his hands. "All right, then. Whatever it is, I'm sure I'll love it."

"Good. You're fired."

His eyes are still closed, but his smirk disappears. "Mhmm. Real funny."

"I'm not kidding, Dex. *You're fired.* But not for performance. You're doing a superb job. You're welcome to consider this a long-term sabbatical if you please."

Now his eyes pop open as his jaw drops. "Have you forgotten what birthdays are? Because that's not a present."

"It is."

Shame splatters across his face as he bites the inside of his cheek. "Look, Grandma. What I said before... I didn't mean to sound ungrateful. I'd be an idiot to complain about the privileges I have. I'm lucky to be a Hessler, I know that. And I'm sorry about Briar and all the other bullshit that's been going on for the past year. I need to be smarter. I've been thinking and I'm going to take some time off of dating, period. I'm going to focus on work. When I'm in my thirties, you can just pick a wife for me for all I care."

"Dex. I'm relieving you of your position *temporarily.* You've been working yourself like a dog since freshman year of your undergrad. I'm proud of you. Hessler Group will be waiting when you're ready. But right now, I'm gifting you a break."

"Thank you, but I don't need a break." He rises from his seat, his jaw clenched. "I've been here since six this morning though, and I do need some sleep—"

"Please, *sit*." I raised this child on my own since he was seven years old. At twenty-seven, he still minds me. Once his behind is nestled back in the tufted cream sofa, I soften my eyes.

"Sweet boy, I had no idea what I was signing you up for when I chose this life for you."

He shakes his head. "*Chose*? You didn't choose this life for me."

"Didn't I?" I fold my hands together as a wave of remorse washes over me, threatening to drown me. "When I agreed to become a Hessler, I specifically had your mother, you, and your future children in mind. I thought money would make my family feel safe. I never knew the magnitude of evil that would come from it. And I know you're going through hell now, but I promise you, it gets worse. You think my husband had never been caught up in a scandal or accused of something unsavory? We just became skilled at acting impervious. We tripled our legal and PR teams. Harrison always used to say that if you were rich enough, you could buy bravery, but it's all still a façade."

Dex squints one eye, looking thrown by my response. "It's weird to hear you call him Harrison. Just say, 'Grandpa.'"

I exhale in exasperation. "Dex, listen to me. Eventually, you won't just be grappling with decisions you're currently making. You'll be wrestling with ghosts. Suffocating from decisions that were clearly mistakes in hindsight. It never gets easier. The load never gets lighter. Wealth will always be a malignant tumor, feeding off your soul. Greed grows, want grows, all while you starve what you actually need."

"Being?" His question comes out a gruff whisper.

"Love. But love isn't about pretty girls and the pretty rings they want wrapped around their fingers. Love is about companionship."

"Grandma, I'm not looking for—"

"But," I say, interrupting him, "you can't find the right someone until you find yourself. Do you understand that?"

I'm sure he'd love to roll his eyes—his natural reaction every time we have this conversation. I don't blame him. I'd be wary of love if I were him as well. The women he's met are far from genuine. None of them with family and future on their mind. Their calculating eyes are fixed on black cards, penthouses, and my grandson's bottomless pocket. I sometimes wonder if they even care that he's good-looking. He'd serve the same purpose to them if he looked like a troll under a bridge.

That's my greatest fear. Nobody will see Dex outside of a *thing* to use and possess.

For so long, I was treated like a doll on the shelf. When my husband succumbed to his excessive drinking decades ago, the responsibility fell on me. I went from a doll to a pawn on a chessboard. All I want is for my grandson's life to be more than a game.

"Well, what do you expect me to do? Sit around the estate all day ordering the staff around until it's time to take over the company?" Irritation lines his tone. He's rubbing his hands together so hard they're turning red.

"Well, now for your actual present."

Barefoot, I stand and make my way to my top desk drawer. I pull out an envelope and balance it on my palm, feeling a thousand pounds of layered guilt. I wasn't supposed to look him up. I made my choice long ago. I owe the Hesslers a lot. But you can't force your heart to obey when it comes to love. Loyalty, however, is an entirely separate matter. That's a choice, and now, a part of me feels truly unfaithful.

Dex stares at the envelope as if it were dangerous. No patience for his hesitance, I open the envelope and show him the deed to the dive shop.

"The friend I'm writing... He used to love diving as much as you do. Maybe even more. We lost contact for a very long time. Even when the internet emerged, I couldn't find him. So, I hired a private investigator to look him up. It took a long time. My friend would disappear off the grid for months on end on liveaboards and other various ships, so he was nearly impossible to find. I thought he was lost forever. But I got a surprise report from the PI last week."

"Really?" Genuine interest is painted all over Dex's face. He picks up his drink and takes a small sip of bourbon, seemingly unbothered by the bitter burn. I blinked, and the little boy I raised is all grown now, drinking like a man. "And how's your friend?"

"He passed a few years ago. I was too late. We didn't get to reconnect. But he opened a dive shop in Las Vegas of all places. It looks like it was employee-run as long as possible, but it just recently went up for sale." I balance the deed on Dex's leg. "I bought it for you. You always said if you had the time, you'd like to be a dive instructor, right?"

He stares at the paper but doesn't touch it. "I'm the Director of Operations of the largest cruise ship conglomerate in the world while being groomed to take over as CEO. Time hasn't been on my side."

"Well, I'm putting time on your side. Go have a life all your own while you can, Dex. Make memories. One day, those memories will carry you through the bad days."

"Grandma, I can't leave you by yourself." He grabs the deed, glances it over while shaking his head, then hands it back to me. "I won't."

Refusing to take it, I answer simply, "You have to. You're fired, and now you own a dive shop. *In Las Vegas.*" Crouching down, I kiss his cheek, then his forehead. "I'll expect you at Thanksgiving, Christmas, Easter, and whenever else you're missing home."

His chuckle starts as disbelief, then turns eager. It's as if I can see the acceptance slowly saturate his face. "What about income? Am I just fired, or are you kicking me off the bank accounts, too?"

I smirk. "I just bought you a dive shop. Perhaps sell some flippers."

He scowls and then mutters, "Sassy," under his breath.

Laughing, I ruffle his hair before taking my seat and cradling my drink once more. "How about an allowance from your trust?"

Dex stands to inherit everything once I'm gone. But for now, his trust is allocated at my discretion. Harrison and I both agreed that no teenager or young man needs immediate and total access to his billion-dollar fortune.

"What'd you have in mind?" he asks.

"I think exercising a little humility in Las Vegas might help you attract a different crowd than you do in Miami. No household staff or personal assistants. Establish your own accounts. Buy a house. I'll release twenty million from your trust. That should be enough to support the dive shop. And you always have your black card for emergencies."

"Okay. Good idea." His words are drawn out and distracted. His eyes shift to the left, and I can feel his trepidation.

"Is that not enough?" I ask.

I didn't raise my grandson to chase luxuries. He's not one to purchase ostentatious cars or houses to prove a point. His only real indulgences are travel and extravagant diving trips. I've happily supported that hobby his entire life. Scuba diving keeps his anxiety under control, and I can't remember the last time he got in the ocean. He finished grad school and then barricaded himself in his office.

He nods slowly. "More than enough."

"Then what's on your mind?"

Dex shakes his head then runs his hand through his hair. "I've never actually had a utility bill in my name. Or grocery shopped, for that matter. I guess I have a lot to learn." Dex pats the tops of his thighs, and the loud clap thunders through my quiet office. He stands. "All right, it's late. Are you ready?"

"You go. I need to finish my letter. Joe has the car outside. He'll drive me home. Are you staying at your penthouse or headed back to the estate?"

"I can spend the weekend at the estate. Want to have breakfast tomorrow?"

"Lovely idea. I'll have the chef make that brioche French toast with the berry sauce and bring it out to the marina."

Dex gently grabs my hand and kisses the top of it. "As long

as there's bacon." He smiles. "Goodnight, Grandma. I love you."

"I love you, too."

He stops in his tracks halfway to the door. "Hey, I have a question about your friend."

My heart knocks, my adrenaline bubbling in my veins. Did I say too much? "What about him?"

"You said he passed away. Why are you still writing letters?"

Because true love transcends death, Dex. "Like you said...lost apologies, sweetheart. Now, get out of here. Give your grandma some privacy."

He closes the door gently behind him. For a moment, I sit in silence. Forcing Dex to move out of this bubble, even temporarily, means I'll truly be alone. My heart sinks at the impending reality but the look of relief on Dex's face confirmed what I already knew. He needs this.

After a few more swigs of my drink, I uncross my stiffened legs and will my aching body to move back to my desk.

I pick up my pen and start off on a new trail of thought.

I missed you by a sliver, and I'll never stop wondering if maybe you looked me up, too. Did I fool you? Did you think I was happy?

Did you honestly think my happiness could exist outside of you?

There was some joy in my life, though. In Melody. In her beautiful son, Dex. I wish you could've met him. He's your spitting image.

And see, the best parts of Dex—his tender heart, his warm smile, his optimism, his sense of adventure—those are all parts of you. And the longer he's buried in this office, the more he loses himself.

Every day, he becomes more Hessler and less who he really is.

So, I'm sending him to a place where he can feel close to you. If you're up there watching over us, please take extra good care of our grandson. He's everything to me. He's all I have left of Melody.

He's all I have left of you.

Goodnight, Jacob.

-Dottie

P.S. Love doesn't seem like a big enough word, but I do still love you.

CHAPTER 1

Lennox

Present Day

Las Vegas

I clench the pink note in my fist, not sure if I should feel relieved or panicked. I can't believe they still give out pink slips. A termination email, sure. But an actual pink carbon copy form dismissing me from my position as a policy service representative is...comical. *It's fine.* I hate this call center anyway. The job was cruel and unusual punishment. I will miss the benefits, though. Not a lot of companies are handing out medical and dental coverage on your first day.

Fuck. I touch my cheek.

And, of course, the minute I lose my dental insurance is when my tooth starts to hurt again. What a coincidence.

I thought I'd need more time to clean out my cubicle. My coworkers have mini cacti, colorful pen holders, or little cubbies that hold their books, keys, and lip balms. Anything to make these bland partitions feel a little more comfortable during our ten-hour shifts. All I have to clean up are a few Polaroids, a magazine, and the Luna bars I buy from the vending machine each day. I don't know why I keep buying them. I don't eat them.

Sighing, I unpin the few pictures I have thumbtacked into the built-in corkboard on the wall of my cubicle. One is of my dad and my old pit bull, Boggle. The next is of me and my best friends, Finn and Avery, sharing an amusingly large cheeseburger at a local restaurant that was featured in Diners, Drive-ins, and Dives. That was a good day. I am blessed with a cousin who is my best friend and his sweet fiancée, who has never once complained about me being their constant third wheel.

Not that I should be third-wheeling. I'm in a relationship. But I'm aware it's a little weird that I'm more comfortable around Finn and Avery than on my own with my boyfriend. Alan is nice, but he reminds me of school. Good for me, but goddamn, am I reluctant to go some days. I know how that sounds, but I'm twenty-seven now. I'm trying to choose grown-up things.

I unpin the last photograph—me and my mom posing at the Grand Canyon. A stranger took this picture for us. We're wearing matching sunglasses. My hair was still vibrantly dyed at the time. In the picture, I'm laughing and my mom is pretending to lick my purple hair because she always said it made me look like a popsicle.

She's going to be furious that I got fired today. Mom stuck her neck out to get me this job. But between training and three weeks on the call floor, I lasted *almost* three months. That's...something. Right?

"*Lennox!*" It comes out more like a shriek than anything else. I know who it is, but I don't see Brooke. Leaning backward, I look up and down the row of cubicles. "*Unbelievable.*" She continues her bellyaching again from an unknown location.

"Where are you?" I ask, mostly to myself.

I flip my small, empty metal trash can over and hoist myself up to peer over the sea of cubicles. *Ah, there she is.* I see the red-knotted bun on the top of her head weaving through the rows.

The massive customer service floor is so poorly designed. I can't believe this place passed a fire inspection. Brooke's desk is in what can only be described as a dead-end cul-de-sac. She has to maneuver through a complex rat maze to get to the break room, elevators, exit, or her work bestie's desk. If this building were to spontaneously burst into flames, half the policy reps on this floor would for sure be goners. Had I been given a proper exit interview, it would've been one of my many complaints about this job.

But I committed the ultimate crime. Grounds for immediate dismissal. There was no exit interview, no severance, *no mercy*. All I did was hang up on a customer.

When Brooke finally reaches my cubicle, she's panting. Her headset is still fastened to her head, the input cord dangling like a necklace. "Fired?" she asks.

I nod solemnly, yet I'm wearing a small grin.

She huffs out, "Let's ditch this bitch. I'm going with you."

My laugh is half-hearted. "How'd you find out?"

"The company chat. All of a sudden, your username is gone, and your email is no longer active." Her big eyes are bewildered, like it's so shocking that someone got fired. People come and go daily—it's a massive call center for auto insurance. At least once a day, someone loses their shit and storms out with their middle fingers in the air. Out loud, we cheer for them. In silence, we envy them. There's freedom right through the glass front doors. The only reason we're all trapped is because the pay is so damn good.

"I'm already deleted? Damn, that was fast," I mutter.

The call that ended my short-lived career at Advantage Insurance was barely an hour ago. The very minute I hung up on that old asshole, I got an instant message from my boss: *Meet me in Conference Room A. Now, please.*

"Fuck 'em. Fuck this place. Like I said, I'm going with you."

I click my tongue. "I appreciate the solidarity, but you know you can't do that. You're so close."

Brooke's been here for six months longer than me. She's near her assistant manager promotion. That's the dream. Serve your time on the phones, get promoted, and become a manager; then, you never have to take customer service calls again. For the go-getters, it takes about a year. If you can survive that hellacious year of verbal lashings and abuse, *all of your dreams can come true...*If your dreams are middle management at an insurance company, that is.

Brooke wraps her arms around me and squeezes firmly. I

wheeze as I hug her back. Her bubblegum-sweet body spray is so strong my eyes are watering. She must've spritzed recently.

"This place is going to suck without you."

"Agreed," Beth says, popping up from her cubicle in front of me.

"Sorry," I say, lowering my voice. "Are we being too loud?"

Beth, another one of my favorite people at this dreary place, points to her headset. "Nah, I've got this fucker on hold. He was rude, now he can wait. I'm escalating him over to sales for a new policy..." She smiles deviously. "In about fifteen more minutes."

"Won't that screw with your metrics, Goody Two-shoes?" Brooke asks her, pointing to the giant electric sign mounted on the front wall of the floor. "You're top five on the leaderboard."

Another joyous aspect of this job is that they publicly grade us. I suppose Advantage Insurance thinks a little healthy competition is motivational, not demeaning. They plaster our names on the digital sign that is constantly ranking us by call metrics such as efficiency, first-call resolution, and customer satisfaction surveys. Only the top thirty reps are displayed at one time. My name's been up there only once, and it was very short-lived. Probably a fluke.

Beth shrugs. "I'll drop a few ranks to punish this one. Real piece of work. He's trying to put his girlfriend on a secret policy that his wife can't access. I told him we could only add a driver if they were living in the same household. Then, he asked me if I was dumb enough to think he had his wife and girlfriend living under the same roof."

Brooke grits her teeth and seethes. "Why are men so open about being pieces of shit? I can't even—" She stops and exhales deeply before closing her eyes. Pinching the bridge of her nose, she mumbles, "*Happy place...happy place...happy place.*"

Poor Brooke was recently cheated on. It was the main topic of many of our break room rants. Men. In a show of solidarity, I join in the disgruntled monologues. I've dated my fair share of jerks, but right now, I'm with a good guy. Alan is a textbook gentleman. He's just a little matter-of-fact. He'd never cheat on me. He'd just end things, wait the appropriate amount of time before dating again, then move forward. Why do I assume that? Quite literally because we had that conversation.

One time in bed, right after sex—and I'm talking cuddling, with our sweaty bodies still glued to each other—Alan asked what the appropriate amount of time was that couples should wait to date new people after breaking up. I probably should've asked him why the hell he was thinking about breaking up while I was still naked in his arms, but I was caught off guard. He said we should wait at least a month for a fling but three months for anything serious. I went with it. My actual answer was *"When I felt like it,"* but that sounded a little sassy for such a vulnerable conversation.

I'll admit, him planning our potential breakup over pillow talk isn't exactly romantic, but I appreciated the honesty. My past relationships, while far more passionate, were volatile, to say the least. They always ended the same way—me getting cheated on, a week of gnarly hangovers, and dying my hair a new color.

I no longer want men who get drunk off belly shots from a stripper's navel. I want the guy who's sober at eight o'clock in the morning because he has a job. I don't want to spend all day distracting myself so I'm not the girl who waits by the phone. I just want the guy who calls. No more Pop-Tarts. These days, I'm buying Luna Bars. So, I consider it a good thing that Alan wears khakis with pocket protectors. Even if pocket protectors are the least sexy thing on the planet.

Alan's safe.

We dated casually for a year before we officially became boyfriend and girlfriend. After almost two years of knowing the man, he *still* opens doors for me and pulls out chairs. Every time I see him, the first thing he does is compliment me. He takes me out to expensive restaurants that I know he can't afford. And when I try to order something small to be considerate, he insists I get the steak, a fancy cocktail, *and* dessert. He's good to me. So, I ignore the fact that we have about as much sexual chemistry as two puffer fish. That's what kissing him feels like sometimes. Two people puckering their lips and bumping into each other face first. I swear he still gets a little startled whenever I slip him tongue.

"Oh, look at that. He dropped off the call," Beth singsongs as she pulls off her headset. "I wonder if his wife came home. Dickhead."

"All right," I grumble as I tuck my pictures into my purse. "Who wants an ergonomic standing desk? My cubicle is officially up for grabs."

"I would, but I have to stay close to my pod," Brooke grumbles. "*Pod*," she reiterates. "Like we're a freaking team of orcas. They are really pushing the team camaraderie lately."

I smirk at her. "Probably because turnover is expensive, and they don't have enough reps as it is."

They both frown, but Beth is the one to speak up. "We'll miss you. Let's do drinks on Friday on the Strip. That new club, Ventura? The minute we're off work, okay? We'll come get you."

I nod. "Okay. Sounds good."

It's a nice sentiment, but it probably won't happen. We're always making big plans and then bailing because a long week at this place sucks the life out of us. Lately, on the weekends, I stay in, watching movies until I fall asleep. Alan works nights and weekends, so I usually pal around at Finn and Avery's place. They never make me feel unwelcome. Unless they're itching to have loud, wild sex. I can usually tell when their game of footsie on the couch is getting a little too intense, and then I see myself out.

"Babes, get back to work before you guys get fired too." I blow a kiss to my friends. "See you on the other side."

"Let us know what sunshine looks like, okay? And fresh water and real food," Brooke says from behind me. "We're going to miss you here on death row."

I'm laughing at her dramatic sarcasm all the way to the building's front lobby. I say bye to the receptionist and tell her to have a great day like nothing's wrong and I'm simply at the end of my shift. I won't lie, there's a little pep in my step. You know a job isn't right for you when you're now officially broke with no insurance and no other job prospects...yet you still feel elated.

But the jolly feeling of relief quickly dissipates when I see my mother waiting for me right outside the building. Her arms are crossed, wrinkling her neat, blue blouse. Her dark gray dress pants hemmed just above the ankle show off her pointed black heels. She's tapping her foot, her obvious tell when she's trying to control her temper.

It brings me right back to high school when I was constantly in trouble. Whenever I'd get C's in school...foot tapping. The time she caught me sneaking back into my bedroom after a boy dropped me off at one in the morning...foot tapping. The time I clipped the curb in her car and busted her front driver's side tire... very aggressive foot tapping.

"Where's your stuff?" Mom asks, her lips barely moving.

I tap my satchel. "Right here."

"They're not going to let you back in the building, Lennox. You need to take all of your belongings." Mom is a director on the sales side of Advantage Insurance. I wonder how she found out. Gossip moves like wildfire in a call center. Someone probably tipped her off the moment I disappeared from the company instant message directory.

"I realize, Mom. *I did.* I didn't have much here."

She exhales dramatically. "I can take an early lunch. Do you want to talk about it? Maybe over some Subway?"

I cinch one eye closed and shake my head at her. "Don't try to butter me up with a footlong Italian B.M.T. with all the fixings, extra pickles, mayo, and the special vinaigrette. I know you just want to lecture me about getting fired."

She raises her eyebrows at my response. "I do. But that description was quite specific. Sounds like you want a sandwich."

I raise my eyebrows right back at her. "Are you paying?"

"Sure," she says.

"Can we skip the lecture?"

"No," she snaps.

But my stomach grumbles right on cue. "Fine. Sandwich and

lecture, then. Your car or mine?"

Mom scoffs. "I'm not getting into that metal death trap you call a vehicle. I don't even like my baby driving in that thing. I thought this job was going to get you a little closer to a down payment on something safer."

We turn left, heading toward the dedicated parking spaces. All directors get a special spot with their initials spray-painted on a parking block.

"What happened, Lennox? I thought the job was going well."

"I hung up on a customer," I answer simply. "They fired me. That's it. There's no big story. I broke a rule, then I paid the price." I keep my eyes down on my ballet flats. The soles are so worn I can feel the cold concrete on my feet. Vegas is never freezing, but in December, the air is brisk enough to cool the sidewalks.

"I understand *why* you were fired. I'm asking what possessed you to hang up on a customer. It's literally the first thing they teach you in training. Advantage's only deal breaker. Simeon Walters from my sales team all but cussed a customer out over the phone. I wrote him up. *But did he get fired?* No. Because he didn't hang up."

"Mom," I say, halting in place. "What's your point?"

She doubles back to face me, hands on her hips, challenge in her eyes. Her foot goes back to tapping. "My point is, you're incredibly smart, Lennox. This was deliberate. You wanted to get fired."

Is that true? *Possibly.*

"N-O-E-L." I say the letters individually.

"What?" she asks.

"How would you pronounce that?"

She narrows her eyes but plays along. "No-Elle."

"Right." I agree with a quick nod. "That's what I said when the caller script came in. 'Good afternoon, am I speaking with Mr. Noel?'" I mimic, in my customer service agent voice. "I was wrong. It was pronounced 'Noll,' like rhymes with toll."

"Lennox, where are we going with this?"

"Well, I apologized for mispronouncing his name, corrected

myself, and asked how I could help him with his policy."

"Okay..."

"Then he proceeded to call me an illiterate, uneducated cunt, and told me to use whatever few brain cells I had to transfer him to someone who spoke English. I had his policy details in front of me. He's seventy-two years old."

Mom's jaw drops. "That was unnecessary of him."

"No, Mom," I grumble. "It was actually *very* necessary. It helped me pull my head out of my ass. I'm not going to spend one more minute at a job that cares more about metrics than their employees getting bullied and harassed. It's not only today. I have a dozen stories just like it. Every single day, I'm getting metaphorically spit on and slapped in the face. I'll work the long hours. I'll come in on weekends. I'll even scrub toilets. But I'm not going to work a job where I'm not respected like a goddamn human being should be."

Mom's arms are still tightly crossed around her chest, but at least her foot stops tapping. "Lennox, as your mother, I want to crawl through that phone, grab that man's cane, and beat him with it. But—"

"Always a but—"

"*Also, as your mother,* I am supposed to teach you about life. Yes, people can be awful. And I'm sorry, but you have to be more resilient than that. You can't win every battle. That man is vile, but who is standing here without a job right now? I mean, did you get your tooth looked at yet? It's been bothering you for months. And you're twenty-seven, old enough where you need an annual pap smear and breast exam. You have to start thinking about saving for retirement. Social security isn't going to do a damn thing for you by the time you can withdraw. You need to buy a car that doesn't look like it could shatter from a light breeze. Lennox, you're floating through life. Pitching in at Finn's studio, these bartending jobs, dog walking...they are not real careers. I am so afraid you're going to end up like your father."

"Happy?" I ask with a heavy dose of snark.

Mom frowns. "Lost. Broke. Feeling guilty. With a wife who has to work overtime every single week to pay off his astronomical debt. I want to buy you a car, but I can't afford to. Because of your father's mistakes, I can't help my baby when she needs it the most. It kills him, and it kills me. Don't end up like us. *Grow up, sweetheart.*"

If my mom were a crier, I'm sure she'd be in tears. But she's not. I think I saw her shed one single tear in my entire life. It was when our house got repoed after my dad lost his job and was blacklisted from the finance industry. It was a downward spiral from there with his hobby-esque coping mechanism. He didn't go back to making money, just spending money we didn't have. We lost my childhood home. We lost everything.

"Why didn't you get divorced?" I ask point blank.

"*Lennox.*"

"What? I just mean on paper, not actually breaking up. Dad said divorce would've given you a fresh start from his record. Why didn't you?"

Mom shakes her head like my question is silly. "Honey, marriage is so much more than paperwork. I'm committed to your father—his mistakes, his burdens, his pain. They are mine as well. I'm not going to walk away from my commitment just because it's financially convenient to do so. I didn't marry your father for what he could give me. I married him because I love him... Also, a little bit for his body, because your dad"—Mom breathes out a low whistle— "is sexy." She pumps her eyebrows twice.

I glower at her as she snickers at my discomfort. "I would endure a lobotomy to unhear that."

"Oh, come on," she teases, "every kid wants cool parents who still have the hots for each other."

"I assure you they don't."

This is the problem. My parents are too happily married, even through the wreckage of my dad's career. My wildly unrealistic expectation of men is because of my stupid parents and their ridiculously healthy marriage. I blame my mother one thousand percent for all of my breakups. She's the one who taught me to walk away at the first sign of disrespect, never forgive a cheater, and not tolerate a man who constantly talks over me.

It's worth mentioning that she loves Alan. On more than one occasion she's forwarded me articles for beautiful, budget-friendly weddings for the money-conscious bride. If only she knew money wasn't the thing holding me back from officially committing to Alan.

"You're a better woman than me," I tell her. "I would've had serious doubts about my marriage the time Dad took up breeding Yorkie-doodles."

Mom rolls her eyes. "Yorkipoos," she corrects. "I never thought I could hate puppies, but my house will forever smell like dog shit now."

I laugh. "Mom, look, don't worry about me. I'll find something. Another grown-up job, *with benefits*."

She blows out a sharp breath and relaxes her shoulders. "Okay. Come on," she says, throwing her head back and gesturing to her car. "I want a double chocolate cookie."

"Weak order. Everyone knows the raspberry cheesecake cookies are where it's at."

"Bleh." She leads the way to her SUV. "It's chocolate or nothing. Fruit doesn't belong in cookies."

"Hey, Mom?"

"Yes?"

"You could be a real jerk right now. You got me this job, and I blew it. But thank you for not making my bad day even worse."

She stands in front of me, placing her palm against my cheek. I nuzzle into her hand. She still smells like the same spicy, floral perfume she's worn for as long as I can remember. "An old man called you a cunt, sweetheart. I think you've taken enough crap today."

I laugh. *Damn straight*. At least it's a fresh start.

Hopefully, it's going to get easier from here.

CHAPTER 2

Dex

Three Years Earlier

Las Vegas

Out of sheer boredom, I filled my new house with strangers on a Friday night. Word spread about my little get-together after inviting just my neighbors and a few acquaintances. I haven't met many people since I moved to town and took over the dive shop a couple months ago, so I wasn't expecting the huge turnout. There are so many people in my four-thousand-square-foot suburban home that we're veering away from shindig and getting dangerously close to mosh pit.

The colored strobe lights highlight random faces in the low-lit room. I don't recognize a single person here. Just strangers, drinking my booze, smoking my cigars, and trashing my new home.

I dropped a few grand on top-shelf liquor, that no one can appreciate at this level of inebriation. The imported German beer, which can only be found at the best Oktoberfest festivals, was left out and lukewarm before being poured into red and blue SOLO cups and used for endless rounds of beer pong. I even fired up the hot tub. It's currently a washing machine of couples' saliva and other bodily fluids that I'd rather not dwell on. Chlorine won't cut it. I'm going to have to drain that fucker after tonight.

I've seen enough. Intent on grabbing a beer for the road and abandoning my party for my bed, I head to my kitchen.

"Excuse me," I say to the women who are lip-locked and blocking my hidden refrigerator, lying behind long, black doors that match my cabinetry. "Just trying to grab a beer."

The blond-haired woman pulls away from the brunette and traces her lips with the tip of her finger. Her smile is wicked. "Pay the toll." She taps her lips, then the brunette's.

It's too dark for them to notice the flicker of agitation in my eyes or the way my jaw clenches. "Not interested."

She takes it as a challenge. The blonde leans back against the fridge door then shrugs her shoulders, purposely squeezing her tits together, making her ample cleavage hard to ignore. "Then no beer for you."

This woman is wrapped tightly in a giant red flag. I don't find this sexy. Just embarrassing. I'd like to pick her up by her shoulders and move her out of my way, but I'm not dumb enough to touch her.

The blonde giggles as I duck down to speak into her ear, clearly thinking I've mistaken her cheap seduction tactics for charm. By now, I've gone through it all. Holes poked through condoms. Full-on nudes in my DMs with no names, just addresses. Court-ordered paternity test requests filed by women I've never met. Most recently, baseless accusations that led to blackmail and extortion. I've sacrificed so much already, what's one more beer?

"Then no beer for me," I grumble in her ear before walking away.

For fuck's sake. Can't get a drink in my own goddamn house.

I slip by the sweaty clusters of people as I make my way to the stairs. Taking them two by two, my feet land heavily with each leap on the wooden steps, my eyes set on the master suite. Ignoring the loiterers in my upstairs foyer, I burst through the French doors and slam them shut behind me. The loud music from downstairs immediately dissipates thanks to the soundproofed room.

But as soon as I peel off my shirt and lob it onto my cleanly made bed, there's a soft tapping at my door. A hesitant, noncommittal knock. I almost don't answer, but then I realize the bedroom isn't locked. The person on the other side of the door could've barged in but chose to knock and wait instead. That kind of intrigues me. Something in the realm of manners, at least.

I pull open the doors and...

There she is.

An elegant, sweet face carved with perfect angles. Her long, thick, dark-purple hair is wrapped around her like a cloak, which is ideal because her white lace top is most definitely see-through, and I have a clear visual of her bra. Her shorts have some sort of iridescent sheen to them. All paired with glittery black tennis shoes.

Basically, this woman is a hundred fucking layers of interesting.

"Hey. What's up?" I'll give myself credit. That sounded pretty damn casual, even though there's a circus show of flips and kicks going on in my chest. It's her big, dark brown eyes and the way they are locked on mine. Her eye contact is intimidating, actually.

Good thing she's pairing her stare with a smile. She's wearing an even-keeled, confident expression like I should have been expecting her at my bedroom door or something. "Here you go." She raises her hands, tightly wrapped around two frosted beer bottles. Both unopened. "I saw all that go down in the kitchen. Sorry about Kendra. She loses all sense when she drinks. That was rude of her." She glances past me into my bedroom. "I'm assuming this is your house and your party?"

"Yeah."

She holds the beers up higher. "Are either of these what you were after? There were only a few kinds left in the fridge."

As if we're in some unspoken game of chicken, I keep my eyes glued on hers, matching her intense gaze. "Kendra was the blonde blocking the fridge?"

The purple-haired girl nods. "Yes."

I smirk at her. "Did she make you pay the toll?"

She throws her head back and laughs, finally breaking her

gaze. "No. Apparently, that's just a hot guy toll. Free passage for me."

A warm flood of satisfaction rushes through me. Not just because she thinks I'm hot but because she says it so casually. I like her bravado.

Taking one beer from her, I say, "Thank you." With the bottle steadied between my thumb and forefinger, I point to the other bottle she's holding with my pinky. "That one is better. It's a Hefeweizen."

She quickly holds out the other bottle. "I brought both for you. To buy you some time before you have to go down there again. Oh, and here." She steadies the bottle between the crook of her elbow and the side of her ribcage as she digs through her satchel. "Do you have a pitch jar or something? I didn't see one downstairs."

"A what?"

She's struggling to hold the bottle as she fishes in her wallet, so I pull it free and hold onto it as I patiently wait to see what in the hell a pitch jar is.

"Everyone downstairs is drinking *your* alcohol, right?"

"Why do you say that?"

She scoffs like I'm missing the obvious punch line to a joke. "Because I know if my friends supplied the booze, we'd be slamming back PBR and chasing shots of Burnett's with Monster energy drinks. You actually have good liquor and beer." She proudly holds up a folded ten-dollar bill. "I had three drinks, so this probably isn't enough." Twisting her lips, she gives me an apologetic smile. "But it's all I have on me right now."

Her pouty, bright red lips are a distraction every time she moves them, so it takes me a little longer to register what she's insinuating. "So, a pitch jar is where everyone financially contributes to the party booze?"

She tilts her head just slightly. "You seem surprised. Is this your first house party?"

I could explain to her the parties I'm used to are usually

hosted in multimillion-dollar mansions, have valet for guests' foreign sports cars, and caviar and cocaine are served on platinum platters. But I don't feel like opening up that can of worms. The whole point of being in Las Vegas is to lead a very different life than I had in Miami. Even if it's temporary.

"I can honestly say my friends have never offered," I answer.

She twists up her face like she witnessed something obscene. "Some friends."

"Apparently, I've been missing out." I lift my eyebrows. "Keep your money. The gesture is appreciated. But I don't need it."

She rolls her eyes. "Such a hero. Just take the cash. Who can't use an extra ten bucks?" She steps forward and the lace of her shirt brushes against my bare skin. Her scent wafts around us. It's sugary and citrus, like candy. It's the kind of smell that makes my mouth water and has me suddenly craving something sweet. Before I can fully process the smell of her, her hand is in my front jeans pocket. With a beer in each of my hands, I can't stop her from tucking the folded bill deep into my pocket and grazing against the tip of my dick with her fingertips.

She knows what she just touched because her big eyes go from large to cartoon proportions as she rips her hand out of my pocket and leaps backward. The thin lining of my pocket and my briefs kept her accidental touch pretty tame, but she still looks mortified.

"There's a purple stripe on the corner. It's just nail polish. It's how I make sure my tips don't get mixed up at the restaurant. But it shouldn't be a problem at the store. I use them all the time," she explains, her eyes now on her shoes.

I want to make a joke and laugh it off. It was an innocent accident. But obviously, she wants to pretend that didn't happen.

She takes another step backward and spins around to leave, but it's poorly timed because a group of sloppy jackasses knocks right into her. One of them empties a full Solo cup of beer on her chest. She freezes with her back turned to me. I hear her sharp gasp. "*Shit. That's cold!*"

"Oh man, so sorry, Lenny. Accident," a man says in a drunken drawl. His hat is turned backward so I can see his red cheeks and bloodshot eyes. Then he's pawing at her as his buddies snicker and leave him behind, thundering down the stairs like a herd of cattle. "Just lemme clean it up for you."

Based on the disgusting smile on his face, I'm convinced he dumped his beer on her on purpose. But he said her name...*Lenny?* Is this her guy friend? Boyfriend, perhaps? His friends walked on by, leaving them together. Obviously, she knows him. Maybe I shouldn't intervene like a territorial—

"Get the fuck off of me, Charlie," she barks out. "Do you think your hands are made of goddamn paper towels?"

It's all the invitation I need.

Within two strides, my hand is on his shoulder, pushing him away from her. Once she's at a safe distance—in case he throws a drunken punch—my hand moves to his throat. I tighten my grip until he's sputtering. "I'm going to do you a favor and not throw you off my balcony. But in exchange for my generosity, you're going to get the fuck out of my house. Right now. Deal?"

I'm taller than him, larger than him, and I'm sure my temper doesn't look worth testing at the moment. He makes a smart move and nods until I release his neck. I keep my eyes on him as he tries not to trip down the stairs. He looks like the kind of sleazy piece of shit who'd strike you with something the moment your back is turned. So, I watch his sorry ass until he's through the front door.

"He's stupid but harmless," she says from behind me. "He's been high for like two years straight now."

"It's impressive he's not dead," I mutter.

"Just high off weed," she explains. "Nothing that could kill him."

I smile as I turn to face her. "No, I mean I'm impressed with my self-control. I really wanted to throw him off my balcony. You think he'd bounce like a skipping stone?"

My smile is wiped clean when I see the front of her shirt. She looks like she's been hosed down. Her flowy lace top is glued to her skin, and her white bra is now see-through, her thick, dark nipples completely on display.

What might be worse is that her shorts must be made out of tissue paper or something because they basically melted, and I can see the outlines of her lower body in great detail.

She cringes when she sees my expression. "Oh no. How bad is it?"

First, I check to make sure no bystanders are gawking at her the way I am. Then, I lean down and ask in a low murmur, "You're not wearing underwear, are you?"

"Shit." She crosses one leg over the other. "Okay, so it's bad."

I clamp one eye shut and nod solemnly. "Want to use my bathroom to get cleaned up?"

"Thank you." She doesn't wait for me to lead, shuffling into my bedroom in a hurry. I'm right behind her, this time shutting the door and locking it behind me. Snagging my shirt off the bed, I pull it overhead before following her into the bathroom.

There's no door to my ensuite, just a large archway that leads into the walk-through closet and then opens to the bathroom. She's busy rinsing her lace top under the sink, so I knock on the doorframe to let her know I'm behind her.

"Lenny, do you want some soap?"

After plugging the sink, she glances over her shoulder. "Did you just call me Lenny?"

"Is that not your name? I thought I heard that guy call you Lenny."

She's standing in just her bra top, already having shed her sheer outer top, clenching it in her small fist. She goes back to watching the running sink water. When there's a deep enough pool of water in the sink, she plunges the entire top in to soak, then helps herself to the navy hand towel to her right. Never once has the right sink in my bathroom been used. That towel has hung there pristine and untouched for a month.

"Lennox," she clarifies. "And that guy is Charlie. My ex. I hate when he calls me that."

"Sorry. *Lennox*, then. I'm Dex."

"It's okay. You didn't know." Her flushed cheeks bunch into bubbly half-spheres when she smiles. "Nice to meet you, Dex."

"So, were you guys serious?"

"I was serious. Him? Not so much. See this?" She taps her collarbone as she abandons the sink and approaches me. I have to duck down to read the small tattoo. My stomach churns when I realize it's Charlie's name in an elegant calligraphy. "My constant reminder of the dumb things I've done drunk. This stupid tattoo... and Charlie."

"Why'd you guys break up?"

"About a week after this mistake"—she rubs her finger against her collarbone like his name is a smudge she can remove—"I caught him balls deep in a girl from the restaurant he manages. And you want to know the gaslighting bullshit he threw my way when I found out?"

God, I feel bad. She's trying to play it cool, but I see the way she sucks in her lips to keep her reaction under control. I know that face. This girl doesn't like to cry. Or doesn't want me to see her cry.

"What'd he say?"

"He told me that I was too high maintenance in expecting him to remain monogamous. All the 'woke girls' are into open relationships these days."

"He said that right to your face?" She nods. "Wow. He's got a pair. I'll give him that. I hope you kicked his ass. And if you didn't, you'll need to excuse me for a moment so I can."

"That's sweet... And you're hot." She scrunches her face. "Just tell me that you're the kind of guy to ignore texts and only call me when you want some ass. And if I have the nerve to call you first when I haven't heard from you for weeks, please tell me you'd tease me for being needy."

I cross my arms. "Now, why in the hell would I ever tell you that?"

A mischievous grin spreads across her face. "Because then you'd be *exactly* my type." She half-curtsies. "My superpower is knowing how to pick the cream of the crop when it comes to dickwads. I'm basically a walking magnet for epic stupidity. Which is why, from now on, I'm only dating men I'm not remotely attracted to." She shrugs. "So, sorry, you're out."

"Ah, damn. I can be less attractive if that helps? Maybe chew with my mouth wide open."

"That'd definitely help."

"Wear khakis with a brown belt and black suede shoes."

She laughs. "Getting warmer."

"Skip a few showers and cut my toenails at the kitchen table."

"There you go. Basically, become disgusting, and I think we'd have a real shot at happily ever after."

Our laughter fades and then we're sitting in the first lull of conversation since she showed up at my door.

"I don't get it. You party with your ex when he was that big of a jerk to you?"

She crosses her arms and hangs her head, looking vulnerable for the first time since I met her. "I don't party with him. He just always pops up wherever I am. We run in the same circles. It's just easier to keep the peace, I guess."

I nod but I must seem unimpressed because she reaches out to touch my forearm, like she assumed I was going to leave and was trying to prevent me from doing so. *I'm not going anywhere, pretty girl.*

"I know how that sounds, but I'm not trying to get him back or anything. He just got to me more than I like to admit, and um..." She stops blinking like she's trying to focus on something. Trying not to cry again. Once she's composed, she adds, "Sometimes if you pretend like something isn't a big deal, it eventually just stops feeling like a big deal. It's the only coping mechanism that's ever worked for me."

"So he just gets away with it?" I ask.

"Well, I mean, he doesn't get to have me." She lifts her shoulders then drops them like their too heavy to hold. "That's all that's in my control."

I pat her hand, still resting on my arm. "Yeah, that seems like punishment enough."

She glances over her shoulder, then back to me. "Is your shower being repaired?"

"No. Why?"

"There's no door. How do you keep the water in?"

He smiles. "No, it's designed like that, doorless. It's floor-to-ceiling tile, so you don't need to keep the water in. It's supposed to feel like a spa."

"Fancy," she mutters. "You know, my cousin Finn just moved in next door. That's how I found out about this party to begin with. He told me the same builder made all the houses in this neighborhood, but his shower is nowhere near this nice."

"It was one of the liberties I took when I bought the house. I had them rip out the old shower and make this instead." I rub the back of my neck, feeling uncomfortable. I've done a pretty damn good job keeping my wealth under the radar since I moved here. I never know which of my eccentricities are going to tip me off.

Finn, Lennox's cousin, actually stopped by a few days ago to introduce himself. He's a good guy. Someone I could see myself being friends with. When I poured my new neighbor a friendly drink, he happened to notice my collection of bourbon and whiskey was worth well over ten grand. Which is why I put those bottles away before tonight. I'm not trying to lie to anyone. I just don't want to attract the wrong kind of attention.

"Then if it's working, may I use your shower? I'll be really quick. I don't know what Charlie was drinking, but I smell awful."

Now that she mentions it, the smell of her sweet citrus perfume has been doused out.

"Sure. You want me to throw your clothes in the washer?"

She twists her lips. "Won't that take a while?"

"I think my machine has a rapid wash setting. Why? Am I keeping you from something?"

"It's your party. Don't you need to get back down there?" She glances over my shoulder.

I find her eyes again. "You brought me beer." I wink at her. "Stay. Hang out. We can turn on the TV."

She tries to hold in her laugh, but it breaks through her lips. "Are you inviting me to *Netflix and chill*?"

"What is that?"

"You don't know what a pitch jar is or what '*Netflix and chill*' means? Are you a million years old?"

I lift my shoulders. "I had a...let's call it sheltered childhood."

Lennox's teenage years were probably filled with public school and house parties. I went to private school and graduated early. And when I drank as a teenager, it wasn't because I was sneaking around. It was because I was spending a lot of time in Germany, where it was legal to do so. I didn't have the urge to rebel. I liked school. I liked traveling. Grandma and Grandpa filled my life with all the extravagant adventures money could buy. Looking back, they were probably trying to keep me distracted. Between never knowing my dad and losing my mom at seven, I could've turned into a troubled, brooding teenager. They just wanted me to have some semblance of a happy childhood.

I did. Childhood wasn't the problem. Adulthood has been the real bitch.

"*Netflix* and chill means sex. Or at least third base. It's when people literally make plans to do nothing except...*you know*. I mean, sometimes you bring snacks."

"Snacks? Really?" I lift my brows.

"Popcorn and such."

"*Oh*. See, I thought—"

She interrupts me with a cute chuckle. "Yeah, I know what you were thinking. Whipped cream, chocolate sauce, warm honey, maraschino cherries?"

I show her a sexy smirk. Now I can't stop picturing her drenched from head to toe in something tasty. "Warm honey? Never tried that one."

She pinches her thumb and pointer finger together, making a sprinkling motion. "With a little cinnamon."

I tuck a few loose hairs behind her ear. "I'm intrigued."

"It's a little sticky."

Completely transfixed on her thick, pouty lips, I say, "Not by the honey."

Her lips part slightly, just enough room to slide mine between them. "Right," she says, her voice cracking. She clears her throat. "Anyway, I wasn't sure if that's what you meant by hanging out."

"Not what I was implying. But if the invitation's open..."

She nods. "Then what? If the invitation was open?"

"*If* the invitation was open..." My eyes drop to her stained bra top. "Then I'd tell you to take that off. Your shorts, too. Then get in my shower while I watch."

Her top teeth drag against her bottom lip. "You sure you're a nice guy? That was kind of forward."

"I'm nice... I'm not a saint. You're standing here in your bra. Kind of hard not to notice."

"It's not a bra. It's a bralette," she mutters. "Like a crop top."

I flash her a devilish smile. "All the same once it's on the floor."

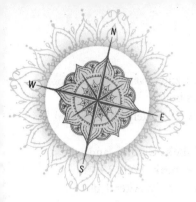

CHAPTER 3

Lennox

I promised I'd stop doing this. One-night stands don't lead to happily ever after. *Get that through your head, Lennox.*

But fuck, Dex makes my knees weak. His body looks like it was carved from marble. And I love that this close, I have to look up to see his eyes. A few feet away, his hazel eyes look more tan than green. But from this angle, where he's so close that I can feel the warmth coming off his body, his eyes are clearly emerald. Completely hypnotizing.

There's also the small matter that I accidentally grazed his dick, and from what I gathered, even the tip seems like it'd be overwhelming. Now he's inviting me to strip down naked and hop into his fancy shower.

Where's the crime, Lennox? You're single. He's...well, actually. Perhaps I should confirm.

"Be honest. Are you single?" I ask Dex.

His eyes were on my lips. Now, they've dipped a little lower, landing on my chest. "Yes," he answers without hesitation.

"But I mean *really* single. So, no wife, no girlfriend, but also no hopeful girl you've been chatting up that's waiting by her phone, expecting you to call her tonight?"

He laughs. "No. Definitely no one I'm calling each night. Well, my grandma. But I usually just text her goodnight."

My face melts into a goofy, bemused smile. "You text your grandma goodnight? Aww."

He laughs but rolls his eyes. "She worries and likes to

know I'm alive. But yeah, maybe we can add that to your list of unattractive things. I'm a total grandma's boy."

"No, that's pretty attractive, actually. Definitely *not* my usual type."

If Charlie has a grandmother, she's Ursula, and she's torturing unsuspecting mermaids as we speak. Well, I can only assume. He never introduced me to his family. After I dumped him for cheating on me, he spent days begging me to forgive him, but my mother taught me better than to believe his bullshit. His apologies weren't genuine. He was just frustrated that he couldn't have his way.

Once he knew it was really over, he grew mean. One time, in a weed-laced, drunken stupor, he told me I was always his placeholder girl anyway. The girl you keep around until you find the girl you actually want to keep.

That hurt.

I mean, it was probably the first honest thing he ever told me.

But it hurt.

"So the shower is a little complicated," Dex says, leading me to the corner of his bathroom. "There are two nozzles. One for each showerhead. But the water gets hot fast, so please be careful. Don't crank the handles all the way."

"Did you seriously just 'mansplain' turning on a shower to me?"

"I was just—" He stops, holding up his hands, a smile breaking free from his pretend-offended expression. "*Wow.* You're just a little shit starter, aren't you?"

"Yeah, I'm trouble. Feel free to kick me out."

His laugh tapers off to a breathy chuckle. "No, Trouble, that's okay. I think I'll keep you. I'll leave you to shower in peace. But just know if you scald yourself, the 'I told you so' I give you will be loud and relentless."

"I thought you were going to stay and watch."

He licks his lips and tries to control his grin. "It was just playful flirting, Lennox. I don't think I could watch you and not..." He clears his throat. "Anyway, I'll be right outside in the bedroom. Maybe I'll go sign up for a *Netflix* account." He winks, and I burst out laughing. A laugh that brews deep from my belly and overflows.

Oh, I'm definitely in trouble. He's so sexy. So flirty. Funny. Protective. Charming. Sexy again. I just want to rub up against his body like a cat and make him my favorite scratching post.

Once he disappears from view, I peel off my stained bralette and toss it in the sink to soak with my lace blouse. I yank down my shorts, which are probably unsalvageable. *Fucking Charlie.* And it's not like I can replace them. I struck gold at the thrift store. These are my favorite summer shorts.

I kick them aside, walk into Dex's enormous shower, and turn both handles. I yelp when the water goes from cool to burning within seconds. I'd dart to the other side, but there are two rain showerheads overhead, spanning the entire shower. I have to endure the boiling downpour as I lunge for the handles and turn them to half-mast.

I cradle my shoulders, now an angry red, until the water feels safely warm. Then, I grab the shampoo and deposit a large dollop into my hand. I take a little sniff. Definitely something fancier than I use. I usually go with Garnier Fructis, whatever scent is on clearance at Walmart. Dex uses something from a salon, I'm sure of it. This smells like lavender and tea tree oil. In fact, Dex's shower, much like his house, is a little over the top. It has features similar to my parents' old house.

My mom poured over the design of their new build. Dad happily indulged in every single upgrade, especially in the bathroom. All the countertops were granite, top-tier finishings for the handles and faucets, and marbled tile laid on top of heated floors. And the tub. Mom loves baths, which is why Dad insisted she go with a jetted tub so large it looked like they shoved a full-size hot tub into the corner of their master bathroom.

Their new house doesn't have a single bathtub. Just a shower, but Mom never complains or dwells on what they had...then lost.

Knock, knock.

I spin to see Dex standing just outside of the shower with his hand over his eyes. He points to the left with his free hand. "Towel and a shirt you can borrow. I'm going to grab your dirty clothes." I know he's not looking at me naked because he thinks he's pointing to the sink, where he left a folded towel and T-shirt on top. He's actually gesturing to the door that I'm assuming the toilet is behind.

"Thanks," I say, poking my head out of the shower so he can hear me. "I'll just be another minute."

I wait until he disappears from the bathroom before I tiptoe to the sink. I'm dripping water everywhere, so after I pat my body down and sop up the excess from my hair, I clean his bathroom floor using the towel to mop up the trail I left.

I have no underwear, so I pray this T-shirt is long enough. It looks new. It's folded very flat, the way shirts are only once when they are fresh out of the factory. Once I shake it out, I'm pleasantly surprised to see a logo I recognize. *Discover Dives*? Excited to ask Dex how he has a T-shirt from the dive shop, I pull the shirt on overhead. It's a literal dress on me.

After scurrying out of the bathroom and through the closet, I find Dex lounging on his bed. He has one hand tucked behind his head as he scrolls through his phone. I let myself admire him for about ten seconds before asking, "Hey, how do you know Discover Dives?" I point to the logo of a hammerhead shark on the chest of my T-shirt.

His eyes lift and brighten, matching my enthusiasm. "You know it? I own it. I'll be running classes soon. That shirt was with some leftover inventory I found in boxes last week. It's smaller than my other shirts. I thought it'd fit you better."

"You're kidding me. You're the new owner? That's...wow. Small world." Looking up at his vaulted ceiling and the elegant crown molding that covers every inch of his enormous bedroom, a realization washes over me. "I would've never guessed you owned a dive shop."

"Why?" Dex sits up, setting one foot on the ground so he can face me.

"I didn't get the impression from Jacob that dive instructors made a ton of money." I rotate my wrist, gesturing around his room. "And you have a really nice place."

"They don't. My old job did," he mumbles. I wait, but he seems unwilling to elaborate.

"Oh."

"You knew the old owner? I think my grandma and him were good friends back in the day."

I nod. "Jacob Hayes."

After joining Dex on the bed, I remind myself I don't have underwear on and to keep my thighs clamped tightly shut. If I relax my legs, this man is going to get much more than a peep show. He'd get a full-on, front-row seat to my at-home, DIY Brazilian wax job.

"Jacob used to come into the restaurant I worked at. I was only seventeen, and the restaurant wouldn't give me the good shifts because I couldn't legally bartend yet. My family had just gone through some tough times, and I needed cash. So, Jacob hired me at the dive shop." I smile at the memory. "He paid me under the table to stock inventory, reserve the pool at the rec center for classes, return customer calls when their equipment was in, that sort of thing. Jacob was the only reason I had some new clothes and gas money my senior year."

Dex smiles. "Seems like a nice enough guy."

"Nice guy? Jacob was...was..." I search my brain for the right word. How the hell do I sum up Jacob Hayes? "*Legendary.* That's the best way to describe him. Everybody loved him. He was always smiling. And he had the best stories. He literally traveled the world diving and sailing. It sucked when he passed away a few years ago. Everybody tried to pitch in and keep the shop running in his honor, but we just couldn't hold it together. I was too young and wasn't certified to teach. Mel moved to Cali. Sanders is even more broke than I am, not to mention he's in a very committed relationship with his bong. And Delilah got married and had twins. She didn't have time to run the shop." I hold up my hands, shaking them around. "I'm droning on but what I mean to say is, I'm so glad someone bought it. It's a really special place."

"It sounds like I have big shoes to fill."

I widen my eyes. "Huge."

"Why didn't his kids do something with it?" Dex asks.

Shaking my head, I shrug. "As far as I know, no kids. No wife. Just a life full of adventure."

"I see." Dex's eyes shift down and to the left like he's debating something. After a quick moment of contemplation, he places his hand on my knee. "So, what's been your favorite place to dive?"

I point to my chest, trying to act casual. But his large hand on my knee has me wanting to jump right out of my skin. "Me?"

"Yes, you."

"I don't have one. I just pitched in at the shop. I've never been scuba diving. I can swim. I just don't do ocean stuff."

Dex stares at me like I've lost my mind. "What do you mean you don't do 'ocean stuff?'"

I feel like I was pretty clear. I don't like the ocean and I don't want to get scuba certified. My top five worst fears go like this: One, getting eaten by a shark. Two, getting bitten by a shark and then bleeding to death in the ocean. Three, being pulled to the ocean floor by a giant octopus and being squeezed to death. Four, getting eaten by a shark again. Five, getting mistaken for a seal and an orca crushing my bones like I'm a doggie chew toy.

"I'm just more of a pool kind of girl. Where there are no sharks."

"Oh, you're one of those," he says, squeezing my knee. I don't appreciate his nonchalance at my paralyzing fear, but his hand is inching higher up my leg, and my brain has gone too fuzzy to snap back with something sassy. "Lennox, you have a much higher chance of drowning in the ocean than encountering an aggressive shark. And if by some miraculous chance a shark bit you, I promise it'd be only once—accidental or exploratory. Most bite victims survive."

"Wow." Now, it's my turn to stare at him like he's crazy.

He notices my vexed expression and asks, "What?"

"Oh, I'm just picturing what the coroner's face would look like as they write 'accidental' or 'exploratory' nibble as the cause of death in my file."

He laughs and gently pats my mid-thigh, sending tingles up my spine. "You can't let irrational fear keep you out of the ocean."

"Oh, I can. And I do."

"Certify with me," he insists.

"Even if I wanted to, I can't afford it. And let me reiterate...*I don't want to.*"

"Free of charge. I'm new to instruction, and I could use the help. You can be my practice student and give me feedback on how I'm doing as a teacher. In exchange, I'll pay for your certs, get you custom-fitted equipment, and everything else you need. What do you say?"

It becomes abundantly clear that Dex understands exactly how good-looking he is and the effect he has on women. He purposely ducks his head and looks up at me through his thick, dark lashes. He even goes as far as batting them a bit. "I'll give you private lessons, and we'll take baby steps. We don't even have to do your open water cert in the ocean. We could do a lake if you prefer."

I drop my jaw. "Lakes are worse. That's where man-eating saltwater crocodiles live. I assure you, their bites would not be accidental."

"Man-eating saltwater crocodiles?" he asks in disbelief. "How much time are you spending watching the *SyFy* network?"

I start counting the killer marine animal movies I've binged on the SyFy network in my head but lose track around eight. "Not a lot."

Dex laughs. "Listen, Lennox. There's a whole other world down there. It's unbelievable. When you're diving, it makes all your actual problems seem so small. There's a peaceful harmony in the ocean that is so intricately perfect that you start thinking that humans don't know what the fuck they're doing up here. When I'm fed up with this world, I find solace in the one below. It's a freedom you can't explain." He holds my gaze. "You just have to experience it."

I swear he could tell me to jump off a bridge or take a nap in a bonfire with that look on his face, and I'd do it.

"Okay, fine," I say. "Teeny, tiny baby steps. One lesson to start. And I want actual reports with statistics about the unlikeliness of a shark encounter before I even consider getting in the ocean."

"You got it," he replies quickly, a triumphant smile on his face.

I push against his shoulder. "Well, see? There you go. Already filling the big shoes. Jacob could never get me to agree to a lesson. He tried."

"Ah, well good to know you like me more than Jacob Hayes. I'm honored."

I flash him a smartass smirk. "I didn't say I like you more. I'm just implying you're way more persuasive."

"Really? Why's that?"

He drags his tongue over his dark pink lips, wetting them, causing a wave of desire to shoot up my thighs. *I shouldn't.* I promised myself that from here on out, I'd only go for guys who ask me out like cordial gentlemen. Three dates, *then* they get dessert. It's not because I'm a prude. I'm just trying to weed out the assholes and heartbreakers.

But Dex is so tempting that it's hard to find my self-control at the moment. I'm no match. He's tall, muscular, tan, with raven-colored hair. His dark hair makes his light eyes pop. I'm such a sucker for hazel eyes. Weak for deep dimples. Completely powerless for a man who's witty and smirks like that.

I don't believe in instant love. But I do believe in chemistry. And yes, I believe it's chemical. Like a physical feeling. Stupid, giddy, butterfly tingles. The kind of overwhelming attraction that makes all reason leave your brain. Two people are either destined to have it or not. Love takes time to grow, but chemistry explodes right out of the gate.

And if my hunch is right, Dex and I most definitely have chemistry.

I place my hand on his knee with no hesitation. My fingertips are on the warpath up his thighs, telling him exactly what's on my mind. "My hair is getting your shirt all wet," I say in a cracked whisper that's mostly from nerves, but it comes out sort of dangerously sexy. I roll with it. "Maybe you should take it back now."

I close my eyes and put my mouth on his, but instead of full, warm lips fervently kissing me back, I feel him pull away.

"Wait," he says.

Dex has fantastic reflexes. He dodges my kiss and catches my hand so quickly that, at first, I don't even register it's his rejection. "That was me trying to *Netflix* and chill." I try to sound playful, but now the nerves bubbling under my skin aren't from desire. It's from embarrassment.

"I'm flattered. I really am. But I'm serious about the diving stuff."

"Is there a no-sex oath for scuba divers I'm unaware of?"

He laughs, which makes me relax a little. I really like the way he laughs. It starts with his eyes first. They crinkle in the corners, and then his lips catch up, spreading into that charming grin. Then there's the rich baritone of the sound.

"Look, if I can be honest, I haven't made a lot of friends here. I normally don't have much in common with people, but you're easy to talk to. I like you."

"Those are all good things, right?"

"Yeah, great things." His expression turns solemn, and I know he's about to say something I don't agree with. "But in my experience, sex is the best way to fuck up a budding friendship. And I guess what I'm saying is, as much as I'd like to see you naked, I think I'd prefer to see you again tomorrow. Is that okay?"

"Oh, yeah, that's actually...nice. We can go slow. I didn't mean to give you the wrong impression here." The flood of excitement returns, making the hairs rise on the back of my neck. I thought Dex would be a fun night, but now he's saying all this stuff about seeing me tomorrow. What are the chances that he's actually a freaking decent guy? *Thank you, universe. I was due for a little good luck.* "I'm not usually a hook-up kind of girl. I think I kind of got caught up in the moment. But, full transparency, I'm a relationship junkie. So, it's great if you want to slow down, hang out tomorrow first, and see where things go—"

"I'm not," Dex interrupts. He sucks in his lips, a look of remorse on his face. "I'm sorry. I'm not a relationship junkie, to borrow your words."

This conversation is giving me whiplash. Hope, then bitter disappointment swinging like a pendulum back and forth with every verbal exchange. "Oh, so you meant see me naked or see me tomorrow."

"Right."

An uncomfortable ache balloons in my chest to the point it might burst. I've had guys pretend to like me, sleep with me, and then never call again. But this is a brand-new form of rejection. It was a little sneaky, and quite frankly, I feel led on. But maybe I led myself on. I knocked on his door. Asked to use his shower. Climbed on his bed. I'm the one who misread every single sign.

"It's nothing personal. I'm just not dating right now. And I don't want to be another guy to waste your time."

I raise my brows at him. *Oh, come on. That seems like a lazy lie.* A guy who looks like him is never *not* dating. But it's not my business.

"Okay. Well, thanks for your honesty." I show him a clipped smile.

He rubs his palms nervously against his jeans. "Are you leaving now?"

Turning my head slowly, I gawk as I meet his eyes. I try to scoff, but what comes out is an incredulous cackle. "Wait a minute, you're going to turn me down *and* boot me out of your bedroom wearing nothing but a thin T-shirt? I didn't kick your cat, man.

All I did was try to kiss you. I meant that to be flattering, at least."

He laughs in relief. "Oh shit, no. I'm not kicking you out. I just thought you'd be pissed at me. You're not about to storm out and cancel all the scuba stuff?"

I draw in a small breath, then release it with gusto. "No. If I cancel the scuba stuff, it's because I will forever be deathly afraid of sharks."

He smirks at me. "Oh, come on, Trouble. I swear on my life I won't let a shark eat you."

"Promise?"

He nods once. "Promise."

"Then, we're cool, Dex." I make a fist with my free hand and hold it out to him. "Friends?"

He taps his knuckles to mine, his charming grin sweet and *relieved*. "Friends."

There's a heavy ball of humiliation sinking deep into my gut. I can almost hear the thud as it settles into the pit of my stomach like a lead cannonball hitting the ocean floor. Hope squashed. Feelings unreturned. Chemistry snuffed right out. But it's okay. I cope how I always cope.

If I pretend like it's not a big deal...

Eventually, it just won't feel like such a big deal.

CHAPTER 4

Dex

Present Day

Miami

I force myself to inhale for four seconds, then exhale for six. I don't allow myself to breathe in short heaves. My panic attacks always start with hyperventilating. Once I lose my breath, I lose control.

I count the small marble tiles beneath my feet. *Cool tile.* Good idea. I step out of my black dress loafers and yank off my socks, pressing my bare feet against the cold floor. Glancing down, I roll my eyes when I see the brand name imprinted in gold scrawl on the heel of my shoe soles. *Christian Louboutin* gracing us with his designer presence at my grandmother's funeral.

I didn't pick my outfit today. I never do when I'm back home. My clothes, shoes, and matching watch are always conveniently messengered over to wherever I'm getting dressed.

Believe it or not, some reporter or another will likely comment on my shoes. These are too fancy. Louboutin loafers retail for well over a grand. No doubt someone will accuse me of squandering away Grandma's fortune on frivolous things before she's even cold in her grave. Then again, had I shown up in Magnannis, they wouldn't be fancy enough. The flip side of the coin is that I'm a disrespectful slob of an heir and just glad to be rid of Grandma so I can piss away her wealth.

Basically, damned if I do, damned if I don't. And this is why when I'm home in Miami, amongst the judgmental social elitists, I let other people dress me.

Fuck, do I hate it here.

I hear Grandma's voice in my head. *Just breathe, baby. Your feet have to stay here, but your mind can go wherever you want. Where do you want to go, sweet boy?*

My answer was always the same... *The ocean.* My other home. Far, far away from all the things I despise about being Dex Malcolm Hessler.

But I don't want to think about the ocean right now. I'm still clouded with guilt. When Grandma died, I was on a liveaboard at Socorro Island in Mexico without any cell service. November is prime season for whale sharks. All I could focus on was my dive students getting their money's worth out of their trip. The travel, equipment, and accommodations were so expensive, and I knew it was a once-in-a-lifetime experience for most of my students. They waited so long for a spotting. I gave myself a headache obsessing, trying to will it into existence. *Just one whale shark.*

We didn't see a damn one.

When we got back to San Jose Del Cabo, I learned my grandma had died alone in her sleep.

She called me the night she passed and left a bizarre message that will live in my head for the rest of my life. Her words were slurred, and she spoke like a broken record. Over and over, she kept telling me that there's a reason she did what she did. That she trusts me, and I need to make the choice with my heart, not my head. Grandma kept saying not to make the mistake she did, because if she could just go back, she would've chosen daisies.

But what choice? And what does she mean by choosing daisies?

I have so many questions, and there's still a lot to sort out with the lawyers.

Fuck.

My heart starts to race as I picture a bunch of suits, foaming at the mouth, wondering to whom Grandma left what. Of course, it's assumed everything will go to me—her wealth, her company.

I'm her only living relative. But there's always the chance of some sort of legal foul play. A loophole. Any excuse for the board to rip my family's hard-earned legacy to shreds and sell it off in pieces.

Goddammit. I should've been there at the meetings. I should've been there every time she signed a piece of paper. To protect her. She was tired. It was my job to help bear the load. But all I could think about was my freedom while I had it. Before I had to put the monkey suit on permanently and accept my fate.

The guilt washes over me like an insurmountable wave, and I forget to breathe slowly. I'm sucking in short heaves now, and the room starts spinning. The bathroom goes from too hot to too cold, back and forth, making me nauseous. I can't see the ocean...I can't see anything.

And now my panic attack is full-blown.

I clutch my chest as the sweat beads on my forehead. I've never had a heart attack, but this has to be what it feels like. My heart toggles from rapid pounding to stunned into stillness. Unable to find a set rhythm no matter how much I try to focus. I can't...

I can't...

I can't fucking breathe.

By the time the door opens, I'm slumped on the ground, my hot cheek resting against the cool tile as I feebly gasp for air.

"*Jesus, Dex,*" Denny squalls. "Oh my God. I'm here. I have them." She rattles a bottle of prescription pills before slamming them on the granite countertop. Hiking up her skirt so she has room to maneuver, she falls to her knees next to me. She grabs my cheeks in both of her soft hands, which feel like relief against my burning skin. "Look at me. You're fine. I'm right here. Just breathe. You are in control."

"Count," I muster out. "Count for me."

"One...two...three...four." Her voice sounds distant, but I hold my breath until I hear her next instructions. "That's good, Dex. Now, let it out. Six...five...four...three...two...one."

Denny counts up to four, then down from six at least ten more times until she's sure I can sit upright.

"Oh, honey. This is why you can't travel without your medication," Denny lectures. She swipes a hand towel from a woven basket and wets it under the faucet. Then, she proceeds to dab along my hairline. Sweet relief. It's a very soft towel. Actually, now that I'm calm enough to notice, this bathroom is oddly lavish for a funeral home.

I point to the transparent orange bottle at the edge of the counter. "Apparently, I didn't leave them. You found them."

"No," she says, rising to her feet. "These are backups from your last visit home."

I shouldn't be surprised she's prepared. Denny, my nickname for Denise, has been with our family since before I was born. She was a childhood friend of Mom's. Even when Mom left home for a while, Denny lived at the Hessler estate. I never knew what kind of family Denny came from, I just know she preferred to be part of ours.

And when Mom passed away, she and Grandma grew very close. They bonded over the grief of losing Mom and the agitation with Grandpa's absence. He chose to cope with Mom's death by doubling down on the whiskey while leaving Grandma to run the Hessler empire. I was only seven. There wasn't anything I could do to help. Denny became a sounding board, the one to hold Grandma's hand on the bad days. Eventually, she took over as Grandma's personal assistant and our household manager— there isn't much she doesn't do for us, including event planning, managing the staff, and making travel arrangements. But more realistically, I think Grandma always saw her as more of a second daughter of sorts.

Not me. I love Denny as a friend. But I only have one mother. She's gone. Grandpa's gone. Grandma's gone. Now, everyone I belong to...is gone.

"Backup?" I finally ask. "Which medication?" I've switched a few times over the past few years. They all eventually lose their efficacy.

"The same you're taking now, but only ten milligrams. What's your current dosage?"

I close my eyes and breathe out with a heavy sigh. "Sixty."

"Jesus," she mutters. "I didn't know they could prescribe that high of a dosage." She shakes the pills into her palm then deposits them into my outstretched hand. "Do you have water here? There are cold bottles in the lounge area. I can grab one."

"No need," I say before swallowing the pills dry. "Thank you."

"I didn't know it was still getting worse. When was the last time you had a panic attack?"

"Not since the Hessler executive holiday party last year, when I had to give the welcome speech."

"They're only happening when you're here in Miami?"

It's not that surprising. Miami used to feel like home. Once I got a taste of freedom and happiness in Las Vegas, home started feeling like a cage. Every time I came back, it was an unpleasant reminder of where my destiny would take me. And what do you expect right before you cage a bird? *It panics.*

"I guess."

She holds out her hands for mine to help me get up. When I notice her bright red polish, I smile at her. "You hate red nail polish. Almost as much as you hate animal print shoes."

Denny's blond hair is twisted neatly at the nape of her neck. Her earrings are modest—pearl studs. The black dress she's wearing is sleek and flattering but not promiscuous. Just classy. Her shoes are the perfect height. An elegant three inches. Everything about her ensemble is strategically subtle...except her bright nails.

She shrugs one shoulder. "She loved red."

"I know," I say.

Denny examines her nails, her eyes drooping with sadness. "She bought me a huge gift card at our favorite spa for my birthday. I never got a chance to use it because we always had a once-a-month 'official business meeting,' which was actually just her treating me to a massage, mani, pedi, and body wrap." She inhales deeply and releases a heavy breath. "I went early this week. When they told me to pick a color for my nails, I asked for the Dottie special."

"I get it. You wanted to feel close to her."

She nods emphatically. "Exactly. I don't know what I'm going to do without her. Dottie was my whole life." She touches my cheek. "It's just us now."

After everything she's done for us, it's selfish, but looking into her light eyes right now, I know I'd trade her in a heartbeat for Mom or Grandma.

It's just not the same...

She's not my family.

But maybe I should pull my head out of my ass because she's all I have left.

"Thank you, Denny. I'm glad you're here." I force a genuine smile.

We're both lost in our thoughts for a moment until Denny lets out a sharp exhale and clasps her hands together, signaling "Let's go." She straightens her already pristine dress then rubs her hands together like she's warming them. She's fidgety and anxious today. I know she's hurting, too.

"Are you ready?" she asks.

I take in a testing deep breath, ensuring my lungs are fully functioning again. "Yeah, I'm good."

"I have your speech." Denny brushes off my shoulders before fetching my suit jacket, hanging behind the bathroom door. After helping me slip on the stiff jacket, she pulls out a folded piece of paper from the hidden pockets in her dress. Wiggling it between two fingers, she says, "Just in case." Then she slips my printed-out eulogy into the inside pocket of my coat.

We rehearsed the speech a dozen times. I can easily recite it by memory. My issue isn't public speaking or making the tough decisions as a boss. My MBA taught me how to understand corporate finances, evaluate the efficacy of partnerships, and know the difference between the incubation, growth, and eventual decline of initiatives. I know numbers. In that aspect, I'm fully prepared to become the CEO of the Hessler Group. It's people that are a struggle. I'm not always good at reading people.

Denny still looks at me skeptically. Her gaze darts from the pills on the counter back to my eyes. "Are you sure you're up for this?"

"Even if I wasn't, who else could speak today?" *Everyone's gone. It's all on me now.*

"I'm just asking, Dex." She twists her lips, and her big blue eyes shift down. "The last thing I want is for you to collapse in front of all those people."

I exhale. "I'll be fine. But I don't think I want to read the speech."

It's a fine eulogy. We covered Grandma's most prominent accomplishments, making sure to mention how she was a pioneer in an industry dominated by men. We go into great detail about her accolades as a CEO, commanding a billion-dollar company yet still finding a way to raise her orphaned grandson. I think the exact words are: *Dottie Hessler was both a widower and a mother who lost her only child. But grief didn't deter her, and she miraculously found a way to raise her grandson while securing her spot amongst Forbes top 100 richest people in the world. She was a pioneer for women in business.*

It's not that it isn't true. It's just shallow.

"What do you want to say?"

"I know most of the company is out there today, but it just seems like such a shame to talk about work. Grandma was so much more than that. I remember this one time when I was eight; I called her and told her the nanny was hurting me. She was on a phone conference with the CEO of Royal Bahamas, Hessler's biggest competitor at the time. They were discussing a huge merger, but right in the middle, she put his ass on hold for twenty-two minutes. She came home, fired the nanny on the spot, then brought me back to the office with her."

"Yeah, that sounds like Dottie," she says with a half-hearted chuckle.

"Grandma kicked off her shoes and sat on the ground with me. She handed me crayons one by one and doodled with me while she finished her meeting on speaker. She ended up acquiring two Royal Bahamas ships that day."

I didn't understand the logistics until much later, but Royal Bahamas thought they got away with a slimy business deal. Of course, Grandma was two steps ahead. She stripped both ships to the studs, rebuilt and rebranded. Today, they are two of the most lucrative ships in the Hessler fleet. In fact, the revenue from those two ships is what knocked Royal Bahamas down a few pegs. We no longer consider them competition.

"Dottie was such a badass," Denny says. "She could do it all. I will forever be in awe of that woman."

I nod along. "Same."

"What did your nanny do to you, by the way?"

"Oh, right. See, that's the funny part. When Grandma finally got off the call and asked me what the nanny did to hurt me, I told her the truth."

"Which was?"

A chuckle breaks through my lips. "She wouldn't let me win during a game of Candy Land. The nanny wouldn't let me lie or cheat. She was trying to instill some morals into an eight-year-old, I think. Anyway, I meant she *hurt my feelings*. Grandma had to call the nanny back, apologize, rehire her, and then triple her salary."

"Oh, I bet she wanted to tear your little butt up," Denny says.

I shrug. "I'm sure, but she didn't. In fact, I distinctly remember going for ice cream that day. A sundae as big as my head with extra whipped cream."

"That's a sweet story." But I see the look in her eyes, like she's confused as to why I'm telling her this today.

I continue to clarify. "Grandma could've had the backup nanny pick me up so she could stay focused on her call. We had cameras all around the estate. She could've asked her security team to look into what was going on. There were always options, but she dropped what she was doing every time I needed her. I was the most important person in the world to her."

Denny's eyes drop to her shoes as she presses her lips together.

"You really were," she mutters.

My voice breaks as I continue, "Do you know how hard it is to be that disgustingly rich and powerful, with so much responsibility on your shoulders, and still make time to bake chocolate chip cookies with your grandson every other day? I was raised amongst rich, arrogant, asshole elitists who think money makes them superior to everyone. They are so out of touch with what matters. Grandma had more than all of them combined, yet her soul was still pure. She started good, and she stayed good. Money never turned her into something else. That's what I'm in awe of."

Denny smiles at me and straightens my tie before smoothing it down over my chest. "Take out the arrogant, asshole elitist part, and then tell *that* story. That's a good speech." She reaches into my inside coat pocket and pulls out the folded speech. "She started good and stayed good. I think that's all people need to know about Dottie Hessler. *She was a good one.*"

"Yeah, she was."

She ducks her head and finds my gaze before showing me a small, hesitant smile. "Are you ready now? Where's Leah?" Denny asks, looking around the bathroom as if I was hiding my ex-girlfriend the entire time.

"We broke up."

Denny's eyes grow into saucers. "Who broke up with whom?" she asks slowly. Her eyelids are twitching, like she's trying to resist the urge to roll them.

"You're going to question me about this the day of my grandmother's funeral?"

"The best way to get out of a scandal is—"

"To get ahead of it," I grumble. "*I know,* Denny. I know. But this isn't a scandal. Just two people who are no longer dating. Our breakup was amicable. Nothing dramatic."

She lifts one eyebrow as she presses her lips into a flat line. "I wonder if she'd say the same. We need to reach out to PR to make a statement."

"No, we don't."

In Vegas, I'm a normal guy. I don't spend a lot of money there. My house is nice, but it definitely doesn't say billionaire. I don't buy flashy things. My dive shop was almost bankrupt until my consultant, Avery, swooped in and saved us with proper marketing. Overall, things have been calm, and I've been flying under the radar easily.

Leah is still unaware of who I really am. None of my friends in Vegas know I'm the sole heir of one of the wealthiest families in the world. Hessler Group owns three major cruise companies. Luxe Adventure, Serenity, and Victorian. While the cruise names may be common knowledge, people rarely look up the owners behind them.

"I hate to say this, but your relationships affect everybody. Over a hundred thousand jobs are now dependent on you. We have to be wary of any women who might have a vendetta against you. What happened with you and Leah? Please tell me she broke up with you."

I grumble. "She stole something. It bothered me."

"She stole something?"

"A Birkin bag."

Denny's jaw drops. "A Birkin bag? The cheapest one they make is ten grand. That's a felony, Dex. How in the world did she get away with that?"

I hold up my hand. "Let me clarify. She stole the bag from her dad."

She squints one eye. "Leah's dad had a Birkin bag?" Denny jostles her head like she's trying to shake her thoughts into a reasonable explanation. "How come the more you clarify, the more confused I get?"

I really don't want to talk about this today, but it's unwise to keep secrets from Denny. She can't protect me if she doesn't know what's going on. So, I let out an exasperated sigh and explain. "Leah's dad is a veteran. He has a TBI from a deployment that's caused a lot of suffering. He's a very kind man, but I can tell his mind isn't all there. Therefore, Leah handles her parents' finances. Between VA pay, social security, and money he saved up during his career, he had a nice chunk of change in the bank. That money was supposed to pay off their house and vehicles and take care of bills. Leah's been slowly draining that account to buy *stuff* without them knowing. She was eyeing that Birkin bag for months. No way she could afford it on her own."

I actually bought it for her. The dive shop isn't particularly lucrative, and I'd been hiding my true wealth. I was going to make up some excuse about my long-term savings to explain why I could so easily buy a fifteen-thousand-dollar purse. But the day I intended to give it to her, she showed up at my place with the exact same bag. When I asked her where she got the money, she simply said her parents weren't using it.

I tried, but I couldn't look past it. It reminded me of the friends I grew up around and what I was trying to escape. Name brand this, name brand that. What you're wearing or driving defines your worth.

Leah's dad could've used a new sitting chair. Their house needed repairs. Leah's mom had a bad back and weak knees, and it was hard for her to keep up with the house. I suggested a cleaning service once a week so she didn't have to bear the burden alone. But instead, Leah drained their account for a purse.

I returned the bag I bought for her and ordered a cleaning service for her parents for an entire year. I had the vendor tell them they won a sweepstakes. Then, I ended things with Leah. She wasn't happy, but I'd hardly call her the vengeful type. It's been six months. I'm sure she doesn't even think of me anymore.

"Did you tell Dottie?"

"Yeah," I say with a shrug. "I told Grandma everything."

"Funny, you'd think she would've mentioned it to me," Denny mutters. "Okay, well..." She holds out her left hand, her large diamond catching a glint of the overhead lighting. She's been divorced for nearly two decades. Her ex is remarried, yet she still wears it. "I'll be right in the front row. If you start feeling any type of way, just give the signal and I will take over, okay?"

I nod. "Okay."

"Dex?" Denny rakes over my hair, making a makeshift comb with her fingers. It's the same way she's been fussing over me since I was a little boy. "I'm glad you're home. It's time to take your throne, and I'll be right here beside you. If no one else, you have me. You're not alone. You can trust me."

Throne? So dramatic. But she's not wrong. There's a lot of responsibility on a man whose total net worth is now a little north of eighteen billion dollars. It's not just my duty to my company but to the economy. Every decision I make from here on out isn't simply about business. It has to be strategic. A declaration of who I am and what I align with. When it comes to money like this, life is a giant game of chess. One you'll never win. Grandma bore the burden for far too long, and now it's my turn. I have a game to play, even if all I want is to disappear into the ocean.

I grab Denny's free hand, squeezing the tip of her fingertips and rubbing my thumb over the bright red polish. The same shade Grandma would always wear. "Thank God you're here, Denny."

She smiles. "Come on," she says, nodding to the door. "Let's go say goodbye."

CHAPTER 5

Lennox

Present Day

Las Vegas

The dim glow of the small TV is the only light in my bedroom. Alan kisses me on my temple before pulling me tighter into his bare chest. My bed creaks loudly, even at the most subtle movements. This mattress has seen better days, that's for sure. But replacing it is low on the priority list. First, see a dentist for my aching molar. Next, figure out why my car is making that wheezing sound. Third, replace my mattress.

Actually, scratch that. Before replacing my mattress, I really need to look into a new living situation. I share a tiny apartment with my roommate, Grace. She's a little quiet, definitely a wallflower, but she's kind and considerate. Oftentimes, she picks me up a soda and a candy bar when she swings by the gas station. She leaves it on the kitchen counter, always with the same little note: *For my favorite roomie.* It's sweet, but I highly suspect it's a bribe, so I don't go poking my nose into her business. I am almost certain Grace is not her real name and that she's using her room to store the drugs she distributes.

I can't be certain. I'm not in the business of raiding people's rooms when they're away. Nor am I a snitch. As long as I don't see any dead bodies or questionable sleepy-eyed women going in and out of my apartment, my lips are sealed. It's Las Vegas. The city of sin. Everybody is drunk, high, or some combination of the two. It could all be in my head, and blue-eyed, blonde-haired, sweet Grace is really just a normal roommate who happens to have four burner phones and pill cutters in every color.

I highly doubt it, though. I'm pretty positive she's dealing prescription drugs.

Alan lets out a low hum, a sheepish, satisfied smile on his face. "I think that was our best sex ever."

"Definitely." Liar. I silently scold myself. *Just tell him the truth. He's sweet, handsome, polite...and has never once given you an orgasm.* Maybe I just need to hold his hand through more adventurous stuff. Perhaps he's waiting for an invitation. "I have an idea," I say.

"What idea, Lennox?" he asks.

Lennox? That's another thing... Alan always calls me by my name, and it makes me feel like I'm in trouble. Okay, this is actually a good first step to opening this conversation. I won't tell him about the leather cuffs and anal beads I have in the back of my closet yet, but I can tell him I am a sucker for cutesy names.

I kiss his pec and nuzzle against his chest. "Hey, you know, you're welcome to call me nicknames if you like. I'm not one of those girls who doesn't like pet names. I think they're sweet, and they make me feel adored."

"Nicknames?" Alan asks.

"Yeah," I say, snuggling deeper into him. "Like baby, sexy, sugar, sweetheart, angel...anything really. Whatever feels natural."

"Oh." His brows knit together. "I uh...okay. I can try that if you'd like. It's just you have such a pretty name, I love to use it."

I exhale in exasperation. Therein lies the problem. Alan says and does everything right. Why aren't we connecting in *that* way? It's been over a year, and it's still awkward. Does he feel it, too? Is he faking it as well?

"What was your idea...um...Muffin?"

Muffin? Oh God. This nickname thing is going to take some work. "I was thinking, maybe I grab you a snack from the kitchen, we cuddle for a little longer, and then round two?" I waggle my eyebrows at him. "Me on top?"

"You're full of energy," Alan says with a worried-looking smile. You'd think I just suggested we snort a line and go base jumping.

"I'd love to be full of *something*," I say, winking.

His face falls in confusion. "Oh, right. You mentioned a snack. Are you hungry?"

The poor man is clueless about dirty talk.

"Sorry, bad joke. Never mind. But if you're hungry, I have a new bag of Funyuns in the pantry. And Grace left me a couple of Cokes in the fridge."

Alan sits up, causing me to slide off his chest. I wiggle upward to cuddle against his side again. "Not the most nutritious dinner choice. Is that all you have?"

I nod wordlessly.

"How about I bring some groceries by tomorrow morning? Sprouts is on my way back here. I'll pick up a fruit tray." I flash him a tepid smile at best. He winks and adds, "And the cream cheese fruit dip you like."

"My hero." I strain to press my lips against his. He pecks me, but I linger. So he awkwardly pecks me again, then pulls away.

He clears his throat. "You love that dip so much. I should keep it at my place, too. Maybe it'll get you to eat a little more fruit."

"And veggies," I say. "I dip baby carrots into that stuff, too."

"Gross," he teases.

We used to stay at Alan's house predominantly. It's much bigger. My apartment is similar to the cardboard boxes you find puppies in at yard sales. Just enough room to wiggle your ass and spin around. But we crash here because Alan's roommate recently got a girlfriend, and they're *loud* when they have sex. My boyfriend considers them lewd. Me? I'm a little jealous.

Through the paper-thin walls, I've heard them fuck, and I've also heard them make love. They seem to connect on every single level. The way I wish I was connecting with Alan.

I let my fingers tiptoe down his chest but before I can reach beneath the covers, he grabs my hand. "Len—I mean, Muffin, aren't you exhausted? We were at it for almost half an hour." He pulls my hand up to his lips and kisses my palm. "Anyway, I have to get home and take a shower. It's end-of-month inventory. I need to be at work a little early so I'm done in time for my shift."

"Such an overachiever," I mutter, crossing my legs, trying to ignore the familiar ache that won't be relieved.

"Actually, my boss thinks so too," Alan says, with an odd look on his face. "He offered me a raise."

"That's great. Good for you," I say, patting his hand. I'm trying to be enthusiastic, but I'm distracted by the itch that most definitely wasn't scratched. And as soon as Alan leaves, I can finish the job in private with my vibrator. "You deserve it more than anybody."

"The raise comes with a promotion to general night manager."

That gets my full attention. I shoot up in bed, the covers falling down, exposing my breasts. "*Alan*. That's amazing. You've been waiting for this for so long. I'm so happy for you." I wrap my arm around his broad chest and rub his shoulder in an awkward hug with my breasts smashed against his side.

"Thank you. And hey, there's a front desk concierge position open during the day shift. I could put in a good word for you at my company."

"Eh... Won't that be a problem, seeing as you're about to be the manager and we're dating?"

"No, not if you're on day shift. I wouldn't be your direct manager. Camden Hotels has really good benefits, and they do career mapping. If you wanted to switch over to corporate eventually, they'd help. There's a lot you can do in corporate— finance, marketing, accounting. They even offer tuition assistance if you want to go to school."

Grimacing, I run my hands through my hair, catching the few loose strands that break free. They're dark. My natural shade, but against the colorful glow of the TV screen, they almost look purple again. I really miss my purple hair. On our first date, Alan mentioned that flamboyant hair colors were fun but a little childish. Looking back, I'm not sure if he was merely commenting or if it was a not-so-subtle hint about my blue streaks at the time. Regardless, my hair has remained its natural jet-black for a year now since we officially became boyfriend and girlfriend.

"Thank you for thinking of me. But I need a break from customer service for a while. I'm seeing Avery tomorrow. I bet she has some ideas. Don't worry about me."

"Okay, just let me know if I can help." After kissing the top of my head, he crawls out of bed. He covers his bare ass when he stands in a show of modesty. Once his boxers are pulled on, he turns around and smiles at me. "You look very pretty."

"Thank you, babe."

His smile goes from wide to small, and then his face turns anguished as he switches on the bedside lamp. "Since we're being honest about things..."

"Yeah?" I ask.

"I'm happy to call you whatever you like, um...Dumpling."

Why did I open my mouth about nicknames? This is even more uncomfortable.

"Okay, I appreciate you trying," I say.

"But, for me, I prefer Alan. Is that all right? I've never been into pet names or any of that stuff."

"What stuff?"

He grimaces. "Like flaunting your relationship. Public displays of affection. I think what we do in private should be private."

I glance over his deep blue eyes and neatly trimmed sandy-blond hair. He really is beautiful. "Oh, okay, sure. I understand."

His smile returns. "Great. I like that we can talk about this stuff. I love you."

"I love you too," I reply, but the words feel empty. I do love Alan. I want to make him happy. I'm loyal, protective, and thoughtful. But I'm not *hungry* for him. Is this grownup love? Is maturity choosing what's good for me, regardless of what I'm actually craving?

Once he's fully dressed, he heads towards the door, leaving me behind, still naked and half-tucked under the sheets. "I'll lock the front door so you can stay cozy as long as you like. I'll see you in the morning," he says. *So considerate.*

"Have a good night at work."

I wait until I hear the front door close.

Then, the eager butterflies flutter in my chest as I open my nightstand drawer to find my sleek black vibrating clit stimulator. Magic little device. Relief is just moments away.

I flick on the vibration to the lowest settings and strip the sheets from my body, feeling the cool air kissing my nipples. I hate having sex under the covers. It's like trying to fuck in a straight jacket. What's there to be ashamed about when you love someone? When you're sharing your body with someone you trust, it should feel like a playground. Every breath should be held in anticipation until it hurts. Every touch should feel dangerous, like a salacious dare. Every time you lock eyes is an invitation to go one step further than you had before. Sex should be invigorating. A treasure, a treat, not a chore to endure.

I'm religious about cleaning my vibrators so I can take my time and use them all over. It's the teasing that really gets me. First, I place the suction divot in the hollow behind my ear. A few seconds later, I'm dragging it down my neck, fantasizing about plush lips leaving a trail of kisses down to my collarbone. Goosebumps begin to rise.

My breath quickens, and the images start to flash through my head. I stay focused on Alan's face, but it quickly morphs into the man who has been occupying my hidden thoughts for years now.

It always happens like this, and I hate myself for it. Because I don't see Alan's blond hair and blue eyes. I try to keep him at the forefront of my mind. But instead, as it always goes, I picture my fists closing around thick tufts of jet-black hair. Hazel eyes—green in small patches, honey-brown in others—hold my gaze. I see the smile that starts in his eyes, spreading to his lips.

As I graze my nipples one by one with the vibrator, I think about Dex's mouth on them. What it'd feel like. I wonder whether he's the kind of guy to gently flick his tongue or suck mercilessly. In my fantasy, he's a different Dex, and I'm a different Lennox. I want him, he wants me, and there aren't so many obstacles in the way. Like friendship. The excuse he's used to keep me at arm's length for three years now.

Friendship. The thing I say I'm satisfied with.

And I am in real life. I truly do care about Dex as a friend. I'd do anything for him.

But in the sanctity of my mind?

His large hands are all-fucking-over my body.

And the mere thought of it is almost enough to make me come.

My clit is aching by the time the vibrator is resting just below my belly button. I bite my lip hard, making myself wait, staying in the fantasy for just a moment longer. I wonder what he'd say to me right now. Is Dex powerful and possessive in the bedroom? Or sweet and tender? If he wanted me like that, would we make love... or fuck?

I guess I'll never get to know.

The vibrator barely contacts my wet clit before I'm sent. I groan loudly in pleasure at my surging climax. No one is here, so I let loose, whimpering, mewling, wishing these were the sounds I made with Alan. I bring him to the forefront of my mind, *focusing on my boyfriend*, feeling too guilty coming to the thought of a different man.

Stay, Alan. Stay with me.

When I hear his voice through the haze, saying my name, I'm certain for once my forced fantasy worked. It doesn't always, so I'm relieved. At least I'm hearing the right man's voice. But then he speaks again, and it sounds a little too real.

"Lennox?"

Yanked from my post-orgasmic high, I fly up into a sitting position to see Alan standing in the doorway. The bedroom door that was previously closed is flung wide open. My jaw drops. As if he didn't just see my entire display of theatrics, I hastily tuck my vibrator behind my back. I clamp my knees together, closing my legs and hiding my swollen sex. But I don't say anything as I try to gauge his expression.

There's no misunderstanding the look on his face. It's hurt and bewilderment mixed with a lot of embarrassment.

"I wasn't spying on you," he says, pointing to the nightstand. "I forgot my wallet. I knocked, but I don't think you heard."

I glance to my right, and sure enough, his worn black wallet is lying on my plastic nightstand. Grasping the edge of my sheets, I pull them up and cover my naked body as best I can before grabbing his wallet off the nightstand. Holding it out to him, I say, "I didn't think you were spying on me."

Why am I panicking? I didn't do anything wrong, did I? Okay, it's wrong to fantasize about another man, but who gets to govern my thoughts? I can't even control them myself. God, I wish he'd make a joke to comfort me right now. Something like, *"Well, that was quite a show."* Or, *"If I wasn't late for work, I'd join you for another round."* But it's Alan, so all he does is politely take his wallet and avoid my gaze.

"I'll lock up again behind me. Have a good night, Lennox."

He doesn't wait for my response.

And it dawns on me as he closes the door that the nicknames are gone, and we're already back to *Lennox.*

Except it's appropriate.

Because right now, I do actually believe I'm in trouble.

CHAPTER 6

Dex

Present Day

Miami

I shouldn't be nervous. I was bred for this. To the advisory board, the executives, and all of the employees at Hessler Group, I'm merely assuming my rightful role.

No one needs to know about the man who is having panic attacks behind closed doors. The man who feels more comfortable around deadly sharks than in large crowds of people.

They need "the closer." Their leader. The man who graduated from Harvard Business School with honors and knows more about corporate strategy than anyone else in the room.

They don't want Dex. *They need Mr. Hessler.*

I loosen my tie and lean back in my seat, looking out the windows at the Miami skyline. The sun is glistening off the still waters surrounding the cityscape. With no boats in motion, the water is stoic. It looks more like glass than water.

This was Grandma's preferred meeting room for everything. She loved this view. She liked looking at the ocean, but she was terrified of getting in. Never once could I convince her to put on a wetsuit and see what was beneath the water line. Grandma couldn't swim, and she wouldn't let me teach her. She told me she'd rather be lion chow than shark bait.

In her favorite chair, looking at her favorite view, I can't help thinking about her favorite movie. The unsinkable ship that sunk. *Titanic*. Completely unfathomable. That's how everything feels right now. *Impossible*. How the hell is Dottie Hessler gone? I wasn't ready. No one was ready.

A vibration on the table pulls me from my thoughts. As usual, I smile when I see Lennox's name flash across my phone. I answer without hesitation.

"Len, have you ever seen *Titanic*?" I ask.

This is my rapport with Lennox. We never answer the phone with "Hello." We're too eager to actually talk. "Hello" seems like a waste of time when it comes to us.

"I watch the 1997 version about once a year. I like to keep a young DiCaprio fresh in my mind," she says.

"I know Kate Winslet survives. But if they were together when everything went down, how did *he* die?"

"Jack?" Lennox asks.

"Who? No, I mean DiCaprio."

"Yeah, Dex. He plays Jack. Kate Winslet plays Rose, who floats on top of a door to survive. Jack's just holding onto the aforementioned door and freezes to death in the water."

"What the hell?" I ask. "How does that make sense? Why didn't he get on?"

"They couldn't both fit."

"And they couldn't just find another door?" *Freaking Hollywood.*

She half grumbles, half scoffs. "You're missing the point. It was beautifully self-sacrificial. He died so she could live. It was some seriously epic romantic stuff. I can't believe you've never seen it."

"No thanks," I grunt into the phone. "I probably feel about Titanic the way you feel about *Jaws* or *The Meg*. Or even serial killer documentaries."

"Actually, I really enjoy those. I live on the Oxygen channel these days."

"See? That's concerning."

"And seriously—being shipwrecked in the North Atlantic Ocean is as scary to you as getting eaten alive or murdered? Because one is a quick call to AAA and an airlift rescue. The other is a gory death."

It's not the shipwreck that's terrifying. It's the mass lawsuits that would come out of a situation like that. "You can't just call AAA from a ship."

"How would you know? It's still a vehicle of sorts," she says.

"I just know," I reply, trying not to draw attention to my expertise. "Anyway, what's up? How are you?"

She's quiet for a minute. I wait patiently for her to respond before she finally rushes out, "I need to cancel my spot on the Cozumel trip."

Ah, typical. At least once before every dive trip, I have to remind Lennox she won't be shark food. "Len, I promise you, there aren't going to be any sharks in that region—"

"No, it's not that." She clears her throat. "I can't afford it anymore. I got fired."

I grip the phone tighter in my hand, pressing it firmly against my cheek. "I want to say, 'I'm sorry,' but you hated that job."

"I did. Don't get me wrong, I'm relieved. But I don't know... Everyone seems kind of disappointed in me."

"Who's everyone? I'm certainly not."

She sighs. "Okay, fair enough. Maybe *I'm* disappointed in me."

"Why?"

"I think I want too much from a job."

If only she could see my vexed expression. "Your job paid like twenty bucks an hour."

"Excuse you. That's good pay for someone like me."

"Someone like you, being?" I ask.

"No college degree, has never kept a full-time job for more than a few months, hates numbers and metrics, and has the attention span of one of the little fish in your tanks...so, yeah, twenty bucks an hour is solid. But money isn't the want I'm talking about anyway."

Leaning back in my chair, eyes fixed on the Miami skyline, I breathe out and feel the pressure in my chest lessen. I always feel better when my mind is on Lennox. "What are you talking about then?"

"I want to love what I do each day. You know the way you feel about scuba diving? Aren't we supposed to feel like that all the time? Or is that childish, head-in-the-clouds thinking?"

"If I breathed through an oxygen tank under water for forty hours a week, I'd be brain dead. Not to mention, the dive shop doesn't pay my bills. You know it's a hobby."

She mumbles something I can't make out, then says, "That's right, I forgot you have a backup big boy job back home. What's your family business again? You guys are in cargo shipping?"

"Just ships," I mumble, then quickly digress. "But anyway, look, there are some people who live to work and others who work for the weekends. Everyone is different. It doesn't have to make sense to anyone but you. Just figure out what you want and go for it. You can make a great living in a more creative, less structured field. It's hard but not impossible. If you're miserable working at an insurance call center, maybe getting fired is the universe's way of telling you it's not for you."

She lets out a little chuckle. "You're so wise, Grandpa. I hope I'm as astute as you when I'm your age."

"When you're thirty? In three years?"

"Yes. I sincerely hope I age as gracefully as you," she teases. "Touch of gray. Bifocals. Your walking cane always adds a touch of sophistication to your outfit."

"Hilarious." I smile into the phone, wishing we weren't on the phone. But it's a little easier to talk to Lennox when there's physical distance between us. I see her, and my mind gets hung up on all the things I tell myself I don't want.

Three years ago, when the quirky showstopper with purple hair appeared at my bedroom door, trying to contribute to a pitch jar, I sucked in a breath I've been holding ever since. I've held on to

Lennox like a troll does its treasure. I keep her close however I can.

For us, that means friendship.

It's not like I'm not torturously tempted to yank her long hair back, tear her eccentric little outfits off, and bend her naked body over whatever surface she'd let me. I'd show her what all these clowns she dates are lacking.

But Lennox has something I've never encountered before. She's genuine. Full of raw honesty and good intentions. It fuels me in the best way. The moment I was ready to give up on people, Lennox gave me hope. She excavated a side of me I was trying to bury.

I needed her friendship so much more than I needed to fuck her, so I had no choice but to keep the boundaries in place. There's no faster way to lose a friend than getting sex, feelings, and money involved.

Therefore, I try not to look at anything except her eyes or be alone with her too often. I shake her boyfriend's hand out of respect. I avoid her like the plague after a dive when she's peeled off her wetsuit, and her tits, barely concealed in string bikinis, are calling out to me like a persistent-as-fuck siren. I keep my dick tucked away and all my secrets hidden. She doesn't know who my family is or my net worth. Lennox doesn't know anything about the other side of me... She wouldn't like him. Or maybe she could warm up to the idea of my life in Miami.

I don't know how to start that conversation or bridge that gap. I never planned to. I knew my time in Vegas was temporary. I just never imagined encountering someone who means as much to me as Lennox. She's probably the longest relationship I've ever had. A pseudo-relationship built on fantasy, denial, and self-control. But still...

"So, what are your next steps?" I ask her.

"Well, step one is canceling trips that are now out of my budget," she says.

I exhale into the phone. "I'd offer to pay for you, but Pocket Protectors probably wouldn't appreciate that very much."

"Don't call Alan that," she scolds me.

"What?" I ask defensively. "You call him that."

"When I call him that, it's a playful term of endearment. When you call him that, you're making fun of him."

I hate Alan more than all of Lennox's other past boyfriends. She's had a slew of dalliances since I passed on my tiny window of opportunity three years ago. She's always capturing some guy's attention or another. But they end up disappointing her quickly and never last long. Alan is different. Not her usual type. He's genuinely a good guy. I roll my eyes just thinking about it. He might actually last. One day, I'm going to be front row at their wedding, smiling at the beautiful bride who should've been mine and daydreaming about beating Alan to a pulp.

"I'm not making fun of him. Just the other day, a blue pen exploded in my unprotected pocket. Ruined my nice new pants. I couldn't help but think how much smarter Alan is than me."

She roars in laughter. *There it is.* My favorite sound. "You're such a jackass. Anyway, are you free to come over to Finn and Avery's tonight? The fridge is stocked with the beer you like."

"As much as I'd love to crash your couples' night, I'm in Miami."

"Alan's working. And what? Since when are you in Miami? I thought you just got back from Mexico."

"I got back, then had to head out again the day after. Something back home came up." *Not technically a lie.* I didn't know how to tell my Vegas friends that Grandma died. They barely knew she existed and certainly don't know what she means to me.

Lennox is, of course, the exception. She met Grandma once a few years ago. Just one dinner, but they bonded so quickly. They both understood how much the other means to me. Maybe that's why I don't want to tell Lennox about my loss. I'm sure she'll say and do all the right things to pull out the emotions I've set aside. Then, I'll have to deal with all the pain I'm effectively avoiding.

I don't have time to fall apart. There's too much work to be done. A legacy to uphold.

"You know something? You get really secretive when you go home."

There's a lull as she calls me on my shit. "I just don't like talking about it. Right now, home is really...complicated."

"Anything I can do to help?"

"Yeah. Don't cancel the dive trip. I planned this whole thing during ray season *for you*. You haven't seen them on a dive before and said you always wanted to."

Lennox typically avoids the dives with possible sightings of big marine life. She thinks baby whales will only attract killer sharks. According to her, dolphins are vindictive enough to drown you. She also has an irrational fear of being squashed between two whales like getting sandwiched between two semi-trucks. Not a completely inaccurate analogy. At any rate, big sea turtles and eagle rays seem to be the exception. She likes those.

"I did. But I'm not exaggerating. I'm broke. I could barely afford it before, and now I'm screwed. I don't even know how I'm going to pay rent next month. And I'm sick of taking handouts from everyone, so don't offer. It's starting to make me feel pathetic."

"You know the stuff that's come up here?"

"Yeah."

"The Cozumel trip will be my last for Discover Dives. I have to go back to working my big boy job, full time. So, if it's the last dive I lead, I'd really like for you to be there. We can work something out financially. A payment plan. Just give me a dollar a month until the end of time. We'll figure it out, okay?"

She's silent again, so I knock my thumb against the table to kill time. But the lull becomes too much. "Len, you still there?"

"Yes. So, you're moving?"

I nod slowly, then remember she can't see me. "Yes. I'm in no hurry to sell the house, though. You, Finn, and Avery can still use the hot tub whenever you want."

"Hm," she says, her tone unmistakably peeved.

"What does 'hm' mean?"

"Funny that you think your hot tub is what I'll miss."

"Aw, okay. Don't get all sad and sappy on me yet. I'll be home in a few days to grab some things, and we can shed a few tears then."

I swear I hear her sniffle which is odd because Lennox doesn't cry. Ever. Or she's strategic about hiding it. In the three years I've known her, I've seen her eyes tear up once, but that was when she closed the car door on her toe and nearly broke it.

"You know I'm always only a phone call away for you," I assure her.

"Really? Because you suck with your phone, Dex. I'm shocked you answered today."

Lennox thinks I'm flaky with my phone. On more than one occasion, I've heard her refer to me as a lovable goof. The truth is my phone is never not ringing. I often ignore it. Even when Grandma dismissed me from my director position three years ago, I still stayed on very part-time in an advisory role. I couldn't completely lose touch of my future company. Not to mention, there is always some kind of familiar affair I get looped into. Someone always needs a signature for something or another.

Between the lawyers, advisors, Denny, staff, and PR, my phone never stops. It's overwhelming. I keep it on silent most of the time, which means I miss more of Lennox's calls and messages than I mean to. That's no good.

Maybe I should just get an extra phone and only give Lennox the number. Is that inappropriate to have a dedicated phone for a woman who's in love with another man?

"I'll get better with it. From now on if you call, I'll answer, Trouble. I promise."

She laughs. "All these years, and you still call me that. Do you remember when you gave me that nickname?"

Of course, I do. "The day we met. You want me to stop?"

"No," she says softly. "I love nicknames. And thank you regarding the trip. I'll figure out how to pay you back."

"So you'll go?"

"Yes," she replies.

"Good."

A light knock on the meeting room door interrupts us. I thought it was the first board member an hour early, but turns out it's Denny. She's in a sharp-looking gray suit today, as if she belongs in the boardroom. She certainly looks the part.

I beckon her in as I rise. "Hey," I say in a hush to Lennox, "I have to go. Duty calls."

I hang up in a hurry, feeling guilty. I don't know why I get like this. So desperately trying to keep my worlds apart. Of all the people in my life, I know Denny and Lennox wouldn't mix.

"Dex Hessler, what in the world are you doing?" She clicks her tongue as she crosses the room. "Security said you were at the office preparing for some big meeting?"

"That is accurate," I say.

"You shouldn't be here today. We buried your grandmother three days ago. You should be mourning in peace, honey. Why was the entire board called out?"

I point to the sealed envelope lying in the middle of the table. "I needed a distraction. I have the will. I figured a little transparency with the leadership team would help break the ice. The lawyer who was assigned as the executor is coming to walk us all through it."

"I'm sorry...*what*?" Denny hisses. "Please tell me you're not crazy enough to read your grandmother's will to your subordinates."

"Denny, calm down. Not my personal finances, just the matters regarding the Hessler Group."

I flew the entire leadership team into the office on a Saturday. Grandma's will was submitted to the probate courts almost immediately upon her death. She had a plan ready to execute like a well-oiled machine. Due to her financial status, the will was immediately sealed. No one knows what's in it besides Grandma and the lawyers who prepared it.

I decided to open and go over the will with Hessler Group's board of advisors and senior executive team. Well, most of it. They don't need to know the full extent of my outrageous wealth, but I do want to go over the fate of the company.

Obviously, I have big shoes to fill. Grandma spent decades earning their trust and loyalty. And some of them probably don't trust my competency. I'm half the age of most of them. Others don't like the fact that while I should've been assuming more responsibility over the past three years, I was living a double life across the country. But unfortunately for them, Hessler Group is privately owned. There's no voting me out. Like it or not, Grandma chose her successor. Hessler Group is now mine. And my first order of business is assuring my new team that their jobs are secure and I will break my back safeguarding the legacy my grandparents built.

Denny finds a seat on the other side of the table. "You have my number, right?" she asks as she leans back in the leather executive chair. She crosses her arms and legs in unison.

"Yes?" What a crazy question. We talk weekly.

"Then use it, Dex. I really wish you'd run these things by me first."

I raise a brow. "Run it by you?" I ask, lowering my tone.

Denny's eyes pop open as she gestures to the long, empty table. "I could've arranged a spread. Breakfast, coffee, tea, and such."

Oh. That slipped my mind. "Is it too late?"

She glances at her watch. "How much time do we have?"

"They should be arriving in an hour."

She winks at me as she rises. "Easy. Let me make some calls to the caterers and see what they can prepare and deliver in a hurry."

"Can't the cafeteria from downstairs send some donuts and coffee up?"

Our headquarters is a 350-million-dollar corporate campus. Thousands of employees spend most of their waking hours here. I specifically remember Grandma wanting to ensure that the dining facilities were top-tier and more than accommodating for all the employees. There's a literal food court on the first floor. Surely, one of those shops can whip up something for a meeting of about twenty people.

"Dex," Denny says with a sigh. "You called in the entire executive leadership team and the advisory board. You can't feed millionaires cafeteria food. Goodness." She might as well pat me on the head and pinch my cheek, the way she talks to me like I'm a child. Probably because she still sees me as a child.

"I don't mind cafeteria food."

Her smile is riddled with condescension. "You're the big boss. Time to act the part. Our private caterers do a beautiful spread of salmon caviar benedict and wagyu beef tostadas."

I don't have the energy for an ethical debate right now. After the leadership meeting, I have to meet with PR. Then, the finance team. Not to mention, I have to sit through about ten different meetings with personal lawyers as I agree to bank transfers and start property appraisals. "Whatever you think. Let's just make sure there's plenty of coffee."

"Yes, sir." Denny flashes me an overenthusiastic smile paired with an eager thumbs up. "Oh, um..." She glances at the sealed envelope on the table. "I know this meeting is just for board members and executives, but do you mind if I stay to hear what's in the will? Just so I understand how to support you, or if you need..." She trails off, shoulders slumping, cheeks flushing. She suddenly looks vulnerable. *Hm, was this the same woman talking about caviar for millionaires a few moments ago?*

"Denny, are you asking me if you still have a job?"

She barely nods, one small bob of her head. "In not so many words."

"You aren't my employee. You're family. You shouldn't even have to ask."

She blows out an exaggerated breath of relief. "Thank you, Dex. And what I said before—about running things by me, it was just to help you. The reason Dottie was such an amazing leader is because she knew how to delegate. You have worker bees now." She clicks her jaw. "Let us handle the brunch spreads, okay?"

"Thanks."

She shuffles to the door, already dialing on her phone to make arrangements.

"Denny, wait," I say, calling her back.

"Yes?"

As I glance at the yellow, still-sealed envelope, it suddenly dawns on me why Denny doesn't have the will. Only the court, the executor, and the named beneficiaries receive a copy. "If you don't have a copy of the will, that means..."

"Right." She nods. "The agreement with your grandpa still remains in place. I have no claim in any sort of Hessler affairs." She shrugs. "We knew this."

"I guess I always thought Grandma would've figured out a way around it," I say.

Denny nods. "I think she tried. That's good enough." The pained look on her face makes my stomach twist. Denny's family, too, whether or not my grandpa wanted to accept that. He never looked too kindly on people who wanted handouts. From what I understand, he saw her as more of a barnacle than anything else. He allowed her to live with Grandma and Mom as long as she was legally bound to an agreement that ensured she couldn't claim anything from the Hesslers nor sue for any various purposes. A bizarre arrangement, but that was Grandpa's style. He built his kingdom behind walls of legal protection.

"What about the Hessler Estate?"

"What about it?" Denny asks, looking puzzled.

"Honestly, you spent more time there than I ever did. It's basically your childhood home. I want to sell it to you."

Her jaw drops. "Dex...that's...very generous, but you know I can't afford—"

"For a dollar. Or is that too steep?" I ask with a wink.

"I...um..." Tears begin to fill her eyes. "I could probably handle a dollar," she breathes out in a whisper.

"Great. I'll have the real estate team make arrangements. I'll make sure we add the amount of the annual taxes to your salary, too. The property will be in much better care with you. I travel too much anyway. This is how Grandma would've wanted it."

Crossing the room, she wraps her arms around my neck, her tears absorbing into my dress shirt. Leaning back, she looks me in the eye. "Sweet boy. It's hard to believe you're a Hessler sometimes." She pats my cheek. "Okay, I'm off."

With that, she's dialing again on her phone, a little pep in her step as the new owner of a forty-million dollar property.

CHAPTER 7

Dex

In the matter of Hessler Group Holdings, I nominate Dex Malcolm Hessler's legal spouse to inherit my majority shares in full, which are then to be locked from transfer or distribution for a minimum of a twelve-month period.

Just like that. One simple sentence has changed the entire trajectory of my life.

At least twenty pairs of eyes are locked on my ghost-white face, but all I can do is focus on breathing. *Stay calm. Stay in control.*

Looking down at the small stack of papers in front of me, I tap the line that just threatened my entire future. I lift my eyes, glaring at the lawyer across from me who has the daunting task of explaining the troublesome matter at hand.

"What the fu—" I exhale. After taking in a few more deep breaths, I collect myself and start again. "Ms. Mendel, what does this mean?" I force out, trying to maintain manners.

The lawyer gulps as I address her directly. She's young. I bet she's barely out of the legal bullpen. Tori Mendel. I've never heard of her before today. She clarified upon her arrival that the will was revised under her guidance a couple months ago. Why would Grandma hire an executor that isn't in-house? We pay a small fortune for a dedicated team of very experienced lawyers. Perhaps it's because she was planning to pull the rug out from under all of us.

Tori clears her throat and speaks with confidence. "Mr. Hessler, it indicates that Hessler Group, being privately owned, has a policy that the majority shareholder of the company also assumes the role of CEO."

"That part I understand. What's confusing me is the part that says my *legal spouse*."

Tori sucks in her lips. "Um, so that would indicate an individual that you are legally married to. We'd need to see a marriage certificate to validate the name—"

"Ms. Mendel, I'm not married. I've never been married. I have no plans to marry," I bark out.

The boardroom is silent except for the subtle sound of people shifting in their chairs. The spread that Denny arranged for has been served, but no one is touching the little white plates in front of them filled with lavish brunch appetizers.

Denny leans forward in her chair, her elbows hitting the table. "Clearly, this is a misunderstanding." Her voice is honey-smooth and unwavering, a direct contradiction to my current fluster. But this is what she's constantly trying to remind me of. A good leader maintains their composure, even in the face of disaster. "Dottie must've put this together when Dex was in a relationship. Perhaps she made some assumptions about Dex and Leah's future plans, but that relationship has since ended. I'm assuming as there is no one to claim the title of his legal spouse, the company inheritance defaults to the Hessler's next of kin." Denny gestures to me. "Hence, her grandson. Problem solved."

I see the first flicker of agitation on Tori's face. She barely glances in Denny's direction and locks her gaze back on me. Folding her hands, she calmly explains, "That's not an option. Mrs. Hessler was extremely clear about her intentions. The company will either be claimed by your legal spouse, or you forfeit the shares to a trust. Hessler Group would be without an acting CEO. And if the trust is unclaimed, the state will likely get involved after a relatively short dormancy period."

I bury my head in my hands as I groan. *Grandma? What the hell were you thinking?* She knew I was nowhere close to marriage. There's not a damn woman on the planet I'd trust to be my wife right now. And especially not one I'd hand my family's entire company over to.

From the moment I turned eighteen, I've been manipulated, tricked, and possessed by women, all in attempts to obtain my wealth. Briar was the icing on the cake. Never again. I dated Leah because, after her divorce, she swore she'd never marry again either. We were in similar boats—disinterested in trusting the opposite sex again. We were comfortable with the boundaries we set. Grandma knew all of this. *How could she do this to me?*

"How about this?" Hank Fowler, our most senior advisor, who has sat on the board for thirty years, speaks up. His voice is grisly, a side-effect from decades of chain-smoking cigars. "What if all the shareholders in this room refused to forfeit ownership to the state? Then we could collectively vote Dex back in as our CEO."

Hank's thick white eyebrows are furrowed, but when he catches my glance, he smiles. A brief rush of gratitude sobers my current horror.

"Thank you, Hank."

He bows his head in a heavy nod. "The seat at the head of the table is yours, son. Harrison and Dorothea set this company up for you. We're not going to let some senseless legal mumbo jumbo stand in the way."

I look around the room and watch the ripple effect of nods and mumbles of support.

"A very nice sentiment," Tori says with a look of reluctance on her face. "But unfortunately, you don't have the power to do that. You're an advisory board. Not a board of directors. Your minimal shares were gifted, and any and all of your input was implemented at Mrs. Hessler's discretion."

Peter Richmond chimes in next, a newer board member but

a pioneer in eCommerce. He was brought on about five years ago as a lynchpin in our new merchandising endeavors. "I don't mean to sound crass here, but all we need is a marriage certificate for the inheritance, right?"

Tori peers at him quizzically. "Yes. It has to be a legal marriage."

"Then...uh, can we just hire a wife?" Peter turns his attention to me and widens his eyes. "Or, pardon me. I shouldn't assume... Wife or husband?" he asks.

"Wife," I reply.

"My niece is an aspiring actress. She's twenty-two and a little ditzy, but I'm sure she could slip on a ring for the right price and pretend to be married to Dex for a year until she could relinquish the shares. She doesn't have a lick of common sense, but she'll sign the papers where we tell her to."

Tori looks at me and lifts her eyebrows. She's probably the youngest person in this room, yet suddenly seemingly the most level-headed and sensible. "I'm going to pretend I didn't just hear a ploy to fraudulently fulfill this will—"

"It doesn't have to be fraudulent," Peter assures her.

Wonderful. Apparently, my board of advisors not only provides counsel for my company but can fetch me a wife at the drop of a hat. The epitome of resourcefulness.

"And anyway, it's a dangerous game to play," Tori advises. "There is no red tape here. Whoever claims the company as Dex's spouse will be directly stepping into Mrs. Hessler's business shoes, so to speak. But she's not inheriting any wealth. Just whatever salary comes with being the CEO of Hessler Group." Tori gestures to me with her palm toward the ceiling. "In an effort to access a mass fortune, she could sell Hessler Group off in pieces, absolve the company, fire you all, dismiss your pensions. She would have the power to drive this company straight into the ground and walk away with history's biggest personal payout."

"She'd never," Peter says.

"Are you sure?" I ask as the sickening realization overcomes me. "What do you think a twenty-two-year-old would choose if billions of dollars were in reach? Sixty-hour work weeks in an office, or a life of luxury, jet-setting across the globe?"

Peter shudders. "Okay, good point. Plan C?"

"There is no Plan C," Denny says as she points to the stack of papers in front of me. "We could continue to offer futile suggestions, but I assure you, knowing Dottie, she already thought of them all. There's only one solution here."

"Which is?" Hank asks, his voice full of snippy agitation. He's always had a mild irritation with Denny, who has no problem inserting herself into business matters of Hessler Group. On more than one occasion, he told her to mind her place. But all she wanted was to protect Grandma and me, and she had no qualms going toe-to-toe with the powerful men in the room.

Denny doesn't address him and instead tilts her head to the side, meeting my eyes with a pitying stare. "Dex, I think you should return to Las Vegas, take a couple days to rest, and get your affairs in order. You should have time to mourn Dottie in peace. I'll take care of all of this for you. I'll find you a wife who can run Hessler Group for a year, then hand it right back. Someone we can trust."

A wife I can trust?

At this point, resurrecting Grandma seems like an easier feat.

CHAPTER 8

Lennox

Present Day

Las Vegas

My ass is aching from the hard ground, but I don't care. I'm in a good mood today. The lukewarm breeze is so pleasant. It's a perfect park day. Alan and I packed a picnic of all things. The weather is unseasonably warm for December, so we thought we'd take advantage of his day off.

I'm munching on baby carrots as Alan tries to prep me for my interview as the day shift concierge at Camden Hotel on Bateman Street. I caved and took the interview he set up. Mostly on accident. After our awkward encounter where he caught me with a vibrator in my hand, I just wanted to do something to stay on his good side. When I brought it up, he was so excited to help me get back on my feet. But it was a stupid move. I don't know what I was worried about. Alan only has good sides. He wasn't angry with me. And now, I'm about to interview for yet another job I'll despise.

"So, I wouldn't bring up the fact that you got fired from Advantage Insurance. If they ask, you do have to say you were terminated, but make sure you mention it wasn't for anything violent or issues with other team members. Camden is big on camaraderie. At least for the management track, so just something to keep in mind."

I'm only half paying attention to Alan as I tuck the extra

fabric of my short sundress between my thighs and clamp my legs together. Then, I lay back on the polka-dot picnic blanket. The breeze catches something delicious-smelling—funnel cake, churros, something fried and sweet. If I had more motivation at the moment, I'd go hunt down a snack.

I grab my phone and turn it face down on my belly, but as soon as I do, it buzzes, tickling me.

> **Dex: Professional panda cuddler. But you'd have to move to China.**

I chuckle out loud.

> **Me: Sold.**

> **Dex: What? Not yet. I have so many more suggestions.**

Dex has been sending me all sorts of odd jobs since I told him I got fired. He toggles between being serious and helpful—like offering to take a look at my resumé—and then just trying to make me laugh. Today he's being particularly playful, which matches my good mood. That's how Dex and I are. Always in sync.

I'm a little surprised Dex hasn't just offered me a job. Discover Dives isn't lucrative enough to really make a living, but Dex mentioned that his family's company is pretty big. Surely I qualify for something entry-level there. Perhaps he thinks I wouldn't be interested in moving to Miami. That'd be correct. I want to stay close to my friends and family. Especially my dad. He needs me.

Not to mention, I still don't know what Dex really does. We've always joked around and called it his "big boy job." He's rather secretive about it; just says it's something with numbers. I once teasingly accused him of running the mafia and printing money.

I mean...he didn't outright deny it. Overall, Dex doesn't talk much about home. Whenever someone brings up Miami, he gets this strange, clouded look in his eyes like he's trying to detach. We don't have to talk about it. I don't like to upset him. And it's not like there's ever a lull between us. Dex could fill hours of conversation talking about scuba diving, beer, good food, and music.

Me: I'll bite. What other jobs?

Dex: Professional sleeper. There's a hotel in Finland that hires people to sleep in their beds and rate their rest quality. That's a full-time job with benefits.

Me: Well, now I'm torn between that and panda cuddling.

Dex: Dog food taster.

Me: Hard pass.

Dex: Well, not so fast. Did I mention it's all organic and grass-fed? And apparently, the company does an annual trade show in Cabo. All-expense paid.

Dex: I'm sure they'll provide you with people snacks for the plane.

Me: I appreciate your cruel humor in my time of desperation.

Dex: Excuse me. I'm trying to help my friend and am taking this very seriously.

Me: Uh huh. And where are you finding all this random shit?

Dex: Definitely not Reddit.

I laugh out loud again, and when I peek up from my phone, I'm met by Alan's narrowed eyes.

"Did you hear me?" he asks.

Oh crap. "Sorry. Dex was sending me funny job listings. He's been trying to cheer me up after getting fired and all."

Alan's lips twitch into a clipped smile. "I thought I had that covered."

I sit up and reach out to him, but we're too far apart. My hands fall aimlessly to my sides. "Of course you do. Dex is just a buddy, you know that." I wave my phone in the air at him. "I have nothing to hide. He only knows I got fired because, after I lost my job, I called to cancel the dive trip next year. That's all." The wind gusts through, and I sniff dramatically in the air just to change the subject. "Hey, do you smell that? Is that churros or funnel cakes? Should we go get some dessert?"

Alan's face is blank. He stares at me for an uncomfortably long time, then finally says, "You said his name." His words seem to come out in slow motion.

"What?" I ask, lowering my phone.

"The night I walked in on you on the bed. When you...you know...you said Dex's name."

A wave of nausea washes over me, and I have to swallow down the bile. It was over a week ago that Alan caught me with my vibrator. We haven't talked about it. It was quite clear he wanted to pretend it didn't happen, so we did just that. Now he's bringing it up?

"No, I didn't," I say.

"Yes, you did. Clear as day. I wasn't going to bring it up. But—"

"I didn't, Alan. I was there."

"Lennox," he bites out. I flinch at his tone, a little sharper than I'm used to. "It's not the kind of thing a boyfriend forgets. You said his name. I'm sure of it."

Did I? Who the hell remembers what they say when they orgasm? I guess... Is it possible? I mean, I distinctly remember thinking about him. *Oh, hell.*

"Alan, I..."

"I'm not mad." He holds up his hands, waving me off. "I'm sorry, I shouldn't have brought it up."

There's a loud ticking sound in my head. *Tick, tock. Tick, tock.* Just counting down the seconds until I say something I'll regret. "You should be mad." It comes out as a plea. "If your girlfriend is calling out another man's name when she's masturbating, especially right after you had sex, you should be *pissed*, Alan."

His eyes bulge to owl proportions as he rotates his neck side to side, checking to see if anyone heard me. The way he moves his head only emphasizes his likeness to the bird. I'd giggle if the tension wasn't so thick, but I can read a room. It's most definitely not the time to laugh. Instead, I survey the park with him and see our company is sparse. The nearest group of people is at least thirty yards away.

"You *want* to fight about this?" Alan eventually asks, his eyes touched with sadness.

"No," I respond softly. "I just want..." The end of my sentence disappears in the thickening air. Maybe I didn't have the words to begin with. *What do I want?* If I could build a boyfriend in a lab and fill him with all the magic ingredients...it'd be Alan. He checks every box except one.

I didn't realize what a huge fucking box it is. I'm not a shallow girl. I don't think lust is all about good looks and muscles, and I don't think mind-blowing sex has to be kinky. But I do believe chemistry is something that can't be forged. *It's gifted.* My old friend and mentor, Jacob, once told me that love is how the universe still has a hand in our fate. And something in me suspects that for the past year, I've been fighting fate.

Alan scoots in closer, wrinkling our picnic blanket. Rubbing his thumbs under my eyes, where tears should be. "Just tell me how you feel."

"What's off with us?" I whisper.

He looks away; suddenly, the green-brown grass is captivating to him. "I guess what's off is the fact that you think something's off. This is all news to me."

"You don't feel it?"

He forces himself to face me. Holding my gaze, he slowly shakes his head. "Not until about ten seconds ago. How long have you been unhappy?"

"I'm not unhappy." I grab his face in both of my hands, his barely-there stubble scraping against my palms. "Not at all."

He glances at my phone. "Then why don't you smile like that when you're texting me?"

"Like what?" I ask, my tone defensive. "And how would you know? You can't see my face when we're texting."

"It's just a metaphor. What I'm trying to say is there have been little clues I've been ignoring. I see how things are going to end with us. And I think..." He exhales deeply.

I shake my head fervently. "Alan, please don't. We were having a perfectly nice picnic. I'll put my phone away. You have my full attention."

"I'd rather we face things now than drag this out."

I ignore the throbbing in my head that's matching the pounding in my heart. A perfect synchronization of rapid pulsing. It's my instincts telling me something bad is about to happen. Pretending like I'm composed, I ask, "Drag what out?"

"Us. You want to break up, don't you?"

"Don't be ridiculous. You are *the best* man I've ever been with. I'm in this. I promise."

"Then why don't I believe you?" he asks. He watches my face like he's waiting for a tear. Some indication of my feelings for him.

"Please stop. You're scaring me," I say. "I'm happy with you, Alan. I swear."

"Lennox," Alan says again. His voice is oddly steady, and his face stoic. It's as if he's already accepted what I haven't. "Tell me the honest truth. I know you love me, but what about a year from now? Five? Ten? How long can you hold out? Am I the guy you want?"—he unsubtly glances at my phone again—"or the guy you're settling for?"

My bottom lip begins to tremble. I didn't expect him to peel back all the layers of my heart and read my secrets out loud. "That's not fair. He's your friend too. There's nothing going on between Dex and I."

"I didn't accuse you of anything. And that's not the question I asked."

I place the back of my hand against my cheeks, feeling the heat that's risen to my face. "I don't want to hurt you. I *never meant to hurt you*. And I want to want this, really badly."

Hooking his finger over his top lip, he nods. Disappointment clouds his face as my words must knock around his head. *I want to want this...*

But I don't.

I was willing to pretend until the end of time to avoid the look on his face at this moment.

There's serenity in the silence before we have to address the inevitable. So, for a while, we just sit quietly, feeling the warm wind brush past us in short gusts. I'm not enjoying it as much as I was before.

Eventually, Alan scoots a little closer and wraps his hand around the back of my neck, pulling me close. His hand is steady, and his breath is even. If he's nervous, he's hiding it well. "It's okay," he says. "I'm going to be okay." He tenderly kisses my forehead, and ironically, it's the most intimacy we've ever had. I should've known it would precede our end.

I give him a weak smile. "I'm not. How could you ever forgive me for this?"

"For what? Your honest feelings?" he asks. His smile is small, but he tries. "How about this? Do you want me to break your heart so you don't have to break mine?"

And those are the words that shatter me. Because even when he stands to gain nothing, even when I'm hurting him, Alan is still taking care of me. Dependable, honest...safe. *Fuck the universe* and its stupid plans. Alan's the perfect guy, and I hate my heart for being unsatisfied. This should be enough. More than enough. After a year, my feelings should've caught up. I tried my best to force them.

My dry eyes are starting to burn. I want to show Alan tears right now so he can see how much I care. But I've spent so long training myself not to. Crying is a reflex I've forgotten how to use.

My head suddenly weighs a thousand pounds, but somehow, I find the strength to nod.

"Lennox," he murmurs in my ear. "I think our relationship has run its course. I want to break up."

He pulls me into his chest, holding me tightly. My ear is resting against his heart, listening to the steady beats that are a far cry from the erratic skipping of my own. I nuzzle into him. I'm sure my makeup is staining his clean gray polo, but neither of us seems to care. For once, we're locked in a precious moment of passion, even if this hug means the end.

It's painful, but at least now I'm feeling something.

CHAPTER 9

Lennox

There's an almost purple-haired girl staring back at me in the mirror. You can hardly see the color against my dark hair, but right now, it's the best I can do. All I have is cheap box dye. No way I can afford for a quality salon to do this properly. And the last time I attempted to bleach my own hair, it all nearly fell out. My friend Kallie was in a high-end cosmetology course at the time. She snuck me into her beauty school after hours and used all the best products to nurse my poor hair back to life.

She owns Vue Salon now, one of Vegas' finest. I could probably squeeze in for a free service. She's told me so many times that the door is always open for me. Back when she had Grover, her bulldog, I'd pet sit when she was out of town, and she'd take care of my hair for free. But he passed, and these days, I don't have anything to offer in return, so I don't want to take advantage. That's how you lose friends.

I always dye my hair after a breakup, but this feels a little different. My breakup with Alan last week wasn't spiteful. He even texted to check on me the day after. The day after that, I checked on him. He was the most mature relationship I've ever had. Perhaps I should've anticipated the most mature breakup as well. He even suggested I still take the concierge interview, but I passed. I told him it'd be too hard to see him. *Half-truth.* I really didn't want that job. Now, I don't feel as pressured.

Pound, pound, pound.

I freeze. That's a knock I don't recognize. It sounds angry

enough that I hesitate in my tiny bathroom, unsure if I should answer the door. Then again, is it Grace? Maybe she forgot her key. I haven't seen her in a few days, but that's not unlike her. She's never been home much in the two years I've lived with her. It's like I pay half the rent but have a whole apartment to myself. A tiny apartment, but still.

Pound, pound.

"Okay, okay, I'm coming," I mutter, making my way to the front door. I peek through the peephole. The shiny police badge is the absolute last thing I want to see at the moment.

"Um, hello, Officer," I say as I open the door.

He doesn't smile. His neatly trimmed stubble is speckled with gray. Mid-forties maybe? Brown eyes, brown hair, medium height. His most prominent feature, however, is his thorough agitation. "Are you Grace Reeds?" he grunts out.

"No."

He holds up a thick legal envelope. "Are you at least eighteen years of age?"

I narrow my eyes. "Yes."

He hands over the envelope. "I've no choice but to leave this with you. This is a lockout order. Grace has twenty-four hours to collect her belongings before the locks are changed."

My jaw drops. "I'm sorry. *Excuse me?*"

He squints at me. "Are you a friend of hers? She's missed several court hearings."

There is a flurry of questions going through my mind and I try to mentally organize them as fast as I can. "Court hearings? Are we being evicted?"

"We?" the officer asks. My eyes drop to his belt, and the severity of the situation hits me at once. That's a real beating stick. A real taser. Real cuffs. This is not a sick joke. "Are you a tenant here?"

Oh, shit. Technically, I'm not on the lease. I thought our landlord was cool, turning a blind eye to it. I wasn't qualified as a lessee when I first moved in. It's an issue with my credit due to a couple of credit cards and a loan I took out to help my dad years back. One my mom still doesn't know about. I've missed so many minimum payments. I don't know if you can have a negative credit score, but if you can, I do. I try not to look anymore. It makes my stomach sick. Grace really saved my ass, letting me live with her under the radar. I thought she was kind of my savior, until right now.

"I am a tenant." *Sort of.*

"Then why aren't you on the lawsuit? Apparently, you haven't been paying rent."

"*Lawsuit?* That's incorrect. I've been paying my portion of the rent. Every month. It's put into a PayPal account Grace and I pay into, then the apartment drafts it from there. This has been happening with no problems for *two years.* Suddenly, there's an issue now? Maybe it's just a misunderstanding. Let me call PayPal."

"It's not a misunderstanding." The officer exhales and shakes his head. "Let me guess, Grace has access to this PayPal account?"

My stomach drops a dozen floors as I realize that for the past few months, I've technically been buying my own Cokes and candy bars. "Fuck. She's been draining the accounts and lying to me, hasn't she?" Her name is on everything. How hard would it be to keep all the notices and documentation from me?

The officer's expression softens slightly, a look of pity overcoming him. "Can I tell you something off the record?"

I nod.

"Eviction is just the tip of the iceberg. Grace"—he makes air quotes at the mention of her name—"isn't who you think she is. The feds are very interested in her and if she has any sense, she's already on the move. If she turns up again, you could try and sue her for fraud and theft, but it'd take a while, and I doubt you'd ever recover your money." He points into my apartment. "But if you could come up with a deposit and about four months of missing rent, I bet the landlord would let you stay. I could get a message out to her today."

I raise my brows at him and clench the thick envelope in my

fist. "Come up with almost half a year's worth of rent in one go?"

He nods solemnly.

I scoff. "Yeah, I'll go pack my shit."

C33 &D

I was able to cram most of my crap in my car, but I need Finn—and Finn's truck—to haul my lumpy, queen-size mattress out of my apartment. I did a lot of work all by myself for the past five hours, but now I need help. After an entire afternoon of Finn and Avery not answering their phones, I ended up on their doorstep pounding away.

I'm standing on their front door mat, cursing their existence under my breath, when it dawns on me that they aren't home. *That's right.* Finn told me a few days ago... They're in Scottsdale. With Finn's mom and her new husband at that mountain resort with next to no service. *Goddammit.* I could call my mom, I suppose. But that'd be opening up a huge can of worms...like why I was living with a potential drug dealer...and couldn't rent an apartment myself...because my credit is shot...because I helped my dad cover the mortgage and car payments for a home and vehicles that we ended up losing anyway.

Calling Mom needs to be Plan Z. I can come up with something better than that first.

There's always Alan, but that feels a little selfish. Of course, he'd come help me, but that's not my right anymore.

I've been in panic-mode for so long, I didn't notice the sky go from bright to dusk. Right on cue, the neighborhood streetlamp planted between Dex and Finn's front yards switches on, illuminating the sides of both houses. It's only then that I notice for once Dex's interior lights are on.

Holy shit. He's home. *The bastard is actually home.* And you know what? He drives a jeep. I bet it's big enough to strap my mattress on top. He'd probably let me store my stuff in his garage until Finn and Avery get home.

Practically skipping with joy that I don't have to call my mom, I make my way over. I ring the doorbell and wait patiently but to no avail. When that doesn't work, I start to knock. I know his house is big, but it's not *that* big. Did he hear the bell and make himself a freaking sandwich first? I know he's home. All the lights are on.

By the time he opens the door, I'm scowling. His face, however, lights up when he sees me. "Oh, hey, Trouble. Your hair."

I grab it self-consciously, remembering my crappy dye job. "What? It's bad?"

"No, it looks great. Purple again. And with you knocking all crazy like that, it's bringing back memories. You want to come in and have a beer?" He looks me up and down. "I warn you, though, the pitch jar rate has gone up. Fifteen bucks."

I try not to laugh, but I can't help it. "Why'd you take so long to answer the door?"

He frowns. "Sorry, I was finishing a work call. I hung up as soon as I could."

"Work? It's like eight o'clock at night."

He shrugs but doesn't offer an explanation. "Are you coming in?" He nods over his shoulder, gesturing inside.

He smells so good. His house smells good too. I'm going to miss him so much. "Don't you want to know why I'm here first?"

He screws up his face like I said something absurd. "Do you need a reason to be here? I just thought you came to say hi."

Dammit, that would've been more considerate. "That too." I cringe.

He chuckles. "What's up, Len? You need something?"

"I got evicted. My roommate fucked me over big time, and now she's on the run. I have to be out by tomorrow. I still have to move my bed, but my car isn't big enough. Finn's out of town and took his truck. I've been breaking my back, moving stuff into my car all day by myself, but now I really need help, and I'm running out of time."

Dex narrows his eyes as he leans against the door frame. Even leaning, he's so tall he looks a little intimidating at the moment. It's not the reaction I was hoping for. I thought we'd spring into action, quick like bunnies. I realize it's not the most fun task at night, but I'd do it for him. Isn't that what friends are for? But judging by the annoyed look on his face, I half expect him to brush me off.

"When did all this happen?" he finally asks.

"Earlier today."

"And where the fuck is your boyfriend? He's just standing by, letting you go through this all by yourself? This whole good guy façade, and then he shits the bed when it matters most?"

I stare down at my blue cowgirl boots, noticing the fringe on the left side is starting to come loose. There's also a black scuff on the top of my right boot. I'm really just noticing anything to not have to meet Dex's stare. I know he's looking at me. I'm sure he didn't mean to hurt my feelings, but he did. I don't need a reminder of how I blew up my entire life in the past few weeks. Got fired. Threw away the best relationship I've ever had. Blindly trusted a freaking drug dealer as a roommate.

I get it. *I'm fucking up.*

"We broke up," I muster out. "So, I didn't call him. I'm sure if I did, he would've offered to help." I finally lift my eyes to meet his, and all I see is sympathy on his face.

"Oh, Len. I'm sorry. I didn't know."

"We're on good terms though," I assure him with a little nod.

The smile that always starts at the corner of his eyes doesn't quite reach his lips this time. "No ass-kicking needed?"

"Not at all. And anyway, I'd call Finn for that."

He clutches his chest, pretending like I broke his heart. "That's offensive."

I turn my hands so the backs are facing him, then wiggle my fingers. "I mean, you're strong, but you're such a pretty boy. I wouldn't want you to ruin your manicure."

His laugh is thick and grumbly. The best sound in the world. It immediately lifts my mood. "Okay, Trouble, you're going to pay for that."

I'm laughing now, too. "Go ahead and kick a girl when she's down."

He exhales and crosses his arms, still surveying me. *What the hell is he trying to figure out? I just told him everything.* "Your mattress is a piece of shit."

"This is fact," I say noncombatively.

Dex is the one who helped me move my mattress into the apartment two years ago. It was already lumpy when I got it from the secondhand store, but I was just proud it was queen-sized and not a dormitory-looking twin mattress. It felt like a grown-up's bed.

"Let your landlord take it to the dump. You can have my guest bed. It's the same size as yours. I don't need it."

"Awfully chivalrous of you."

He pumps his eyebrows at me. "Or maybe I just don't want to ruin my manicure by moving your bed."

I roll my eyes. "I was kidding."

He smirks. "All right, let me grab my keys." Standing up straight, he stretches his arms overhead. His thin T-shirt hugs all the tight muscles of his abdomen, and as usual, I'm hypnotized. Alan and I aren't together, but I still feel guilty gawking at Dex.

"Are you headed somewhere?" I ask, taking a step back off his porch.

"*We*," he says, pointing to his chest, then mine, back and forth, "need something stronger than beer. We're going out."

"I'm in jean shorts, a tank top, and cowgirl boots. And I'm sweaty and smelly from moving stuff into my car all day."

"Yeah, what's up with the boots?"

"As I was clearing stuff out, I found them in the back of my closet. I put them on to see if they still fit. They're so comfortable, I forgot to take them off."

"Well, they're perfect for where we're headed." He steps out of the house onto the porch right in front of me. I normally don't let myself get this close to Dex. My knees get weak when he's *this close.*

To Dex, every look, touch, and smile is normal and friendly. To me? It's an exercise of self-control. It's been three years since I made a move, and he clearly indicated he'd rather be friends. For three years, I've pretended like we made the right decision.

When he leans down, he puts his face near my breasts, and I pray to every god, shadow, and spirit that exists that he can't hear how hard my heart is pounding. He sniffs twice. "You're good. You smell fine to me. Come on, let's go have some fun."

CHAPTER 10

Dex

Lennox sways her hips to the loud country music as she makes her way over to where I'm sitting at the bar. She even goes as far as shaking her head side to side so her long, purple hair fans out and drapes over her bare shoulders.

Fuck, it's too sexy.

Stop walking towards me like that. It makes me want to do something about it.

"Hey," she shouts over the music, still rolling her shoulders to the beat. "Can I convince you to come dance with us?"

"Not a chance," I say definitively.

"Do you suck at it? I can teach you."

I nod over her shoulder. "Like you did your new biker buddies?" Only Lennox could get a gang of late-aged, tattooed bikers doing the electric slide and drinking razzle dazzle cocktails. It's her superpower. She can make friends with anybody, anywhere. Her spirit is contagious.

She looks to the opposite side of the bar, where the bar-goers pushed tables and chairs to the side to arrange a makeshift dance floor. "I'm proud, actually. Only five minutes of instruction and they look pretty good out there, right?"

No. You look good out there. "If you say so."

She pushes against my shoulder with two fingers. "Come on. Scared?"

"I can dance. I'm choosing not to."

She reaches over me and grabs my drink. After taking a hefty swig of my bourbon, she cringes. "Bleh, I didn't know they had lighter fluid on the menu." But she takes another small sip before handing my glass back as the song's chorus starts to kick up. "All right, you'll find me on the dance floor if you need me."

"Hey," I say, stopping her.

"What's up?" She catches my gaze, her big brown eyes a little hazy from the booze. Her cheeks still flushed from all the dancing.

"Are you feeling better?"

Her big eyes light up. "You know what? I really am. I think this was exactly what I needed." She looks around at the grimy bar with the run-down tables that look like they could spontaneously fall apart and the scuffed-up, chipped wooden floors. Then, her eyes snap back to mine. "By the way, why are we here? I thought you hated dive bars."

"I do. But you love them." I tell her how I feel about her the only way I can. I get as close to the line as possible without crossing it.

She smiles, but it disappears quickly. "I'm going to miss the shit out of you, Dex Hessler."

Before I can say anything else, her long hair is swishing behind her as she slides right into place with the line dance.

"Another?" A voice behind me startles me. A bartender with a short blond ponytail and a small lip ring taps the glass top counter, and I swivel around in my stool to face her.

"No, thank you. I have to drive when she's done dancing."

The bartender lets out a low whistle as she looks over my shoulder. "You might be here a while. She looks like she has stamina."

I laugh as I shake the ice cubes in my almost-empty glass. "That she does."

"How about a Coke with a lime?"

"Sure. Thanks."

"How long have you guys been together?" The bartender grabs a glass from under the bar and stuffs it to the brim with ice before filling it with the soda gun.

"She's just a friend," I automatically reply. After three years of my odd friendship with Lennox, I'm used to this question. I shut it down every time.

She scoffs. "Yeah. Okay."

"What?" I ask, acting like I don't know where her skepticism stems from.

"Oh, nothing. I also stare at my friends longingly from the bar when we go out." She smirks as she places the soda in front of me. "Want a straw?"

I roll my eyes. "No, thanks."

"So, what's the problem? Is she with someone?"

I widen my eyes at the nosy bartender. "Do you have other customers? Don't let me keep you."

She cackles. "Come on. Humor me. It's a slow night. I'm bored and curious."

Grumbling, I fold my hands together and rest my chin on my knuckles. "We're from two very different worlds. I might've given her the wrong impression about what I really am."

"*Who*," the bartender corrects, then shrugs sheepishly. "You meant 'who' you really are. Sorry, I have a reputation as the grammar police."

I give her a curt nod. "Who, then."

Except, I actually did mean "*What.*" Mass wealth has made me feel more like a thing than a person. I don't think anybody from home sees Dex Hessler as a person, just an embodiment. I wonder if Grandma felt the same. She married into the name. She could've sold the company and walked away when she lost Grandpa. But I know she felt the same burden. The same painful obligation. I learned from her example: how to sacrifice your life to fulfill a legacy that's bigger than you are. How to accept that your life is just a tiny piece of a bigger puzzle.

Hesslers breed CEOs who graduate in the top ten percent of their class from Harvard Business School. Hesslers do *not* breed anxiety-ridden, scuba-diving nomads who have panic attacks behind closed doors.

My own personal form of rebellion is ensuring the Hessler line ends with me. There'll be no one left to play Atlas and carry the goddamn world on their shoulders.

"So, how exactly did you mislead her?" the bartender asks. But before I can respond, my phone buzzes in rapid succession from my pocket. When I check the notifications, it's Denny.

Normally a text message from Denny wouldn't make me so jumpy, but there's the pressing matter at hand of finding me a wife.

"Excuse me. It's work," I say before swiveling around in my seat and diving into the messages.

> **Denny: Here's a picture of Allie.**
> **Very pretty girl.**

The next message is a picture of a blonde. It's a professional headshot. It looks like the photo she probably uses for LinkedIn. Her full name is Allie Conner. She's 34, so only four years older than me. She graduated from Harvard Law, so we have Harvard in common. No kids. Comes from a good family. Denny has apparently already run her through the details of the will. She's already agreed to hand the company back to me after the one-year holding period.

I've said no to all the other women Denny has sifted through. At least eight now. All the other girls she suggested were text messages but when Denny found Allie, she was so excited, she called, urging me to commit right then and there. I was relieved when Lennox interrupted. I rushed Denny off the phone, saying a friend had an emergency. I didn't realize it was somewhat true.

Denny: So, what do you think now that you've seen her picture? We'll need an iron-clad prenup, but I think we should move forward. Can I confirm?

Denny: She won't wait forever. And she's really not asking for a lot of compensation.

Me: How much?

Denny: 128 million. And whatever property she purchases while she's your wife.

I scowl at my phone.

Me: That's not a lot to you? Then what in the world do you consider "a lot of compensation?"

Denny: It's a big favor, Dex. There has to be a big incentive. I need your decision. Fast. The lawyers will have a mountain of paperwork to prepare.

Me: You're not asking me to pick a place for lunch. You're asking me to pick a wife. I need a moment to think.

Even if it's just a year, it's still a marriage. That's a long time for a miserable marriage if we don't get along. Especially during a very difficult first year of transition. Grandma ran Hessler Group like a well-oiled machine because she had been doing it for decades. Even while Grandpa was still CEO. He was either frowning or drunk, so Grandma filled in all the gaps.

Fulfilling the responsibility was no easy feat. Grandma prepared me best she could, but I still have some things to learn. And my future wife is in for the surprise of her life.

Still, I can't help but think...

Should it really be this fucking complicated? Should I have to bribe my wife with 128 million dollars to tolerate me for a year? I've only ever known advantageous women. The kind who smiles like a Disney villain when they know they've got me by the balls. Just be a good person, and I'll be one right back. It's not that hard.

I grumble out loud, my agitation drowned by the loud music. After turning back around, I set my phone face down on the bar. It goads me—*flip me over...just one text.* I could get this over with. It's inevitable and I'm sure Allie's fine. But...

What's stopping me?

"Need something?" the bartender asks, suddenly reappearing as if I summoned her.

Fuck it. "Changed my mind. May I have a double? I'll grab a ride home."

"Sure." She grabs the bottle of bourbon already on the counter from my drink before. "Problem with work?" she asks as she pours my drink.

"In a way," I mumble. "Is she still dancing?" I point my thumb over my shoulder.

The bartender looks over me to the dance floor. "Dancing her heart out."

"Good, then I'm fine. My bullshit doesn't matter tonight. I came out to cheer Lennox up. She's just gone through hell—got fired, went through a breakup, lost her apartment. She has no job, no money, nowhere to live. She really needs someone to cut her a break right now—"

My heart jolts so hard that, at first, I'm worried I'm on the brink a panic attack. But my breath is steady. My head is clear. In fact, I'm thinking more clearly than I have been in a while.

I realize it's simply that my heart has made a decision before my head has gotten a chance to catch up.

The obvious answer to everyone's problems is clear as goddamn day.

I pull my black card out of my wallet and toss it on the counter. Rotating my pointer finger, I gesture around the bar. "Pay everyone in this bar's tab. On me. And give yourself a one hundred percent tip. If anyone asks, don't tell them who it was."

"Wow, thank you. That's generous, but"—she nods towards the bikers, still line dancing with Lennox—"do you want to see the bill first? You realize those guys have been here drinking since three, right?"

"Pretty sure I can handle it," I say before I throw back the bourbon in two gulps. The first one burns. The second goes down smooth, coating my throat like honey. I point to my card. "I'll be back for that."

"Where are you going?"

I slide out of my bar stool, eyes locked on Lennox. "To close a deal."

CHAPTER 11

D e x

Three Years Earlier

Las Vegas

I swear on my life, she wore that sexy black bikini to torture me.

I emerge from the locker room shirtless with two fresh towels. One for me, one for Lennox, who is sitting at the edge of the pool, lazily stirring the water with one foot.

She watches me approach, and when I'm close enough, she exhales heavily. "Dude, I'm exhausted."

"Breath control will do that," I say, then throw my thumb over my shoulder, pointing to our discarded regulators and tanks resting behind us. "And the equipment is heavier than you think."

She says, "Thank you," as she reaches for the towel, but she sets it aside and continues to disturb the pool water with her toe. She even goes as far as kicking against the water line and splashing me across my chest.

I plop down next to her. Leaning forward, I scoop a handful of pool water, lobbing it at her exposed stomach. "You don't want to play that game." I nod toward the deep end of the pool. "I'll drag you right back in."

She smiles and rubs her eyes like a sleepy child. When she opens them, they look slightly red. "Hey, let me see," I instruct her, leaning closer to her face. "Your eyes look irritated."

"It's the saltwater," she says. "I'm used to chlorine pools."

I squeeze her shoulder. "I know. But saltwater pools are better for practicing your buoyancy. I have some eyedrops. Let me go grab them."

She seizes my forearm as I try to rise. "I'm okay. Just sit with me for a bit."

I do as she asks. Laying backward and flattening myself against the ground, I tuck my hands behind my head, creating a makeshift pillow. From this angle, I can admire Lennox's silhouette from behind. The way her waist narrows before her hips curve outward. It takes every ounce of restraint not to reach up and yank on the black bow of her bikini top. Because fuck... I can't stop thinking about her. It's been three months since I met her. The fantasies won't cease. Her smile...her laugh...her naked. I've never been in this position before. Usually, it's about three dates with a woman before I realize the sex isn't worth the company.

I could fall asleep talking to Lennox. That's how comfortable I am with her. It's a different kind of love, I suppose. Friendship. Something you don't risk by getting sloppy in the sheets. What would happen? When Lennox finds out what I'm worth, either she'll change, or our friendship will. It's what always happens. The moment the word billionaire is floating around...people change. I like the way things are.

"So, what's next?" she asks, resting her elbow on her knee and cupping her chin.

"You know what's next," I quip back.

She narrows her eyes, one corner of her plush lips curling into a smile. "Right. I need more practice on the test where I lose my mask in the water and have to find it. I panic when I can't see. I should work on that."

I close my eyes and shake my head. "Nope, you're solid. It's natural to be nervous when you're blind underwater. And you recover very nicely."

"What about learning to use a dive watch?"

"Those are most helpful when you're diving solo or mapping out a dive. You're not ready for either of those things."

"Well, maybe next week we could—"

"Lennox," I singsong. "Dodge it all you want, but it's time to get into the ocean."

"I'm not ready."

"Yes, you are," I assure her.

I've been giving Lennox private scuba diving lessons for months now. She's a natural. Strong swimmer, quick learner, and she handles her tank like a master. Her breath control is that of an experienced diver. She could probably even dive with me, stretching a single tank out to over an hour at a thirty-meter depth. She doesn't need more lessons or pop quizzes. It's time for Lennox to get into open water. Except, she's still scared.

She's stalling. Maybe a better instructor would encourage her to conquer her fear. I, however, have been savoring my Lennox time. So, we meet at the Lakewood community pool after hours once a week, going over the same technical skills. At this point, I think we're both pretending like this is useful. I like to think she looks forward to spending time with me, too.

If I planned to stay in Las Vegas, I would've told her how I feel about her. But I don't want to be one more guy who recklessly falls for her and then leaves her high and dry. But what if...

What if bringing her to Miami was an option?

I sit up and nudge her shoulder with mine. She flinches when my bare skin touches her. "Hey, can I ask you something?"

"Of course."

"Would you ever consider leaving Las Vegas?"

She raises one eyebrow. "Odd question."

Shit. Yeah, that was tactless. I make up a lie to quickly recover. "My family's company had a job become available that I think you'd be good for, but it's in Miami. I was just curious."

"*Oh,*" she responds, easily believing my weak excuse. "Thanks for thinking of me. But no, I'm stuck in Las Vegas."

I'm relieved when she doesn't ask more about the fictitious job I just made up. Honestly, there's not a corporate job in the world I think Lennox would enjoy. All Hessler Group has as far as open positions are accounting and legal, which I'm sure sounds mind-numbingly boring for a girl like her. But curious, I ask, "Why are you stuck? Love the Strip that much?"

"Not for the nightlife or anything. I'm really close to my family. Finn's not just my cousin; he's my best friend. My mom, Aunt Hannah, and I still do a weekly lunch. And most importantly, my dad..." Her face flattens, and she stares out across the pool for a while. Then, hastily, she yanks her feet out of the water and hugs her knees. "I couldn't leave my dad."

"Why?"

Her eyes snap to mine. "How are you with secrets?"

She doesn't understand the irony of her question, seeing as I'm basically keeping my entire identity secret from her. "Excellent."

"I've never told anybody this because I don't trust anyone to understand. But maybe..." She studies my eyes. "Just don't let me down and go blabbing. Especially not to Finn because he'd worry sick. This is a burden I have to carry alone."

"Promise. My lips are sealed."

She gazes back across the pool. "My parents used to be very well off until my dad lost his job. I was in my sophomore year of high school when things dramatically changed. Everything he worked for over two decades was gone like that"—she snaps her fingers—"and it broke him. I did what I could at sixteen. I got part-time jobs and tried to take care of my own lunch and gas money. I studied hard, knowing I needed a scholarship if I had any chance of going to college. My mom reentered the workforce. She got a job at an insurance call center and has been working her way up in the company. But it wasn't enough. Eventually, they took the house, our cars, and his retirement. My parents went bankrupt." She lifts her shoulders then drops them as if they're heavy.

"This economy," I offer as a lame excuse. "It's rough right now."

Lennox's face twists in disgust. "It's not the economy. It's evil, corporate greed, and finance assholes. My dad was spectacular at his job. He got screwed over. Then, all of his supposed friends, who he broke his back helping for decades, turned on him when he needed them most. If I've learned one thing...never ever trust people with money."

I wish I could disagree. But I've learned much the same lesson. "I'm sorry to hear that," I muster out. "It sucks about his friends, but it sounds like he has a really supportive family."

"He did...he *does*. I just think he had this ridiculous notion that it was his fault, and he let me and my mom down in an unforgivable way. It was so far from the truth. But he felt so bad. I've never seen anyone so down on himself. It's like someone sucked the life right out of him. I think he was too proud to admit he was depressed, but I remember not seeing him smile for months in a row—almost as if he completely forgot how to. And just when I thought it couldn't get worse, one day I came home from school, and Dad was napping, or so I thought."

My stomach sinks, understanding where this story is going. "Oh, no. You don't mean..."

She still doesn't look at me but nods. "Mom was working a late shift... By the time eight o'clock came around, I realized Dad was going to sleep right through dinner. So, I made him mac n' cheese and brought it to his room. I tried to wake him up, but he wouldn't budge. That's when I noticed the empty pill bottles on the nightstand."

She suddenly hunches forward, bending at the waist so her face is inches from the water. Lennox splashes her face and hair like she is suddenly burning up and needs to cool off. But I don't buy it. The pool water drenches her face, enough to cover the tears.

"What happened?" I ask when she sits back upright.

"I was hysterical. Shaking him, wailing, smacking his cheeks, pouring ice-cold water on his face. I had the phone in my hand. I started dialing 9-1-1 when his eyes popped open. I'll never forget the look on his face. Like he was shocked to wake up and even more surprised to see me. The way he reached out to touch my face like he wasn't sure I was real." Lennox touches my cheek to demonstrate. Gentle fingertips across my cheek, tracing my jawline. "He told me later that he thought he died, and he couldn't believe that he made it to heaven." She drops her hand, returning it to her lap while muttering, "So fucked up," under her breath.

"He thought you were an angel?" I ask.

She closes her eyes and nods in response.

My heart beats in slow, steady knocks as I watch her compose herself. She presses her lips firmly together. It looks like she's trying not to cry. Here's a woman who tries so hard to make lemonade with all the bullshit life seems to throw at her.

"Anyway, it messed me up for a while. I couldn't sleep. I was paranoid, glued to my phone, and physically ill whenever he didn't text me back right away. I should've told someone. That was too much for a sixteen-year-old. But..."

I grab her hand, cupping it tightly. "He begged you not to tell anyone, didn't he?"

"Yeah." She tries to take her hand back but I hang onto it tightly.

"It's okay. I won't tell a soul, Len."

"I would've told someone if I saw any signs. I swear. But he seemed to get better, like what he did was just a moment of weakness. He had to hit rock bottom before he could start climbing back up. And he found peace with being broke. Eventually, Dad stopped worrying about his reputation or getting his fortune back. Things mellowed out... But there's still a part of me that can't unsee that look on his face."

I know better than she realizes. "Once you know real grief, trauma, or betrayal, you can't go back to living in a world where that doesn't exist."

"*Exactly.* That's exactly it." She squeezes my hand back. "You must've gone through something heavy, too, if you understand."

I could elaborate on how my mom died when I was seven. I never knew my dad. My grandpa was on my ass constantly, trying to ensure I grew up to be a replica of him with his inflated, elitist ego. It eased up when he drank himself useless, but then I watched my grandma slowly begin to work herself to the bone. Maybe

I should tell Lennox I feel so fucking lost in my own skin, and Miami feels more like a life sentence than a privilege.

But I don't.

Because here I'm just Dex—the scuba diving instructor. That's the guy Lennox likes. The guy she talks to.

"Not really. Just a guess," I tell her.

"Oh, okay. Anyway, I don't know...sometimes I wonder what if it gets bad again? What if no one knows what he did when he was sad, and therefore, no one else can protect him?" She hangs her head. "I should've told my mom, but I made a promise. Now, if anything happens to him, it's on me."

"That's a pretty big responsibility to carry, don't you think? How can you constantly breathe for someone else?"

She tugs on her bottom lip with her top teeth. "Well, that's what happens when you keep secrets."

I wrap my arm around her bare shoulder, pulling her close. "And now you're scared to leave home."

"Something like that. Las Vegas is just where I belong."

And there's my answer. A bond I could never come between.

"Lennox, I'm sorry." I have her smashed up against me, but right now, I'm not paying attention to her half-naked body pressed against mine. I'm just trying to make her feel safe.

"When I was little, I used to tell everyone I wanted to have a high-powered career and be important. I mean I was an ambitious little thing. Screw doctor or lawyer, I wanted to be a surgeon or supreme court justice. But after what Dad went through..."

"Now, what do you want?"

She leans away from me, breaking free of my embrace. "To be happy. I don't want to get caught up with money, things, status, or any of that bullshit that made my dad go to the pit of despair. I don't want money to ever make me feel failure the way it did for my dad. It was painful enough to make him want to end his life."

I think Lennox's dad and my grandpa have quite a bit in common. Money ruled their lives, but it also ruled their emotions. Except there was a stark difference between Lennox's dad and

Grandpa. I don't think Mom would've ever stayed anywhere to be close to Grandpa. In fact, she ran away from it all—that's how she got pregnant with me.

"Your dad is far from a failure. He has a daughter and wife who love every single version of him. You stuck by him through thick and thin. He built a real family. That's way more success than money can ever bring."

Her face relaxes into a small smile. "I like that. He did, didn't he? He built a real family. Thanks for listening." She holds up her pinky. "Our secret, right?"

Hooking my pinky around hers, I promise her, "Our secret."

A loud ring from behind us echoes through the empty community pool. It costs double to rent this place out after hours, but it's worth it. These moments are precious...just me, Lennox, and the water. My favorite part of the week.

"Shit. What time is it?" she asks, grabbing my wrist and checking my dive watch.

"Eight-thirty," I say as she reads the time for herself. "You in a rush?"

"That's probably my date. I was supposed to call him at eight to let him know if I was still free tonight."

"Oh." I have no right to feel disappointed. I'm the one who said we should just be friends. Regardless, it feels like a slap in the face.

"I don't mean to run out on you." She looks over her shoulder at the equipment. "I still want to help you load everything up."

I ignore the beast of jealousy roaring in my chest and try to approach this conversation like an actual friend would. "Is he a good guy?"

"Too soon to tell," she says quickly. "But he has a nine-to-five, doesn't drink, likes sitcoms. He volunteers at the children's hospital once a month. He calls exactly when he says he's going to."

"So, basically, Charlie's polar opposite," I add.

Lennox taps her nose twice, then points at me. "Exactly."

"And where the hell did you meet a guy like that?"

She widens her eyes. "The grocery store of all places. He saw me knocking on watermelons, trying to find a good one. He helped me pick one out." She holds her hands shoulder-width apart, demonstrating the size of the watermelon mystery guy picked. "Then he gave me his number and told me if the watermelon was sweet, I had to call him." She rolls her wrist, swiveling her hand in the air. "It was pleasantly cute and innocent. I kind of felt like I was in a movie."

Fuck. Pretty smooth of him. "And how was the watermelon?"

She pops the tip of her finger into her mouth and holds it between her teeth. There's a dreamy look in her eyes, like she's reliving the moment of that first bite... *For fuck's sake.* Some random dude stole my girl with a piece of fruit.

"The sweetest I'd ever tasted," she finally answers. "So, I owe him a date." I really don't like the way she's smiling now. Obviously, she was charmed. "But I can see him a different night. I'll help you get this all sorted." She stands, stretching her arms overhead, then massages one shoulder like she's sore.

"Nah, I got it. Get out of here." I run my hand over my face, reluctant to add, "He sounds like a good guy. You deserve a good guy, Len. Good luck. I hope it works out." *What a bitter-tasting lie.* He better not hurt her in any way, shape, or form, but I hope this dude is corny as fuck.

"Are you sure?" she asks. "I really don't mind. We could maybe grab a bite on the way home."

I tap her nose. "You don't need to babysit me. Plus, I told Leah I'd call her this week." I shrug. "Maybe tonight's a good night."

"*Leah*?" Lennox asks, unable to mask her surprise. "You asked out Leah? She's been working at the dive shop for what—a millisecond?"

"A month," I correct. "And I didn't ask her out. She asked if I wanted to"—I tilt my head back, looking at the ceiling—"let's say *Netflix and chill*."

"Oh, I..."

"You don't like her?" I ask, surprised. "You're the one who recommended her for the job."

"No, I do. Leah's great, it's...she just got divorced, and it was—" Lennox stops midsentence. "It's not my place to tell you, but I don't think she's looking for anything serious."

I raise my eyebrows, admitting to the uncomfortable truth. "Yeah, I know. That's kind of why we—"

"*Ah*," Lennox interrupts. "Got it. Say no more. You guys are actually perfect for each other."

I hold up my hands. "She was your friend first. I don't have to hang out with her. I can tell her it's unprofessional. Me being her boss and all."

Lennox grunts in laughter. "Boss," she mumbles.

"What?"

"I'm trying to picture you in a suit and tie." She makes a square outline with her fingers, framing my face, then squints one eye. "I don't see it."

I've let this ruse go on too far. I own at least one hundred suits. And at least as many pairs of business shoes. Back home, a quarter of my closet is dedicated to ties. Whatever Lennox is struggling to picture is exactly who I am.

Rising to my feet, I hold my hands out for hers. As soon as her small palms are in mine, I tug her up. "I own a few suits."

"Sure you do." She winks before her playful smile fades. "Leah likes Junior Mints. Addicted actually. They're her catnip. She buys two boxes when we go to the movies, and she inhales them before the previews even start. It'd be a nice touch if you picked a box up for her before you guys, you know...watch a show."

I ruffle her damp hair. "I'm not an animal. When I say *hang out*, I do mean hang out. I'm not going to sleep with her tonight. Hey, actually, how about you call your watermelon guy? I'll bring my Junior Mints girl, and we can bring this picnic to the movie theatre. We could double."

I regret the words as soon as they're out of my mouth. That sounds like torture, actually. I don't want to watch Lennox all night cozying up to another man. I also don't feel like Leah is actually interested in going out anywhere. She made her intentions pretty clear. It was refreshing at least. I like an honest woman.

"I think that'd be distracting," Lennox says barely above a whisper. "Watermelon guy deserves my full attention on our first date."

I agree about the distracting part at least.

"Yeah...makes sense. You're considerate. One of my favorite things about you."

"Thanks." She nods but hangs her head, examining her painted toes. They were perfectly intact this morning. So much time in the pool tonight did a number on her polish, which is now chipped and peeling. "Hey, you know what?"

"What?" I try to find her eyes, but she's still staring down.

"I think I'm ready to try the ocean."

"Really? Wow, I thought I was going to have to resort to bribes."

She finally looks up, smirking. "What kind of bribes?" Pointing to my dive watch she asks, "Do they make that in purple?"

"I'm sure it could be arranged."

She rolls her eyes. "I'm obviously kidding, Dex. No bribes necessary. I'm just nervous. Can we do a beach entry instead of rolling off the boat?"

"Definitely. We'll pace ourselves," I assure her.

"And you'll stay with me the whole time?"

"*I promise.*"

"Okay, just let me know when." She bends down to pick up her towel, wrapping it around her already dry body. At this point, it's just for modesty. "If you're absolutely sure you don't need me, I'm going to go return that call."

I nod. "I'm sure." Lennox is three strides away when I ask her, "Hey, what's watermelon guy's name, by the way?"

"Alan," she calls over her shoulder.

CHAPTER 12

Lennox

Present Day

Las Vegas

Sitting, I glide my fingers over the grain and grit of the dirty curb, waiting for Dex to speak. Moments ago, he interrupted my flamboyant rendition of the electric slide and led me outside of the dive bar with urgency. He said he needed to talk to me about something important in private...but he has yet to say a word to me. Instead, he stepped a few paces away and started making calls, muttering in hushed tones. I didn't bother trying to hear what he was saying.

It's dark except for the flickering glow of the streetlamp across the street. The odor of the dumpsters across the street is really rounding out the ambiance. All we need is cop sirens in the distance or the screeches and wails of an alley cat fight to set the mood.

The effects of all the alcohol are finally wearing off. I'm tired. My bones feel heavy, and I imagine my blood is thick and sluggish in my veins. I'm also aware that I reek of smoke. Several people were chain-smoking cigarettes in the bar. Now, a headache is most definitely in the works.

I just want to go home and crawl into bed.

Except I don't have a home. I no longer have a bed.

That's the problem with pushing off your problems. They

will, in fact, catch up with you the moment you stop dancing.

"Sorry to keep you waiting," Dex says, waving his phone in the air as he approaches me. "I was working out some logistics."

I barely lift my shoulders, too exhausted to put in any more effort than that. "No big deal. I needed some fresh air anyway. Actually, I think I'm ready to leave if you are? I just need to pay my tab."

"I already took care of it."

"Oh, okay. Thank you." I'd tell him he didn't need to do that, but tonight...yeah, I kind of need the help.

Dex sits down next to me, too close. Our shoulders and thighs press into each other, and while I go rigid like a board, he seems entirely unfazed. I want to smack him when he acts like this. It's frustrating when he doesn't understand how reckless his touches are. This is why I'm accidentally mumbling the wrong man's name when I'm using my vibrator.

"Are you cold?" Dex asks.

"No."

"You're shivering." Maneuvering around my back, his hand finds the outside part of my arm, and he rubs rapidly. *Goddammit.* But I let it happen. "Sorry I dragged you out here. I couldn't hear in there."

"It's fine. So, what did you want to talk about?"

"My grandma died."

My mouth falls open, but nothing comes out. Stunned into silence is the only explanation I have. Of all the things I was expecting...not that. *Oh, Dottie.* I feel the tension in my chest, an instant ache of sadness. Dorothea Hessler is the kind of woman that leaves an impression. If it hurts my heart that she's gone, I imagine Dex is devastated right now.

Dex can be a chatterbox but usually only talks in circles about inconsequential things. At first, I used to think he was a little goofy. Or smoked pot. I always imagined Dex saw the world in kaleidoscope colors, with The Beatles greatest hits on repeat in his head. It took me a little while to realize that Dex is just strategic with conversations. He's skilled at making you focus on what's unimportant, not what he really wants to say. His way of keeping the world at arm's length.

So why is he opening up now? *Grief?*

But I choose not to focus on why he didn't tell me. More importantly, I want to know how he's holding up. "Dex, I'm so sorry. How are you?"

He takes his arm back then leans forward, planting his elbows on his knees. Staring across the street, he's looking into dark shadows of nothing. "I don't know. There was the funeral, the will, and all the business affairs afterward." He shakes his head. "I'm still wrapping my head around it. Everything's felt transactional since she passed."

I only met Dottie Hessler once. Over one dinner, I learned her favorite flowers are daisies. She and Jacob were dear friends. Like me, she had an irrational fear of the ocean, so she never learned to scuba dive despite the enthusiasts in her life. Her French perfume was by far the most glamorous scent I'd ever experienced. The only cocktail she enjoyed was a Long Island Iced Tea. Otherwise, she took her red wine French and her liquor neat. She always gets her nails painted red. And most importantly, Dex was the light of her life.

That's it.

The extent of my knowledge. The way Dex is staring off into the abyss has me wishing I knew more so I could say the right thing. It's clear he's hurting more than he knows how to convey. "When?" Is all I can think to ask.

He glances at me briefly in his periphery, then goes back to staring at the street. "When I was in Socorro. I didn't have service." He buries his face in his hands. "The one week I didn't have service...and then she died. I'm told she went peacefully in her sleep," he mumbles through his fingers.

"Has anybody been helping you through all this? Any family?" I cringe, wondering if it's an inconsiderate question. Dex doesn't like to talk about his family or lack thereof.

"Like who?"

"Cousins? Family friends?"

"I don't have cousins. My mom was an only child. You already know she died when I was little. Never knew my dad. My grandma and grandpa raised me until he passed away, too."

"Dex," I exhale out, now feeling breathless. "That's everybody. How are you—"

"It sounds dramatic when I say it like that, but I'm fine Len," he rushes out, brushing off the intensity of the conversation. "Anyway, I was thinking about our current situations and—"

He stops mid-sentence, and his gaze rises with me as I stand.

"What are you doing?" Dex asks.

He's so handsome, it's a distraction. I don't usually pay attention to how strained his eyes look behind his thick, full lashes. *It's like tension.* It's as if he's always holding his poker face, worried he might break at any minute under the tremendous pressure.

"Stand up," I say.

Once he does, I wrap my arms around his stomach and turn my head so my cheek is pressed against the middle of his chest. It's admittedly a little awkward because Dex is so much taller than me. This is the best I can do in the territory of friendly hugs. I even try not to breathe in the sexy smell of his leathery, spicy cologne that makes my head foggy. It's when he hugs back that I step away, realizing that I'm enjoying the warmth of his body too much. Not the best time to take advantage of my friend.

I even go as far as offering him an explanation he didn't ask for. "I can't afford to send beautiful flowers like your grandma deserves. And the kitchen is not where I shine, or I'd offer to make you a casserole. Bear hugs are all I have to offer. I'm sorry."

"Don't apologize," he says with an exhale. "That felt really nice. Can I have one more?" Dex holds his arms out as an invitation.

"Really?" I ask.

"Yeah, why are you surprised?"

"You're not really a hugger."

He stares at me, eyes wide and pleading like I'm missing the obvious punch line of a joke. "I'm a hugger, Lennox. You just never offer. In fact, you usually treat me like I'm contagious. I always assumed it was out of respect for whoever you're dating."

Incorrect. It's actually because I see his face almost every time I come, so I'm trying hard not to blur even more lines by touching him too much. "Yeah, I guess something like that."

"But you're single now, right?"

"Right." I pretend to be nonchalant as I step back into his arms, fully prepared to give him another awkward cheek-against-chest, butt-out, pat-on-the-back hug, but Dex has other plans. After ducking his head, he grabs my hands, one by one, securing them at the top of his shoulders. He rests his chin in the nook where my neck meets my shoulders and then his muscular arms are squeezing the life out of me. He's holding me so tight against his body, I'm almost certain if I open my mouth, a squeal will slip right out. It doesn't hurt, it just feels desperate. I wanted this hug. He apparently *needed* it.

"No one offered this," he mumbles into my neck.

"What's that?" I ask. My face is buried into his pec, and screw it, I breathe him in. I breathe him the fuck in and let my legs go completely numb. *Just one tiny moment.* This moment belongs to me.

"Endless handshakes, pats on the back, and *goddamn,* do elderly people love to brush fictitious crumbs off your shoulders... but no one hugged me. Think about that. My grandma died, and no one offered me a hug. *Until you.* Thank you," Dex says against my ear.

He kisses the top of my head, then finally lets me go. It feels like we just crossed some sort of boundary. I'm not sure what it was but that was more than friendly. For a moment, I think I just admitted all my feelings for Dex with one hug. That would've been humiliating.

His embrace is gone, so I cross my own arms, cupping my elbows with opposite hands. "Dex, if you want your friends to help, all you have to do is ask."

"Well, I'm asking now."

I raise my brows. "For another hug?" I'm game for another. Only one more moment, though, because any more time spent in fantasy land and I might accidentally get stuck.

"No, something a little more involved than a hug. A job." Dex holds up his hands like he's telling me to halt, but I haven't moved a muscle. "What if I offered you a job for just one year that would set you up for the rest of your life? You'd never have to work or worry about money again. *Your kids* would never have to worry about money again."

His cool, casual demeanor makes me wonder if he's not exaggerating. Pretending like his cryptic offer is for real, I answer with the first thing that comes to mind. "I mean, provided I don't have to take my clothes off or put anything in my mouth, I'd say that sounds pretty damn good. What are you suggesting?"

He smirks at me with a touch of humor relaxing his tense brows. "As long as you don't have to put anything in your mouth?"

"We live in Vegas, don't act like that's a weird thing to be worried about."

"Fair enough. But no—nothing like that. My grandma..." He exhales. "How do I sum this up as quickly as possible?"

"I don't mind a story."

His lips twitch into a half-hearted smile. "I'm not a good storyteller."

That's a lie. Dex's scuba diving stories are legendary. "Fine. What about your grandma?"

His sigh is heavy like he's reluctant to talk about the conversation *he* brought up. "I think she got caught up in this idea that I shouldn't take over the company alone."

I nod along, but I'm not really understanding.

"My family's company is bigger than I've alluded to. There are a lot of jobs and money on the line. I've been preparing to take over the company my whole life. Everyone assumed my grandma would leave the business to me."

"But she didn't?"

"No, she left everything to my wife."

The first thing I feel is a paralyzing zap of shock. Ice-cold shock.

Then, anger.

"You have a wife, Dex?" I ask in a harsh whisper. I don't notice I'm backing away from him until he steps forward to close the growing gap between us.

He rolls his eyes, and for the first time in my history with him, it doesn't make me laugh. "Don't, Len. Not you, of all people," he says.

"Don't what?"

He clamps his giant hand on my shoulder, holding me in place. "Jump to conclusions. It's not what you think."

I narrow my eyes. "Then choose your words more carefully. Because I don't want to be outside of a bar this late, flirting with a married man."

The hard lines of his chiseled jaw slacken. He cracks a smile. "We're flirting?"

"Or talking, I mean," I rush out, scrambling for words. *Shit.* I didn't mean for that to slip out. My thoughts are ricocheting off the walls like a pinball machine. "I just know what it looks like. I don't want people to get the wrong impression. All our friends think we secretly hook up. I'm pretty sure Alan's convinced I'm in love with you. It's why he dumped me. The very last thing I need is an angry, jilted wife pounding on my door, threatening to kick my ass over something that's never existed between us." As soon as the last words leave my lips, my open palm finds my forehead. I hang my head, looking down at my metaphorical word vomit spilled all over the ground.

"Alan dumped you because of me?" Dex asks.

I peek up. He's also looking down, staring at my boots like he's ashamed.

"No. I mean, yes, but there's more to it than that. He just thought... He was feeling insecure, is all. Don't read into it."

Dex rolls his hand over my shoulder, then down my back,

leaving a blazing trail of goosebumps wherever he touches. "I'm sorry. The whole point of resisting you was to not make your life so messy. But shit, since I'm screwing everything up for you anyway, might as well dive in."

"Oh...I..." I can't seem to form a lucid response.

"I'm not married. I've never been. My grandma left the business to my wife to force me to get married. It's either find a wife or forfeit the company. So, I need to get married, have my wife assume the role of CEO, then she'll hand everything right back to me after a year."

"*What?*" I squall. "How? Are you even dating anybody?"

"It's just paperwork, Lennox. Afterward, we'll get amicably divorced, and everyone can move on with their lives. As of right now, I have someone lined up."

"Oh. Who?" I do a terrible job biting back the jealousy in my voice. Dammit. "Never mind. Not my business," I quickly backtrack. My head is spinning. There are too many competing thoughts and emotions flooding my mind. I'm going to drown in the confusion. How is Dex talking about all this so nonchalantly? He just lost Dottie. He should be in shambles. They were so close. And what the hell does he mean his grandma is forcing him to marry some woman—who I swear I don't already resent—from beyond the grave?

Dex is still elaborating, but I'm only catching portions of his explanation. As I repeat the conversation in my mind, a new realization comes over me. Wait... Did Dex just say he's been "resisting me?" What the hell does that mean? Are all these touches reckless for him, too?

"...she's a Harvard grad, plenty of business experience, familiar with the social elitist circles, already lives in Miami. She checks all the boxes, apparently..."

"Right." I try to refocus on the logistics of the conversation, but my mind wanders. If we've been feeling the same way for three years... *What the hell, man?* And then why is he telling me all of this now? Is it possible he's been holding back his feelings, too?

I fixate on Dex's moving lips, trying to concentrate on what he's saying and stop wondering what kissing him would feel like. *Focus, Lennox.* I'm staring so intently, my eyes ache. *Are my eyes dilated? They feel dilated.*

"...but this is going to be the hardest year of my life, and I'd rather do it with a friend. I know it's a big ask. But I will take good care of you every step of the way. I'll do all the heavy lifting; you'll just have to sit in the boss' seat, sign paperwork, and attend a few events. Then, after a year, the nightmare will be over, and you'll be financially set for life. I promise. Name your price."

I stare at him, trying to fit the missing puzzle pieces together. "My price for what?"

His eyelids clamp shut, and he exhales like he's exasperated with me. "How much to convince you to marry me? I just inherited *everything,* Len. When I tell you I don't have limits, I mean it."

I roll my eyes. "A million dollars," I tease.

"How about twenty million?" he asks, holding my gaze. Not a hint of humor in his quick reply. Dex looks completely serious, and it all hits me at once...

Why he's never really cared about the scuba shop bringing in money. The reason he doesn't talk about his other job. How his monthly fish food costs more than what I make in a month. He's been sharing his life with half-truths *for years.*

"What the actual fuck, Dex?"

"I can go higher. And I don't mind because you might be the only woman I've met who actually deserves it." He cradles my shoulders. "I typically don't like to ask for help, but..."

"You need my help?" I ask, finishing his thought. He nods.

I wet my lips and consider my answer. I'm in debt. My credit sucks. I don't have a home. Dad's in financial ruin. My family needs help. My tooth is getting worse. One day, I'm sure my kids would appreciate a mom who isn't such a hot mess. Money would definitely make things easier...

But I don't think money would make me happier.

I silently stare at Dex, still half expecting him to burst out laughing with a giant "Just kidding." But judging by the look on his face, he'd probably give me anything I want right now.

"The position will pay like a normal job, right?"

"What do you mean?" he asks, looking caught off guard.

"As in, I'd work for you and then earn a paycheck. I'm assuming it'll be enough for rent, groceries, gas, and all that stuff?"

"Technically, if you accept, I'll work for you." Dex smiles my favorite smile, the one that starts at the corner of his eyes. "But full transparency, I should explain—Hessler Group pays its CEO a lot less than industry norms. It's a decision my great-grandparents made to help with employee gainshare because they never needed the income. Cut down the CEO's salary, then all the entry-level employees can get paid a little more. So, the salary is marginal compared to other Fortune 100 CEOs, but I promise, it'll more than cover rent, groceries, and gas."

"Did you just say Fortune 100? Dex, what are you even talking about right now?" As much as I try to avoid corporate conversations, I'm not completely clueless. I know what a Fortune 100 company must be worth from my dad's days in finance.

He tilts his head as he looks into my eyes with a strained expression. It almost seems like a silent plead for me to not overact. "Have you ever heard of Luxe Adventure, Serenity, or Victorian cruises?"

"Of course." My parents splurged on a Serenity cruise for their twentieth anniversary. Luxe Adventure is apparently the cruise line to go on if you want a celebrity spotting. Victorian is an international cruise line if you want to live on a boat for a month. "Your company works with those cruise lines?"

"They *are* my cruise lines. Hessler Group owns all three, among other commercial vacation ventures."

"You said your family was in cargo shipping," I blurt out, accusing him.

"No," he replies, defensiveness lacing his tone. "I said we were in ships. You filled in your own blanks."

"And you let me," I argue back.

"All you've done since I met you is talk about how much you hate corporate, money, 'the man,' and basically everything I am. How else was I supposed to—" He blows out a sharp breath instead of finishing his sentence.

"To what?"

Dex holds out his hand, but I don't take it. It's not anger, it's fear. Three years I've cherished this man, but who the hell is he really? Have I been falling for an idea instead of a person? "Look...I'm a different guy in Las Vegas. I took some time to explore the other things I care about. But now, vacation is over, and it's time to get back to my actual life. I guess I've always been worried you wouldn't like the real me."

"So, you lied?"

"I..." He looks up, then down. Eyes fixed on his shoes, he continues, "I kept you. It's as simple as that. You're my best friend, Len. I said and did what was needed to keep you close. Can you try to understand that?"

He drops his hand to his side, accepting I have no intention of taking it. The guilt seeps through me as I see the defeat grow in his eyes. All I want to do is fix it. Mend the pain. Fill in the gaps. It's dangerous how much I care about Dex. Telling me the truth created all these holes, now my first instinct is to patch them.

"Tell me more about this job, Dex. You know I'm wildly underqualified to be a CEO, right?"

"It's more of a figurehead position. Basically, your job is to just spend time with me for a year. Hopefully not the worst thing in the world." He winks, trying to add his signature playfulness into the conversation.

There are multiple red flags flapping so hard in my mind. My logic and reason take over, scolding me: *No. Bad idea.* One, don't marry someone when the end goal is divorce. *You'll end up getting hurt.* Two, and more worrisome, don't marry someone just for money. *You'll end up getting screwed over.* Three, this is Dex. Freaking Dex Hessler. Lie all you want but you know how you feel about him. Don't marry a man who doesn't want you back. *You'll end up getting annihilated.*

On the other hand...

I bet even half a hot-shot CEO's salary is enough to clear up some of my debt and maybe help my parents as well.

"How much is the CEO's salary?"

Dex grimaces. "A little north of six million. I know it's modest, but like I said, I'm personally offering you—"

"*Modest*? Do you live on a different planet?" As soon as the words are out, I realize the truth of it all. It hits me like a train. All the tender touches, the way Dex smiles and lights up when he sees me. How he laughs with me. The first time we met, the way he was looking at me like he was hungry for me. It never really made sense why we didn't cross that line together...until now.

No way Dex sees me as compatible. He couldn't end up with the broke, hot-mess, purple-haired girl. It's probably why he doesn't mention his family or talk about home. Why he keeps the distance between us...

"Len, are you okay?"

All the times I felt more than comfortable opening up to Dex about my life and money problems. Now, I'm a little embarrassed. My eyes lift to meet his, and it suddenly dawns on me that Dex is so much taller than me. He's been looking down on me since the moment we met.

"How much do you make?"

"That's complicated," he says, pinching one eye shut. "It's my family's money...old money. I don't technically make it."

He stops his explanation there, probably thinking he's off the hook. I narrow my eyes and point right at his chest. "No. No way. You just asked me to marry you. No more secrets, half-truths, and most definitely no more family deaths that you hide from your friends. If you want my help, you better start talking."

He blows out a long, steady breath. "It's not like it's all cash in my pocket or anything, but with assets, property, the company...I don't know. My net worth is somewhere in the ballpark of eighteen billion." He scours my face, reading something I can't see. "And that look right there is exactly why I didn't tell you all this."

"What look?" I relax my face, wiping away the evidence of whatever he just saw.

He sucks in his lips. "Money changes people. And a *lot* of money usually changes them in bad ways."

His words knock the wind out of me, mostly because I wasn't expecting that response. Like when a punching bag swings back and knocks you down on your ass. "So, you lie to all of your friends because you don't want us coming after your money?" I let out a bitter chuckle and nod. I'm too sober for this. *I'm tired.* I've carried this stupid crush for three years on a man I obviously don't know.

"No. That's *not* what I meant," he pleads.

"Dex, you don't need me," I say, looking over my shoulder at the bar entrance. "You clearly have options. And right now, honestly, it feels like you're a stranger. So, no. I can't marry you, even for a year." But I reach out and run my fingers lightly across his forearm. "But I'm really sorry about your grandma. If you ever want to talk, I'll be here."

I turn to head back to the bikers and booze but am yanked back. "Please, wait." Inhumanly fast, Dex weaves his fingers between mine, holding my hand with a death grip.

"I'm not into fancy things. My only real vices are expensive liquor and dive trips." He rushes his words out like he's on a timer. "One time, I wanted to see this shipwreck in a remote part of Nova Scotia, and they didn't have enough passengers to justify the tour, so I just bought the whole damn yacht and made them take me out. My favorite food is Cubanos—but only if they're authentic. I've never broken a bone, but I have had stitches. Sliced my foot open on a broken glass bottle on the beach. Um, let's see what else... My birthday is February eighteenth. I have the same birthday as my mom. I never tell anyone that because I don't celebrate outside of this tradition I have with my grandma. Every year for our birthday, we'd eat at a burger place called Rooster's. They have the most ridiculous menu, and they are always changing it and trying crazy stuff. There's a peanut butter jelly turkey burger on the menu."

I pinch my face in disgust, and Dex raises his brows.

"Don't knock it 'til you've tried it. And anyway, it's not about the food. It's just a place my grandma and I felt close to her. I was only seven when she died from a stroke nobody saw coming. I lost my mom; Grandma lost her daughter. As devastating as it was, after a while, my grandpa, her friends, and everyone else just seemed to move on. But not Grandma and me. We kind of stood there, watching in shock as the world kept spinning for everybody. So, once a year, on me and Mom's birthday, Grandma and I would go get a burger and a confetti birthday shake and sit there dumbfounded that no one else seemed to still be missing her like we were."

I'm quiet and completely still, like I'm trying not to startle a deer away. I've known Dex for three years, and I've learned more about him in the last two minutes than I have in all those years combined. I want to hear more, except now he's staring at me like it's my turn to speak. I clear my throat and say the first thing that comes to mind. "Dex, that's the most heartbreaking story I've ever heard. Are you...trying to guilt me into marrying you?"

He shakes his head like it's preposterous. "No." Then his smile turns just a touch mischievous. "Would that work?"

"So, you made all that up?" I ask, my tone turning glacial.

"No. Not at all. Rooster's is very much real. The confetti birthday cake shake is epic. They put little frozen pieces of cake in it and globs of chocolate frosting." His smirk fades before he adds, "This year, I'll be there alone because I just lost the last person on earth that I love. Len, I'm not telling you all of this to get you to do anything. I'm simply trying to open up because I can't stand the idea of you feeling like I'm a stranger." He squeezes my hand. "I'll tell you whatever it takes to keep you from walking away from me. I don't know how to explain what you mean to me."

"Try." I wiggle my hand free of his and place it on my hip. I'm sure I have an unsettling resemblance to my mom at the moment. I'm even fighting the urge to tap my foot. But I stare into Dex's eyes and prepare myself to ask the question I've been wrestling with for years. "What do I mean to you, Dex?"

He fishes his wallet out of his back pocket. I never paid attention before, but after tonight's shocking revelation, I can't help but notice that Dex's wallet is sleek and black. There's no huge wad of cash in there. There also aren't many cards. Just one black card that's probably as powerful as one hundred high-limit credit cards.

He pulls out a faded folded bill from behind his ID, resting in the dedicated plastic compartment. "Here," he says, then hands it to me. I see the thick ten on the right corner.

"I'm not a gold digger or anything, but knowing how rich you are, this is kind of insulting." I smirk.

"So sassy," he mumbles under his breath. He takes the bill back and unfolds it carefully so I can see the purple nail polish mark at the top right corner. Looking pleased, he places it back in my palm.

It literally feels like the air is sucked out of my lungs. I try to inhale, but nothing happens. "This is?" I ask, somehow managing the two words through my breathlessness.

"From the first time we met. My souvenir," he says.

There are little tells that he's nervous. Not on his expression, that's completely composed. Dex has a bulletproof poker face. It's how his thumb is subtly twitching, so he tucks it into his fist. His jaw is clenched and he's so still, like he stopped breathing as well.

I run my finger over the glittery purple nail polish streak. The polish is still vibrant even though the bill looks worse for wear. All this time, he didn't just keep it.

He kept it close.

I'm stuffed to the brim with conflicting emotions. When they finally burst free, what comes out of my mouth is an awkward, almost-deranged chuckle. "I gave a billionaire ten dollars for beer."

"What?" Dex asks, his brows furrowing.

"You must've thought I was pathetic."

"Lennox, that ten-dollar bill told me everything I needed to know about you in only one gesture. Look...people typically either like me or hate me for what I have. They judge my worth by what I can or can't do for them. I've had disposable relationships my whole life until you. I think you were the first person to..." He shrugs.

"Like you for you?" I offer.

Nodding, he says, "Something like that. I guess I wanted to keep things simple between us to keep our relationship safe. Losing you just wasn't an option for me. I'm sorry I was dishonest."

Dex gently takes the ten-dollar bill out of my hand and then carefully folds it back up exactly as it was. He tucks it back behind his ID card.

"Wait," I say with a chuckle. "You're not giving it back? I could use ten dollars. You clearly don't need it."

He looks at me like I've lost my mind. "No. Sorry. You can have literally any bill in my bank account except that one. It means way too much to me."

It only takes one line. Just like that, my fate is sealed.

"Okay, I'm in. I'll do it."

"Do what?" he asks, a little glint of hope in his tone.

"I'll marry you."

"You're serious?"

I nod. "Yeah, serious." I hold out my hand, intent on shaking on it. But Dex doesn't take it. His eyes are glowing under the flickering streetlamp as he focuses on my face.

"Right now," he says. "Before we change our minds."

Dropping my hand, I ask, "Why would you change your mind?"

"I'm about to piss off a lot of people. The lawyers will want a prenup. My execs will be nervous about their positions. Denny will be livid—unless you have an Ivy League degree you haven't mentioned to me yet." He laughs absentmindedly.

Who the hell is Denny? "No, definitely not," I answer.

His smile fades. "What's wrong?"

"I'll sign a prenup," I assure him. "I understand you want to protect yourself. I have no ulterior motives. Not to mention, you're offering me a get-out-of-jail-free card for my life right now. I'm just glad I can help you."

"That's exactly why we don't need one. I trust you, Lennox. You're the only person I trust. I don't need a prenup to protect myself or my company from you." He brushes the tip of his thumb against my cheek. A gesture of affection that feels like way more than friendship, confusing the shit out of me.

Last chance. Run. My logic begs me not to do this. But three years later, I'm still powerless before those hazel eyes.

"Okay, tonight. Let's go," I agree.

The flood of nerves starts at the top of my head all seeps down to the very tips of my toes, because after three long years of wrestling with my feelings...

I'm now just minutes away from marrying Dex Hessler.

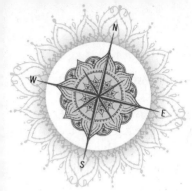

CHAPTER 13

Dex

"Lucky number eighteen," I say, holding up a white ticket. I plop down next to Lennox on the wooden bench outside the chapel doors. "There are four couples ahead of us. But apparently, the officiant used to be an auctioneer, so he'll have us in and out like that." I snap my fingers.

The whole bench is shaking because she's jiggling her knee aggressively. She's hunched over, her elbows resting on her thighs, holding her phone between both hands. "Mhm," she mumbles.

"What's on your mind?" I ask. Lennox wasn't this nervous an hour ago at the courthouse when we got our marriage license. She was cool as a cucumber, but now she seems out of sorts.

"Nothing, you?" she mutters distractedly. Her eyes are fixed on her screen and the death grip she's sporting might snap her phone in half.

"I'm debating how much tongue I'm going to slip you during our first kiss after we say, 'I do.'"

She's glaring at me through her peripherals, but at least that grabs her attention. "Funny."

"Will you lighten up? Who are you texting?" I nudge her knee with mine, and it calms.

"I need to text my mom, but I don't know what to say." Her tone turns pleading. "Do I say I got married, or I got a job? Honestly, she'll be equally shocked at both."

Sometimes I forget other people have families that care about their life choices outside of the financial implications. "Is she going to be mad? I've met your mom a time or two. I thought it went fine."

"Mom likes you, Dex. It's not that. It's just..." She trails off, shrugging.

"What?" I prod.

"I haven't been making the best decisions for my future lately. This seems like piling on."

I scoff. "What's that supposed to mean?"

"What happens when you're done with me in a year? Then what?" she asks. "What kind of jobs do you apply for after being a CEO, except you weren't qualified to be one in the first place? How do you tell your future boyfriends that you're a divorcée but your marriage wasn't real? I'm just"—she jostles her head—"trying to think it through. These are the questions my mom is going to ask. I'm preparing my defenses."

I pull her phone out of her hands and set it aside. "Do you not want to do this? We can walk out right now."

She rolls her eyes. "And let you marry Blonde Harvard Barbie? I don't think so. Who is going to call you pretty boy and build you perfect Subway sandwiches? You need a friend, not a stranger, Dex. You need me."

Subway sandwiches aren't why I need her, but I do, in fact, need her. I laugh. "I'm not going to be done with you, Len. I already told you I'd set you up. If you don't want money, I'll help you figure out a stable career. All you have to do is figure out what you want from your life."

"That's sort of the problem." She pats her thighs, resulting in a loud clap that echoes against the walls. "I don't know what I want to do. I'm twenty-seven and I still have no idea."

I grab her hand and squeeze twice before releasing it. "I'll call your mom tomorrow and explain everything. How's that?"

A bewildered smile claims her face. "You're going to call my mom?"

I nod. "Yes. I'll take the heat. And anyway, there's the matter of your dowry we need to discuss. I'm not greedy. I don't want their money. Just a few cows, an ox, and some grain will do."

She rolls her eyes. "You ass."

"There she is." I nudge her shoulder. "And if it makes you feel better, I'll explain to all of your boyfriends until the end of time how your divorcée status is simply evidence of what an incredible friend you are."

She shakes her head. "That won't be necessary. Good to know we'll stay friends until the end of time, though."

"Can I tell you something?"

She already looks more relaxed. Her shoulders slack as she leans back against the bench that creaks in protest. "Of course."

"You're not just my best friend; I think you're my only friend."

"That's not true. You have everyone at the dive shop. Finn, Avery, and even you and Leah are still on good terms, right?"

"Surface level, sure. But you're the only person I really talk to."

She peers at me from the corner of her eyes, skepticism painting her face. "That can't be right. You have a whole other life in Miami. What about all the friends you grew up with?"

I scoff. "I was very much raised in a bubble."

"Who'd you have to talk to?" Lennox asks. She pulls one knee up onto the bench. It brushes against my thigh as she turns to me.

"Grandma."

"And now she's gone," Lennox says softly.

I nod with a clipped smile. "Pretty much."

"Dex, that's so sad. I'm very sorry. I feel terrible for you."

Running my finger over her forehead, I try to smooth out the wrinkles of her concern. "You don't have to do that. I'm not trying to play the sad, little rich boy card. Nobody likes that."

"Can I tell *you* something?" she asks.

"Sure."

"You can be rich *and* sad. I don't think money fixes everything. In fact, if I learned anything from my dad, it breaks far more than it fixes."

My smile grows and I feel the warmth I always do around

Lennox. She's a twenty-seven-year-old temp, but she doesn't see her superpower. A fancy career or degree isn't necessary. She's already got everything she needs to be okay. Lennox, with her sassy outfits and purple hair, is always the wisest person in the room. The world just needs to listen.

I tuck a lock of hair behind her ear, and the touch feels different. It's not friendly, more laced with intimacy. But this time, she doesn't pull away. Instead, she gulps so hard, I hear it. Then, she licks her lips. Probably self-consciously because I'm staring at them so intently.

I want to feel them. The urge is getting to be too much to resist. Lennox should be mine. She's actually moments away from being mine. *Those lips belong to me.* I lean in a little closer as I decide consequences be damned...I have to taste them—

"Sir!" The chapel's assistant comes barreling down the hallway, making a ruckus, ruining my moment of opportunity.

"What?" I grumble in agitation.

She's holding out a white plastic bag. "You forgot this at the front. This comes with your package. Her veil is in there as well. Congratulations," she says before hurrying back down the hallway.

"Package?" Lennox straightens up in her seat, her eyes bright and big. Our moment of temptation over.

"I splurged and got the Deluxe package," I say with a little sarcasm. "It comes with a commemorative shot glass, and you get to keep the veil. I just wanted to give you the wedding of your dreams." I bat my eyelashes innocently at her.

"How much is splurging?" She grabs the bag and pulls out a pathetic-looking plastic tiara with a short white veil attached. The ruby gems glued to the crown look like the end result of a kindergarten homework assignment. "Seriously, what a scam. How much did they charge for this cheap crap?"

"I don't know, Len. I usually don't look at prices."

I don't register the effect of my words until I see her bewildered expression. "So, when you go out to eat at a nice restaurant, you don't even check the dinner bill?"

I shake my head. "Not really."

"When you buy clothes and shoes?"

I lock eyes with her, slowly realizing what's going through her head. But why lie? She's going to find out soon enough. "In Miami, I have personal staff who shop for me and fill my closets."

"What about when you buy a car? You don't even check the price?"

"No," I reply flatly, growing weary of the conversation.

"How about a house?"

I clear my throat, listening to it echo off the walls. The music from the chapel behind us dies down, and suddenly, it's very quiet in the hallway. "Grandpa, Grandma, and I would typically make real estate offers under a trust not associated with our names. If we were to purchase under 'Hessler,' the seller would probably try to charge me ten times the actual value."

"Which you could still afford?" She's twisting the tiara in her hand nervously. It's so cheap and thin that it easily bends back and forth.

"Yes. Careful, you're going to snap that in half."

But she doesn't stop. "How much is your house in Miami worth?"

Why do I feel like she's staring at me naked? But not in a sexy way. Just in a way in which I feel uncomfortably exposed. "Which one?"

"The biggest one."

"That'd be the Hessler Estate. And technically, it belonged to my family, not just me. Not to mention, I'm selling it to Denny—"

"Dex, quit avoiding the question."

"A little north of forty million. What are you getting at?"

Crack! The tiara snaps in half. She grabs her palm where the sharp edge of the plastic bit her. "Ow," she mumbles.

"I warned you." I take her hand and pull it to my lips. *Kiss.* As if a little peck will fix everything. I meant it as a sweet gesture but she rips her hand away, her cheeks flushing crimson.

"That thing you said earlier about Denny being upset I'm not

Ivy League... Who's Denny?"

"She's my family's household manager. A personal assistant of sorts but with more authority. Right now, she's the closest thing I have to family. She's been around since before I was born. But the thing I said about Ivy League was just a jab at Denny. It bothers me how pretentious she is sometimes. Len..." I wait until her eyes are on mine. "That's my world, but I'm not like that."

"You sure?" she asks with a reluctant smile. "Because for three years, I've wondered why you turned me down the night we met. You haven't made a move since. You're sweet, considerate, and flirt with me shamelessly. You hate my boyfriends. It didn't make sense. *Until tonight.*"

My face screws up in confusion. "What makes sense now?"

"You cared about me too much to hit it and quit it. But I'm also not your pedigree. So, I guess friends made the most sense."

"Len, that's so out of—"

"Who's my number eighteen? *You're up!*" The officiant busts through the chapel doors with his auctioneer voice. I might've laughed if his timing wasn't piss-poor.

I hold up our ticket between two fingers but keep my eyes on Lennox. She looks like she's about to cry. *Just stay with me. Let me explain how you've got this all wrong.* "We need a minute," I say, but he doesn't hear me.

"Oh, hey there, missy, you broke your veil." He looks at Lennox's lap. "I can grab another from the front."

"That's all right." She clears her throat and stands up. "We're ready."

He glances between me and Lennox, finally cluing into the tension. "You sure?"

His gut is begging to break free of his beige suit. And apparently, I just hurt my bride's feelings. Not to mention she's in cowgirl boots and we both smell like the bar we were drinking at. This isn't right. She deserves a dress and a real veil. Lennox should get married knowing how her groom actually feels about her. This wasn't how anything was supposed to go.

Nothing in the past few weeks is how my life was supposed to go.

Every time things would get too far off course like this, and I didn't know what was best, I'd call Grandma. If I could, I'd ask her what to do in this moment, but she already made her intentions clear from beyond the grave. Her decision is why I'm in this mess to begin with.

"You still want to do this?" I ask Lennox.

Her nod is too eager. Overcompensating. "I gave you my word."

"And now I'm giving you an out."

She holds out her hand to me and wiggles her fingers. "Dex Hessler, get your ass up and let's get married."

Lennox

Dex didn't slip me tongue. In fact, after it was all said and done, he pecked me on the cheek. Even the officiant gave him the side eye. I was so embarrassed I stormed out of the chapel like a child and hunted down the nearest rideshare driver.

I knock on the darkly tinted passenger window. Once it rolls down, I point to the neon pink rideshare sign visible through his windshield. "Hey, are you waiting for someone, or are you free?"

"Are you headed to the Strip?" he asks.

He looks like a freaking kid. *Eighteen, maybe?* I bet he can't drink. He looks barely old enough to legally hold this job. His hat is backward, and he's wearing a cut-off gym shirt with two gold chains around his neck. Yet, there's a blazer neatly folded and lying in the passenger seat of his nice SUV. It's safe to say I am confused about everything going on in front of me. Then again, I just came barreling out of a wedding chapel in a white tank top, jean shorts, and cowgirl boots with my groom nowhere in sight. I'm hardly in a position to judge.

"No," I answer. "Opposite direction. Near Calico Springs. It's about thirty minutes from here."

He twists his lips. "That's too far. I can make, like, three trips back and forth from the Strip in that time. I don't like to venture from my normal route."

There are footsteps on the concrete approaching me, but before I can turn, Dex wraps his forearm around my shoulders from behind. He pulls me backward into the firm wall of his body so when he leans through the open window, he's not squishing me against the door.

"Can you make an exception?" Dex asks the kid.

It's too dark for me to see how much cash Dex handed him, but it's enough to earn an eager, "Yes, sir. I'll get the door for you guys." The kid opens his door in a hurry.

"Just sit down and start the car," he grumbles. He's rubbed the wrong way. Probably because the driver gave me a hard time before he showed up. I'd say this newfound protectiveness is because now I'm his wife, but Dex has always been this way. Whenever I'm with him, he doesn't tolerate anyone cutting me in lines, talking over me, or bumping into me without an immediate "excuse me" or apology. I thought it was manners. Maybe it was more.

I shuffle to the backdoor and grab the handle, but Dex plants his hand on the door, making it impossible for me to open it.

Spinning around to face him, I ask, "What?"

He moves in a little closer to me. "Are you okay?"

I nod. "Yeah. Why?"

"Because I think you just tried to ditch my ass ten seconds after marrying me."

I make a face, pretending like he's crazy, even though he's spot on. "Not at all. The smoke machine mixed with the strobe lights were making me nauseous. I had to get out of there unless you wanted vomit on your shoes."

The look he's giving me tells me he's unconvinced. He sees right through me as usual. "Yeah, that was a little much. I didn't realize the fog machine came with the Deluxe package." He cracks a smile, but it quickly disappears. "It was hard to see you in there.

I was just repeating whatever bullshit the officiant was telling me to. It felt like I was making promises to a cloud of smoke."

I turn down the corner of my lips and nod. "Well, husband, nice to know you think our vows are bullshit." I chuckle, but Dex's eyes are too intense. He's not laughing or smiling. I feel silly, like I'm the only one laughing at a cruel joke. So, I stop.

"They weren't real. To have, hold, and obey? That doesn't mean anything."

I shrug. "Well, neither does this marriage. So..."

"Do you want this to be meaningful? You want me to tell you how I really feel about you? Because once I do, there's no going back."

I lean back so hard into the door, I'm sure the metal is going to bruise my spine. "What do you mean?"

"There's another side of me, and he is the antithesis of the man you want. Corporate, money, politics...that's the version of me I've been hiding from you. And it's a big part of me and my future. The side of my life that'd sink any potential for a relationship for us. And I'm not interested in losing you, Len. But it's your choice. Do you want us to stay where it's safe? Or do you really want to cross this line and risk ruining our friendship?"

I slump forward, my forehead knocking against his chest. The thin fabric of his shirt is cool against my hot skin. "Ruin it," I mumble against him. "Tell me how you really feel about me."

His chest lifts as he takes in a drawn-out inhale. He's breathing deeply while I'm holding my own breath, waiting for an answer to the question I've had for three long years.

"Trouble...my heart stops every time you walk into a room. I am fucking obsessed with you. I have been from the very first moment you showed up at my bedroom door and gave me that ten-dollar bill." He reaches out to cup my cheek, running his thumb along my bottom lip. "But how do we make sense? My destiny is everything you despise. I didn't know how else to keep you close except with...lies."

I gasp like I've just come up for air after holding my head

underwater for too long. Finally, here's my answer. I was never alone in the needy ache. It's been torturing us both for so damn long. And now I'm going to put us both out of our misery. "I can handle it, Dex. All your sides. I'll be right next to you for all of it."

"Promise?" he asks.

"Promise."

I press my ear against his chest, and his erratic heartbeat gives him away. His breath is ragged, and while this is a moment of solace for me, he seems unnerved.

"What's wrong?"

"Absolutely nothing." He wraps me in his arms, his embrace a blanket against the cool night air. I cross every line. I wrap my hands around his hips, grazing the top of his belt. All I can think is it needs to come off. Every single barrier between Dex and I is over now—the half-truths, secrets, our clothes—it's all coming down tonight. "So what's next?" he asks. "What are we now? Married? Friends? Dating? All of the above?"

His body is a playground I finally get to explore. After taking my time running my hands across his lower back, then tracing his hard abs, I place them flat against his pecs. Leaning away, looking for his eyes, I allow myself to get fully lost in the green and honey-colored patches. "I don't know. We said, 'I do,' and then you pecked me on the cheek."

"I was trying to maintain boundaries," he answers defensively. "I didn't know what you wanted."

I grab his shirt and tighten my fist, pulling him closer. "You. For three fucking years, Dex. *You*."

Then, his full, cool lips are on mine. The woodsy, rich, sweet smell of his mouth-watering cologne is all I breathe in as he kisses me. He's pressed so tightly against me, I can't tell where his body stops and mine begins. We're melted into one, the car barely bracing our interwoven bodies.

Breathless, he breaks away. Searching my eyes, he asks, "How'd that kiss feel?"

The answer is so simple. "Completely addicting."

His lips are on mine again, and I'm kissing my husband back like I'm starving for him.

Tongue and all.

CHAPTER 14

Lennox

The car ride is mostly silent besides the low hum of French rap music. Apparently, our driver, Colton, has very specific taste. It's been thirty minutes, inching through bumper-to-bumper traffic on the highway, and his entire playlist is what sounds like French club bangers. Colton's onto something. This playlist is my newest obsession.

I bob my head along to the beat and roll my shoulders when the melody of the bridge drops. "What is this?" I call out to the front seat.

Colton smiles through the rearview mirror. "You like it?"

"I do." I glance at Dex right next to me, who is wearing a satisfied expression with his eyes locked on me. I don't think he's enjoying the music. It seems like he's enjoying me smiling.

"This is GIMS," Colton replies. "One of the best. You should see some of these French rappers live. Mind-blowing. Way more passionate than American rap. The concerts are an artistic experience." He cranks up the volume.

Dex weaves his fingers between mine and squeezes. "We could go, you know."

I raise my eyebrows. "To France?"

Dex nods. "I owe you a honeymoon. How about Paris?"

So this is the life Dex has been so hush-hush about. Jet setting to Paris like it's no big deal. "That sounds nice one day."

I run my thumb over the back of his hand. How quickly everything can change. One kiss later and suddenly Dex is mine. The moment is so satisfying. I'm sad it's fleeting. It's like I was desperately craving a piece of chocolate for as long as I can remember, and now it's melting on my tongue. I want to freeze this moment, not let it slip away. Then again, what's the worry? I have a feeling I'll crave him until my dying day.

Dex unbuckles, leaning in close so he can speak right into my ear. "Not 'one day.' Right now, if you want. I can have the jet here in a couple hours."

"What would we even do? We don't speak French."

"Actually, I do," Dex says nonchalantly. "Well, exaggeration. *Juste un petit peu*," he says with a perfect-sounding French accent. "Enough for us to maneuver around on our own. Then again, we could book a nice room with a view and never leave the bed."

I squint one eye. "How much more am I going to learn about you tonight, Dex?"

He checks to ensure Colton's eyes are on the road, then smooth as silk, he pulls my hand slowly up his thigh, then drapes it over his crotch. "Hopefully a few more things. So, what do you think?"

"Six inches, give or take," I squeeze his bulge and reply with a sly smile.

He levels his stare as his jaw tenses. I can't tell if he's trying not to laugh or if he's honestly offended. Since when is six inches a bad thing? "I meant about Paris, Lennox."

I chuckle. "*Oh.* Um...Paris sounds incredible, but not tonight. I just want to crawl under the covers and sleep next to you. Are you a cuddler?"

He kisses my temple sweetly. "With you? Yes."

I'm busy swooning and trilling my fingers against the outline of his cock when Dex pulls out his phone and starts typing away. I don't know who he's messaging past midnight, but if that's a CEO's schedule, he's going to be sorely disappointed to learn I need eight hours of sleep each night. I have no intention of becoming a slave to an inbox—email or text. But my mental tantrum is cut short when my phone pings loudly from my purse.

Dex flashes me a satisfied smirk. "I believe you got a message, Mrs. Hessler."

Mrs. Hessler. Why does that give me goosebumps in an eerie way? Is it the "Mrs." or the "Hessler" part that's more uncomfortable? Because one make-out session doesn't make this real, does it? I have feelings for my friend. And I married him. But does that make this a real marriage? We have quite a bit to sort out.

Dex's eyes are on me as I fish out my phone. His text is simple.

Dex: Six inches? Not even close. You're going to pay for that, wife.

Me: I meant it as a compliment.

Dex: It was not. Now, you're in trouble.

Me: My punishment?

He pumps his brows at me as he composes his text.

Dex: How about a few swats to that perfect ass of yours?

Me: Okay. But after that, what's my punishment?

Dex tucks his phone away and leans over to whisper in my ear. "Bad girl." His deep voice comes out in a decibel lower than I'm used to. With his warm, stubbled cheek pressed against mine, I try to keep my breath under control. But the surge of need I always feel around Dex is ten times stronger than usual. Probably because tonight, I plan on doing something about it.

"This car ride is taking too long. I want you so fucking badly. We're going to cross all sorts of lines tonight."

My smile is teasing. "What makes you so sure? There's this two-letter word that gives me so much power. Starts with 'N,' ends with 'O.'"

He bats his eyelashes at me, reminding me of the way he did three years ago in his bedroom when he was trying to talk me into scuba diving lessons. "True. But how could you say no to your sweet bridegroom who just wants to love on you and give you the world?"

"Eh. If you're sweet on me tonight, you'll be sweet on me tomorrow. After I take a shower, rest, and eat something."

Dex frowns, the corner of his lips turned down, yet he nods like he understands. "Mmk, Trouble. I see what you need. Check your phone." He pulls his phone back out and starts tapping away aggressively. There's a *swoop* sound as he sends the message and then locks his eyes on mine. "I'm very eagerly awaiting your reply."

> **Dex: I'm not waiting one more night for your sweet pussy, Lennox. You're my wife. All mine. I'll have you when I want, where I want. Clear?**

My cheeks fill with heat as a swell of desire brews below my navel. I turn to him and raise one brow. His face is stoic, an expression that clearly translates to, *"I said what I said."*

> **Me: Well Mr. Hyde, will Dr. Jekyll be joining us again? Or am I stuck with your dark side for the evening?**

**Dex: Depends. Are you interested
in my dark side?**

I set my phone down. Stretching my arms overhead, I make a
meal out of a slow, giant yawn. He lets out a breathy chuckle from
beside me as if he knows I'm purposely trying to dangle him on
the thread.

I don't text him back. I answer out loud while giving him my
sexiest smile. "Mr. Hessler, I would very much like to meet your
dark side."

Dex scoots forward in the seat. He enunciates so Colton can
hear him clearly from up front. "How much longer?"

"Would only be twenty minutes, but traffic isn't moving,"
Colton replies. "GPS says at least another hour. It must be a really
big wreck ahead. I'd find another route, but the highway is the
only way back to Calico Springs. You guys need a snack? I have
Nutter Butters." He reaches for the compartment in front of the
passenger seat, and the car swerves.

"Stop. We don't need cookies. There's a shopping center just
up the way. Take the next exit," Dex instructs him.

"Why would I do that?" Colton asks.

Dex shoots me a side glance. The flash of irritation is brief,
but I catch it. Definitely a different side of him. As an instructor
and friend, he's so patient and kind. But I get the feeling "Boss
Dex" wants people to do what he says immediately without talking
back.

"Haven't I paid you enough to stop asking so many questions?"

"Almost," Colton says with a punk-ass little smile.

"Take the exit," Dex bites out. "I'll make it worth your while."

"Fine," Colton grumbles. He flips on his turn signal just to
prove a point. The exit is still a half-mile away and we're inching
forward maybe five miles an hour, tops.

"Dex, the next exit takes us to Primrose. It's past midnight,
and everything is closed besides a Taco Bell and that 24-Hour

Walmart. What are we going to do?"

"*He*"—Dex nods toward Colton, who has gone back to ignoring us—"is going to entertain himself in Walmart for a while. *We're* not leaving the car. Private party. Your shorts aren't invited."

"Pity," I say.

He winks. "Those boots are welcome to stay, though."

CHAPTER 15

Dex

After Colton shifts into park, he unbuckles as he pivots in the driver's seat to address us. He smiles sweetly at Lennox, then narrows his eyes at me. "I still expect payment for my time if I'm waiting in here for you guys to grocery shop. And you should pick up cooler bags if you buy anything cold. I don't know when traffic is going to let up. Don't want your spoiled milk in my car."

"Fair point," Lennox adds.

"Get out," I snap.

"Wow, man. You talk to your lady like that?" Colton asks.

Pressing my fingers against my temple, I grumble, "*You*, Colton. Get out. I'm sure you can figure out a way to kill thirty minutes in Walmart."

"Uh, no," he sasses back as he rubs his bare arms. What kind of man wears a cut-off gym shirt with a suit jacket? Am I that out of touch, or is this seriously considered fashion? The day my stylist starts stocking my closet with cutoffs, she'll be looking for a new job.

"I need to have a private conversation with my wife. Go into Walmart and fill one cart with whatever the hell you want. Doesn't matter the cost. When I'm finished, I'll meet you at checkout and pay for it all."

He rolls his eyes, but I know he's intrigued by the offer. He was compliant the moment I handed him half a grand to take me and Lennox home. "I know what 'private conversation' means. I'd rather you just give me more cash."

"I made you an offer," I say flatly. "Take it or leave it."

"Fine," he huffs out as he drops his car keys into the cupholder. Then, he opens his door. "Don't ruin my leather. I'll be charging for any incidentals."

"The way this kid thinks he's driving a Bugatti or something," I grumble to Lennox, eyes on Colton until he disappears through the sliding door of the supercenter.

"This is a nice SUV, Dex. For us poor people anyways."

I reach over her legs and release her buckle. With my hand firmly wrapped around her hip, I guide her onto my lap. For a moment, I ignore her crotch pressed against mine, causing my cock to pulse. We'll get to that. I need a moment to explain to Lennox what she clearly doesn't understand.

I smooth out her long, purple locks, tucking her thick hair behind her ears. Then, I press my hand against her chest, feeling her heart beating fast. "You're wealthy in the ways that matter."

"Ah, a rich man's mantra," she teases.

"I'm serious. Money doesn't make me a better person. Wealth has never made me feel confident that I'm doing the right things with my life."

I don't know how she does it, but Lennox smiles with her heart. Her lips glide into an upward curve and I know when she's looking at me like this, she's genuinely happy. I want to freeze this look on her face permanently. "What makes you feel confident, Mr. Hessler?"

"The times I feel lost in myself, I think about you. Every time I have a good dream, it's about you. When I don't know where I belong, you remind me."

She traces the outline of my lips gently. Lennox stares into my eyes, but I know she's looking deeper. Maybe she's searching for all the pieces of me I've been hiding from her. "You're right where you belong. With me."

"Shouldn't have taken us so long," I murmur.

"Maybe we had to have what wasn't enough first. So, when we finally got together, it'd be—"

"Forever?"

"Is that what you want?" she asks. "Because I thought this marriage was about your company."

"Len, this marriage can mean whatever you want it to mean. As long as I can keep you. Whatever you want." I say the last line against her lips. Her skin is smooth. My fingers glide underneath her top, up the divot of her back. She raises her arms in the air so I can strip off her tank top. I barely pinch the fabric of her bra together before it effortlessly unhooks, like the clasp is begging to be freed. I kiss below her collarbone as I pull her bra straps down over each shoulder.

Her arms are clamped against her ribs, holding her bra in place. It gives me time to glance at the tiny "Charlie" tattoo she never had the money to remove. Running my finger over his name, I say, "I'm getting rid of this."

"You want me to get a Dex tattoo instead?" she asks with a chuckle.

"No. I don't need to put my name on your body to claim you."

"Then how are you going to claim me? A fancy ring?"

I yank her bra off, discarding it to the side.

Suddenly, she's sheepish. Covering her breasts with one arm, she looks nervously out the window. "I don't want to get in trouble. This is a public parking lot."

"We're alone and these windows are tinted way past regulation. Not to mention, most cops are willing to look the other way for the right price."

"You'd pay a cop off just to screw me in a car?" We shouldn't be doing this in a rideshare for the first time, but we've wasted too much time already. I don't feel like I can wait another minute.

"I'd pay the world off to keep you in this moment." I pull her arm away from her bare chest, catching her fleshy tit in one hand. I cradle it like a treasure while running my thumb over her dark, firm nipple. "What are you thinking about?"

"It doesn't feel right."

I release her tit and lean back. "Am I fucking this up?" I shake my head. I thought I was being passionate. Lennox isn't a wine-and-dine kind of girl. She likes spontaneity and being lost in a moment. "I'm trying to show you how bad I've wanted you all this time. But maybe I shouldn't be undressing you in a car."

"No, not that," she assures me. "The fact that you can't wait until we get home is such a turn on. I can't tell you how many times I thought about you ripping my clothes off, pinning me against a wall, pulling my hair, and telling me all sorts of dirty things. I always pictured us being explosive."

I weave my fingers in her hair and playfully tug. "That can be arranged."

"But right now..."

I smile at her. "It's your wedding night, and tonight you want me to be sweet to you, don't you?"

She nods sheepishly. "Even if it's in a car."

"From now on, tell me how you feel and ask me for what you want." I hunch over to engulf one nipple then the other, sucking hard so she feels the pressure. "We can make love. We can fuck. I can do whatever you like."

She nods as she climbs off my lap. Standing upright best she can in the backseat, she unbuttons and unzips her bottoms. She shimmies down her shorts and thong together. When she lifts one leg to step out of her bottoms, I take advantage of her position. I hook one hand underneath her thigh, my other arm behind her back, and carefully lay her down on the leather bench.

I position her so she's comfortable. One foot planted on the floor, the other on the seat. Her knee is bent and her thighs are spread so I can see everything that's mine. How quickly my friend can go from a fantasy to my most important reality. I don't care how this started...a deal, a marriage, whatever—I know how this ends. With us falling right into where we should've been all along. In lust. In love. Tonight is the beginning of everything.

"Stay right there, baby. I've got you." I press against her inner thigh, keeping her open for me. I have to hunch over and half hang off the seat to get my mouth where I want to be. If it's uncomfortable, I'm not aware. I lose my mind at the noise she's making. That first little whimper the moment when I drag my wet tongue over her slit. Fuck, that sound. So goddamn satiating. I blow against her sex like I'm breathing life into her.

"*Oh, fuck. That's...yes...perfect,*" she groans.

"Careful. Keep moaning like that and you're going to drive me feral. There'll be nothing sweet about tonight."

I let the saliva pool in my mouth, then I drench her smooth, pink pussy. Her clit becomes a playground for my tongue. Circles then quick flicks; the more she moans and gasps, the crazier it drives me.

She's bridging her hips like she needs more. I feel the muscles of her thigh start to tense, and her clit pulses against the tip of my tongue. "Oh, God...so good...so close," she mumbles in needy rasps.

If we were in a nice bed, I could make love to her properly. I'd keep her dangled at the edge, dragging this out as long as she could possibly handle it. But right now, she deserves relief. "What do you need, baby? Tell me. How do I get you there, hm?"

"Bite it."

Two little words I'll never forget for the rest of my life.

I oblige, barely nipping at her most sensitive area. Then I hollow my cheeks, lips latched around her clit, like I need to soothe the ache.

"Harder," she pleads as she hooks her ankle around my shoulder.

Make that three words I'll never forget.

"Good God, Lennox. You're so fucking sexy. But I don't want to hurt you."

"Trust me. *Please.* I can take it. I'm about to come so hard."

After a couple of sweet strokes, I clamp her little button between my teeth, giving her a little pressure. Her hips buck so hard my whole face is buried into her pussy as she fists my hair, gripping it like she's holding onto a handle for dear life. The symphony of hisses and gasps coming from her has me so hard, I have to unbutton my jeans to relieve the pressure.

I kiss her inner thighs, staying close until her breathing calms and her legs relax. She pushes back on my shoulders as she sits up. I wrap my hands behind her back, supporting her weight. Using her thumb, she wipes her arousal from my lips. "You're ridiculous. I've been packing boxes, dancing, and drinking all night. You didn't have to do that."

I smile at her. "Want to know what you taste like?"

"No," she says flatly.

I laugh and answer anyway. "Delicious. Like the last pussy I'll ever crave."

She places both palms against my cheeks. "How the hell did this happen in just a few hours? Are we really about to start our happily ever after?"

"All I know is right now, my happily ever after is between your thighs. Lay down. Let me take care of you again."

She smiles. "How about you let me take care of you?"

I lift my brows. "I thought you wanted sweet."

"I changed my mind. I just want to make you happy."

Leaning forward, I touch my lips to hers. "You do."

She kisses me back, slipping her tongue between my lips briefly. Then a kiss to each cheek before she tugs at the hem of my polo. I hunch over so it's easier for her to pull off my shirt. She lobs it to the driver's seat. Biting her bottom lip, she scours my bare chest. "I used to never let myself look," she mumbles. She follows up by dragging her nails gently from my shoulders, over my pecs, and down my abs. Her nails are short, and she's far from breaking skin, but she leaves light pink streaks against my skin. *How does she know how much this turns me on?* .

"Mr. Hessler, have me your way." The expression on her face is sugary and clouded over like she's lost in a haze.

"You'll meet my dark side later. Right now, you need to know my real intentions."

"Which are?"

"Taking care of you. So tell me, how do you want me to fuck

you for the first time?"

She blinks a few times, carefully considering her response. "Fuck me like you've been waiting to for three whole years, Dex."

The look on her face is tortured. Full of lustful need. As much as I want to stay lost in her eyes, I stand up, head knocking against the roof of the car, and unbutton my pants. "Climb on. I want to see your eyes and your tits."

She waits patiently as I push down my pants and free one leg completely. I can feel her eyes on my erection. Once she's aware of what she's getting into, she straddles my thighs.

Fisting my hard cock in one hand, I run my hands from her shoulder over her soft, round breast, pausing to roll her nipple between my fingers. I used to get hard just imagining what her nipples must look like. I'd always seen the outline in her bikini tops or a few glances through thin, white tank tops when her wet hair was soaking her shirt after a swim. My mouth would water thinking about how'd they feel against my tongue.

I duck my head and take a mouthful. Swiveling my tongue around her taut nipple, teasing it with my teeth. Toggling to the other side, my hand replaces my mouth.

My attention is fully lost in her chest when she asks, "Do we need a condom?"

"Do you have one?" I ask, glancing at her satchel on the ground. That'd be surprising. She's had a boyfriend for a long time. I doubt she carries protection.

She nods. "Alan doesn't trust birth control. He always insisted."

As much as I don't want to talk about her ex at the moment, the oddity of it makes me pause. "Every single time for years?"

"There was one time it broke, but we finished anyway after—"

I hold up my palm to stop her. "I got it. No need to elaborate." Hooking my finger under her chin, I tilt her gaze up to mine. "I have every intention of being your last." Wedging my hand between her thighs, I cup her sex. "This is for me and only me moving forward. I want you bare."

"Okay," she says, scooting in closer. "Then let's—"

"Say it, Len." My words come out as a low growl. All this time, I've been controlling my feelings around Lennox. I have no idea what side is going to come out of me once I let go. Apparently, it's aggressively possessive.

"Say what?" she asks.

"Say I'm your last. If you mean it, say you're mine and I can have you however I want."

I flinch when she grabs my hard length in her fist. She grinds on the tip, coating me with her arousal. "I shouldn't have to say it, Dex. Don't you know by now? I've been yours."

A little hiss escapes her lips when I nudge into her an inch. She's still dripping, and I have to resist pummeling into her fully. Instead, I let her lower herself over me at the pace she can manage. In this position, she's too fucking tight. It'd wreck us both.

She lets out another sweet moan as she lowers down another inch. I have to bite the inside of my cheek. "The way you sound, baby... I can't handle it."

"Slow," she instructs. I'm not sure if she's telling me or herself.

After taking another inch, she buries her head into my neck, groaning. Her toes curl tightly and I smirk to myself, thoroughly pleased. "Does that feel like six inches to you?"

"Maybe a little more," she moans.

"Maybe a lot more." Bucking my hips, I give her my full length, enjoying the sound of her guttural wail. Music to my fucking ears. It sounds like satisfaction. Like I'm exactly what she was craving. *I'm what she's needed all along.* I hold her firmly in place against my chest, pumping into her slowly, embracing the almost painful tension of her walls that feel like they're swelling more every time I drive into her. Deep breaths are all I can focus on. In and out. Slow it down. The hip bruising thrusts and her pink-colored ass from the swats of my palm can all come later. Right now, I just want her to feel happy and secure.

"How's that, baby? You're so fucking wet. Tell me what it feels like."

"I love it, Dex. Stuff of fucking dreams. All the way in and stop moving."

I do as I'm instructed, and she clenches around me. Such a clever move. Every muscle in her thighs and calves are tight and tension-ridden as she bears down as hard as she can, squeezing the life out of me. "My wife knows how to work her sweet pussy. God, I love it. Use me."

"So close," she murmurs. "Just—"

Instead of finishing her sentence, she lets out a weak whimper. Between the tremble of her smooth thighs and her pulsing around my cock, I know she's coming for me, hard. "That's all it takes, baby? You have no idea how much more I can do for you."

She pants out something incoherent, trying to talk through her orgasm. I wait until she relaxes, then grind into her a few more times. I give her slow, languid thrusts before I start to pick up the pace again. It's when I let out a growl of pure pleasure that she pulls off of me. Before I can ask what's wrong, she drops to her knees, then pushes me back into the seat. My wife's head is between my legs, her mouth wide open.

"We can't leave a mess in here," she explains before clamping her lips onto the head of my cock. The warm, wet sensation is bliss. There's no other word. Pure fucking blissful heaven as Lennox works my cock like an expert, disregarding the fact that I'm covered in her orgasm. She leaves a sloppy trail of her saliva up my shaft, then quickly laps it up, over and over, until she hollows her cheeks.

Throwing my arm out to brace myself against the door must give me away. She sucks harder, her hand cradling my balls, both coaxing out the impending explosion. She doesn't flinch as I spill down her throat. She drinks my cum like she's thirsty for me. Like I've kept her locked up in the desert, and I'm the only thing that can quench her thirst.

She waits until I'm still, licks my tip playfully, ensuring not a drop is wasted, then crawls into my lap, cuddling into my embrace. Our skin, slightly damp from sweat, glues together as we melt bare-assed back into the seat. At this point, I'm going to have to buy this car as a show of basic human decency.

We christened this backseat...or maybe defiled it.

Lennox reaches out to trace a heart against the fogged-up window before nestling back into my chest. "I can't wait to do that again."

I chuckle. "Insatiable little thing, aren't you?"

"Oh, no," she mumbles, tickling my bare chest with her breath. "I'm so satisfied I feel high. That was just as good as I imagined it. I don't think I'll ever have my fill."

Holding her in one arm, and reaching out with the other, I retrace the heart she drew that's already fogging over. "I hope you never do."

She lifts her eyes and answers with a small smile. She doesn't have to say anything else. That look tells me everything I need to know right now. She's mine. I'm hers. It's that simple.

"You should get dressed. Who knows what Colton's up to in there. He's probably expecting you to buy half of the store."

I scoff. "The rules were clear. I told him one cart." That's one big flat-screen TV. Maybe a Mac desk if they are even in stock. What else would a kid his age really want? It's not like Walmart sells cars.

"He's a weasel," Lennox says. "I can't wait to see how he hustled you."

"I'll be fine."

She slides off my lap and reaches for her bottoms. Once her shorts are on, she fetches my clothes for me. She takes her time staring at my softening dick. "Like what you see?" I ask with a smirk.

"It's beautiful," she says with a wink. "Like the last dick I'll ever crave."

I chuckle and kiss her forehead. "Don't steal my lines."

After buttoning my pants and pulling my shirt overhead, I crack open the car door. The swell of fresh air purges the car of our cozy, foggy heat. I miss it instantly. I like to be surrounded by

Lennox—her warmth, scent, the feel of her chest rising and falling against me. It feels like home.

"Can you grab a bottle of water while you're in there, please?" Lennox asks.

"Of course. Do you want some snacks, too?"

After securing her bra and putting her tank top back on, she hunches over the dash, reaching for Colton's glove box. There lies the aforementioned package of Nutter Butters. "Aha!" she says with enthusiasm. "Yes, grab snacks. May I have some Chex Mix? And we'll need to replace his cookies," she says, sliding out one peanut butter treat from the package. She holds it out to me. At first, I shake my head, but she insists again. "Fuel up, mister. I'm not done with you yet tonight."

I take the cookie and plant a wet kiss on her forehead. "Okay. I'll be right back."

Reluctantly, I leave her behind to enter the store and seek out my far less pleasing company for the evening.

Lennox

Two cookies later, I still taste him.

Normally I avoid cum in my mouth. But with Dex, I had to know what he tasted like. Riding him wasn't close enough. I had to get closer. I needed to turn over every stone and allow myself to cross every single line I'd been toeing all this time.

I run my tongue over the roof of my mouth, then over my teeth, before I wet my lips. I'm chasing the sensation. It's been a long time since sex had this kind of power over me. With Alan, I was instantly deflated after sex. Pulled out of the moment the minute he'd finish. But one car fuck with Dex, and I've been sent to la-la-land. Head in the clouds, droopy-eyed, feeling like I'm about to slip into a dream. He left me here in this sexy, sweet, sultry hideaway to wait for him.

Any other night I might be chilly, but my skin is still hot and raw. I'm so comfortable, in fact, that I must doze off for a moment because I'm startled awake by the abrupt opening of the trunk. My heart rate spikes then settles when I see Colton a few paces away, key fob pointed at the car. Dex is trailing just a few paces behind.

Colton is practically skipping, pushing a cart loaded with at least twenty plastic bags. They are barely balancing on top of each other, smashed together in a haphazard attempt at Tetris. Every time the cart wiggles, it looks like one of the bumpy-filled bags might topple over.

Colton continues his lazy stroll, but Dex's feet hit the concrete in an angry trek to the car. Brows tightly furrowed, lips in a hard line, he looks so pissed.

"Oh common, sourpuss," Colton calls out as Dex passes him. "A deal's a deal, right? Be a gentleman and help me load these up."

Dex ignores him and climbs into the backseat next to me with one bag in his hand. He doesn't bother buckling or setting his bag down. He wraps one arm around me and squeezes, like he's desperately clinging to me to calm his nerves.

I sit patiently as Colton slings bag after bag into the trunk, humming to himself.

"You okay?" I ask Dex.

"Mhmm," he answers, which isn't much of an answer. Eventually, he pulls out an ice-cold Dasani from the plastic bag. He releases me to twist open the water bottle. "Here, sweetheart."

Hm, I like that. Sweetheart. Trouble. Baby. Len. I love the way he addresses me. Fueled by either tender, playful, or sexy affection.

"What's wrong?" I ask after taking a small sip of water. But the answer becomes apparent as I turn my head to peer into the trunk. Two bags have tipped over, revealing a handful of smartphones. *"Oh, shit, he—"*

"Yup," Dex says through a clenched jaw. "Fucker bought sixty-eight iPhones, Len. Cleaned out every single version they had in stock."

Clever little weasel. I clasp my hand over my mouth and chuckle-gasp through my fingers. "You should've offered him cash. Oh, Dex...I must be the most expensive lay you've ever had."

He pulls out the black bag of Chex Mix—Bold Party Flavor from the bag on his lap. Dex knows exactly what I like without me having to tell him. As he opens the bag, a puff of the salty snack mix wafts underneath my nose, making my stomach churn eagerly. He fishes out a rye chip and places it into my mouth.

With a little wink he says, "Worth it, Trouble. You're so, so worth it."

I munch away happily, knowing he means it. It was a long time coming, but Dex and I are explosive. Worth the fucking wait.

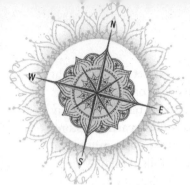

CHAPTER 16

Dex

Three Years Earlier

Las Vegas

"She'll be here any minute," I tell Grandma as I quickly text Lennox back.

> **Me: Take your time. The front door is unlocked. Come right in.**

"She was next door helping her cousin finish up a photo shoot. She said we can start eating without her if you'd like." I nod toward the bags of takeout on my kitchen island.

Grandma scowls at me. "Where are your manners? We'll wait for our guest of honor."

"Fair enough." I start unpacking bags, intent on at least plating them and setting the table. I ordered way too much food for three people. Probably out of nerves.

I'd been in Las Vegas for nearly half a year when Grandma's curiosity got the best of her, and she wanted to see how my new life was going. My life here is a far cry from the luxury back home. I've barely touched the money she released from my trust, but Grandma seems more impressed with me than ever. She raved about my guest room, which was fake generous of her because, basically, it's a bed topped with a comforter set that I bought solely for her visit. The walls are bare outside of one Ansel Adams photograph I hung opposite of the bed. I also did remember to buy fresh towels—the fluffiest one I could find at the department store, along with some hand soap. But I'll admit, it's the bare minimum. Without any personal staff, my home décor skills are nonexistent.

I'm not nervous because of Grandma's visit. It's because on her last evening here she asked if she could meet my girlfriend. There were a hundred different options besides inviting Lennox over, especially because she is not the girl I'm currently entangled with. But the truth is, I wanted Grandma to know Lennox. Subconsciously, it's important to me.

"So, Leah is a photographer?" Grandma asks as she fetches wine glasses from my cupboard. "I'd love to see her work."

I hold up two fingers. "Just two glasses, Grandma. *Lennox* doesn't like wine. She drinks beer or cocktails. And she's not a photographer; her cousin Finn is. When she's not waitressing, she pitches in at his studio next door."

"Lennox?" Grandma asks, raising her brows. "I thought you were dating a young woman named Leah?"

"Sort of. It's complicated," I lie. It's really not. Leah and I get along just fine. We've fooled around a few times now. We mostly talk about diving. Her ex-husband would never let her spend money on scuba diving, so now that they're divorced, she's fully indulging. She likes my stories about deep-sea diving, and she thoroughly enjoys the employee discount on equipment. I care about her, but it's hard to tell if I have feelings for her.

It's been the same routine for the past three times we've hung out. We talk, she sucks me off, I return the favor, and then she leaves. I always invite her to stay, even though I'm not much of a cuddler. But, like me, I think Leah prefers to sleep alone.

"Leah's a nice girl," I add, feeling guilty.

"Why am I not meeting *her* this evening?"

"We're not officially dating. We're...taking it slow." I really don't want to say the words *fucking around* to my grandmother, so I omit a further explanation. "Lennox is my closest friend here. You said you wanted to know what kind of company I'm keeping... She's my favorite person in Vegas, so I wanted you to meet her. That's all."

"Dex, honey, would you like to know how juggling two women typically ends up?" Grandma runs her finger across her throat, flashing me a mocking smile.

"I'm not juggling two women, Grandma. Lennox is seeing someone." At least, I think.

Lennox has been rather secretive about Alan. Which makes me even more uncomfortable. She's keeping their private life *very* private. All I know is that Alan is looking for something serious. They are taking their time to get to know each other before making any real commitments. *Prick.* That's the perfect way to get a girl all weak-kneed for you.

I know he's taking her out weekly. She's slower to respond to text messages lately. A few Fridays ago, after Leah had left me for the evening, I asked if Lennox wanted to grab a decent meal. I was sick of quick takeout and was craving her company. She turned me down, saying she already ate with Alan, but she highly recommended the new sushi place that just opened right outside the Strip.

It's driving me crazy. I want to know if she's sleeping with him. Does she have real feelings for him? But she's been nothing but tight-lipped, treating her budding romance like it's sacred. I'll admit, paying this guy to disappear and forget her name has crossed my mind several times. It's good I don't know his full name, where he works, or what he looks like.

"Do you remember the last time you had a girl who was your best friend?"

"I don't," I reply. I can't even remember the last time I had a best friend, period. People walk in and out of my life like I'm a revolving door.

The large paper bag crinkles loudly as I pull out several round aluminum containers of plain pasta. I ordered sauce on the side, unsure what Lennox preferred. Grandma's order is usually the same. Eggplant Parmesan with a side of vodka sauce paired with a cabernet or pinot noir. I am a fan of simple—spaghetti with meatballs. When I asked Lennox what she wanted, her reply was, "Whatever is great," which was zero percent helpful. So, I ordered everything off the menu.

"Her name was Maddie. Sweet girl. You met her in a children's music class. You were four. She was almost six."

"Older woman," I murmur. "Nice."

"You two were inseparable for about six weeks. Your mother and I were positive you'd met your soulmate."

I laugh. "What happened?" I have no recollection of this, so no chance Maddie stuck around. "Did she move or something?"

Grandma yanks the stopper out of the bottle of Pinot Noir she started yesterday. "She asked to be your girlfriend and hold your hand. You said no and she never forgave you. She mooned you and then refused to speak to you ever again."

"She mooned me?" I ask.

"I'm assuming it was six-year-old speak for 'fuck you.'"

"Lovely." I find the baguette of crusty bread in the second oversized bag of takeout. Grandma raises her brow at me as I tear a piece off with the gusto of a caveman. "Why are you telling me this?" I ask Grandma before tearing off a piece of bread and popping it into my mouth.

"I thought I'd warn Ms. Lennox that if she wants to stay in your life, not to reveal her feelings for you, keep her hands to herself, and her ass fully covered." Grandma smirks as she fills two wine glasses halfway.

"What makes you think Lennox has feelings for me? You've never even met her."

"Oh, Dex. So smart, yet still such a man. She's spending her Saturday evening having dinner at home with you and your old grandma. What does that tell you?" Cradling the bulb of the glass in her palm, Grandma takes a long sip of wine.

In any other circumstance, I'd make an excuse. But I can't lie to Grandma. I've tried. She sees right through me.

"Have you ever met someone who tethers you to the earth? All those times before when I wanted a different life... I don't know. She helps me see the world differently. I like her reality better than my own."

I can't read Grandma's expression. Her face tenses as she studies my eyes. Her bright red lips are pressed together but not pursed.

She's silent, so I continue, "That's why you wanted me to come out here, isn't it? Perspective?"

Grandma sets her wine glass down. "You love her." It's a statement, not a question.

"No, Grandma. Nothing like that, I just..." Well, I don't know. *What the fuck else is this, then?* A lonely, rich boy's puppy love? Wanting what I can't have? "I think I could one day," I admit. "But I also don't think I'm destined for love. I know how Grandpa treated you. I don't want that for Lennox or any woman I love."

"Don't want what for her, Dex?"

"A lonely life. It's not fair. I know what my duties are. What you and Grandpa left me to take care of. My life here in Vegas is a break, not an escape."

Grandma steps towards me and places her palms on either side of my cheeks. Her cool hands are trembling. "Choose love over *fair*. Over duties. *Escape*, Dex. Do you understand me? Love, love, *love*. Fight for it. Obsess over it. It's the only thing that makes sense at the end of your life. How do I get you to understand that? You should have loyalty to absolutely nothing else except love."

I place my hands over hers. They feel smaller than usual, and the tips feel icy as she rubs them under my eyes. "Grandma, are you okay?" This is not the Dottie Hessler I'm familiar with. She's strong, determined, and takes no shit. I don't recognize her pleading tone, and I can't help but wonder if I've left when she needs me most. "Do you need me to come back home?"

She shakes her head, her eyes nearly watering. "No, Dex. Stay. Just please don't make the same mistakes as me. It doesn't have to make sense for it to be exactly right. Tell me more about her."

"She's a ferocious little thing. She's so honest and earnest. Heart wide open all the time. She's a philosophical genius and doesn't even know it. Unlike the rest of us, it doesn't seem like she's alive to accomplish or acquire anything. She just exists to get to know the best version of herself. She's brave because she's completely unashamed to admit when she's scared. Her honesty is addicting. I don't know how to explain it...she's changing my mind about everything. Maybe changing my heart."

Grandma returns to her wine glass and smiles. "I like her already."

Lennox

They didn't hear me come in. Dex told me the front door was unlocked, so I slipped in without knocking, but I halted in the hallway when I heard his grandma telling him to choose love. It didn't seem like a conversation I should interrupt. Instead, I shut my mouth and listened.

Love, love, love. Fight for it. Obsess over it. I think I'll hear her words on repeat in my head forever. Such persuasive conviction in her plea.

The moment would've stayed sweet and endearing had I not heard Dex gushing over Leah right afterward. *She's changing my mind... Maybe changing my heart.* Those words are engrained in my brain, too.

It's odd, though. I talked to Leah a couple weeks ago when she and Dex started hanging out. She likes him. Of course, she does. Who wouldn't? But she seemed so nonchalant. She even told me she had no intention of becoming exclusive. I guess I didn't realize how quickly and deeply they'd connected in the seemingly five seconds since Leah and I had that conversation. I think I've been on more dates with Alan than Leah's been on with Dex. Admittedly, I've been moving so slowly with Alan we're practically moving backward. There was a little part of me still holding onto the idea of me and Dex. But apparently, I'm pining over a man who's falling in love...with another woman.

And his grandma is just as smitten. So, what the hell am I doing here?

I grip the shoebox in my hands a little tighter. This is why. *Stop it, Lennox.* Dex said he wanted to just be friends. Accept that. Get this stupid fantasy under control and actually be his friend. The kind of friend who digs up an old shoebox of memories for his grandmother's long, lost friend.

This is why Dex asked me to meet Mrs. Dottie Hessler. She's actually the one who bought Jacob's dive shop as a present for Dex. *Weird present.* If my grandparents bought me a labor-intensive small business for my birthday, we'd have some words. But I have a feeling for Dottie, it's nostalgia.

Sucking in a deep breath, I announce myself before I have to endure the painful stab of Dex proclaiming his love for Leah out loud.

"*Knock, knock,*" I chirp as I enter the kitchen, holding my fist in the air, doing knocking charades. "Sorry to keep you guys waiting."

Grandma Dottie takes my breath away. I don't think I've ever seen anyone so elegant. She's wearing a cream-colored flowy jumpsuit. While she looks comfortable, all she'd need is a stiletto to wear that outfit right to the Met Gala. Her jet-black hair, which matches Dex's, looks fluffy and soft, but it doesn't move an inch as she makes a beeline to me, arms outstretched.

"I'm not usually a big hugger, but you are just..." Grandma Dottie wraps her arms around me and squeezes tightly. I didn't have time to put my shoebox down, so I'm unable to hug her back. Instead, I rest my chin on her shoulder, trying to return her enthusiastic affection. She pulls away to get a good look at me. "So beautiful," she finishes.

"Thank you. You smell incredible, Mrs. Hessler."

She doesn't say anything. She just continues to beam at me,

holding the outer sides of my arms. Naturally, I feel the need to fill the awkward lull.

"I didn't mean for that to come off weird. Is that, um...well, your perfume is very nice. It smells rich." *Shit. Did that sound accusing?* "Not overly fancy. I just mean very warm and full. Like amber or cashmere...or, now come to think of it, maybe it's laundry detergent? Or, I don't know if you can put that outfit in a regular wash." *Dear Lord. What the hell am I rambling about?*

I look over Grandma Dottie's shoulder to see Dex silently laughing. He clutches his chest. "What?" I snap at him.

"Oh, I've just never seen you this uncomfortable before. It's pretty adorable."

"Ass," I say, then immediately cover my mouth, clutching tightly to my box with the other hand. "I'm sorry, Mrs. Hessler. Forgot my manners. But I'm not uncomfortable, I promise." *Just fucking nervous.* I really want her to like me for some reason.

She smirks at me. "He is being an ass, isn't he?"

"Two against one. Wonderful," Dex murmurs.

Grandma Dottie ignores him and drops her arms. "First of all, none of this 'Mrs. Hessler' business. Please call me Dottie. And thank you for noticing. It's my favorite perfume. It's called *Pardonné,* or *Forgiven* in English. It's from a little boutique in France. I stock up every time I visit. You can't get it anywhere else. My attempt at staying a touch unique in a world where every woman seems to smell like Chanel No. 5."

I chuckle. "Right on the nose. My mom wears that," I say. "So you spend a lot of time in France?"

"Not anymore. Infrequent visits. Dex and I lived there for about six months in his adolescence, though."

"I think closer to four," Dex says from behind us. "Just enough time for Olivier to completely give up on me learning to cook French cuisine."

Dottie drops her arms and laughs heartily. "Oh, goodness, he nearly burned down the kitchen."

"Well, flambé is not a skillset for a preteen. We learned that the hard way."

A loud chime comes from Dottie's smartwatch. She briefly glances at the notification, and the tiniest flicker of irritation crosses her face. She recomposes herself quickly and says, "Pardon me for a moment. Emergency on the East Coast. I'll be right back." She doesn't walk, she glides with elegance right out of the kitchen, through the open-concept living room, and up the stairs.

As soon as Dottie disappears from view, I set my shoebox down on the counter and make my way to Dex. I wrap one arm around his thick frame, giving him a friendly hug. "Thanks for inviting me. You smell nice, too. Like food."

He chuckles. "Are you hungry?"

"Famished."

He looks me up and down and grimaces. "Is this a new dress? Did I mention we're eating in?"

"It's not a new dress." Lie. No...half-truth. I borrowed it from a friend and paid zero dollars for it. I needed a "meet the grandparents" dress. "Why would you think that?"

"It's not your usual colorful flair. You look very nice. I'm just used to your outfits being an adventure."

I shrug. "I have layers. Sometimes I like simple."

We actually match tonight. My black dress is sleek and form-fitting, but the length touches my knees so it's a combination of allure and elegance, or so my bartender friend Cass, whom I borrowed this dress from, told me. Dex's dress shirt is also black, sleeves rolled up just below his elbows, showing off his thick, masculine forearms.

"Well, now I feel bad for not taking you guys out somewhere nice."

"Out?" I scoff like the notion is ridiculous. "Then I would've had to put on underwear. Staying in is perfect."

Dex levels a stare at me, his expression flattening, and I feel the heat in my cheeks. "You're not wearing—"

"Just a bad joke, Dex. Sorry." The guilt floods through me for hoping that sparked his interest. For constantly wanting what's not mine. "Is Leah joining us tonight?"

Dex barely jostles his head. "No."

"Is something wrong?"

"I mentioned my grandma was in town, and she said she'd give me some space. Haven't heard from her all week. I figured that was pretty clear."

I lift one eyebrow. *Yet, you say she's changing your heart and mind?* Men. Literally walking contradictions. "Oh, okay. Do you think she'll be bothered I'm here?"

He shrugs simply. "I'd hope not. We're not an item."

"But all that stuff you just said? I'm confused."

He squints at me as he crosses his arms, leaning back against the kitchen island. "What stuff?"

I palm my forehead and let out a low grumble. "I wasn't eavesdropping. I was trying to wait for the right moment to cut in. I heard what you told your grandma about Leah. That was all so sweet. If you're that into her, I don't want to jeopardize your relationship. You should tell her I'm here just to clear the air. I asked Alan before I agreed to come."

Dex opens his mouth, stalls, then clamps his lips shut. Whatever he was about to say, he changes his mind. "Why did you need Alan's permission?"

I scowl, my hand finding my hip. "I didn't ask for his *permission.* I asked if he'd be uncomfortable. I keep saying how sick I am of men who play mind games. Why would I behave exactly in the way I'm asking him not to?"

"Okay, then what'd he say about you coming over tonight?"

"He said that he likes how important my friendships are to me and he'd never try to come between that. I think mostly he appreciated that I was honest with him. I tell him about every time you and I hang out."

Dex swallows hard, anguish strewn across his face as his Adam's apple rises then falls. "Yet you never mention a thing about Alan to me."

I bite the inside of my cheek, debating my response. I know

that look. There's absolutely no mistaking it. He's jealous. "I don't kiss and tell, Dex. When you and I hang out, I tell Alan how much I'm learning about scuba diving and craft beer. Do you really want to hear about me and Alan sucking face?"

"Fair point. I don't," he answers flatly. "Speaking of which. Want a beer?" He tries to step by me to get to the fridge, but I catch his forearm. His eyes narrow in on the spot I'm touching him, so I immediately let him go.

"But...we're okay, right? I mean, I don't ask about when you and Leah hang out, purely out of respect. But if Alan bothers you, then maybe that means..."

I mentally beg him to fill in the blank. Here's his chance. One little declaration. A small moment of honesty and if Dex is feeling remotely close to the way I do, we could—

"It doesn't," he says. "I'm happy for you."

"Good. And I'm happy for you and Leah, too."

I hope I'm hiding my disappointment. I keep my eyes big but there are pins and needles dotting my face. What the hell? He's acting jealous... Why won't he admit it? Then again...why don't I? Probably because every single time I have hope with this man, it's theatrically squashed.

"Can I tell you something?" He locks eyes with me. "Sometimes with Leah...it's really hard to read her because she so easily misses all the signs. I don't want to come on too strong. But I'm into her...*really fucking into her.* So much so, it's driving me insane." It feels like salt in the wound but I smile and nod like it's good news. I step out of his way, and he squeezes my shoulder as he passes.

"Why not tell her how you feel?"

He spins around and sucks in his lips as he looks at me. Once again, he's taking his time to calculate his response. I hate how he does that. It makes me feel like our conversation is a game of chess I'm about to lose. He finally answers, a faraway look in his eyes, "It's simple. She's a flight risk. And I can't afford to lose her."

CHAPTER 17

Lennox

Dex ordered enough food to feed the whole block. I sampled everything and it has me reconsidering the dress I wore. Pretty, but not remotely forgiving.

With my hands strewn across my full belly, I sink back into Dex's couch. He's busy in the kitchen, repacking leftovers and putting dishes in the sink, refusing to let me or Dottie help. I'm so stuffed I can barely move. I'm in a trance, watching the little fish in his giant aquarium under the low lights. It's past eight o'clock, so the tank lights automatically switched to dim. The fish look so still, it's like they are sleeping.

"He's become quite domestic since he's moved out here," Dottie says, taking a small sip of her red wine.

"Dex doesn't do dishes at home?"

Dottie points to Dex's giant aquarium in front of us. "This kind of thing usually ate up most of his chore time."

The first time I saw this tank was the night I met Dex. I didn't even realize it was supposed to be a giant aquarium. I thought it was art—some sort of glass wall. But after a few weeks, Dex's tank pieces came in. He had the filters, pumps, and lights meticulously installed. Once his masterpiece was set up, he never threw a rowdy party like that again.

"There's another one in the bedroom," I say. "He let me feed the Damselfish up there once. They are prissy little things. They eat live mealworms for clean protein and get daily vitamins through an eyedropper. They are healthier than I am." I laugh thinking about the rundown Dex gave me with their feeding schedule and how to gauge their health by watching their swim patterns.

"Damselfish," Dottie muses.

"Is that the big, flat black one?"

"Oh, no, no. That's his Black Tang, Zeus. He's very fond of that one. The way he sweettalks Zeus is going to cause that poor fish lots of problems. Everyone is going to gang up on Zeus out of jealousy. The tank upstairs is a little angsty. I keep telling him he should move Zeus down here, but for some reason, he keeps all the smaller fish down here. To be honest, they are less impressive."

"See that little red one?" Dottie says, pointing to the bright red fish that seems to be staring right back at us.

"The Cherry Barb?"

Dottie smiles. "Yes. It's his favorite. He puts one in every single tank."

"Really?" I ask, squinting at the fish. It's not that they aren't cute. But they aren't that impressive in comparison to their tankmates or the exotic beauties upstairs.

"It was the first fish his mother bought him. They are small and easy-going enough for a five-year-old to care for."

"And yet I've still managed to lose so many," Dex says, startling me. I didn't notice him approach. He sets a tray of drinks down. Coffee for me and Dottie, and a glass full of amber liquid for him. He settles on the couch next to me and hands me a cup of coffee. "Lots of cream and sugar for you." After grabbing his glass, he slides the tray closer to Dottie. "Black for you, Grandma. Careful, the mug is hot."

"Thank you, honey," she says, sitting back and letting the burning cup cool.

I take a small sip and give Dex an appreciative smile. "It's perfect." He gives me a quick flash of a smile, but it's gone so fast, it seems something's bothering him. "I take it your mom likes aquariums, too?"

"She did." His response is flat and he doesn't elaborate. It's apparent from the anguish on his face that this is a tough topic for Dex.

"Dex's mom, my daughter Melody, passed away when she was twenty-nine," Dottie clarifies.

"I'm so sorry," I say, unable to find bigger, better words to convey my feelings.

"Thank you. It happened a long time ago," Dottie assures me. She points to the tank at the little red fish. "But we try to keep parts of her close."

"Len, I've been wondering all night...what's in that old shoebox?" Dex looks over his shoulder to the kitchen island, unsubtly changing the conversation. "Because I'm half worried you bought me a hamster or something."

"Oh! Geez, I almost forgot." He's blocking me into the sectional, so I pat his knee. "Would you grab it for me?"

He's on his feet immediately, crossing the living room to fetch the box. He shakes it aggressively, then holds it up to his ear.

"Dude! Careful," I squall. "What if it was a hamster?"

He laughs. "Sounds like paper," Dex says as he hands the box over.

Setting it on the table, I open the lid so it's facing Dottie. "Dex told me you and Jacob were friends a long time ago. After he passed, I saved some of this stuff from the dive shop. Mostly just pictures and notes he'd jot down. I thought maybe you'd like a little insight into his later life. Seemed like you two were close once if you felt compelled to buy his dive shop?"

"Thank you, Lennox. This is..." Dottie trails off as she slides the box into her lap. She handles it so delicately, you'd think it was a baby. Holding up the folded stack of papers on top, she murmurs, "This says Business Plan. Was this an idea of Jacob's?"

"Oh, that's my college admissions essay. Jacob helped me." I slide my coffee cup aside and scoot closer to Dottie. "For my college application to UNLV, Jacob had this idea to write out a legitimate business plan instead of a typical admission essay. Just to stand out. So, I made all these big pretend plans for the dive shop like I was actually planning a future for Discover Dives. He wrote a statement as the owner claiming he was going to implement my plan and had intended to give me a percentage of the profits. That little stunt got me into business school and a partial academic scholarship. Jacob was so proud of me that he kept a copy of the plan."

Dottie flips through the pages, reading line by line. "You and Jacob did all this together?"

"It was just a cute bonding thing." *Cute?* Why did I say that? I hate that term so much. Cute is for puppies and babies, and it always feels aggressively condescending when people use it against me. Although, from what I understand Dottie runs a pretty big company. This might indeed seem *cute* to her.

"Did Jacob implement any of this?"

"No, he never got the chance. And anyway, it wasn't a real plan, just a way to get me into a good college."

Dottie's eyes snap to mine, and she surveys my face. "But this business plan is very good. You wrote this when you were eighteen?"

I nod. "Just about."

"Do you know how many pitches and business plans come across my desk? All from professionals who never once think to include ethical business practices, checks and balance systems, and giving back to the community in their five-year plans. You wrote this based on how the business could better society instead of simply how the business could drive revenue. That takes maturity far beyond your years, Lennox. Very impressive. I have a feeling you were a natural in your business ethics classes?"

I feel the flicker of shame I always do when this topic comes up. "I never ended up going to school. My scholarship wasn't enough, and my student loans got messed up. I... I couldn't afford it."

"Oh, that's such a shame," Dottie says. "It's impossible to afford school for many students these days. It wasn't like that in my generation."

I shrug like it doesn't bother me. "All for the best. I probably would've failed out. Numbers and statistics aren't my strength. I've heard those pesky things are necessary in business school." I shoot her a playful wink.

"Sweetheart, I've been in business for a very long time. Numbers aren't what you need to be a successful leader," Dottie says, setting the box down.

"What is it, then?"

"Heart and resilience," Dottie answers. "And you, Lennox, seem to have both."

I turn to Dex and lift my brows. "Hear that? I think your grandma likes me."

Dottie chuckles as she continues to sift through the box. Dex reaches over and pats my knee. "I think you won her over. Clever."

It wasn't strategic. I was just interested to learn Jacob had friends. He was such a warm spirit, yet a lone wolf. It didn't make sense to me. I was relieved there were people who cared enough to seek him out eventually. Even if it was long overdue.

"These are incredible," Dottie says, holding up each picture and article. Some of the images are crystal clear. Underwater photos of giant sea turtles and manta rays. There are a few news articles about ocean anomalies that Jacob witnessed. Rare marine life sightings, environmental movements to protect the ocean, and mass community cleanups of oil spills and garbage dumping. Jacob always volunteered when he could.

As she nears the bottom half of the box, the pictures become poorer quality, faded, and in desperate need of restoration. Evidence of the antiquated photography equipment used at the time.

"He lived a really full life," Dottie murmurs. "What was he like? Happy? Was he in love?"

"I only knew him for about three years before he passed away. From what I know, he was never married. No children," I answer.

Dottie's eyes are down, scanning images slowly, like she's savoring them. "Marriage doesn't always mean happy...or in love."

I hold out my hands. "Actually, may I see the box? I might

know..."

Setting the box on the table, I remove the photos and clippings in small chunks, laying them out on the coffee table. *I think it's at the bottom.* "Ah, here," I say, finding the image that's paperclipped to a folded-up piece of paper. I carefully detach the flimsy half-picture of a woman sitting on a dock. Her back is turned, so all you can see is her feminine silhouette and long, dark hair hanging in a thick braid down her back. "Be careful, it's delicate," I say, handing the photo to Dottie. "My cousin Finn has access to the photo lab at UNLV, and he said he could restore it. But it'd be so much better if we had the other half."

"Maybe it's in there," Dex says, leaning forward, starting to gently lay out the images one by one.

"No, I've looked. I think it's with *her.* Daisy."

"What did you say?" Dottie asks in an urgent whisper. "Who?"

"Daisy." I hold up the square, folded note in my hand. "That's what I nicknamed her. I don't know her real name. He wrote this letter for her. Or maybe it's a poem. I'm not sure. But I always imagined this was his long-lost sweetheart. I asked him about it once, but he told me Daisy died. You should've seen the look on his face. I couldn't pull at that thread. Seems like it would've broken him."

Tears fill her eyes as she scours the photo. "Will you read it? My eyes are not so good without my reading glasses." I hardly believe that. She read the tiny print of the business plan just fine. It seems like Dottie needs my help, though. So, I unfold the note and read her the short poem:

Daisies, daisies, daisies,

They follow me into the ocean. They haunt my sweetest dreams.

My heart is detached from my body, lying in a field of white flowers.

A long, full life is a curse.

Every single breath that staves off death keeps me away from you.

Pink lips. Rosy cheeks.

I let you go in this life.

But you're mine in the next.

I promise.

"Len," Dex says softly. "Maybe we should stop."

I look at him. "I'm done. That's the whole poem."

"Look," he says, gesturing to Dottie.

I turn to see her face tear-streaked, the picture pressed tightly against her heart, ignoring my warning to be careful. Her head is hung, and she's silently sobbing.

"Grandma? Are you okay?"

She inhales and exhales deeply a few times as she nods. Surprisingly, her makeup didn't even move. She gently dabs her cheeks with the back of her hand. After a deep sniffle, she's completely recomposed. Dottie Hessler is elegant even in the throes of a meltdown.

"I'm sorry. Just years of emotions bubbling to the surface. That's what happens when you go gray. Too much bottled up." She traces her hand over her perfectly curled hair, but there's not one gray hair on her head. Her hair is dyed a rich black. "I'm okay. I'm just sad I never got to say goodbye to my friend."

"Grandma, can I get you some water?"

"I'm fine, Dex. Thank you. I think it's well past my bedtime, though. I'm still on East Coast hours. I think I'll excuse myself for the evening, but Lennox?"

"Yes?"

"I know it's a tremendous thing to ask but may I keep this

185

picture?"

I nod eagerly. "Dottie, you can keep whatever you like. I brought it all for you. Do you want me to sort out the pictures? Or do you want—"

"Then I want it all," she says with firm resolve. "If I may... I want every single piece, if you're offering."

I nod again. "Of course."

"Grandma, I'll clean all this up, and we'll leave it for you. You just get some rest," Dex instructs.

"Okay, yes," she breathes out. But she doesn't replace the cut polaroid. She holds it in her palm as she shuffles around the coffee table to stand in front of me. "I can't tell you how glad I am to meet you, Lennox. Thank you for these memories, and thank you for being such a good friend to my precious grandson." Stunning me, she kisses me on the cheek. The smell of her fancy French perfume envelops us both as I hold my cheek, fighting the urge to cry. I'm not even sure why. I think she transferred everything she was feeling when we touched, and now my heart aches miserably.

We sit in silence until Dottie is up the stairs, and I hear a bedroom door gently shut.

"She liked you, I promise. I have no idea what that was. She's been having breakdowns left and right lately. I think she might be sick. I'm starting to really worry about her," Dex says.

I turn to face him. "She's not sick, Dex. Don't you see it? Your grandmother and Jacob were obviously lovers."

"What?" He looks torn between disgusted and offended. "She married my grandpa at twenty. Are you suggesting she had an affair?"

"No. I'm saying you don't have to *be* with someone to love them."

"Len, I'm not saying my grandma had the perfect marriage, but she loved my grandpa a lot. She loved my mother and her family. She was a faithful woman."

I pat his knee and apologize. "I never meant to question your grandma's integrity. Forget what I said."

But I got a glimpse of the truth based on the look in Dottie's eyes.

There's love. And then there's *love*.

That kind that gives you no choice in the matter. Jacob once told me that love is an innate force beyond our will and comprehension. It's how the universe humbles the stubborn human race, hellbent on forging destructive new paths. Love is how the universe stays in control of our fates. Some people can see that and accept it. Others ignore it and let it slip right by, living half-lives.

Dottie's tears tell me there's more to the story than just a long-lost friend. Did she and Jacob live their lives full of regret?

"Do you want some dessert?" Dex asks, pulling me from my thoughts. "I have a whole sheet of tiramisu in the fridge. You don't have to rush out, do you?"

I hold onto Dex's soft eyes and feel the ache of sadness. Are we headed down a path of regret? Maybe in sixty years, we'll be kicking ourselves for what could've been.

"I should actually head out. I told Alan I'd swing by his place if dinner didn't run too late."

Dex's eyes shift down, and he subtly nods. "Probably for the best." Then, he rises. "I'll pack two slices up for you guys."

CHAPTER 18

Lennox

Present Day

Las Vegas

These aren't my taupe-colored walls. This isn't my bed. Not my sheets or pillows. But they smell like Dex, so now they feel like home. Right now, my new home is empty.

I sit up and run my hand over the empty space next to me in the California King. I don't hear the shower running. I don't see his clothes in the pile we left on the floor.

Was last night a dream? I could've sworn I married my friend and we finally confessed that we're both equally obsessed with the notion of us. I think we made love in a car, came home, and then proceeded to fuck all night. I'm almost positive Dex fell asleep in me. Not just next to me, but in me. Once the dam was broken, we couldn't get enough. It feels like close will never ever be close enough.

But here I am, alone this morning, staring at Zeus moping around his tank, wondering if I got too drunk at the bar and made the whole thing up in my mind. I climb out from under the covers, shivering as the cool air conditioning shocks my naked body. As I stretch my arms overhead, I say, "I'll find your daddy and get you fed, Zeus," to the big, black fish slowly gliding around.

"No need," Dex says from the doorway. "Fed him this morning right after I took a shower. You sleep like the dead, do you know that? You didn't even flinch."

I cross my arms over my chest and nod toward the tray in his hand. "Did you cook me breakfast?"

"Uncross your arms," he scolds with a smirk. "Don't hide from me. I like the view."

"I'm not hiding. I'm chilly."

"Then get back under the covers, Mrs. Hessler. I'm here to feed you."

I gleefully oblige. Once I'm settled, Dex joins me on the bed, showing off his tray of goodies. This is not takeout. Everything is homemade. Fluffy scrambled eggs lie next to bacon that looks like it's been grilled. Thick slices of French toast are topped with berries, powdered sugar, and whipped cream. My empty stomach grumbles, making all sorts of embarrassing noises, ratting me out. I'm starving.

"Since when do you cook?" I rub my hands together in excitement and scan the tray for a fork but don't see one. My only option is the finger food on the plate. "Oh my God, what fresh hell is this? This bacon is impossibly good." A rich sensation of sweet and salty coats my mouth, making it water.

Dex laughs. "You're just hungry. It's center-cut bacon slathered in honey, then grilled on a pellet smoker."

"You made all of this yourself?"

"Yes."

"You *cook*?"

"Yeah, I like to cook and eat. You can't tell?" He pats his stomach as if he has a round gut, but his hand simply bounces off his tight abs, visible through his thin gray T-shirt.

"You're kidding, right?" I roll my eyes.

"You seem surprised. You've been to many of my barbeques. You know I grill out."

"Anyone with a Y chromosome knows how to grill out. It's in your DNA. I'm talking about actual *cooking*." I point to the French toast. "Did you make that batter yourself?"

"I did."

"Can I try it?" I ask.

"Go ahead, what's stopping you?"

"Silverware."

"Right." He kisses my temple and crawls off the bed. "Hang tight. I'll be right back. I have another tray."

"Dex, wait!" I call after him. But he must already be down the stairs. We're two people. How much food could we possibly need?

In the meantime, I help myself to another slice of the candied bacon. *Fucking lottery, Lennox. Good girl. You fell for a guy with eyes like a mermaid's tail, a rock-hard body you can climb like a tree,* and *he knows his way around the kitchen? That does it. I'm convinced. There's a God after all.*

After I run out of bacon and drain half a glass of orange juice, I set the tray aside on the nightstand. I'm saving the rest of my appetite for that mouth-watering French toast and whatever else Dex has whipped up. But when he returns, he's holding another tray that doesn't contain food. It's displaying what I refer to as my naughty box of secrets. I gawk for an uncomfortably long time, then finally manage to croak out, "That's not more food or a fork."

"*Au contraire.*" Dex is smiling at my horrified expression. He lifts up a small silver fork from the tray, proving me wrong. I didn't see it. I was too distracted by both of my vibrators lined up, my anal beads, a slim jar of honey, and a small glass canister of cinnamon.

"You went through my car?" I ask incredulously. "Talk about invasion of privacy."

"I'm sorry, but I had the best intentions. Being the incredibly thoughtful husband I am, the first order of business was to get rid of the clunky, rusted death trap you call transportation. I emptied it out so a tow truck could take it to the dump. As I was moving your boxes in, naturally, some of your belongings caught my eye. But of course, I'd never get rid of your possessions without talking to you first." He narrows his eyes. "But I want to warn you if any of this touched Alan's genitalia, it's going in my furnace."

Stunned at his audacity, I sidestep around the topic. "You

don't have a furnace."

"Fine, my grill then. As long as I can burn it to a crisp. I have to say, I'm shocked you two were this..." He teeters his head back and forth like he's trying to find the right word. "Let's say *adventurous*. Alan strikes me as the kind of guy who keeps his socks on in bed."

I thought this was our happily ever after. The guilty shame cloud of Alan has no business here, but Dex brought him up and now I feel terrible. I cower, pulling the covers up to my chin. "Those are mine. Alan never touched those. He doesn't know they exist. And please stop bringing him up. You're making me feel awful."

I feel the soft thud at the foot of the bed as Dex places the tray down. He makes his way over to sit beside me. Breathing me in, he plants a soft kiss on my temple. "I'm still navigating this. I have to joke so it doesn't bother me as much. I've been jealous for so long. You don't understand."

"Yes, I do. You dated Leah. I hated that."

He shakes his head. "Not the same thing. You knew as well as I did that Leah and I weren't ever going further. But you and Alan..." He sighs heavily. "When you showed up at my door yesterday, I checked your left hand. I knew how good Alan was to you. I also knew that if you got engaged, you'd be so excited you'd run right over to tell me. I know it's what I said I wanted, but to be your friend like that was excruciating."

I place my hand on his smooth cheek. Not only did he shower this morning, he also shaved. I didn't hear any of it. I slept so long and hard because I was finally at peace. The gnawing ache of longing soothed. "Dex Hessler, we were never friends. We were just waiting."

"Waiting for what?" he asks.

"I have no idea. Something big." Something kept me and Dex apart. A something I'm not sure we've fully addressed and to be quite frank, I'm terrified to face it. He keeps warning me about Miami and what lies ahead, but I don't want real-life problems right now. I deserve a few more days of the fantasy, so I push the blanket down, exposing my chest. As if by a magnet's pull, his eyes lower.

I rake my fingernails against his scalp before cradling his cheek in my hand. *Alan, please forgive me for saying this...* "No one's ever touched me like you do. I come at the mere thought of you. Stop being jealous, Dex. I've been yours since the very moment we met. And now that we've established that, you can have what's yours, however you want." Holding the back of his neck, I guide his mouth to my nipple and throw my head back.

Dex sucks and nips while yanking the covers from my hips. He cups my eager sex but is careful not to touch my most sensitive spot. I try to grind into his hand, but he keeps his fingers tented around my outer lips, protecting my clit from any attention. "How do you want me?" he murmurs as he switches to my other breast.

"Greedy, Mr. Hessler. Angry. Hard. I want to meet your dark side this morning."

His sexy smile disappears instantly. Lustful need filling every inch of his expression. "I'm done with the jealousy, Lennox. If I ever find out you're thinking about another man, I won't end us. I'll end him. Don't ever make me miss you again. Do you understand?"

I nod.

"Use your words if you want to come this morning," he growls.

"Yes."

"*Sir.*"

With obnoxious exaggeration, I look around the room. "Is someone joining us? Who the hell are you calling, 'Sir?'" I cackle at my own sass, expecting Dex to laugh along. Instead, he thrusts two fingers inside of me with no warning. I yelp and clamp my legs shut, but that just ignites something even more grisly in him. He rips his hand away and stares at me like I just slapped him.

"Did you close your legs on me?"

I shake my head, spreading my knees, putting myself right back on display.

He clicks his tongue. "And now you're lying. What am I going to do with you?"

Outside of my tongue wetting my lips, I'm frozen in anticipation. The nerves dancing up and down my spine seem enough to send me straight to an orgasm. This is what I wanted. I know my sweet husband cares for me. Now, I need him to own me. I want proof that we can be everything. The passion, the pleasure, the pain. It's all part of the package of a full life.

"Flip over. Don't make me ask you twice." He unbuttons his shirt while his eyes stay locked on mine.

I debate fighting him on it. I want to see what comes out if I push him even further. But I'm too excited to hold my cards close to my chest. I turn onto my stomach, elbows buried into the mattress under the thick, fluffy pillow that smells like Dex. I poke my ass up in the air expecting him to slip his fingers in again, but instead—

Whack! There's a sharp sting where Dex's palm collided with my right ass cheek. The dull burn radiates across my entire ass. "That's for closing your legs on me."

Smack! He addresses my left cheek the same way he did the right. "And that's for lying to me about it. Two things I won't tolerate, wife. Denying me and lies."

"Understood," I murmur.

It doesn't really hurt, it's just deliciously igniting. I wiggle my hips, craving the sensation again, except now he's rubbing where he swatted. His lips follow quickly, planting sweet kisses against my warm flesh. "Oh shit, baby. Your ass is already bright pink. I took that too far." He hunches over me, his stomach pressed against my back. "I'll stop."

I turn my head, looking over my shoulder. When I find his cheek, I plant a firm kiss. "Don't you dare. Just a little harder. And don't let me come until the end. We'll both come once."

His cheek twitches against my lips. I can't see his expression in this position, but I can feel his smile. "Why? If I could come multiple times in a row, I would. If you've got the superpower, use it."

I chuckle. "The teasing makes me feverish, Dex. I'm telling you what I want. I like the anticipation as much as finishing. Maybe more."

"I want that in writing so I don't get in trouble for keeping you on the edge for hours."

"Fine. Fuck first, sign later. Now, back in character. Chop, chop." I peck his cheek again, then bury my head back in the pillow, hoisting my hips up as high as I can.

He jostles me as he straddles my calves. Even going as far as grinding his growing hard-on against my sex. I bet I could soak right through the fabric of his jeans just from him brushing against me. That's how crazy Dex makes me. The fact that I can't see what's going on is making me nervous, but my unspoken instructions are clear. *Head down, ass up. Take it like a champ. You asked for it.*

"So fucking sexy," he murmurs. "Are you getting wet for me, baby? Or are you *still* wet for me? Hm? I thought I wore you out last night, but you can't get enough, can you?" The clank of his belt unbuckling makes my stomach lurch. I freeze, now alert and tense. Oh no. How dark is his dark side? There's a *whoosh* as he yanks his belt free of the belt loops.

"Wait, wait. Dex, please wait. I've never been belted. Not too hard."

"Are you fucking crazy?" He sounds so aghast, I can't help but peer over my shoulder to check his reaction. Dex looks exactly like he sounds, as if I just admitted that murder turns me on. "Do you trust me?" he asks, and I nod in response. "Good. Lie on your back and hold your hands out in front of you."

Flipping and flopping, foreplay with Dex is starting to feel like exercising. I do as he says, folding my hands together. He wraps his belt around my wrists twice, then secures the hook so my arms are inseparable.

"I appreciate your kinky spirit, Trouble, but I'm here to pleasure and protect you. Not to traumatize you, sweet wife. I can make you feel so fucking alive without the welts and bruises. My belt is to keep you still. Now hold your arms over your head. You move them and there'll be no teasing. I'll make you come in a heartbeat, and then we're finished."

"Yes..." I narrow my eyes. *"Sir."*

"That's much better, sassy." The smile he wears is of pure satisfaction. "Such a quick learner. You're so much more obedient tied up like this. What's on your mind?"

"Honestly?" I ask. His response is a sultry nod. "I'm still kind of hungry."

He laughs. "You know what? Me too. I could go for something sweet." Stretching his long frame, he reaches for the tray at the foot of the bed. He rights himself then straddles my hips, honey in one hand, cinnamon in the other. "Remember this? You mentioned it the first night we met. I've been curious ever since. Stick your tongue out."

He uncaps the lid as I poke my tongue through my lips. The honey drips in a thick flood, drenching my tongue, then overflowing down my cheek and neck. Forgetting my arms are bound, I instinctually try and catch the thick liquid slow-dripping into my hair but my movements are strained.

Dex makes a warning sound. "Stop moving, baby. You want this to be over?"

I shake my head, rubbing my lips together, tasting the sweet glaze again. "No."

"Then be still." He pumps his brows as he shimmies down my legs. After squeezing a thick glob of honey on each of my nipples, he pours a line down my stomach, letting it pool in my belly button. "Spread your legs."

I do, but he's not satisfied. I pant as he spreads my pussy wide open with two fingers. He drips the warm honey down my center, ensuring it thoroughly coats my clit before releasing me. Oh, for fuck's sake. I'm so turned on. I want him to take good care of me, so I dare not move. Instead, I curl my toes, trying to control the urge to bridge my hips and beg him to put me in his mouth.

After replacing the cap and twisting the lid tightly shut, Dex tosses the plastic bottle over his shoulder. He grabs the cinnamon resting by my knee and sprinkles it over my chest and stomach. He seems thoroughly pleased with his sticky artwork. "Now, where should I start, wife?"

"You know where," I reply.

"Beg me."

"Please," I say half-heartedly.

Dropping to his stomach, he puts his head between my thighs. But he doesn't lick up the honey. He blows on me, causing me to buck and moan. The warm salve mixed with his cool breath nearly sends me. "Not good enough. Try again," he growls.

"Oh fuck, Dex. That feels amazing."

So naturally, he stops blowing. "Good to know."

"Do it again," I command.

"Try some manners," he quips back. Stroking against my inner thigh, he covers his thumb in the trails of dripping honey, then raises up to his knees. He pushes his thumb deep into my mouth. I clean his finger with my tongue before he traces my lips, a heady fog clouding his eyes. Then, he starts his assault on my breasts. It's unclear if he's trying to clean me up or suck my nipples right off. I close my eyes, focusing on how much I love the pressure that's sending me to the cusp of discomfort. It's such a drastic difference from the way I've been having sex for the past couple years.

With Dex, all I do is *feel*. Every touch lights me up.

My eyes pop open when I hear the soft buzz of my vibrator. Dex hovers over me with a menacing look on his face, holding my clit stimulator up warningly like it's a weapon. "Let's see if this makes you beg."

He touches my inner thighs, outer lips, then hovers over my clit, so close that I can't feel the pleasure but I'm dripping with need. It's not funny anymore. Now I want relief. I bridge my hips, but his reflexes are too quick. He pulls his hand back like we're sharing a puppet string. I push, he pulls. I relax, he advances.

"Okay, Dex. Enough. Make me come."

"Frustrated?"

"Yes. Please, please, *please*," I beg. Still as a statue, I add, "I'm cooperating."

"Can you cooperate a little more? Then, I'll take good care of you," Dex promises. He rolls me back over and lifts my hips before pushing my knees apart.

I can barely balance with my arms bound. When he turns the vibrator up to the highest speed, I nearly fall over. He presses it firmly against my little button, and I moan loudly, the way he likes.

"Good girl, keep going," he whispers as I mewl like a woman possessed with pleasure.

Then, his tongue is somewhere else.

I try to pull away, but he grips my hip with his free hand, keeping me in place as his tongue dances around my tighter hole. Never has a man done this to me before. There was no awkward, hesitant conversation of "should we" or "do you want to." Dex just takes what he wants. He laps around the tight muscle of my ass until there's no honey left, just his saliva. "How's this, baby? If I'm sweet to you, can I have this too?"

"Yes," I respond, like an instant reaction. *Yes, yes, yes to everything.*

He tenderly presses the tip of one finger against my ass, and I try not to tense. It'll hurt if I fight it. He's trying to ease me in, and it's going to take a lot of TLC. Dex's dick is monstrous. A delight for my pussy, but probably would be the end of me fully shoved into any other hole. I have no idea how this'll work.

But there's no time to debate because the moment his finger is knuckle deep in my ass, I come so hard I scream into the pillow. The surging ecstasy is too overwhelming; every nerve in my body is on fire, and I can't handle it. My hips collapse and I fall onto my side. I'm shaking so hard from my orgasm I have to grind my teeth together to keep them from chattering. I desperately want my hands so I can hold myself.

"Free me," I whimper.

Dex is quick to unbuckle his belt, unbinding my arms. As soon as I'm able, I wrap my arms around my waist. "Too much?" he coos in concern, tossing the vibrator aside.

"I'm just feeling everything," I tell him.

As soon as I catch my breath, my short break over, I lunge for his cock. Using it like a leash, I guide him until he's sitting on the edge of the bed. I sink down to the floor, ignoring how my knees bear uncomfortably into the hardwood floor. Toggling between sucking on his head and swirling my tongue around his tip, I coax out his salty precum. But it's not enough. He wants more.

"Give me your whole throat, baby," he rasps out. "Can you do that for me?"

I pull as much of him into my mouth as I can, but he's too big. I have to wrap my fist around the base of his cock to cover him completely. I try my best not to succumb to my gag reflex as he bumps the back of my throat. My eyes are watering and it's hard to breathe. But the way he's praising me encourages me along. I like the sound of his moaning so much, I seriously consider suffocating on this man's erection. "Such a good girl." He holds the back of my head and bucks his hips a few times. Now, I can't help coughing and sputtering. He must like the sensation against his cock because he's a little slow in releasing me. "You're so fucking good, Len. Do you think I'm as sweet as you? Can you swallow for me?"

"Yes." *For you, always yes.*

I stick out my tongue, and he places his tip into my mouth, stroking his whole shaft almost violently until he groans in relief. Every drop of his warm release fills my mouth. We lock eyes as I swallow his warm release. I lick my lips and he looks so pleased with me.

"You like that?" Dex asks.

"I love it." With Dex, this isn't a chore. Just my pleasure to do.

He wears a sleepy smile as he falls backward on the bed, scooting up the mattress until his head is on a pillow, pressed up against the leather headboard. He pats his chest, wordlessly telling me where I should rest. I climb on top of him and cozy into his cuddle.

The aroma of French toast finds my nose and I'm tempted to grab the fork and return to my breakfast tray. But Dex's chest begins to rise and fall rhythmically, pulling me into a sleepy daze that overwhelms my appetite. With my last bit of energy, I pull the covers over our naked bodies and fall asleep next to my husband.

CHAPTER 19

Dex

"Another bite?" I ask Lennox. She's sitting on my kitchen countertop, wearing my button-down shirt like an open robe draped over her naked body. With her ankles crossed, she's swinging her legs, her heels tapping the cabinets with a soft rhythmic thud.

Nodding with wide eyes, she answers, "Like five more bites. You're such a good cook. If I could, I'd marry you again. How come you've never cooked like this for me before?"

"Seemed too intimate while you were dating someone else," I say, cutting another hearty square piece of French toast and dabbing it in whipped cream before popping it into her mouth. It would've been much better when it was hot two hours ago, but there were more pressing matters at hand. Now, she's enjoying the leftovers, still looking happier than I've ever seen her. My chest is full. Maybe I'm bursting with pride. *I did that.* I put that smile on her face. Now my whole life purpose is to keep it there.

"Cooking for someone is intimate?" she asks after chewing and swallowing.

"Oh yeah," I say. "Even more so than sex. If I caught another man in your bed, I'd ruin his life. But if I caught another man cooking for you, the police would have to scavenger hunt for body parts."

She squints one eye. "Yeah, okay. That seems...reasonable."

I smirk at her. "Glad you agree." Uncrossing her legs, I wedge myself between her smooth thighs. "How are you doing?"

"What do you mean?"

"You went from a breakup, to homeless, to married, to screwing your best guy friend in the timespan of a week. I'm sure your head is still spinning."

"Technically, inaccurate. Finn's my best guy friend." She flashes me a close-lipped, smartass smile.

"I resent that." I tap her nose. "But did you tell him we got married yet?"

"No," Lennox answers.

"Why not?"

"Same reason I haven't told my parents yet."

"Being?" I prod.

"I've been trying to avoid my feelings for you for years. Then, the minute money and your company are on the line...we give in? It doesn't look good, and I don't expect people to understand."

I run my thumb against her cheek. "Since when do you care about what people think?"

"I'm not concerned what anyone else thinks of me. But my parents, Finn, and Avery? They aren't just people to me. I look up to all of them and I don't want them to perceive me as a gold digger. If we had gotten married for any reason outside of Hessler Group, I'd want to parade you around, shouting from the rooftops that I'm happy. But...I don't know. It feels a little weird outside of our bubble."

"It feels a little weird?" I watch the worry lines form on her forehead.

"Yes."

"Forget how this happened, Lennox. Let's just be glad it did. It doesn't feel weird to me."

She smiles. "How does it feel for you?"

I search my mind for the best answer. All I want is to put her mind at ease. "It feels like my favorite memory. Like I returned to a home I didn't even know I had."

She puckers her bottom lip. "You are so good at that. The way you speak to me..."

"It's all the PR and public speaking training. I was born to be in corporate or politics."

She shakes her head and wrinkles up her nose like she smells something disgusting. "I think you have more potential than that, Dex. But I do wish I could borrow your confidence in the matter. You're not worried about what anyone is going to say? You just appointed a CEO whose most impressive business accomplishment is an unimplemented dive shop business plan she wrote out when she was eighteen years old. You're going to have hell to pay with your leadership team."

"First of all, you underestimate yourself." I kiss her forehead. "You know what my grandma used to tell me?"

"What's that?"

"Leadership is less about what's in your head and more about what's in your heart. Business can be learned, but a cold heart will starve potential every single time. You have the best heart, Len. That's all you need."

She rolls her eyes. "Sappy."

"Roll your eyes at me again," I say, dropping my voice to a husky whisper. "I'll bend you over this counter and spank you."

She chuckles as she clamps her knees tightly around my waist. "Go ahead and do your worst, Mr. Hessler."

"Second of all," I say, refocusing before I get too distracted. Now, bending Lennox over this counter is at the forefront of my mind. Every three hours, like a biological timer, the urge bubbles up and I need to have her. Let's hope the obsession fades or I'll become the most unproductive, useless piece of shit on the planet, unable to function without my body locked into my wife. "This was my decision. *You* were my choice. The only other person who gets a say in that is you. If the executive team has a problem with it, they can leave their jobs and pensions at the door and walk the hell away."

Lennox still doesn't have a full grasp on how much power I have. How much power she now has. I don't think she'd care though. It's my favorite part of her. We could be happy together with absolutely nothing. That's the kind of love Grandma wanted for me. The kind that withstands all the changes and challenges. She knew from the moment she met Lennox what I wanted. I was too stubborn and distracted to move my feet, so she had to force my hand.

Thank you, Grandma.

Scooting the plate aside, I plant my hand on the counter and lean into Lennox's body. I bury my nose in her neck, smelling the light traces of my shampoo that she used. It smells so much better on her. "Are you still hungry? Or can we move on from lunch?" I kiss down her neck and across her clavicle. When I run out of skin, I push my shirt off her shoulders, exposing her tits and pert nipples.

"I'm never going to get enough of you," I murmur.

I scoot her to the edge of the counter and reach between her legs. The tip of my finger is barely slick from her entrance when I hear a loud, *"Oh, shit! Dex, I'm sorry."*

It's not Lennox's voice.

I whip my head around to see Denny standing at the entrance of my kitchen, covering her eyes murmuring, "Sorry, sorry, sorry," as she blindly backs away, getting dangerously close to falling down the stairs that lead to the basement. She'd break her neck tumbling down those stairs.

"Denny, watch out! Stairs," I shout. Eyes popping open, she dodges the stair landing and pivots before scuttling down the hallway.

"I'll wait outside," she calls over her shoulder.

I blink a few times, trying to make sense of the situation. Denny is here in Las Vegas...in my home...and just saw me fingering my wife. I check Lennox's face. She looks mortified as she pulls my shirt back over her shoulders and wraps herself up as tightly as she can. Her cheeks are scarlet red and her jaw is tense.

"I'm sorry," I mutter.

"So...that's Denny, huh?"

"That's Denny," I respond.

"Denny with a key, hm?" Lennox looks pissed, but I can't imagine she's jealous. Denny is old enough to be my mother. Maybe it's just embarrassment, but we weren't doing anything wrong. An uncomfortable sight for an outsider, but there's nothing wrong with enjoying my new marital bliss however I please in my home. Why she's here is the big question.

Then again...

"Not a key," I explain. "She has the code to the front lock. Denny was in charge of arranging the moving and cleaning crew. I gave her the code last week so she could schedule everything." I grimace as I tuck Lennox's hair behind her ear. "She was also the one trying to find me a wife. And I ghosted her last night when I asked you to marry me." I shake my head realizing I caused this uncomfortable situation. "I haven't opened her texts or answered any of her calls. She probably thought something happened to me."

Lennox crosses her arms even tighter. "Were you ignoring her because she's going to be pissed we got married?" There's a touch of sadness in her eyes.

"Not at all." Running my hand over her shoulder, then down her arm, I try to relieve the tension. She looks so on edge at the moment, like prey that senses a predator. "I've been ignoring everyone. Apparently, I'm a little neglectful of my responsibilities when I'm this happy."

Immediately, she relaxes. "Well, that's sweet." She places her hands on my cheeks. "Now, duty calls. Give me a two-minute head start to get up the stairs then hurry up and bring her back in. It's chilly out today." Stepping aside, I let her tiptoe away. She peeks down the hallway before darting across the living room, then upstairs.

I don't retrieve Denny immediately. I scrape Lennox's plate clean into the trash then rinse it in the sink. I even wash my hands and take my time drying them off on the kitchen towel. I'm trying to come up with a reasonable explanation before I address Denny. The last conversation we had, she was expecting me to commit to Allie. Canoodling with Lennox was enough of a surprise for her.

Finding out she's my wife, and now the CEO of Hessler Group, might send Denny into a coronary.

When I pull open the front door, I see Denny sitting on the porch. She's in a tight pencil skirt that goes past her knees, forcing her to sit awkwardly like a land-stranded mermaid. She turns around, and before I can address her, she blurts out an explanation. "You dropped off in the middle of an important conversation and I never heard back from you, Dex."

I quirk my brow. "It's been eighteen hours, Denny. Not even a full day."

She pauses. "Doesn't matter. Every alarm in my mind was going off. I rang the doorbell, but it didn't sound. I knocked, but no one answered. So, I used the code because I thought..." She plants her hand across her chest which is rising and falling with her panicked breathing. "I could've been walking into a bloody crime scene. You're so secretive here. Dottie was the only one who could get through to you, and I thought...I thought... What if something happened to you? Who would know? Who would tell me? It's my job to know, and I couldn't..." Tears streak down her cheeks as she heaves.

"Oh, Denny." I cross the short width of the porch and help her to her feet. I pull her into a hug, patting her back. "I'm sorry. I didn't realize you'd worry so much."

She returns my hug but smacks my back hard. *"Didn't think I'd worry?"* Her tone is scolding. "I'm your family. Of course, I was worried!"

I hold her for a while until she calms down. "Feel better?" I ask as I pull away.

She glares at me. "Somewhat. I'm glad you're breathing."

"Sweet of you," I say with sarcasm. "Would you like to come inside?" I peer up and down the street. "How'd you get here?"

"The family jet and then a car service. The driver went off to get gas the moment I got into the house. He'll be back shortly if you want me to leave."

"Don't be silly. Come in." I nod to the door.

"Is your guest still..."

"Getting dressed. She'll be down in a moment, and I'll introduce you."

Suddenly recomposed, Denny crosses her arms in a way that tells me a lecture is on the tip of her tongue. "Dex, I understand you have your life here, but out of respect for your new wife, it's probably best to keep your dalliances minimal. The last thing we want is people insinuating that you're having an affair mere moments after getting married. Allie, or any woman for that matter, wouldn't want to be embarrassed in the media like that."

I let out a heavy sigh, deciding to rip off the Band-Aid right here, right now. "The *dalliance* you're referring to is not a one-night stand. Her name is Lennox Mitchell. She was a very good friend of mine. Now, she's my wife."

Denny gawks at me. "I'm sorry...*what?*" she hisses. "What do you mean 'your wife?'"

I clear my throat and give Denny a warning look. I understand she's shocked, and my communication has been pretty piss-poor, but disrespecting Lennox is not a line she nor anybody else is allowed to cross. I mentally plead for her to respect some boundaries before I have to kick her off my porch. "Denny, I won't be marrying Allie or any of the other women you suggested. Last night, I asked Lennox to marry me, and she agreed."

Denny breathes out in relief. "Oh, you mean you're engaged. So, there's still time to talk you out of—"

"And then last night we got married at a chapel just outside The Strip."

She goes back to jaw-dropped gawking.

"Denny—"

"I thought we talked about you running this stuff by me?"

I pinch the bridge of my nose, controlling my temper. If Denny was a normal employee this condescending attitude wouldn't be accepted, but this woman helped change my diapers and used to buy me rubber bath duckies. I have to grant her a little grace. "There was no changing my mind. And I'd like to convey how completely devoted I am to my marriage. Please understand that anything you say moving forward about Lennox is *about my wife*. You know how unreasonably protective men get when they're in love, right?"

"In love?" she practically spits out. "How come I've never heard of her once? Now you're in *love*? Dex...be with whomever you want *after* Hessler Group is yours again. Surely you can wait a year. This isn't what Dottie wanted."

"I'm pretty confident it's exactly what she wanted," I chide.

It seems like we're both puffing up our chests, trying to prove who has the superior point in the argument. But it really doesn't matter what Denny wants. She's not the heir of Hessler Group. I am. Denny doesn't need to obsess about my company. She'll be well taken care of for the rest of her life. I'll make sure of that. She doesn't need to bear the burden of my business decisions...or my personal ones, for that matter.

She rubs her arms when the brisk breeze cuts through the porch.

"It's cold. Come inside, Denny. You'll love Lennox. She's the most amazing woman I know. You guys will be fast friends, and she'll need your help just like Grandma did. I'm adding to our family, not taking away. I'd really like your support in this because I don't want to say goodbye to any more members of my family."

I'll admit, I'm laying it on a little thick. But maybe if Denny realizes she's safe, she'll see Lennox as less of a threat.

Denny hangs her head, her eyes watering again. She wipes her nose with the back of her hand and sniffles in a very un-Denny-like fashion. "I stood by Dottie through everything. She lost Melody and was left to raise you. Harrison all but abandoned her with an empire she was unprepared to run. I watched this woman become a phenomenon, never cracking under the pressure that would've broken anyone else. She worked so hard for everything we have, Dex. I don't want to see it fall apart in front of my eyes. Protecting you is the only way I know how to honor her now. So, please pardon me for being skeptical of any woman who says she loves you after you wave a billion-dollar company in her face."

My eyes drop to the ground. "Isn't that exactly what Allie and the other women did? They agreed to be my wife in exchange for a payout?"

"No, those were business transactions. Love is an entirely different matter. You can trust one, not the other."

"I agree." But I know we're talking about two different things. Denny trusts paperwork. Grandma wanted me to trust my heart.

Denny's driver returns, slowly pulling up in front of the house.

"Denny, she's everything to me. *Everything*. So can you please play nice?" I point to the car over her shoulder. "Or are we about to say goodbye?"

I swear she glares at me before adjusting her expression. She pats my cheek, which should feel like an affectionate gesture from a maternal figure. Instead, it feels condescending. "If you're happy, I'm happy."

"You sure?"

She nods. "I'm just scared, Dex. What you have now, the world wants to take it away. And they will attack the moment you let your guard down. You need to be surrounded by people you can trust. That's all."

"Don't be scared." Gently placing my hand on her back, I guide her into the warm house. "Come inside and meet my wife."

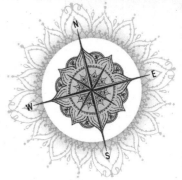

CHAPTER 20

Lennox

I didn't sleep well last night. I've been up for hours. I'm outside, curled up on Dex's patio furniture, sipping on my third cup of coffee alone. My honeymoon is apparently over.

Dex keeps telling me it wasn't a real one and he'll make it up to me. He thinks a honeymoon is a luxurious vacation overseas where I'm wined and dined and treated like a princess. But I didn't need all of that. I already got everything I wanted. We spent full days naked, exploring each other. After sex, he'd take his time holding me, whispering sweet nothings in my ear. I fell asleep to pillow talk where we confessed to each other over and over again that we were feeling all the same emotions for three years. I've never felt less alone knowing every painful stab of missed opportunities were at least shared. Maybe we wasted time, but we didn't let it completely get away. Maybe there's something even sweeter about a second chance.

For the past three days, I've been walking around his house like I've always belonged here. It's just a house to Dex, but it's magic to me. This house is where my best friends, Finn and Avery, found each other and fell in love. In fact, this house is where I fell in love. It's full of magic and memories, and for a few blissful days, I was in heaven...

Then Denny showed up.

I'm trying to keep an open mind. This is as close to a mother-in-law as I'll have with Dex. So, yesterday after she barged in on me and Dex, I hugged her, trying to force a genuine smile and shake off the embarrassment of her catching me and Dex in the act. I'm ignoring her intrusive nature and how uncomfortable it is that this woman has the key code to Dex's house.

When the glass patio doors slide open, I turn my head, expecting to see my husband, but instead, it's Denny. Her blond hair is pulled back into a low, neat ponytail. Even though she's wearing a robe over her silk pajamas, her makeup is fresh and she's wearing diamond studs in her ears. An odd contradiction. She looks like she's getting ready to pose for a magazine shoot.

Holding up a mug of coffee, she says, "I hope you don't mind. I finished the pot."

"Not at all. I can make some more." Uncrossing my legs, I move to sit up, but Denny tuts her tongue.

"Nonsense, this is plenty. I didn't mean for you to get up. In fact, may I join you?"

I look to my left, but there is no one and nothing to save me. Not an excuse in sight. "Of course. Is Dex still sleeping?"

"I wouldn't know." Although there are three wicker sofas surrounding the coffee table, Denny opts to sit right next to me. "He's not my husband," she adds with a wink.

"Right. Dex is normally an early bird. I'm surprised he's sleeping in."

"He's been that way his whole life," Denny adds. "Melody liked to sleep in until eleven and stay up until three in the morning. Dex whipped that right out of her. From infancy, he wanted the bottle and his toys by five a.m." She chuckles fondly.

I nod, taking a little sip from my cooled-off coffee. "You and Melody were close?"

Denny's eyes drop to her lap. "You want the truth?"

"Only if you don't mind sharing..."

"I never told Dex this because I dare not speak ill of his mother." Her eyes open wide. "*And I'm not.* Melody was amazing. Beautiful, smart, funny, and so full of life. Wealth aside, all the boys wanted her. I envied her since childhood. I was too skinny, awkward, and clumsy. I would follow Melody around like a lost puppy, just hoping to soak up some of the magic."

I'm afraid to ask, but I do anyway. "She didn't like you?"

"Melody was always kind to me, but I know spending time with me was a chore her mother mandated. You see, my own mother was a supermodel when that term meant everything. I'm talking about the era of Cindy Crawford and Claudia Schiffer. I was nothing but an inconvenience to her. To this day, I think she's still angry she risked stretchmarks to bring me to term." She scoffs. "Anyway, my mother and Dottie met at a mother's group, and soon playdates for Melody and I turned into Dottie babysitting. That then turned into my mother dropping me on their doorstep for days at a time while she went on a bender. She treated cocaine like a vitamin—took it faithfully every single day."

Denny hadn't exactly been warm and welcoming during our first introduction, but I can forgive her, especially because she's grieving as well. From the sound of it, Dottie wasn't just a friend and employer...she was more of a mother to Denny than her own. "That's awful you didn't get that time with your mom," I say in a hush. "I'm so sorry."

"I'm not. It was better to spend my childhood and adolescence at The Hessler Estate than my own empty home as my mom got passed around like a baton in European sex clubs." She chuckles bitterly before taking a sip from her mug. "You make really good coffee."

"Thank you... But, um, Denny, why are you telling me all this?"

"To try and connect with you."

Her blatant response catches me off guard. "Oh."

She relaxes her shoulder and pats her knee. "I usually have a hard time relating to people, but I think you and I are a lot alike. I also grew up on the outside looking in, Lennox. Had an opportunity like Dex presented itself, I would've jumped as well. It's just good sense. I'm not faulting you. This can be a win-win situation for everyone."

I sigh heavily, unable to mask my frustration. "Dex is not an opportunity to me. I'm not trying to win anything. I care about him. I have for a long time."

Denny holds her hands up in surrender. "I'm sorry, poor choice of words. I just mean I'm trying to understand the situation. Look, Lennox—obviously, you're very important to Dex. Which means now, you're very important to me too. I'd love it if we could get along. I want to help you both however I can."

There's something about Denny I just can't put my finger on. It's like tiptoeing by a sleeping crocodile. I most certainly don't feel safe. On the other hand, if Denny is truly all Dex has left in Miami, I can't imagine me being at odds with the only other person he calls family. I don't want to make his life even more complicated. Denny deserves a chance, at least.

"Thank you, Denny. I appreciate that. I'd really like for us to be friends."

She exhales, a relaxed smile spreading across her flawlessly smooth face. Denny may be in her fifties, but she could easily pass for late thirties. "Me too, Lennox," she says. "Not to mention us women have to stick together. I hate to be the one to break it to you, but Hessler Group is a boys' club. There's not one woman on the advisory board and the entire executive team is comprised of white, middle-aged men who love to mansplain how to properly drink bourbon." She rolls her eyes dramatically as she makes a "C" with her hand, pretending to pour a drink into her mouth. "In my experience, it's as simple as getting the liquid into your mouth, but who am I to speak, right?"

I chuckle at her sarcasm until I realize her message is laced with a bitter undertone.

"I thought Dex mentioned you were their household manager. Do you also work at Hessler Group as well?"

She shrugs, leaning back into the seat before crossing her legs. "In a thankless way."

"Meaning?"

"I was Dottie's sounding board for the better part of two decades. When she first took the helm, nobody respected her.

They thought she was a silly housewife playing dress up in a suit, trying to run a company she had no business running. There was a lot of pressure for the company to go public, take on shareholders, and more investors who—and I quote—'knew what they were doing.' Nobody wanted her making the big decisions." Denny purses her lips and shakes her head like she's trying to brush off a memory that still bothers her. "It was so damn satisfying to watch her prove all their judgments wrong. Dottie was more equipped to run Hessler Group than Harrison ever was. He was a mean, coldhearted drunk. I'm shocked Dottie married him, and even more shocked Melody came from him. Those women deserved better."

From what I remember, Dex has never mentioned his grandpa was mean. "I thought Dex and his grandpa got along?"

Denny nods. "Oh, yes. Because he's the male heir Harrison always wanted. He was mostly a cruel, arrogant, insufferable old man, but he minded himself around Dex. His little protégé." She bites out the last part of her sentence. "Meanwhile, poor Dottie did the backbreaking work, and he never once told his wife how proud he was of her. Never gave her the credit she deserved. I was right there with her, talking out every business decision, picking her back up after every mistake. I probably know more about the inner workings of Hessler Group than any executive or advisory board member... That's why they don't like for me to be in the meetings. I'm happy to call them on their shit." Her cackle is shrill, and the corner of her mouth curls up into what is unmistakably a snarl.

She must've worked very hard her entire life just to be told her opinion was only useful in whispers, behind closed doors. I thought Denny was arrogant and elitist. Turns out she's just pissed neither she nor Dottie got the credit she feels they deserve. The woman I disliked is now the woman I pity. I feel the overwhelming need to comfort her.

"Do you want to be?"

"Pardon?" Denny asks.

"Do you want to be in the meetings? Is that what you wanted

all this time? To work for Hessler Group instead of as a household manager?"

She takes a moment to consider her response. "No, I can't," she finally replies with no further explanation.

"Why not?" I ask. "If I can, I want to help you. I'm sure Dex does, too. Why couldn't we hire you at Hessler Group? You obviously have the experience."

"We," she parrots absentmindedly. "I'm still getting used to that. Dex with a wife." She pats my knee. "Dex with a kind, empathetic, loving wife who already reminds me so much of his mother and grandmother."

I know she's kissing ass, but I still melt into a puddle. It's the highest compliment in the world to be likened to Dottie Hessler.

"I'll talk to Dex," I say. "I'm not sure how to promote someone or what that entails, but I'll figure it out. If you don't want to be a glorified personal assistant, I don't want that for you either. I know my position as CEO is mostly a placeholder until Dex takes the reigns, but if I can do some good, I promise I will. I'd love to help you however I can."

Denny beams at me. She stretches out her arm and wraps it around my shoulders. I steady my mug, trying to keep the liquid from sloshing over the rim as she yanks me into an awkward hug. Pressing her cheek against mine, she makes a kissing noise. This close, I recognize the scent... Dottie's fancy French perfume.

Poor thing. I'd do the same if I lost my mother. I'd wear her perfume to keep her close, surrounding myself in the comfort of memories. Maybe I'd also distrust anybody who suddenly came into my family, threatening to disrupt the foundation the matriarch built. Denny just needs some time to heal.

"Lennox," she finally says. "You're too kind."

"Thank you." I show her a sheepish smile of modesty, but her expression grows grim, and she slowly shakes her head back and forth.

"No, sweetheart, you're too kind. They are going to chew you up and spit you out in Miami."

My heart thuds heavily at her bizarre warning, but I don't have time to ask for clarity. The sliding door opens once more, and Dex appears, fully dressed in slacks and a dress shirt, holding the empty coffee pot. He's wearing a huge smile.

"Well, I was going to give you guys shit for leaving me no coffee, but you two hugging is a much better start to my day."

Denny turns her head and smiles at him. "Your wife and I were just bonding."

"Thank you," Dex mouths to me.

"Did you enjoy sleeping in for once? It's nice, right?" I pump my eyebrows at him.

"Trying to lure me to the dark side, Mrs. Hessler?" He winks. "I wasn't sleeping. I just didn't come downstairs. I've been in my office for the past hour or so attending to emails. I'm just now coming up for air and some coffee... What?" he asks, surveying my perturbed expression.

"You've been working since about six a.m. with no coffee?" I stare at him like he has two heads.

"Yes. People can function without coffee, Len."

Highly incorrect. "And why are you already dressed?" I ask. "Did you have a meeting?"

Dex steps through the glass doors and grabs the small suitcase behind him. He grimaces as he holds it up, then sets it back down. "I have to take care of something in Miami."

"What's going on?" Denny asks, ears perking up.

"I received an interesting email from Royal Bahamas this morning. Richard offered his sincerest condolences and asked if Grandma's merger offer was something I'd still be willing to honor. He wants a meeting."

Denny rolls her eyes. "Sharks smelling blood in the water."

Dex crosses his arms, standing a little taller than usual. He carries a different demeanor when he talks business. It's a stark contrast to the easy-going scuba instructor I know so well. But I like this new Dex, too. He seems confident and so sure of himself, like he's in his element. "It's worth hearing him out. A merger like that would create a lot of opportunities for our workforce. The one partnership I'd be very eager to acquire is their exclusivity agreement with Balton Hotels."

"True," Denny adds. "That'd be maybe an extra billion in revenue potential a year?"

"Somewhere in that ballpark. I woke Fisher up to run the numbers and come up with an implementation plan. He said he'd have them for me by the time my flight lands."

Denny pivots to face me. "Lennox, to catch you up, Richard Spellman is the CEO of Royal Bahamas Cruises. He's finally realized that a merger with Hessler Group might be easier than trying to compete in a market that we dominate. The only bargaining chip he has is a deal he signed with Balton Hotels twenty years ago. Balton is behind several major hotel chains, and they have an ironclad partnership that's kept Hessler Group out of some promotional opportunities that could be very lucrative revenue-wise."

The way Denny's explaining this, it sounds like she should be the CEO of Hessler Group. I guess that's what happens when you spend so much time with the person in power—osmosis.

"I thought Hessler Group was already very successful... Why do you need more revenue?"

Denny opens her mouth, but I appreciate Dex beating her to an explanation.

"At this point, it's not about how much money is in our pockets. It's taking care of the workforce. There's over a hundred thousand jobs within our company, scattered across the globe. The more revenue we have, the better gainshare. Better benefits. Happier employees, less turnover. Fewer lawsuits. All in all, it's like going the extra mile to have the best for your family."

Oh, that I like. That makes more sense than the rich getting richer. I mean, when you have billions, what's left to strive for?

"Do you need me to go with you?" I ask with a grimace, nearly choking on the words.

Dex smirks. "Wow, Trouble. Please try to control your

enthusiasm."

"Funny," I sass. "But I said I'd do this job...I'm ready. If you're considering a merger, doesn't that involve the CEO? I have a lot to learn. Best to get started."

Dex crosses the patio to sit down in the chair adjacent to me as there's no room with me and Denny on the sofa. He squeezes my knee. "The shares were yours the very moment we said, 'I do.' Only a handful of people know about Grandma's will. A lot of people assumed I'd be taking over as CEO, so this is going to take a bit of an explanation. I think we'll start with a meeting introducing you to the board and executives. Then, we'll do a company-wide introduction via email. Once we do that, we'll have you sit in on meetings. But I told you, I'll do all the work. I don't want you to have to lift a finger." He sweetly strokes against my outer thigh, tickling me through my sweatpants.

Dex is unabashed in his affectionate gesture. Denny seems suddenly very interested in her coffee mug, as if a hidden treasure, merely a few gulps away, is at the bottom of her mug.

I kiss Dex's forehead. "Sweet...but condescending. I'm not going to sit around and be a bump on a pickle for a year, Dex. Even if it's fetching everyone coffee, I have to do something to earn my paycheck."

"Bump on a pickle?" Dex asks.

"Useless," I explain. "Literally serves no purpose."

Denny lets out a sharp laugh. "Never heard that one before. I may need to borrow that," she says.

I smile wide. "All yours." The ice is melting, and I'm far more comfortable now. Maybe a little transparency and vulnerability is all we needed.

"Speaking of a paycheck," Dex murmurs, then rises and disappears into the house. He returns with a document mailer. "Denny, thank you for having this overnighted."

She smiles and ducks her head in a short nod. "Of course."

After settling back into his seat, he rips the envelope open, then surveys the documents inside one by one before handing them to me.

"What's all this?" I ask.

"Your new bank account information. This one is your private account. The card is attached," Dex says, flipping to the second page of the document. "It's already activated and here is your current balance at the bottom. I deposited your entire year's salary as an advance. This is *your* account. I'm not even on it. Do as you please without worrying about anyone invading your privacy."

I nearly vomit when I see the bottom line. I've never seen seven digits on anything except math problems in school. It's surreal. And even more so because I don't feel like I earned this in any way. "Dex, you shouldn't have given that to me upfront. You're supposed to work and then earn a paycheck. I haven't done anything for this."

He wets his lips and pulls out another envelope. Inside, there's a sleek black card with no markings. At the bottom corner, it simply reads Mrs. Hessler.

"Don't worry about the name. It'll work as Lennox Mitchell or Lennox Hessler. Whatever you decide. There's no limit on this one. This is a shared account, but whatever you want, it's yours." I don't take the card, so he sets it on the table in front of me. Dex grabs my hand between his. "Len, everything is about to change. If I'm not traveling, I'm in meetings. I work sixty-hour weeks and that's just my professional obligations. Then, there are the personal responsibilities that accompany the Hessler name. I'll never be able to spend as much time with you as I want. There are very few perks to being my wife...this is one of them. Try to enjoy it at least a little, okay?"

I wish Denny wasn't here. I just want to crawl into Dex's lap and comfort the anguish right off his face. "Okay. Actually, there are some things here I need to take care of. When do we need to leave for Miami?" I ask.

"Well, I'm headed there now." He glances towards his suitcase through the glass doors. "I can come back for you or arrange a flight for you to meet me at home."

Home. It takes me by surprise. Dex just referred to Miami as home. My new home. I committed to blindly following this man wherever he leads, and for the first time since we got married, this makes a little less sense.

"You put over six million dollars into my bank account. I think I can afford to arrange my own flight. I just want to talk to my parents first."

"Shit," Dex exhales. "I forgot we were going to do that. I can come back."

In lieu of calling the day after we got married, Dex and I decided showing up in person to explain our unexpected nuptials and my new job might be a better idea. "It's okay. Go take care of what you need to. I'll meet you in Miami by this weekend. How's that?"

He tilts his head. "You sure? I feel like I'm letting you down."

"I'm a big girl," I say with a wink. "I can talk to my parents by myself. All is well."

"We'll fly them out sometime, maybe? Show them your new place. Which reminds me"—he turns his attention to Denny—"could you arrange for the condo to be cleaned and the fridge and closets stocked? Len can give you her sizes. We'll need an on-call chef. Then, she'll need a driver."

Denny nods along, holding up her fingers one by one as if she's keeping a mental list. She seems completely unbothered by the way Dex is listing out chores for her. "Security?" Denny asks Dex.

"Just for travel," he replies. "But I want candidates run through the most thorough background checks possible."

"Got it," Denny says with a short nod.

"One more thing," Dex says, his eyes now on me. "Can you set up a private meeting with that jewelry designer Grandma worked with? I forget his name—something Italian. I want Lennox to have her dream ring made."

Denny nods again. "Sure. Anything else?"

"What do you think, baby? Did I forget anything? Just ask Denny. She runs the Hessler's lives better than we can, I promise you that."

"Um..."

"What do you need?" Denny asks. "Don't be shy in asking. It's literally my job to take care of the family."

It's a calculated, robotic response. I see it in Denny's eyes. Like when somebody is on autopilot.

"You don't need to buy my clothes, Denny. I can do that. And I really don't think we need a chef, do we? Dex cooks. I'll grocery shop and do dishes. I mean, a driver? Security? Is that all really necessary?"

Dex blinks silently for a moment, darting his gaze to Denny, then back to me. "Not if you don't want."

"Lennox?" Denny asks. "What's wrong? You look uncomfortable. Do you want to help me hire staff so you can choose who's working for you?"

"No. I don't want anyone working *for me.*"

"Why?" she prods. "You can more than afford it now, honey."

"It's something my dad would tell me... He had a lot of wealthy clients who had personal staff. He said that the less people did for themselves, the more they lost their identity. So, if I'm not choosing my clothes, cooking my food, taking care of my home, and earning my money...I'm not really living. Right? I'm just existing."

"Len, I..." Dex starts but doesn't finish his sentence. It seems he doesn't know what to say. Maybe neither of us realized how jarring of a change this whole arrangement was. We were just focused on how we felt about each other and the bliss of being able to finally admit that.

"Your dad sounds wise. What industry is he in?"

"He used to be a VP at Seaguard."

"The wealth management firm?" Denny asks in surprise, scooting to the edge of her seat and sitting up a bit taller. "Your dad was a *VP* at Seaguard? That's impressive. My mistake. I was under the impression you came from humble beginnings."

"Denny, don't mention—" Dex starts.

"It's okay," I jump in. Denny was open enough to tell me about her past. I can match her vulnerability. "My family's broke now. My dad was wrongfully terminated while I was in high school. It was messy, and we lost everything. I've been taking care of myself with temp jobs ever since." I raise my brows at her.

Dex kisses my forehead. "All right, baby. I have to return a few more emails and then get going." Dex turns to address Denny. "How quickly can you get packed? The jet will be here shortly. I know how much you hate flying commercial."

Denny hops to her feet. "Yep. Ten minutes. Let me get my bag together." With one more quick thank you, she's through the door.

"If you want Denny to move like The Flash, just threaten her with main cabin seating," Dex says with a laugh. His smile disappears when he sees my face. "What's wrong? You don't like her?"

"No, it's not that. I was just wondering about something."

"What's that?"

"Earlier I asked Denny if she wanted a position at Hessler Group. I was thinking that maybe after thirty-some years she was tired of being a glorified assistant."

"She's not just an assistant. She's a manager. She has enough power and access to set up your bank accounts, access our homes, and arrange medical care. She was my emergency contact growing up if Grandma couldn't be reached."

"That's a lot of trust." I widen my eyes.

"Grandma raised her. She was my mom's best friend. When Grandpa got sick, Denny arranged his care and would sit by his bedside for hours watching Westerns with him. She's not just an employee, she's family."

I choose not to correct Dex in that Denny and Melody's best friendship was more of an obligatory situation. But there is one puzzle piece out of place. "She said she couldn't work at Hessler Group. Why's that?"

He rubs his finger back and forth along his hairline as he cinches one eye closed. I can't tell if he's trying to remember something or is completely disinterested in this conversation. But eventually, he explains.

"From what Grandma told me, when Denny hit middle school, her mom took off to Europe and Denny didn't want to go. Grandma was happy to let her stay at the estate and finish school, but I think my grandpa had an issue with it. He didn't trust her mom, who was willing to abandon her child. He suspected ulterior motives. The compromise was Denny could stay and Grandma and Grandpa would assume responsibility for her with a couple of parameters. Denny could not inherit anything from the Hesslers, she couldn't be employed by Hessler Group, and she forfeited the right to any civil lawsuits against anyone in the Hessler family."

"Civil lawsuits?" I ask, repulsed. "What kind of controlling—"

"It's like if she's living at the estate, trips over a rug, and breaks her leg—she can't sue my family for negligence. That sort of thing."

"That can't be a thing... No way..."

"You can imagine how people would exploit any circumstance for financial gain." Dex leans over and rubs his hand sweetly across my knee. "Then again, maybe you can't. One of my favorite things about you."

His hand creeps up my thigh. "Don't even, Dex. You have a flight to catch."

"I have an idea," he says with a sinful smile. "How about you catch this flight with me? You know there's a really nice bed in the cabin in case of overnight flights. Have you ever wondered how it feels to come at 30,000 feet in the air? Because I could show you."

I lift my eyebrows. "So, in this scenario, are we just going to throw Denny some noise-canceling headphones and ask her to cover her eyes for a few minutes?"

He scrunches his face. "Excuse me, a few minutes?"

"That's your takeaway?"

"I tend to have a one-track mind around you, Trouble." He

winks. "Let me know when you book your flight, Miss Independent. But do me a favor?"

I nod before even knowing what he wants. "Sure. What's up?"

"Try first class. Just for fun."

"Maybe out of curiosity." I shrug with a cute smile. "Also, I'll need our new home address so I can catch a ride from the airport."

Dex shakes his head. "No ride. I'll be there to pick you up."

After one more kiss to my forehead, he's through the door, and once again, I'm alone in the quiet, wondering if *alone* is something I'm going to have to get used to.

CHAPTER 21

Lennox

Dad and I sit in the driveway inside his beat-up Honda. He cuts the car engine off and unbuckles, but he doesn't open his door. Instead, he reclines a few degrees and tucks his hands behind his head.

"Aren't we going inside?" I ask, clutching the bag of canned apple filling Mom sent us to the store for.

"Give her a few more minutes. She's probably frantically running through the house with air freshener as we speak. Don't want to spook her."

After dinner—and my confession about my unexpected marriage to Dex—Mom ushered us out the door saying she forgot a few ingredients for the apple pie a la mode she was planning to make. The shopping list was premade pie crusts, apple pie filling, and vanilla ice cream. It was clear she just wanted an excuse to kick us out of the house so she could sneak a cigarette.

I laugh. "You should just bust her. You know exactly what she's doing."

Dad smiles. That warm smile that easily gives him away—after thirty years of marriage, he still finds Mom completely adorable. "Your mother sneaks about four cigarettes a year. Only when she's really upset. After the bomb you dropped on us tonight, I'll sit out here patiently while she smokes an entire pack."

Exhaling, I hang my head. "You guys like Dex," I mutter. "Don't forget that."

Dad grumbles something inaudible under his breath.

"Okay, asked and answered... Do you wish I married Alan instead?" I place the plastic bag between my feet and recline to match Dad's angle. He reaches across the center console and pats my knee.

"Did you love Alan?"

My heavy heart aches like it always does when this comes up. The guilt hasn't absolved, but the truth is getting easier to tell with each day. "Not in the way he deserved."

Dad's eyes are forward, the flickering lights hanging on either side of the garage illuminating his face. It's time to change the bulbs. "And Dex?"

"Yeah," I breathe out. "I love him. I haven't told him yet."

Dad pulls down on his face, tugging on his skin. "Do you see the central issue we're having? You haven't admitted to your husband that you love him?"

I groan. "I already explained how sudden everything was and why."

"I understand helping your friend with a legality, and I'd understand falling in love with your friend. It's this gray area you're in that has me worried. Does Dex feel the way about you that you do about him? Because I've seen men like him go to greater lengths than falsely professing their love to see a deal through."

"Daddy, you don't understand. He's different."

Dad's smirk starts small and then stretches all the way across his face. He rolls his head to the right to stare at me, a little glean in his eye.

"What?" I ask.

"Moments like this, it's like you're sixteen again, or eighteen, or twenty...twenty-two...twenty-three... So many sweet memories of me wanting to take your boyfriends out back like Old Yeller. You telling me they are *different*."

"Fiiine," I grumble. "So we've had this conversation before." We both laugh. "You don't believe an old broken record, huh?"

"I don't need to believe you to stand by you, baby girl. But I do need you to make me a promise."

"Okay."

"I was in investment banking for twenty years. You don't have a career for that long without knowing Hessler Group. What waits for you in Miami...it's not the life I would've wished for my little girl. Money like that snuffs the soul out of people. It's what happened to me."

Dad has the wrong impression of Dex, and of Dottie too. It's possible to have so much and still have a heart. "What promise?" I ask, clearing my throat.

"I want you to promise me that every single decision you make for the next year is with love in your heart and not money on your mind. Stay true to yourself because I refuse to lose you, Lenny. Not while I'm still breathing."

Ladies and gentlemen—Sam Mitchell—the only person on the planet I don't mind calling me Lenny.

"I'll promise to lead with my heart if you promise to keep breathing," I say softly. I'm dancing dangerously close to the line we never cross. But if I'm leaving, I have to know Dad's okay.

"I promise."

"You know, Dad, you think wanting money is evil, but the fact is, we still need it. It can be a good thing. It can give second chances."

He turns fully now. "What do you mean?"

I was going to wait until after dinner and dessert and linger around after Mom went to bed, but now's as good a time as any. I pull out my phone and put it on speaker as I dial the 1-800 number that I programmed in this morning.

After a brief automated menu, the hold time is minimal. A woman finally answers the line in such a cheerful voice for a student loan call center. "Thank you for calling Better Ed Student Loans. This is Gloria. How can I help you today?"

Dad's eyes widen. He grabs the seat handle, returning to an upright position. "What are you—"

I press my fingers to my lips to silence him. "Gloria, my name is Lennox Mitchell and I'd like to make a payment on my account."

Obediently, Dad stays silent as I give Gloria my social security number and the password on the account. Tears form in his eyes as Gloria reads the painfully high totals on each of my private student loans. The debt I racked up never went to my education. I dropped classes, forfeited school, and used every extra penny of the loans to try and save my family's home—a futile attempt that landed me in financial ruin. There are seven different maxed-out loans accruing interest at ridiculous rates. Gloria explains that some of the loans are delinquent, dangerously close to going to collections. Dad has to cover his mouth as he begins to heave, now fully crying at the damage he thinks he did.

It's not your fault, Daddy. It's not your fault. It was my choice. I could tell him over and over again, but he'd never believe me. We don't need to bleed over this anymore. It's the main reason I said yes to Dex and this job before knowing how he felt about me. My motivation was to absolve my dad of guilt. It's the only way I could leave him and Las Vegas.

"Ms. Mitchell, that's all of them. What payment would you like to make on which loan?" Gloria asks through the speakerphone.

I clear my throat, eyes fixed on Dad's. "All of them. All of it."

She pauses. "The entire balance? Did I hear that correctly?"

"Yes, I want to pay it all off, right now." I fish in my purse and pull out the document Dex gave me yesterday with my new bank account information. "I have a routing and account number when you're ready."

I have to give Gloria the number seven times. One for each loan. One by one, I erase the demons that have been plaguing me and Dad for over a decade now. When we're finished, Gloria congratulates me and assures me that I should see my credit score positively affected within sixty days or so.

I hang up the phone and say to Dad, "It's the same thing the credit card companies told me yesterday when I paid them all off. Apparently, in just two months, my credit score won't be negative twenty anymore." I laugh, but this time, Dad doesn't join me. He buries his face in his hands.

"I'm sorry, baby girl. I'm so sorry. You should've never had to... My burden, and I couldn't take care of you..."

He's soaking his short, dark brown beard, so I pull his hands from his face and wipe the tears away with the back of my hands. "It's okay. Everything is okay. I'm free now." I hand him my phone. "Your turn."

He looks horrified, the skin on his forehead scrunching in tight folds. "What?" he croaks out.

"Every single loan, creditor, debt collector... Start calling." I wave the bank document in the air. "We're all starting over tonight."

Dad shakes his head, blubbering. "No, no, no. I can't let you do that."

"It's not just for you, Dad. It's for Mom, too. Make the calls."

His bottom lip trembles as he speaks, making his words come out in a vibrato. "Daughters aren't supposed to save their daddies. That's not how the fairytales go."

I smile. "Dad, I love you... Fuck fairytales." I point to my phone tightly clutched in his hands. *"Make the calls."*

He sucks in a breath and holds it for so long I'm pretty confident that, at this point, Dad could out-dive even Dex. He finally releases a slow, controlled breath. "He doesn't deserve you, Lenny. None of us do. You kept this family together when I failed to. When I was weak, you were strong."

I reach over the center console and grab Dad's hand. "If we're going to take this to the studs...you taught me what family means. If I'm strong, it's because you and Mom showed me how to be. I'm your little dividend finally paying out."

He finally smiles through his tears. "At least I did one thing right in this life... I chose your mom. She gave me you."

One call at a time, Dad and I stitch together the open wounds, clearing debt, wiping the slate clean. It takes a giant chunk out of my new bank account but I'm not bothered in the slightest. I got everything I could ever want.

I'm safe. My mom and dad are safe. And I'm about to spend

every day with the man who has been starring in my dreams for the past three years. The muddy waters are behind us now.

This is my fresh start.

CHAPTER 22

Lennox

Present Day

Miami

The Miami skyline is almost more majestic than Vegas at night. Not to be a traitor to my beloved home, but I've never seen a city like this, balancing right on the edge of the water. I like the bright lights of Vegas, but Miami has them, too, reflecting off the water and making its presentation a touch more impressive than Vegas. My eyes were glued to the view as I flew into the city, first class, a glass flute of champagne in my hand. Now, in the limousine, I'm seeing the same view from the ground, once again, with another glass of champagne in my hand. I'm learning that when you're rich, every ride is basically a booze cruise.

Despite his best intentions, Dex couldn't meet me at the airport. Duty called, and he had to take a last-minute flight to L.A. to attend to yet another pressing business matter. He briefly explained, but I was so busy assuring him I was a big girl and could handle myself, I didn't catch the details of the deal he was working out.

Instead, a chauffeur in a cliché driver's hat greeted me at the airport with a sign that read "Mrs. Hessler." He ushered me into a limousine then proceeded to go back into the airport to fetch my luggage from baggage claim. I was a little embarrassed to tell him that my luggage was the big one with bright purple zebra stripes.

I haven't purchased new suitcases since my teenage years, and it was the largest one I owned. I shoved everything into it, all the necessities of my life condensed into one jumbo hardcase. I have more clothing, but nothing I own belongs in a corporate work setting. I need to go shopping.

While I may not particularly care about name brands and "looking a certain part," I'm acutely aware of the fact that, as Dex's wife, how people view me may be how they view him by extension. Therefore, the first item of business in Miami is to find some tops that aren't so sheer and bottoms that aren't denim with holes and frayed edges. I brought the few sundresses that I thrifted when I was with Alan. Those look presentable enough in the meantime.

Once the limousine is parked, I reach for the handle and yank on the latch to no avail. The driver rolls down the partition. "Just a moment, Mrs. Hessler. I'll come around."

Apparently, I no longer have the arduous task of opening my own doors anymore either. Once Jeeves—as I've dubbed him—frees me from the back of the vehicle, he points to the elevator behind us.

"This is a private access elevator that will take you right to the entry of the penthouse. The temporary override code is two-nine-six-four-eight-three. That code changes daily, so we'll get you set up on the fingerprint verification system soon. I'll bring your suitcase up through the service elevator. Would you like me to arrange for the housekeepers to unpack your luggage?"

"No!" I emphasize, my voice echoing loudly through the concrete parking structure. I clear my throat. "I mean, no, thank you. I have some personal items in there I'd rather, um...set up myself."

He nods with an uncomfortable-looking smile.

"Fragile photographs and things like that," I add, rolling my eyes at myself because I most definitely just insinuated that I stuffed my suitcase full of sex toys. Which is accurate... I only brought my toothbrush, a few of my favorite hoodies, some framed pictures, and the contents of my naughty box, which Dex requested I pack.

But Jeeves most certainly doesn't need to know that.

"I understand," he answers, politely dodging any further talk of the matter. "Is there anything else I can help you with?"

"Nope, I think that'll do it. Thank you for the ride." I point to the back of the limo. "I can just shlep my suitcase up with me though. It's really not a problem."

"Oh, no need to strain yourself, ma'am." His dimples deepen as he smiles.

"I mean...it rolls. Really not a strain, I promise."

His smile turns into a grimace. "If you don't mind, Mrs. Hessler, it's protocol. Part of my job."

"Oh. Okay. Well, then um"—I pat my pockets like I'm searching for something—"will I be seeing you again? This is embarrassing but I don't have cash for a tip. I'll have Dex take me to an ATM tomorrow, though. Can I get you back? You did a really good job."

His smile before was polite, but now it's clear he's trying not to chuckle at me. "Ma'am, I'm your personal driver. Anywhere you need to go, I'm at your service. No tip necessary. I'm part of your staff." He winks. "You pay me more than plenty."

"Well, now I'm embarrassed."

He shakes his head. "Don't be. That was quite endearing."

"If we'll be seeing each other daily, please call me Len or Lennox, whatever you prefer. And also, I'm sorry—I didn't catch your name."

He clasps his hand over his chest. "Oh, I thought you knew." In a fluid motion, he unsnags the button from his suit and stretches out his hand. "I'm Joseph or Joe. Whatever you prefer." Eh, I was close. Jeeves, Joseph...not that far off.

"Thank you, Joe. Also, one more thing."

"Sure, what is it?"

I nod behind me, gesturing to the extended limo. "Do we have to take this everywhere? It's a little flashy."

He lifts his salt and pepper brows. "Not at all. Do you have a preference?"

"I really don't. I just don't want to look like I'm headed to prom every time we go to Target."

He laughs. "Dually noted. Tomorrow morning when I retrieve you for your interview, I'll bring something simpler. Just out of curiosity, will we be making trips to Target often?"

My smile grows wide and wicked. "I got an advance on my salary, Joe. *Oh, yeah.* Strap in, buddy."

He lets out a thunderous belly laugh. "Good to know. Okay, well, have a good evening, Lennox. I'll see you in the morning."

"Wait, one more thing, Joe. You mentioned an interview... what interview?"

He shrugs. "I'm sorry. I'm not privy to the details of your meetings. I only know that Mrs. Lockleer sent over a note that you are to meet her at the corporate campus at eight-thirty to prep for your interview. I'll be downstairs by eight o'clock, but take your time, it's only a ten-minute drive."

Lockleer? "Oh, do you mean Denny?"

"She prefers I call her Mrs. Lockleer," Joe says, with the slightest begrudging hint in his voice. "I'm to standby tomorrow until your day is complete; then, I'll bring you home."

"Oh...well, okay then. I'm glad one of us is on top of my schedule."

Joe nods. "In case Mrs. Lockleer didn't give you my number." Joe reaches into his inside coat pocket and retrieves a sleek black business card. "Call me anytime if you need anything."

I take the card then wiggle it between my fingers. "Thank you, Joe."

He ducks his head in a show of *you're welcome.* Then, he steps forward to call the elevator for me with the push of a button. "Two-nine-six-four-eight-three at the top, don't forget," he says as I step into the elevator door. As soon as the doors close, I'm propelled upwards automatically.

This is fancier than I expected. Maybe I'm still having trouble wrapping my head around Dex's wealth. Why wouldn't a billionaire have a penthouse in the heart of Miami with private access elevators? I was always impressed with Dex's house in Las Vegas. I didn't realize that was technically slumming it for him.

Dex insisted we live at the condo until he has a chance to find our dream home. He apologized for it being a bit "cozy," but he gifted the Hessler Estate to Denny. I was slightly disappointed to know that Dex wouldn't be living in his childhood home. A little piece of history lost. But he doesn't seem bothered.

After I put in the elevator code and the doors open to the main living room, I realize that Dex needs a dictionary, because he outrageously misused the word "cozy."

Maybe a four-thousand-square-foot penthouse suite *seems* modest and cozy in comparison to the Hessler Estate, which I'm mentally equating to the lifestyle visuals we get on Keeping Up with the Kardashians. But the condo is far from cozy and meager, which is how Dex described it. My footsteps echo as I walk through the main entry. That's how tall the ceilings are. Every piece of décor looks like it belongs in a museum. So much so, I don't want to touch anything. The furniture is oversized, almost triple the size of a normal couch or coffee table, yet it still looks doll-sized in the large open spaces.

Even Dex's bed looks larger than a California King. It's like a giant resides here. The bed, framed with a simple leather headboard and footboard is set on a platform in the middle of the room, facing an electric fireplace. I don't see any fish tanks so far, which makes sense. Dex is never here enough to maintain them. I suppose all that has changed now.

This is my new home...which is empty as can be.

I kill an hour by taking a bath in the massive tub. A tub mom would appreciate. I rummage in the pantry and fully-stocked fridge to find some crackers, cheese, and deli meats. There's a wine rack stocked with fancy red bottles but none of that sounds appealing. Instead, I settle on seltzer water. And finally, after watching a few episodes of mindless sitcom reruns on a TV so large it feels like I'm front row at a movie theatre, I break down and call Dex. I know he's at a meeting, but it's nearly ten. Surely my early bird husband is getting ready for bed by now.

He answers on the first ring.

"Oh hey, Trouble. Your ears must be burning because I was just telling Emmett here about my beautiful new purply-haired bride."

"Purply-haired?" I laugh. "You're drunk."

"Hardly. I *am* however, having drinks, trying to close a bitch of a deal." There's a low hum of chatter wherever he is. Sounds like a restaurant. "But Emmett is a stubborn ass," Dex adds in a comically loud whisper.

I laugh. "Careful. I'm willing to bet your friend heard that."

"I meant for him to," Dex says returning to his normal voice. "He won't agree to my idea until I promise him my bleeding heart on a platter."

"*Exaggeration*," a male voice in the background says.

"What deal?" I ask, nonchalantly.

Dex laughs. A rich, grumbly laugh. The one that used to make my stomach flit with nerves. It's bizarre he's mine. I can listen to that laugh whenever I want. I can tell him how much I want him. It's impossible for Dex to offer up his heart in this deal because it's already mine. "Are you asking to be polite, or are you genuinely interested?"

"Mostly to be polite but I promise I'll listen to every single word."

"Emmett's dad owns Visionary Records label. He's an executive there and right now they work with some of the top world artists. I want some of his roster to make scheduled appearances on Luxe Adventure's cruises. We have some Hollywood A-listers but I'm trying to recruit from the music industry. Wouldn't it be cool to spot your favorite Grammy winner on a cruise?"

I shrug. "They're just people. I don't know if I'd buy a cruise for a celebrity spotting. I'd spend every last dime I had on a cruise if my favorite musician would serenade me for a week straight though."

"What?" Dex asks.

"I don't like big concerts. As much as I love to see the hyped-up world tours, I can't stand having to watch the performance with a slight lag on the jumbotron. Bless Taylor Swift's soul for putting that performance on TV. I don't want to spend my life savings watching an ant in a sparkly leotard from 100 yards away. Now, if she was performing on a cruise, it'd feel so much more intimate...a once in a lifetime experience. I'd pay top dollar for that."

"Once in a lifetime..." Dex mutters. "Baby, I'm putting you on speaker. Say all that again."

I awkwardly repeat myself and when I'm finished Dex drops his voice to a murmur. "We'd call it 'Once in a Lifetime,' Emmett. A concert cruise. What do you think? One headliner per cruise and five to six supporting acts. Each a unique set."

"Exactly. We'd have to play on scarcity," Emmett says. "Create some buzz with surprise performance reveals. Then preorders. Once the tickets are gone, they're gone."

"Could you get Shaylin?" Dex asks.

I'm so glad they can't see my eyes bulge in surprise. Shaylin is the world's darling pop princess and my shameless girl crush. She bought a micro pig and named it Piggie Smalls, aka The Notorious P.I.G., so basically, we're soulmates.

"Are you kidding? She's on her world tour. She's basically scheduled back-to-back for three years straight."

"We can't get her for a week? Cancel a couple shows next year? I'll pay her quadruple what she'd miss out on ticket revenue," Dex pleads. "We need a major name for this to work—"

"Dex, she's also a billionaire. Money isn't much of a motivator," Emmett explains.

"Guardian," I say. They don't hear me the first time as they start throwing out terminology I don't understand about investments and profit margins. I clear my throat again. "What about that charity called *Guardian*?"

"What, baby?" Dex asks.

"Yeah, baby, what was that?" Emmett asks, mocking Dex. I distinctly hear a loud thud and Emmett groans, "*Ow.*"

I snicker before elaborating. "She's really big on social media about the charity she supports called Guardian, which fights sex trafficking and domestic violence. They fund all sorts of things from legal guidance, safe houses, relocation, witness protection—everything. Every birthday, or every time she hits the number one album release, her only wish is for people to donate to Guardian. She's so passionate about it. What if you donated half of the cruise revenue to the charity? I bet she'd do it."

"Half?" Emmett squalls.

"Half would bankrupt the cruise," Dex explains to me. "But a hefty percentage could work. Plus, that's a huge PR move for her..."

"So, take a personal loss to launch the concept," Emmett adds. "Then you attract more headliners who are trying to follow in her footsteps."

"Exactly."

"That's actually fucking brilliant. Why didn't we think of that?"

"Because my wife is smarter than both of us combined," Dex says, his tone full of pride. In reality, it's probably because they have never had to choose between a month's worth of groceries or sitting in the nosebleeds at a concert. It's painful when you have to pinch every penny just to be shafted with the bare minimum. I wish the world was paid based on effort and hard work, not luck and connections.

"It was just an idea, Dex."

"Lennox," Dex says, the background noise settling and his voice crystal clear. He must've taken me off speakerphone. "When you have wealth like we do, ideas become real change. Don't forget that. You have the power to make big moves now."

I smirk. "I thought you wanted me to sit here and look pretty. I'm just your muse."

"Please excuse me while I pull my foot out of my mouth. I shouldn't have said that. If you want to take on some responsibility—"

I laugh. "I'm one grad degree and about ten years of corporate experience away from calling the shots. Let's not get ahead of ourselves."

"Hey," he practically barks. "Mrs. Hessler, I'm going to need you to start trusting yourself as much as I do. Your heart makes you regal, and even in your white tank top and pink pajama shorts, you look like royalty to me. We're all listening. Speak up whenever you want to."

"Dex, thank you. That is so sweet and...wait"—I glance down at my pajamas—"how'd you know what I'm wearing?"

"Security app sends me an alert every time someone passes the motion sensors. I'm surprised you went for sparkling water, by the way. In three years of knowing you, I've never once seen you drink Perrier. There's beer in the beverage fridge."

"The beverage fridge?" I ask.

"It has more specific temperature controls. It's underneath the bar in the living room where you set your purse."

I turn down my lips and nod. "I'm not really feeling the stalker vibes right now," I say sarcastically. "Maybe you could turn it up a notch."

"Sassy," Dex murmurs. "I had them installed when I moved to Vegas. It's for security with the staff. I'll have them taken down now that we're moving in."

"Watch me all you want. I have nothing to hide. I'm just surprised you didn't call."

"I'm sorry." He's quiet for so long, I know I made him feel bad. "I was in back-to-back meetings and I just..."

"Oh, hey, I'm messing with you. I'm not trying to be clingy."

"Please be clingy," Dex says simply. "Lets me know you're thinking of me, which is nice because I'm always thinking of you. Len...I'm sorry. I promised I'd be there and I'm not there. Clearly, I'm under the Hessler curse."

"It's fine," I assure him. But it's not lost on me that we're already starting this marriage with broken promises. Dex said he'd be here, and he's not. I said I'm okay with it... Am I? "I understand you have to work. It's okay."

Still, Dad's warning circulates in my mind. He told me good businessmen know how to say and do whatever it takes to get a deal done. Am I simply a deal to Dex? If he wanted to be here, he could be. His attention is where he feels it's most needed right now.

"I'll make it up to you," he hurries out. "I'll wrap up here and call you when I get home."

"No need. I think I'm going to get some sleep. I'll see you in the morning after that interview?"

"Interview?"

"Denny set something up, I guess."

Dex grumbles underneath his breath. "Did she send you talking points?"

"No. But she's meeting me there first to prep me."

"Please be careful. Reporters can be a little invasive. Believe me, I've been burnt a time or two. Just stick to whatever Denny advises."

"Okay, got it." I blow out a deep breath. "I have to admit, it would've been nice to have a day to shop. Now, I'm going to have to show up to this thing in a sundress." I think back to the time I met Dottie and the outfit she wore. Elegant and professional. I'm going to look laughable in an outfit suited for a low-budget backyard barbeque.

"It's probably just the interview portion. The photo shoot is usually scheduled separately. I'll double-check with Denny. I don't like her putting things on your schedule without running it by me first."

"Uh oh... Are my babysitters about to fight?"

"Hilarious. But by the way, what's wrong with a sundress?"

"It's too casual. My most sophisticated sundress is light blue with feather outlines on it. Basically, I'll look about as professional as a puppy."

He laughs. "For the record, I like feathers, I like sundresses, and I really like when you're just you."

"Good to know." I smile into the phone. "Goodnight, Mr. Hessler."

"Goodnight, wife."

CHAPTER 23

Lennox

I've never seen such a bland room in my life. Dottie's office looks like it was a blank coloring page, and the artist had exactly one crayon in their possession—taupe. A Martha Stewart-style pantsuit in beige would be the perfect camouflage in here. Throw one on and I could disappear leaning against the wall or lying down on the area rug. No wonder she loved red nail polish. It was the only pop of color she had in her office—which I'm guessing was more of a second home than a place of work.

The office still smells like her, though, the fancy French perfume which I love. I can sniff it out like a bloodhound. It makes me feel close to her. I very badly wish she was here. Although, if she was...I probably wouldn't be. Yet, if I had to choose, I'd rather Dex have his grandma right now. Someone who could guide him and make him feel secure with all this change.

All he has is me.

And I most definitely don't belong in this luxury CEO office in my bright blue sundress, hiding my chipped toenail polish inside ballet flats that are worn on the sole, with fake diamond studs in my ears. That's it. Today, after work, Joe and I are going to find some upscale boutique or another and do some damage. I will demolish their section with the professional blouses and slacks. I don't particularly care about my reputation. I just so badly don't want to embarrass Dex.

I kick off my shoes and pace back and forth in front of the coffee table in the sitting area, loving the feel of the plush office rug against my feet. There's a flattened path where I'm treading, but it's not from my footsteps. This wear is from years of footsteps in the same pattern. Meaning...Dottie paced where I'm now pacing. I smile to myself.

"You're looking down on me either extremely pleased or wildly horrified, aren't you?" I ask out loud. "I hope that you're happy Dex chose me. I promise you, Dottie, I'll take good care of him. I love him." I wave my hand around the office, gesturing to the luxury finishings. "Not for any of this, but I fell for him because..." Actually, I don't know how to finish my sentence. I want to say it's because Dex is kind and sweet to me. But so was Alan. No, with Dex, it just feels like fate. Like I had no say in the matter. We met, and then my entire romantic life became a game of resisting fate and then finally succumbing to it.

About two minutes into pacing, a small glint catches the corner of my eye. Something metal, reflecting off the sunlight pouring in from the large floor-to-ceiling windows. My curiosity pulls me to the large built-ins behind Dottie's desk, the wood cabinetry matching the finish of her desk perfectly. Clearly a set. Everything is blended so carefully I almost miss the ivory-colored keepsake box tucked against the far edge of the middle shelf. The little silver clasp must be what caught my attention. I try to undo it, but it's locked. I turn away, deciding it's not my business, but then there's a loud thud, and suddenly, there's a pile of envelopes scattered around my feet. *Oh, shit.*

I must've pulled the box too close to the edge, tinkering with the clasp. It busted open when it fell, spilling what looks like at least a hundred letters. "*Dammit,*" I grumble, dropping to my knees to pick up the contents. I pick up the box, set it upright, and begin to replace the letters, but when I come across a Polaroid mixed in with the letters, I gasp out loud, throwing my hand over my heart.

It's the very same Polaroid I gave Dottie three years ago. Except it's not just half. It's been taped together...the missing piece is a twenty-something-looking Jacob staring back at the camera, a big smile on his face.

That's not the surprising part. *I knew it.* The look in her eye when I spoke about Jacob. I tried to tell Dex they were in love. I am not remotely shocked that it's Dottie and Jacob in this picture together, clearly lovers in their special spot, legs dangling off a dock, a glimpse of a large, white gazebo on Jacob's half. That all makes perfect sense.

What shocks me is that twenty-some-year-old Jacob looks unsettlingly identical to my husband—

"Holy shit," I murmur as the realization washes over me. "*Holy actual shit.*"

"Everything okay?" A woman's voice from the door startles the life out of me. I quickly flip over the pictures, trying to hide my newfound secret as if this strange woman at the door has any clue what I just—might've—discovered.

The red-headed creeper woman darts across the office and drops to her knees, collecting the letters in small piles, completely disinterested in their contents. "I'm so sorry I startled you," she says. "The door was cracked open and Mrs. Lockleer said you'd be expecting me."

She must think she scared me and caused me to drop the box and make this mess. "No problem." I scramble to collect more letters, but she's faster. Already having done most of the work, she places the neat piles of envelopes back in the box. She proceeds to gently close the lid before setting it on the desk.

She holds out her hand and says, "I'm Katherine—or preferably Kat—Tearney, journalist for Peak Publications."

As I shake her hand, I glance to the open door. *Where the hell is Denny?* "Lennox Mitchell. Nice to meet you."

"Mitchell, not Hessler?" she asks as she cocks her head to the side.

"I just got married last week. It was sudden and I haven't had time to start the name change process."

She unsubtly glances at my stomach. "Yeah, I would've expected a huge reception for a Hessler wedding. Why the rush and secrecy?" she asks with a sly smile and a wink. There's a glaring alarm going off in my head. *Don't say too much.*

I look around the office. "There'll be time to celebrate later. Our family is enduring a painful loss."

Kat's buggy green eyes relax as she nods. "Right, I'm so sorry for your loss. You and Dottie must've been very close if she chose you as her successor." Kat scours my face. She must sense my apprehension because she adds, "I know it's not public knowledge yet. Mrs. Lockleer gave me the cliff notes for interview context. Dottie wanted a woman CEO in charge of Hessler Group, so she chose Dex's wife. I think that is a powerful statement for feminism."

Presumptuous on Denny's part. But still, that narrative sounds better than, *"I literally have no clue why Dottie Hessler would risk her entire company in the hands of an amateur like me."*

"Would you like to sit down?" I gesture to the cream-colored sofa opposite of me as I plant myself in the single high-backed chair.

Kat takes a seat and pulls out a recorder, placing it on the table. She has no pen, no paper. She merely crosses her legs and smiles at me expectantly. Her shoes must be a half-size too big because her heel keeps sliding out of her pointy stilettos every time she jiggles her foot.

"So, Ms. Mitchell—tell me about you. Where'd you get your education? What companies have you worked with before? What charities are you involved in? I tried to do some background research on LinkedIn, but I couldn't find your profile."

I wet my lips and gulp, buying time to calculate a dodgy response. "I um...I'm not big on LinkedIn. Most of my references are word of mouth." *Not technically a lie.*

She studies me for a while as she squints one eye. "You're uncomfortable," she finally states.

"Very."

Laughing, she breaks the ice. "Honestly, me, too. I hate these things. I like the writing aspect, but the interviews always make me uncomfortable. Everyone is so stiff and disingenuous. Do you even know what this interview is for?"

"Not a clue," I admit. "Denny—or, I guess Mrs. Lockleer as you know her—was supposed to meet me beforehand so I'd be better prepared for you."

Kat sucks in her lips. There's a loud *smack* as she releases them. "Clearly a miscommunication because when she purchased the feature, she said you'd requested it."

"I didn't request this interview."

"Ah. Must be PR scheming on your behalf," Kat says with a crooked smile. "Okay, let's approach this differently. Do you know much about Peak Publications?"

I shake my head. "I'm not really a magazine girl." The last time I read a magazine, CosmoGirl and Myspace were still relevant.

"Right, well, print media has dwindled. We own several digital publications." She lists off several websites that I'm not familiar with. But when she mentions BuzzLit my ears perk up.

"BuzzLit, as in the celebrity gossip feed?"

Her smile is clipped. "More or less. But that's not where we'll be featuring this interview. Our business publication, Elite, wants to feature a woman CEO as an inspirational story. That's what this interview is for."

I nod. "Okay, sure. That I can do. Although, I'm pretty new to the job so I'm not sure how much insight I can give you."

She leans forward and turns off the recorder. "Listen, Ms. Mitchell—"

"Lennox," I correct.

"Okay, Lennox. I have a boilerplate interview with all the perfect answers I can use. It'll say how humbled and thrilled you are to assume the role of CEO at Hessler Group and how you have all sorts of plans for growth and innovation, of course, lined with philanthropic motivation. Yada, yada." She smiles. "Don't stress about the interview. I'll make sure you come off looking fantastic. You'll get to sign off on the article prior to publishing. Most of the CEOs I interview don't even show up to these things. Their PR teams email me their responses and then they show up for about five minutes to the photo shoot. You've already been far more generous with your time than I expected."

"Okay, that sounds great, actually." I don't think I have a PR team, but I have Dex. Whatever she writes, I'll run it by him.

"Relieved?" she asks.

"Incredibly. I just moved across the country *yesterday*. My head is still spinning."

"Where were you prior?"

"Vegas. That's where I met Dex."

She lifts her thick, red eyebrows so high it looks like they might fly right off her head. "Now, that's an interesting story... consider me intrigued."

I laugh. "It's nothing like that. Dex was living in Vegas for the past three years. That's where we met."

"Ah, I love this. You're giving *Pretty Woman* vibes, especially with your purple hair. How'd you guys meet?" she asks, rubbing her hands together. She kicks off her shoes and tucks her feet underneath her thighs, sitting comfortably like a child would.

I squint one eye. "I'm going to pretend like you didn't just insinuate I'm a prostitute, but for the record, Dex was my scuba diving instructor. I actually didn't have the money to learn to dive and so he gave me lessons for free."

Clasping her hand over her mouth, Kat gasps into her palm. "I'm so sorry, I didn't mean *Pretty Woman* in that way. I just meant Dex Hessler has been on Forbes most eligible heirs for almost a decade. I'm glad to see he ended up with someone with a little... pizazz. You seem far more interesting than the Stepford Wives robot drone we all assumed he'd marry. You know the type—slim, perfectly curled hair, delivers exactly two and a half children, maybe gardens a bit."

I smile, growing a little more comfortable at her feisty nonchalance. "Gardening isn't my strength."

"So, friend to friend, what's the secret? How do I land a billionaire because early retirement is calling my name."

I laugh. "My relationship with Dex wasn't strategic. We knew each other for years. I didn't even know who he really was. I only found out last week about his wealth."

"What? How did you not know who Dex Hessler is? He's literally royalty in Miami."

"He doesn't act like it. He was pretty lowkey in Las Vegas. All I knew is he was so passionate about diving and teaching. He makes me laugh. I'm never not smiling around him. It's why I fell for him."

"Not to mention, he's pretty fucking hot."

I smirk. "Also, that."

"Is he packing?" she asks, snorting in laughter at her own question. "Please tell me he has a tiny penis because he can't be that hot, rich, and have a giant shlong. God isn't *that* generous."

"Just between friends, right?"

She laughs. "Obviously, the word 'shlong' has no place on a business editorial."

"Yeah, his dick is magical."

We both break out in laughter. Actually, I'm glad Denny isn't here. She has a way of railroading conversations. Kat's easy to talk to, and I can tell she's even less interested in this business interview than I am.

"Are you into breakfast tacos?" Kat asks.

"Only on days that end in 'y,'" I reply with a big smile.

"I know a place that serves the best chorizo tacos and spiked horchata. Want to ditch this stuffy office and grab a bite? My treat?"

Right on cue, my stomach rumbles. "Yeah, that sounds great. Do you want me to call my driver to take us? He's on standby." My jaw drops. "Wow, that sounded pretentious."

Kat lets out a deep belly laugh. "Sure did."

I hang my head. "Okay, honestly? I'm very new to being rich. So far, I'm not loving it. It's a lot of coordination to do just regular stuff. Last week I had a beat-up piece of shit Honda. This week, I have a driver and an SUV with blackout, bulletproof windows. I already miss normalcy."

Kat smiles. "Lucky for you, I'm parked right out front, and while I drive a Ford, not a Honda, it is most definitely a piece of shit. You should feel right at home."

I laugh. "Great. Thank you."

She pats her thighs before she stands. "All right, let's go."

I return her smile, feeling relieved. And here I thought it was going to be difficult to make friends in Miami.

CHAPTER 24

Dex

Present Day

Miami

Memories of Grandma flash through my mind as the plane touches down on the tarmac. She was always alone. Even before Grandpa's health declined, every memory I have of her is by herself. There was always a business trip or a pressing matter. He was skilled at finding an excuse to avoid spending time with his wife and family. I think he regretted it after Mom passed away, but there was no time to rectify anything. By then, Grandma had found comfort in self-sufficiency. She stopped wanting his attention. Grandma didn't check on Grandpa's schedule when she arranged trips, parties, or events. She just lived her life regardless of whether Grandpa wanted to be a part of it or not.

I never really pictured getting married, but I know I wouldn't want my wife to have the small touch of sadness in her eyes that Grandma did. Except it seems I'm following in my grandpa's exact footsteps.

Lennox has spent an entire week in Miami by herself. My very first big act as her husband was asking her to meet me at our new home and then basically abandoning her to navigate on her own. Crisis after crisis came up. Every time I made arrangements to get me back to Miami, something else popped up.

First, it was flying to L.A. to loop Emmett into my new

business idea. Luxe Adventure took a major hit this quarter. We're going to have to retire a ship if it doesn't start turning a profit soon. That also would entail letting go of about ten percent of our workforce. Not ideal. So, that agenda was necessary. Next, after three cancellations back-to-back of one of our most prominent port of calls, I had to fly out to the Caribbean to untangle egregiously rising port fees. Further investment can only buy me so much time. Now, we have at least thirty itineraries to rearrange, and I need marketing to package this as an upgrade versus a change in schedule to avoid losing even more revenue.

It's always fires. Sometimes I envy the publicly owned companies who have a team of shareholders and stakeholders to make these decisions together. Privately owned status gives me all the control...and all the burden.

"Thank you, Rhodes. See you next time," I say to my pilot, Art Jones, as I descend from the jet.

"Good evening, Sir. Looking forward to meeting the missus next trip."

I nod, remembering the plans I mentioned to Jones on our way to Los Angeles to meet Emmett. I have every intention of taking a week off before the end of the year and treating Lennox to an actual honeymoon.

I hustle to my transportation. Joe stands dutifully next to the passenger door. "Welcome home, Mr. Hessler."

I smirk at him. "Really? We're back to this 'Mr. Hessler' bullshit?"

He laughs. "Force of habit. Welcome home, Dex."

"That's better."

He glances over my shoulder to the stairs where the pilot set my luggage. "Is that your only bag?"

"Yes. A lot of last-minute trips, I've been washing and wearing the same outfit for a week. God, it's good to be home."

Joe hustles to the stairs to grab my luggage. Once he pops it into the trunk, he asks, "What time should I retrieve you for the office tomorrow?"

"No need. I'm going to take tomorrow off. Spend a long weekend with my wife."

"Good idea," Joe says as I climb into the back seat. "She's having a rough day. I think she'll be happy to see you."

He shuts the car door behind me before I can ask him what he means. And as soon as I pull out my phone, I don't need to. An email from my PR team with the subject line: *Crisis Management Action Plan*, clarifies why Lennox is having a bad day.

The email contains a link to a BuzzLit article that I *know* I don't want to read. It's the trashiest, sleaziest bullshit gossip publication in the market today. Usually, their interest is in major celebrity scandals. Cheaters are their bread and butter. But I've been on flights and in meetings with men in suits for four days straight. Even if news of my recent marriage is circulating, no way they have ammo already to accuse me of infidelity.

I click on the link and nearly choke when I see the article title.

Hessler Group: from legacy to laughable. How one Las Vegas hussy swindled American royalty into handing over his billion-dollar fortune and his huge, magic schlong.

Hilarity brought to you by Kat Tearney

Fucking Kat.

I don't even need to read the article to guess how baseless and cruel her feature is. This woman's job is humiliating every poor, unsuspecting sap she can get her hands on. She seems to think roasting people and spreading toxicity is a talent.

Her latest victim is apparently my wife, but how the hell did she get her hands on Lennox? Denny told me she arranged a cookie-cutter business interview for Lennox to be released after we announced her as CEO. She didn't mention BuzzLit, and she most certainly didn't mention Kat Tearney. I would've nipped that shit in the bud.

I click out of the article without reading it and open my contacts. Denny answers on the third ring.

"Dex. I've been trying to get ahold of you all day. It hasn't been going through."

Why do I highly doubt that? "Denny...start talking. Fast," I bite out. "What the fuck happened? I take it you saw the article?"

"I scheduled an interview with Business Elite. Not BuzzLit. I have no clue why Kat Tearney was sent. I would've never agreed to that. This is what I've been telling you, Dex. Sharks in the water. You can't trust anybody."

"Why didn't you run it by PR?"

"*I was trying to handle it.* What else am I good for?"

I sigh, hating the pleading tone in her voice. "I take it you read it in its entirety?"

"Burned right through my eyeballs. I hate a lot of reporters but Tearney takes the cake, you know? I don't know how she has such a huge fan base. She's the kind of woman that you just *know* has a coat made of real Dalmatian fur."

"How bad is it?" I ask, my eyes fixed out the window, watching traffic pass by. "I couldn't bring myself to read it." Roasting me is one thing. Going after my wife makes me feel a little murderous.

"The stuff they said about her is absolutely ridiculous. Just Kat up to her usual graceless bullshit. She toes that 'off-the-record' line like the fucking Riddler. People in the comments are already calling Kat out for her bitchy behavior."

"Okay. Then it'll blow over. I'll just have to do some damage control with the executive team. This isn't exactly the way I wanted them to find out about their new CEO."

"Do you want me to call a meeting?"

"No, I'll handle it. But anyway, where were you? You were supposed to be there with Lennox. Had you seen Kat walk through that door, you would've had the good sense to send her right out.

You left my wife high and dry when she needed you most. Help me make sense of that."

"I know..." She takes a few deep, steadying breaths as I wait for her excuse. "My mom passed the night before the interview. I, um...had some things to take care of."

That effectively shuts me up. The shock paralyzes me for a moment before I force myself to speak. "I'm very sorry for your loss, Denny. I had no idea. Why didn't you call me?"

"You know my mother and I were estranged. She had health issues, and her husband handled most of the arrangements; I needed some time to process because..." She sniffles heavily into the phone. "I didn't expect it to hit me so hard."

"Well, you just lost both of your moms in the span of a month."

"My family is gone." She cries silently into the phone, and there's nothing I can do. "I tried to call Jeff, but he didn't answer."

Jeff and Denny have been divorced for almost two decades. That's a long time, but I'd like to think he'd have at least some sort of empathy to comfort a friend in a time of need. Their divorce wasn't messy, to the best of my knowledge. She was also under the Hessler curse as a workaholic, and he grew sick of it. He made her choose...us or him. In hindsight, I wonder if she's happy with her choice.

"That's shitty of him."

"No, he's remarried. It was probably inappropriate for me to call."

"Denny..." I don't know what to say. I try to think of how she comforted me at Grandma's funeral. "Your family isn't gone. I'm here."

"Thank you," she breathes out, then clears her throat. "Anyway, back to the interview. I can call the PR team to do some damage control. Josie Rivers or Jay Prudence would love to do a rebuttal on anything Tearney writes. I'm still in New York City, going through some of my mother's things, but I can come back in the morning—"

"Denny. Stop. Don't worry about any of that right now. Lennox and I will figure it out."

"Okay, that sounds good. By the way, while most of that bullshit in the article was fictitious and exaggerated, there was one thing..."

"What?"

"How much do you know about your new father-in-law, Sam Mitchell?"

I met Mr. Mitchell a time or two in passing. Mostly just a wave when he stopped by Finn's house. Once, he came into the dive shop with Lennox. I know his sordid secret about trying to take his own life, not that I'd ever speak about it. "Not too much, yet. He's a nice guy."

"Did you know he's a white-collar felon? Unfortunately, of all Kat's allegations, that one has merit. Do you remember that huge embezzlement scandal with Seaguard Investments about ten years ago? They stole from their employee's pensions to pad some up-and-coming Silicon Valley investments, and it all tanked? They lost hundreds of millions."

"What does that have to do with Lennox's dad?"

"He signed the transfers, Dex. *He did it*. It's a miracle he's not in prison. It just doesn't look good that his daughter is now the CEO of Hessler Group. Kat made some snarly statements about the apple not falling far from the tree."

"Fuck her," I mutter into the phone. Feeling nauseous, I roll down the window, letting some air into the vehicle.

"It's obviously a stretch, but there are some comments... Um, how close is Lennox to her dad?"

"Very," I answer.

"Then tread with caution. If she read the article or anything online pertaining to that article...she's having a bad day."

I sigh, feeling my heart twist in my chest. Lennox has been alone all day. Plenty of time to cry in private. I bet I'll get home, and she'll pretend like she's perfectly okay, making a mental note to never rely on me. Had I come home when I said I was going to, none of this would've happened. "Denny, I'm going to take the weekend off, but if you need anything, call me. Take care and take as much time as you need. We'll be okay."

CHAPTER 25

Dex

My heart stops when I see the open suitcase on my bed. It's half empty, just some shorts and shirts folded and tucked into one side. A few pairs of Lennox's underwear are shoved into the mesh zippered compartment. To the right of the suitcase, there are two chargers with the cords neatly coiled resting beside her phone. No matter how much I investigate, I can't tell if she's in the middle of packing or unpacking.

Her phone lights up, and I can't help but see the notification flash across the screen. A preview of a text from Alan catches my eye.

Alan: It was good to talk. Thanks for calling.

My whole body tenses. I try to relax my jaw, but jealousy seeps into my blood, making me jump to the worst conclusions. We just need to have a simple conversation.

She's in the bathroom. I see the light under the door. I'm assuming the worst as I sit down on the bed and brace myself. *Did I already fuck this up?* One week... That's all it took to completely ruin the shot at happiness my grandma was trying to give me. I turn my back for a few days, and now she wants Alan again?

The pounding in my heart becomes painful as it accelerates. Beads of sweat pour down my forehead, and no matter how hard

I try to focus, the room starts to spin. *Fuck, fuck, fuck.* I press against my chest firmly with my palm as if I can hold my heart steady but it's no use. The sequence of events are as they always go.

I can't breathe. My hands are unsteady.

I can't support my weight and slump to the ground.

There's no use fighting it. I'm gasping for air on the ground, feebly waiting for it to pass.

"Dex?... *Oh my God, Dex.* Babe, can you hear me?"

She drops to the ground and scoops up my head, cradling it as best she can in her lap. The towel she's wearing untucks at the top and falls into my face. Lennox rips it away from my nose and mouth, exposing herself completely. I look up at the underside of her bare tits as she strokes the side of my face. She makes no moves to cover herself, unwilling to release me.

"Dex," Lennox says very calmly. "Are you feeling any pain in your left arm, neck, or shoulders?"

She thinks I'm having a heart attack. I shake my head. "Count..." I murmur. "Just count for me."

"What?" she asks. "No, here, listen...stay with me. You're safe. Are you hot or cold?"

"I don't know," I gasp.

She continues to stroke my cheek. "Think about it. How do my fingers feel? Cool or warm?"

"Warm," I answer.

"Yeah," she says. "I was just in a hot bath. I should feel warm. What do you smell?"

I focus on my senses one by one. Her thighs are smooth and soft. There are still a few water droplets on her legs, probably dripping from her wet hair. I nestle deeper into her lap. "Something sweet. Like candy."

"The Starburst I was eating. I had a whole log. It's probably molting out of my pores at this point."

I laugh. "Smells good on you." My breathing settles as my heartbeat slows. "Keep going."

She mops up the sweat on my forehead with the edge of the

towel. "What do you see?"

I smile as I look up. "Your nipples."

She chuckles. "How do they look from below?"

"Perfect." Relief spreads as the hot, anxious tension in my body subsides. I sit up and lean against the side of the bed. Lennox refastens her towel but stays seated, giving me space.

"Can I get you some water?" she asks.

"You know, I came home fully prepared to comfort *you*. But then I saw this." Using my thumb, I point over my shoulder to her laid-out suitcase. "I'm so sorry."

"For what?" she asks.

"For not being here. For not protecting you from all this bullshit... I was just informed about the article."

"I should've called you, but you were flying, and I didn't want to worry you."

"I don't care, baby. All I care about is how you're doing. Are you okay?"

Her eyes drop to the floor. "Mostly." When she looks up, she shows me a weak smile. "Honestly, I've been better."

"Oh, Len—"

"It's my fault. I fucked up. I carelessly told her everything, no idea she'd use it all against me. We were just chatting—girl talk. I had no idea she would... She seemed like—"

"A friend?" I ask. Lennox nods solemnly. "That's how they get you. Len, listen to me—"

She holds up her hands, stopping me. "No lecture needed, I promise. I will be extra careful moving forward. My lips are zipped unless—"

I yank her into my chest and hold her tightly, my forearm braced against the back of her shoulders. "Don't even go there. None of this is your fault," I whisper into her ear. "It's mine. *I'm sorry.* I should've been here to protect you. It won't happen again. Please don't leave me over this. I can fix it."

She pushes away from me, her face scrunched up in confusion. "What?"

Staring right at her open suitcase, I ask, "Were you going to say goodbye or just disappear in the night?"

Her eyes pop into big circles. "You thought I was leaving you? I ran out of clean underwear, Dex. I had to dig into my backup stash. I can't find the washing machine in this place."

"There isn't one. We just send laundry off with the housekeepers."

She rolls her eyes and lets out an exasperated grumble as she balls up her fists. "Okay, *enough*. Surely, this place has washer and dryer hookups somewhere. We're buying our own machines, Dex. I can't live like this. Having to be so reliant on everyone. I don't want anyone managing my schedule, I want to do my own laundry, and I want a car for fuck's sake. I don't want to call Joe every time I'm craving Taco Bell. Maybe all the convenience works for your schedule because you're actually working. But all I have going on is humiliating my family members in interviews, so I have plenty of time to do my own shopping."

"Okay...okay," I say. "Whatever you want. Just promise me you'll stay."

"Of course I will." She kisses my cheek. "But out of curiosity, why do you want me here if you're not going to be?"

I inhale deeply then release my breath in a loud exhale. "Fair point. Do you want to get dressed, and we can talk?"

"Let me drain the tub first," she says, rising to her feet.

"You didn't finish your bath?"

"No, I heard my husband collapse so I hopped right out mid-soak."

Standing up, I grab her hand, leading her back into the bathroom. The thick white foam is still coating the top of the tub, looking like a fresh layer of snow. There's bath salts and little bottles of oil lining the tub rim. Starburst wrappers are bunched into tiny balls and tucked into the corner of the tub. A beer, dripping from condensation, sits next to them.

"You really went all out, huh?"

She laughs. "I was hoping to just move into the tub forever, never having to face the world again. I'm so embarrassed."

I squeeze her hand. "It'll pass. No one's going to care about it tomorrow."

"I don't care what people think, Dex. What bothers me is how Kat made our marriage sound like it was some kind of money grab. I know this all fell into place in an unexpected way, and we've been on a giant friendship detour for the past few years, but...this is real to me. I want to be with *you*. If anything, your money and your company are a real pain in the ass right now. You don't believe any of that stuff she said about me, right?"

I hang my head and shake it. "Not a goddam thing," I say.

"And the stuff about my dad—"

"I don't believe that either," I assure her.

"It's true, though." She wraps her arms around herself, clutching her towel tightly. "In a way."

Crossing the space between us, I stand in front of her, rubbing the outside of her arms. "What happened?"

"It's so far over my head, my mom had to explain to me why so many lawyers and law enforcement were involved, tearing our house apart, asking for phone records, confiscating all our laptops. She said my dad's bosses were doing some shady shit. He found out they stole a lot of money from their clients and employees and lost it. Many families were going to be impacted, so he said that they should do the right thing and fess up. I guess declaring bankruptcy would help recover some funds. They all agreed...to his face. But when my dad went to give his statement to the SEC, his bosses pinned it all on him. They forged documents, put his name on secret accounts he didn't know about... They set him up. Even their lawyers were in on it. They created an iron-clad case, and no matter how much my dad told the truth, nobody believed him. A fall guy was easier than watching such a lucrative company crumble to pieces. I would've told you sooner, but I didn't think I would ever be called a criminal by association. Especially when my dad didn't do anything wrong. He was the good guy."

"Oh, Len. I know."

"To make matters worse, the company recovered. A few stocks went the right way. They invested in some big tech companies that had a great return on investment. Had my dad kept his mouth shut—"

"He'd be complicit," I say.

"And his life wouldn't have been ruined. I feel like over and over again, the universe teaches me that when it comes to money, assholes reign superior."

I give her a sheepish smile. "You think I'm an asshole?"

"No," she whispers. "You tricked me, Dex Hessler. You got me to fall for you well before I knew the stakes."

"I'm sorry, baby... About not preparing you. But making you fall for me was the smartest thing I ever did." I tap her nose, then make my way back to the tub. Dunking my hand in, I confirm it's still warm. "Join me?" I pull my shirt overhead, then unbuckle and drop my pants and boxers before kicking them to the side.

"I just got out and dry."

"Come on, Trouble," I singsong. "I missed you so much. Me and my magic schlong want to take a bath with you."

She breaks out in a cackle, then covers her eyes. "I did not say 'schlong,'" she grumbles.

Taking her hand, with her eyes still covered, I pull her towards the tub. Barely tugging at the top of her towel releases it to the ground. "But you did say magic, right?"

She opens her eyes and rolls them. "Is your ego asking?"

"Perhaps."

Using my shoulder as leverage, she steps over the ledge and settles into the warm water. Sinking down until her neck is covered, she moans appreciatively. Then, she scoots forward, making room for me behind her.

The water level rises to the brim with both of us seated, a mere inch away from spilling over. "Lean back." I trail kisses from her ear down her neck, nipping at her shoulder. "Thank you," I murmur against her skin.

"For what?"

"After business trips, I usually return to a house. This time, I'm returning to a home."

"You're returning home to a hot mess express of a wife who just humiliated you in the media. I gossiped like a schoolgirl about my boy toy to a fucking rat of a human being."

"Embarrassed me?" I ask, smirking into her neck. "I didn't actually read the article. What else is in there about me and my dick?"

"Nothing. Just that you're well-groomed and have long, thick fingers and know how to use them," she mumbles hurriedly.

I burst out laughing. "None of that is embarrassing for me. Flattering, actually."

"There's a forum on Reddit of women who say they'd be willing to—and I quote—'skull and crossbones emoji' me if it meant they'd have a chance with you."

"Hence the need for security."

"Dex—"

"Len, I'm not going to let anything happen to you. What do I need to do to make you feel safe?"

She turns her head so her lips are close to mine. I'm just grateful she's in my arms. Naked, wet, warm. All I want is to taste her lips, but the worry lines on her forehead are keeping me from claiming what's mine. "Just be here with me as much as you can. Help me do a good job at all this. I don't want to let you down."

"Okay." I run the back of my fingertips across her chest, grazing her nipple, then dipping below the water line down her stomach. Something primal in me takes over when I touch her like this. *Mine, mine, mine.* The beast in my chest chants. No one gets to hurt her. No one gets to touch her. I waited so fucking long... *She's mine.* "The article doesn't bother me, baby. But you did let me down."

"How?"

I wedge my hand between her thighs. "I'm your husband now. I take care of you." I slip my fingers between her center, and she moans. "You stay wet for me and *only* me."

Her breath quickens as I tease her entrance, just slipping the tip of my finger into her warmth.

"Next time you get into trouble, or you need help, you call me first. Not Finn, not your dad, and most fucking definitely not Alan." I slip my finger fully into her, and she groans. But the moment she registers my words she clamps her legs shut so hard she makes a wave in the water, causing it to slosh over the side.

"You read my texts?" she asks, her tone devoid of arousal and instead borderline pissed. She turns her torso so she can look me in the eye.

"No. A notification popped up on your phone right when I walked into the bedroom before..."

"What did it say?"

"It was from Alan, and he said he was glad you called him."

"And then you got so pissed you had a panic attack?" she asks in a whisper.

"No, Len. I have a lot of stress that causes panic attacks... more often than I like to admit. But yeah, I don't love that you called Alan today instead of me."

She buries her head in her hands. "I didn't want to distract you during your meeting. You said you had a lot of important issues to iron out. But so did I. Avery was the one who called to tell me about the article. She begged me not to read it and she was calling all her PR contacts in the industry to try and have it taken down. Finn was tasked with keeping my parents off the internet. The stuff they said about my dad was vile. I didn't want him to see it and get hurt. I got so many calls and text messages from friends who were offended I didn't tell them we were married or dating. I'm not just a prop, Dex. I have a life, too. I gave up my friends and family to come here and support you. Then, you weren't even here."

"I..." I can't finish my sentence because I have nothing reasonable to offer. I wasn't thinking about what Lennox left behind. My mind was fixed on where we were headed.

"And then I got a text from Alan who asked me to be honest

with him... He wanted to know if I had been cheating on him with you the entire time. He and I broke up and I married you not even a week later. Tell me, how does that look? I owed him an explanation, at least."

I promised myself I wouldn't feel bad for Pocket Protectors anymore. *But fuck.* "What did you tell him?"

"In a nutshell, I told him that while I was his, I was his alone. And when we broke up, I became yours *and yours alone.* But that doesn't mean I don't still care about who I hurt."

"Was being with Alan easier than being with me?"

"Yes," she says, spinning around, leaning back into my chest. "But I don't want easy. *I want you.* I want my whole heart feeling like it's going to explode every time you enter a room."

I laugh. "That sounds terrible."

"It's not so bad."

Now that she's relaxed, I go back to trailing kisses on her neck. "My grandpa worked incessantly. His dad was the same. I never actually knew my own dad. My mom got pregnant out of wedlock. Grandma told me after she passed away that my grandpa threatened to disinherit her if she married that man. I don't know what was so awful about my dad that my grandpa didn't want him to be part of our family...but at any rate, my mom was willing to leave the money behind to be with him."

"Then what happened?"

"When the threat didn't work, Grandpa offered my dad a check to disappear. He took it. I was curious about the amount. How much is enough to walk away from your kid, you know?"

Lennox bends her arm, reaching backward. She holds my cheek tightly in her hand. "That's awful."

"I want to be more like the men in your life and less like the men in mine. I want to be as loyal to my family as your dad is. I want to be as enamored with you as Finn is with Avery. Basically, I promise if you stick around, I'm going to do better. I think that was the whole point of Grandma leaving the company to someone else for a while. She didn't want me to focus on being a good CEO.

She wanted me to focus on being a good man. All I want is to be a good man to you." I press my hand against her stomach. "If you let me put some babies in here, I promise I'll be a good dad."

"Since when do you want kids?" she asks with a scoff. "I thought that was off the table. You always said you didn't want kids."

"When did I say that to you?" I ask.

"About five million times over the past few years." She squeezes my knee under the water.

"No, I asked, when did I say that *to you*?" I smile into her neck before tugging on a loose tendril of her hair. "Maybe I just always wanted my kids to come out with purple hair."

"You sure you graduated from Harvard? Did you miss the class where they explain how hair dye works?"

Reaching around her body, I playfully pinch her nipple. "Are you making fun of me?"

"A little."

I pinch harder, and she squirms. "Hmm, two things to address now."

"What do you mean?"

"Your sassy little mouth and the fact that you closed your legs on me." I bite down with pressure on her shoulder and she gasps. "You know how I feel about that."

CHAPTER 26

Lennox

I never thought a *suit* would be my type, but watching my husband all put together in his nice button-down, business slacks, and a matching tie kind of has my stomach flipping. I stare at him in the backseat of our ride, blinking heavily as a wave of desire rushes through me.

"What?" he asks, studying my face.

I flutter my eyelashes at him. "Nothing," I mumble.

He exhales and sets his phone aside. "Len, we'll get you a car. When Denny gets back, she'll call our usual dealer and have them bring some options over. And I know you don't like being chauffeured around, but I like to work on the commutes. Maybe it means I can get out of the office five minutes faster and home to you."

I place my hand on his thigh. "It's not a problem, Mr. Hessler."

He smirks. "You only call me that when you want rough sex."

"Look at you, reading between the lines this morning." My hand creeps up an inch higher.

Joe clears his throat from the front seat. "Sir, we're here. Right up front." I look out the window to see the grand entrance to the Hessler Group corporate headquarters. It looks more like a palace made from glass windows than a corporate office.

"Thanks, Joe," Dex says, "Throw the hazards on. We need a minute. Also, I'd recommend you close the partition now."

Laughing, Joe presses a button, and the partition automatically closes. When I asked Joe if we could switch from a limousine to a less ostentatious car, I wasn't expecting an upgrade. The outside of the SUV looks somewhat normal, but the inside of this luxury stretch Escalade looks like a swanky lounge. There are even swiveling trays that pull out to set up a laptop or tablet. I'm assuming it's so Dex can complete private meetings while he's traveling, but it bothers me his schedule is packed so tight that he can't just sit down and relax for a fifteen-minute commute. Every second of his day is accounted for.

"My insatiable, kinky wife, I thought I handled you thoroughly last night. At this point, I'm going to have to start bringing in mechanical support."

I laugh. "I guess happiness makes me horny." I kiss his cheek.

"As much as I'd love to pull your panties to the side and fuck you senseless in this car right now"—he turns his wrist—"I have a video conference in twelve minutes."

"I thought that meeting you're dragging me to isn't until ten-thirty."

He chuckles. "I'm not *dragging* you to anything. The weekly leadership meeting is technically the CEO's meeting. *Your meeting,* baby."

I roll my eyes. "Dex, everyone knows you're the one who's actually in charge. Don't patronize me."

Hooking his finger under my chin, he turns my face so he can hold my gaze. "Today, I'm announcing to the executive team that we're moving forward with the 'Once in a Lifetime' idea for Luxe Cruises. We're going to start in-house fundraising for a mega-marketing plan. Our CFO has already assessed the numbers, and if everything goes off without a hitch, this endeavor could save a division and a lot of jobs. I want you to wrap your head around that."

I raise my brow. "Around what?"

"This idea is going to save jobs, create opportunities, and benefit a lot of charities. Everything has a trickle effect. Not only can it change the industry, but ideas like this can also change a lot of people's lives for the better. *Your idea.*"

"Is it, though? Because I don't know how to navigate the business stuff. Just because I said a concert in the middle of the ocean would be cool doesn't make me a business mogul. This isn't my wheelhouse and I'm trying to be a help, not a hindrance. I honestly think it's best in these meetings that I sit back and let the professionals do their thing. They'll probably like me more if I don't get in the way."

"I don't care how you got here. You're here." Dex shakes his head. "Be loud. Lean in. Take your seat at the head of the table. I want the whole room to know when my wife speaks, it's time to sit down and listen. You have what most people in this industry don't. Better priorities. You have so much more potential than you realize. You know what Grandma used to tell me?"

"What?"

"You can teach numbers, but you can't teach heart." He touches his lips to mine. "You've already got all the stuff you need. The team is going to love you, I promise."

I hike up my new business pencil skirt and climb on Dex's lap.

"Woman," he says, looking at his watch again. "What'd I just say? Meeting in now eight minutes. I have to get to my office."

I stroke against his growing bulge. "Can you skip it?" I whisper-growl in my most seductive voice.

"No. It's with Peak Publications. A personal vendetta, if you will."

"What do you mean?"

His eyes narrow. "I don't take kindly to people fucking with my wife. I'm going to buy the company and then fire Kat. Then, I'm going to call up all my new publication partners and blackball her from the entire industry. When I'm done with Kat, she won't even be allowed to publish on a Reddit forum."

An uncomfortable pang flashes through my body. Yes, I'm furious. I was taken advantage of, manipulated, and bullied. The petty side of me wants revenge and to see her suffer. But what would that really get me? She hurt me. I hurt her. Then we're just all hurting... Not to mention, I made a promise to my dad.

"How much are you buying the company for?"

Dex raises his brows. "A substantial amount. Suddenly, you're interested in numbers?"

"I just want to know how much revenge is worth to you?"

He nods, wrapping his arms around me, then rubbing the small of my back. "Don't you want a man who defends you?"

I shake my head. "No, I want a man who tells me to rise above. I'm not interested in petty games. Let Kat spew her poison. Let the world judge and laugh. I realized after everything my dad went through, it's usually the most miserable, insecure people that have the loudest opinions and want the biggest say in other people's lives." I shake my head. "Let's not be those people. Let Kat learn her own lessons. It'll catch up to her one day and I want no part of it. I want bigger and better things than revenge."

"Such as?"

"A family. A future. Our happily ever after. I want Dottie to be proud of us."

His eyes shift down and to the left. For a moment, it's just the sound of our breathing and muted chatter outside the car window as Hessler Group employees make their way into the building. "You remind me so much of her," Dex finally says.

"Your grandma?"

Dex shakes his head. "My mom. What I remember of her, anyway." He touches my cheek, then my lips. "Okay, my sweet wife. What do you want me to do?"

"Don't buy Peak. Take the money and donate it to something that can help people. Let some good come out of all this."

Dex nods. "You got it. Pick a cause. I'll sign a check to whomever you want, baby."

I kiss his forehead before climbing off his lap.

"Wait, now that my next meeting is canceled..." He grips the bulge in his pants. "Come here."

Bridging my hips, I smooth out my skirt. "Well, now I have important work to do. I need to go research some charities before my next meeting."

He rolls his eyes. "It can wait."

I open the passenger door then wink over my shoulder. "Have your people call my people, Mr. Hessler. We'll try to pencil you in for this afternoon."

He's still chuckling as I exit the car.

☙ ❧

I almost forgot about Dottie's letters. Last week was such a shitstorm that the cream-colored box completely slipped my mind until I returned to her office—my new office—and saw the box sitting where I left it last Monday.

The mystery calls me. Dex...with Jacob's eyes. Could it be? I need a picture of Dex's mother. The snapshot of Dottie and Jacob together isn't enough. Of course, they were lovers...but did they produce a child? Is Dex a Hessler...or Hayes? And does he know? It's a delicate line to toe. I'm not sure if Dottie was keeping secrets from her family or if Dex is keeping secrets from me. There'd be no need. My love is not remotely conditional on Dex's last name. If I had it my way, Dex and I would've professed our feelings, dated for a while, then got married. I could picture us raising our children in his beautiful Vegas home. Meager to him, but still much too much for me. I'd love to invite my parents over for Sunday barbeques and open up the gate that separates Dex's yard from Finn's. That's my happily ever after. Me and my family. Everybody safe.

Looking at the clock, I have exactly twenty minutes before I'm needed in the grand conference room on the third floor of the campus. Dex's morning is filled with meetings and reports, but he promised he'd meet me there five minutes early.

With time to kill, I open the first letter on top of the pile.

I was expecting sweet love notes between long-lost friends and lovers. But the first few lines leave me speechless as I realize what a can of worms I've opened.

Dear Jacob,

This stack of letters is growing tall, and I'm worried I'll never find you in time to give them to you. Where in the world are you?

I hope from the bottom of my heart, you're fairing better than I am right now.

I'm struggling with forgiveness.

Harrison had an affair. Apparently, it was a few months after our wedding. More than anything, I'm numb. I wanted to be so angry at him for being unfaithful, but haven't I been, too? In matters of the heart, I'm just as much of a cheater as Harrison is. My mind is always on you. My heart, still yours.

I thought after some time with Harrison my feelings for you would fade. But it was the opposite. Now that Melody's here, I feel more tethered to you than ever before, even though I can't see you or touch you...you're more real to me than ever.

The woman Harrison slept with...he said it was simply physical. If you want to know the truth about it, we didn't even consummate our marriage until after Melody was born. He was so scared of a miscarriage. He barely let me walk on my own while I was pregnant with her. So here Harrison was, treating his pregnant wife like a princess while he worked out his primal urges with another woman.

But that's not all Harrison confessed to this morning. That affair produced a child to a mother who is not fit to be a mother.

Harrison's parents were furious. They begged me not to make a fuss. Their reputation as American royalty is far more important than actual lives, of course. Apparently, they handled it. From what I understand, the payout was substantial. They paid her to essentially disappear from our lives. Harrison's indiscretion erased with a hefty deposit.

With the scandal handled, I'm the only wildcard. I suppose I could ruin him if I wanted to, but what good would that do? Maybe I'm supposed to feel brokenhearted, but I suppose I'm not because my heart is safe and sound with you, wherever you are.

If I'm being honest...my mind is on the baby. From the timing, it'd be near Melody's age. Harrison wants nothing to do with the child...

That innocent little baby deserves a mother who cares and a father who protects it.

What life did we choose, Jacob? We thought we were giving Melody the life she deserved. We chose wrong. She deserved us...together. Parents who loved each other. Poor, happy, and madly in love. That's what we should've given our daughter.

See, when I told you I was struggling with forgiveness...it wasn't about Harrison. It was about me. That's why my life is so complicated, Jacob. It's because I'm living the wrong one.

And I don't know if I'll ever be able to forgive myself.

-Dottie

P.S. Love doesn't seem like a big enough word, but I love you. Always.

I re-read the letter two more times to make sure I didn't miss anything. My heart is racing as my brain connects the dots and fills in the half-drawn picture. Flipping through the letters, I'm frustrated to learn that Dottie didn't date any of these. All the envelopes are unmarked.

I open a few more and read manically, trying to gather more context—anything to contradict what I read first. But the rest of the letters are a little less scandalous. Some of the envelopes include Polaroids with captions. *Melody's first time at the zoo. Melody's first spelling bee. Melody's first car. Melody, six months pregnant.* Basically, this box is a memoir. Dottie trying to document parenthood and save a piece of his family for him. A snapshot of the life they were supposed to have together.

She never got a chance to send these. Jacob missed everything. He died never knowing how much she still loved him.

CHAPTER 27

Lennox

There are two minutes before my meeting is supposed to start and nobody is here in the conference room. Dex was supposed to meet me first, but I would not be surprised if his prior meeting ran late. I suppose I need to get used to him being tied up.

One pleasant surprise in this room is the large espresso machine resting on the built-in countertop and shelves. One of my many underappreciated talents is actually knowing how to work an espresso machine, thanks to my brief time as a barista. I'll admit, in a day and age where there's a Starbucks on every block, knowing how to work an espresso machine is a pretty useless skill, but finally, here is my moment to shine.

Maybe I can win over the board by making everyone a perfect latte. Except there's no milk... Okay, fine. Americano then.

I try to flick on the power switch, but it doesn't turn on. After toggling it on and off to no avail several more times, I contort my body, bending over the counter. My feet come off the ground as I try to examine the small slit between the back of the machine and the wall, in case it's come unplugged.

"That's really just for show," says a woman's voice from the meeting room entrance. Planting my sensible heels back on the ground and straightening my skirt, I turn to see a young, tan woman leaning against the doorway, her arms crossed. "I saw you through the window, and it looked like you were struggling. That machine is décor. It won't turn on for you. I just made a pot in the breakroom down the hall, though. You're more than welcome to partake."

She gives me a pitiful smile. Her thick, dark hair is braided neatly to the side. She's wearing a form-fitting navy business dress that accentuates her generous curves.

I point to the little espresso cups that are flipped over and lined neatly next to the machine. "A little deceiving. Why have cups here if you can't actually make coffee?"

She laughs. "I'd need a whole day to explain to you the pointless things we have to do at this office. Are you new here?"

"Yes. New and clueless, apparently." I cross the room with my hand outstretched. "I'm Lennox. Nice to meet you."

"I'm Spencer. I'm the coffee-copy girl."

I screw up my face in confusion. "The what?"

"The coffee-copy girl." She sighs. "I think it started off as a joke. But now I'm pretty sure it's on my actual personnel file. Some of the managers around here have a funny sense of humor."

"Being?"

"I'm sort of stuck in a forever internship. My freshman year, I took a paid internship as an office assistant. My job was to make copies. I'm graduating this coming spring, so a few months ago, I made my pitch for an official role. My manager, Casey gave me a fifty-cent an hour raise, then promoted me to copy *and* coffee girl. Super condescending."

I roll my eyes. "Yeah, I was warned that this entire office was filled with middle-aged men who know more about cigars than their jobs."

She chuckles. "Pretty accurate. There are a few exceptions..."

This woman's smile is genuine, though. Unlike with Kat, the hairs on the back of my neck are unbothered. I sense no danger here.

"Such as?"

"Well, the former CEO, Dottie Hessler, was incredible. I finally got the nerve to schedule a meeting with her. I was going to go above Casey's head and ask about getting a job on the marketing team."

"But you're still getting coffee? She didn't agree?"

Spencer drops her head. "She passed away a few weeks ago. My meeting was scheduled for next week, actually."

"Oh, I'm sorry."

She shrugs. "Just wasn't meant to be. I'm not worried about it at the moment. Right now, we're all mourning. If the office seems a little gloomy, that's why. Dottie will be sorely missed. She was the kind of CEO who would hold doors open for entry-level employees and actually ate in the lunch cafeteria with us. That was her thing. She always tried to be around and approachable."

I'm not remotely surprised to hear this about Dottie. "That's really nice."

"Yes, and I don't mean to make the leadership team sound awful. Casey's a douche, and unfortunately, I report to him. But the other department heads are great. I don't know who you report to, but most of them will do a monthly career mapping meeting with you. My advice for you here is to speak up and ask for what you want. There's a lot of opportunity to climb, and if they know you're hungry to grow, they'll help you. What department did you say you're in?"

After that article was released, I assumed everybody at the company already knew about me in the worst way, but I suppose not everybody subscribes to gossip media. Not to mention there was no picture with the article. "I report to Dex Hessler."

"Ah. Lucky." She winks. "Total dreamboat. He's fantastic eye candy. He used to never be here, but I've seen him at headquarters a handful of times since Mrs. Hessler passed. Actually, your boss is here today. I saw the entire exec team in some big meeting upstairs."

My stomach drops. "What time is it?"

"Ten-forty."

I grumble. "You said *upstairs*?"

"Yes. All the executive meetings are on the fourth floor."

"Shit. I need to be at that meeting. I thought it was the third floor." *I swear Dex said third. Dammit.*

"Oh, come on, I'll take you. Stairs are a little faster if you're late." She leads the way down the hall. After climbing the stairs at warp speed, and banking a sharp left, Spencer points to a large meeting room with windows for walls at the corner of the hallway. I can see Dex sitting at the head of the table with an empty chair beside him. *Fuck.* So much for good first impressions. The entire board and executive team are already seated, eyes fixed on a PowerPoint presentation projected on the board behind them.

"Thank you, Spencer," I say, moving toward the glass door.

"Wait, Lennox, may I ask you for a little favor?" she asks in a hurry.

"Sure."

"If you get a chance to talk to Mr. Hessler, would you mind putting in a good word for me? *Spencer Riley.* I think I'm going to give it a few months and then see if I can apply for the marketing team again. Casey would never approve a transfer. I'm the only one who makes his coffee right, apparently. So, I need his boss to sign off. It'd help to have a good reference."

I smile at her. "I like your odds."

Dex

I press my lips together, trying my best not to laugh as my poor wife sneaks in late to the leadership meeting. She pushes open the door slowly, so as not to interrupt our CFO, Casey. He's droning on about call center efficiency and how they've managed to increase our profit margins by a whole percent thanks to first-call resolution. Unfortunately for Lennox, the door needs a hearty coat of WD-40 and creaks miserably as she pushes against it.

With every tiny step she takes forward, the door wails. Eventually, she must decide, "fuck it," because she hurls the door open with gusto and scurries to the chair right next to me.

Casey continues talking, but now all eyes are fixed on Lennox.

"Sorry to interrupt, but may I have the room?" I ask.

Casey nods, abruptly ending the presentation no one was really paying attention to, and then takes a seat across the table.

"I'd like to introduce everyone to my wife, Lennox." There's a low murmur of awkward "hellos" and "welcomes."

Normally, Lennox approaches everything she does with what I'd call blind ferocity. Complete confidence even when she's ill-equipped. But right now, her knee is jiggling so hard she's shaking her chair. The only time I've seen her nervous like this is the first time she went scuba diving in the ocean. I place my hand on her leg under the table, gently squeezing and massaging until I feel her quad relax.

"Everyone in this room is aware of the complicated nature of my grandmother's intentions with the future of this company," I continue. "Lennox has graciously agreed to step into the role of CEO in the interim. I'll be in the role of president until she feels comfortable handing her shares back over."

I'm expecting smiles...maybe some encouraging nods, but as I look around the room, it's clear why Lennox is so nervous. We're met with scowls, pinched eyebrows, and shifted gazes. Reading a room is half my job, and every warning alarm is going off, telling me this is bad.

As something of a peace offering, I'm eager to brag about Lennox's quick cunning with the Luxe Adventure cruise solution. "Lennox, would you like to tell the team about your plans to reestablish Luxe Adventure?" I nudge her shoulder.

She clears her throat and leans forward like she's speaking into a mic on a witness stand. "No, thank you. It's probably best you explain."

Okay, so everyone is uncomfortable. It's normal with a shift in leadership. It'll be fine. I had the same fears after Grandma's funeral, and I wasn't sure how my new team felt about me.

"Obviously, this is completely confidential, and we'll follow up with more details, but Lennox inspired the idea of drawing in a new source of revenue by using our upcoming itineraries as ticketed concert experiences. We're partnering with some artists from Visionary Record Labels, and I'd love to see marketing concepts in A/B testing by—"

"We have an idea as well," Dean Walsh, Hessler Group's COO, says. "Sorry to interrupt, but if you don't mind, we all got together and found a loophole we wanted to run by you."

I raise my eyebrows. I'm not exactly the tyrannical type of leader, but since when does my team eagerly talk over me when I'm making an announcement for a new endeavor that I expect them to see through?

"Okay, go for it." I lean back in my seat. "Are you presenting?" I ask Dean.

Dean smooths his hands over the top of his hair. "Um," he says, glancing across the table, "It was kind of a group discovery. Does anybody else want to hop in?"

The room is silent, and now the nervous throat-clearing and awkward exchanges of looks are starting to irritate me.

"Somebody speak up...*now.*"

"Dean, you brought it up. Go ahead," Hank barks out. I'm also relieved that Hank, our most senior advisor, is in the room. He's the closest thing I have to a mentor. He was Grandpa's close advisor, then Grandma's...now mine.

"Hank, what's going on?" I ask.

He turns his attention to Lennox. "Mrs. Hessler, it is a pleasure to meet you. May I offer you the warmest welcome to Hessler Group. How incredibly rude of us not to begin with that." He glances around the table, throwing dirty looks like daggers at several advisors and executives. "Please understand that I have nothing to do with, nor want anything to do with the bullshit that Walsh is about to spew."

Another rumble of disapproving grunts and mumbles surfaces and by now my patience is completely gone. I slam my fist on the table in a fashion similar to my grandpa when he was agitated. "Get to it," I snap, making Lennox jump beside me.

Dean nervously blurts out, "We found a loophole. After we saw the um...article from BuzzLit and discovered you were married, we kind of figured based on the contents of the article that perhaps the newest Mrs. Hessler wouldn't feel she was the best fit for leadership at the company."

Lennox's eyes lift, a glint of irritation in the corner of her eye. Dean struck a nerve. She hasn't said a word thus far, but now she speaks up. "You don't even know me, and you're going to make assumptions about how I feel?"

Dean looks at me expectantly, but he must be confused as to where my loyalty lies.

"That article was outrageously exaggerated," I say calmly. "It exploited a very private conversation. Surely, you're not trying to ostracize my wife based on a pathetic gossip column."

"That's exactly what they're doing," Hank grumbles.

"Hank, please. You're the only one in disagreement." With a sharp exhale, Dean continues, "There's a clause in the company policy that if the stakeholders can prove illegal activity by the CEO within the company, we can dismiss them from their position. The majority shares will default to the next eligible Hessler heir..." He gestures to me with an open palm. "Hence, you."

"I don't know what you're accusing me of, but I haven't committed any crimes," Lennox says defensively.

"But your father has," another exec, Jensen adds. "It wouldn't be so farfetched. The apple not falling too far from the tree."

"What the hell did you just say?" Lennox's voice drops to an icy whisper.

I inhale and exhale, feeling my temper bubbling back up to the surface. Before I can speak, Dean hops in to clarify. "We're not suggesting Mrs. Hessler is already involved with any wrongdoings. Sorry for the misunderstanding," he says, shooting a nasty look at Jensen. Everyone is tense, fighting amongst themselves and apparently attempting to stage a coup against my family. "We're simply suggesting that if Mrs. Hessler would sign an affidavit admitting to something along the lines of embezzlement, bribery, any sort of fraud, with your status, she'd get a little slap on the wrist from the SEC, if that. No real consequences, and then it'd absolve the ownership issue we're having. You could take your place as CEO."

"She could stop embarrassing the company and risking all our jobs," Jensen adds.

My normally feisty, quick-with-a-rebuttal wife has her head hung and for the first time in my entire time knowing Lennox, I see her cry. A single tear drips down her cheek and she makes no move to remove it. I watch it cradle her cheek and fall onto the table, leaving a tiny splash mark. Another joins it. Then another. I clench my jaw as my stomach twists. The heat rises in my body.

"Jensen," I ask, "what's biting you in the ass right now?"

He shakes his head. "We've all worked really hard to get to where we are. We plan on retiring comfortably here. None of us want to see this company take a nosedive because of Dottie's lack of good judgment in her late age. We've all been thinking it since the reading of the will, and we're trying to protect you, Dex. This is a solution and nobody wants to see Mrs. Hessler hurt. But even with a record, she'll be fine. Unlike us, she'll never need to actually work again."

Jensen pulls out a manilla folder and passes it down person by person until it lands in front of me. "Here's one option. That's an admission for Mrs. Hessler to sign, saying she established an offshore account. Just a couple million dollars taken under accounting's nose and put into a private holding. All just staged. We can bury the documentation. No one outside this room has to know, but it'll serve the purpose of the necessary legalities for the transfer of ownership. We could be done with this today—"

"Enough," I interrupt. I glance over the document and I'm further enraged. Part of me was hoping this was some sort of twisted hazing and somebody was about to jump out and say "Just kidding," then proceed to give Lennox the proper welcome she deserves. But no. This document is boilerplate, and at the bottom...a line ready for her signature.

"You're fired," I say simply. Jensen's jaw drops.

"I...I..." he stammers.

I lift my eyes ensuring he sees the seriousness in my expression. "End of discussion. Leave my meeting. I'll let HR know you're stopping by for your severance arrangement."

"On what...what grounds?" he manages, looking around the room. But nobody wants to meet his gaze.

"Loyalty. It's something I require on my leadership team. You showed your hand; I'm showing mine. Get the fuck out, Jensen. Don't make me repeat myself. Find your hard-earned retirement at another company. It won't be here. Let me be explicitly clear with everyone in this room that I am a team with my wife. Disrespecting her is disrespecting me. I have zero tolerance for it."

After the shock wears off, Jensen rises and storms out of the room. I tuck the document back into the manilla folder, then lift it up and let it fall on the desk with a heavy thud. "Whose idea was this?" I ask. Nobody responds. Leaning back in my chair, I add, "I could just start firing you all one by one until somebody fesses up."

Hank clears his throat. "Dex, let's take a breath. You made your point. No need to go on the warpath. It was a senseless suggestion. Now we can move on, unless anybody else would like to make their opinion known?" He raises his brows and looks around the room.

There's a quiet knock at the door, and then it pushes open. The young woman who brought Lennox to the meeting room pokes her head through. "I am incredibly sorry to interrupt, but Mrs. Hessler, you just got a call from home. It's important." They exchange a glance, and the woman at the door pumps her eyebrows. "Extremely urgent matter. They need you right now."

What? What calls are Lennox getting at the office already? And who is this woman? As far as I know, Lennox doesn't have an assistant.

Obediently, Lennox rises, smoothing down her skirt. She looks around the room, then her eyes land on me. She gives me a tepid smile before turning her attention back to the leadership team. "Well, as much as I'd like to say it was nice meeting you all...I'm not a liar. Nor a criminal. Have a good day."

With that, she slips out of the room. I watch her disappear down the hallway through the glass walls. Her hips sway side to side as she power walks to keep up with the woman who freed her from the meeting. The way I'm watching her walk away reminds me of the bar the very night I asked Lennox to marry me.

She had no idea the shitstorm I was pulling her into. *Did I?*

I thought I'd go to my grave never seeing Lennox cry...

But marrying me was the thing to push her over the edge.

CHAPTER 28

Lennox

Spencer leads me silently down the hallway toward the elevators. I don't bother asking her what the home emergency is. I'm more than positive it was just an excuse. The elevator dings, and the door peels open. I step inside, and Spencer darts her gaze to the right, turning the toe-end of her stilettos inward. She's wearing the most earnest expression I've ever seen on another human being.

"So...you know how to find your office from here, right?" she asks, biting her bottom lip.

"Do you have somewhere to be?" I ask, leveling my stare.

"No, ma'am. Not particularly."

I nod over my shoulder. "I think I'm headed down to the cafeteria. Join me? My treat."

The doors start to close, and I have to kick out my foot to stop them. Spencer scuttles inside the elevator, and the minute the doors close, she blurts out, "I'm so sorry I called your husband man candy. I had no idea who you were. I would've never—"

I burst out in a relieved chuckle. "That's why you're acting so nervous? He is man candy. Thanks for noticing."

Spencer's eyes bulge. "You're not mad?"

"Not in the slightest...well, not at you anyway." I take in a deep breath, my lungs straining. It took every ounce of restraint not to pop off in the boardroom. I wanted to give each of those rich, arrogant bastards a piece of my mind, but I didn't want to dig a deeper hole and let Dex down. And anyway, he was just as livid for me. "How'd you know to come rescue me?"

Using her top teeth, she pulls on her bottom lip. "The breakroom on the fourth floor. The meeting rooms are soundproof, but there's a vent, and when it's open on both sides, you basically get a front-row seat to the action. My friend Cade and I are basically trauma-bonded because we have the worst bosses at the office. We were chatting in the breakroom when he told me who you were. Apparently, his boss Jensen mentioned something. Anyway, they were being so cruel to you over some stupid article. I couldn't stand you getting attacked like that for another minute. Plus, it sounded like Mr. Hessler was about to punch through a wall."

"Yeah...I suppose we'll be finding Cade another boss soon."

"I heard." She scoffs. "Good riddance. Jensen is..."

"An asshole?" I finish for her. "Yeah, I'm not the kind of CEO you can't say 'asshole' in front of."

She laughs. "How about prick? That's what I was going to say."

"Fine by me."

"Do you still want to go to the cafeteria?" Spencer asks, glancing at the number panel inside the nonmoving elevator.

"Yes," I answer simply. "I just don't know what floor it's on."

"Oh," she says, laughing before hitting the number one. It lights up a bright red. "First floor. Second floor is the mail room and copy center." She rolls her wrist. "Also known as my second home." Spencer points to the number three on the elevator. "Marketing directors and a few meeting rooms. Fourth floor, more meeting and education rooms. Fifth through tenth are cubicles and customer service. Starting at eleven are the executive offices... which is where you are, of course."

I blink at her. "I'm never going to remember all that."

She smiles. "I'll show you around later if you'd like?"

I touch the back of my hands underneath my eyes. "Does it look like I've been crying?"

Spencer holds out her hand, pausing just an inch away from my face. "May I?" I nod, and she immediately wipes under my right eye, cleaning up my makeup. "There you go. Good as new."

"How old are you, Spencer?" I ask as we reach the first floor, the elevator doors pulling back apart. She smooths down her neat dress and then runs her hands over her braid. "Twenty-two...in six months."

I raise a brow. "That was a weird way to say twenty-one." I follow her lead as she crosses the main lobby heading toward the back of the building where all the delicious smells are coming from. I lift my nose and sniff twice like a drug dog that caught a whiff of the good stuff. There's teriyaki somewhere in this building.

"I hate telling people I'm twenty-one. I know the impression that leaves. But I have great grades, I've never once been to work late, and I'm not some party girl. I'm engaged, actually." She wiggles her left hand in the air, but it's ringless.

"Are you missing something?" I ask.

"Oh, I meant it as a gesture. We're still picking one out." Her eyes drop down to her moving feet. "If I'm going to wear it forever, I just want it to be the right one."

I'm picking up on a weird vibe, so I take my best guess. "There's nothing shameful about humility. My dad proposed with a cheap ring, and then my parents upgraded when they could afford it. Married for over thirty years, now." I smile at her.

"Oh, it's not that. My fiancé actually has a great job. He's a junior partner at a big law firm."

"Ah, an older man."

She shrugs. "A little. We just haven't had time to really do any of the wedding stuff...or ring shop. He works nonstop."

I nod. "I'm becoming quite familiar with the notion."

We stop in front of the bustling cafeteria. I was expecting a little coffee shop and maybe a lunch line similar to my grade school. But this is unbelievable. It looks like the food court at the mall. There are about ten different cuisine options shoved into one corridor. My mouth is watering. All of my tastebuds are awoken... confused as all hell, but awake nonetheless.

"Spencer, I don't even know where to start. This is like a food festival."

She laughs. "The French bistro, you have to call ahead with your order, but everything else has short lines. What are you in the mood for?"

"Teriyaki," I answer.

"Ah, Fuji Mountain," she says, pointing to the back corner. "You can build your own hibachi. Come on."

She holds out her elbow like a hook, a giant smile on her face. Well, here it is, folks. My first official friend in Miami. And she's a chipper, twenty-one-year-old copy-coffee girl who reminds me so much of myself at twenty-one. Outside of the stable job and great grades, that is.

"Spencer, how about a fat raise and a new boss?" I ask, returning her smile. She blinks at me, looking dumbfounded. "Or would you prefer to stick with Casey?"

"Not even a little bit," she musters out.

"Good. Then from now on, you work directly for me. My executive assistant." I link my arm in hers. "Please don't leave my side. Your job is to make sure I don't do anything else stupid."

ଓ ଊ

After lunch with Spencer, I told her to go home early for the day. I spent the rest of the afternoon locked in my office, comforting myself with Dottie's letters. There are so many different stories. Her letters read like a stream of consciousness, like she was narrating her life to Jacob so he could have a piece of her.

Every picture containing a Polaroid is a treat. A little glimpse into memories almost lost. What would've happened if I never found this box? Who else would've been curious enough to open it? Would anyone else treasure the memories like I do?

One letter, in particular, eases the ache of my uncomfortable first day at Hessler Group and the obvious disapproval of the leadership team.

Dear Jacob,

If you could've seen the stares they were giving me today, I bet you would've whisked me right out of this place. Maybe you would've thrown a few punches on our way out.

It's official. I was named the CEO of Hessler Group today, and one thing is abundantly clear: nobody wants me here.

I'm in over my head. My responsibilities are manageable enough. I've been carrying the load for Harrison behind the scenes for so long, not much with this business is a surprise. But winning over Harrison's team is a different story. They didn't even want to give me the keys to my new office at first.

Maintenance was convinced I showed up at the office to spy on my husband, wanting access to his personal space behind his back. I don't know how to explain that Harrison's drinking has officially consumed him. He can barely peel himself out of that armchair of his. His drinking was always excessive, but lately, it's clear he is incapable of running his own company.

We can't trust anyone else to take on this responsibility. It took me decades to earn Harrison's parents' trust. I suppose naming me as their successor should feel like some sort of accomplishment, but sitting here in this big, grim office, I feel like a shell of myself.

I daydream about the gazebo. Daisies in my hair. The very first time you told me you loved me. And the day you left and told me you were letting us go so Melody could be raised by a man capable of giving her all the things you couldn't.

In my daydreams, I rewrite the story. You kiss me on the forehead and tell me this rich suitor is my chance at a happily ever after. Instead of agreeing, I plant my feet, grip your arm, and scream until you promise to stay. Maybe we'd never own a home. We'd just be nomads, port to port, as you scramble up odd jobs here and there on the boats. One day, you teach us to swim...

And right now, instead of me being alone in this empty office, we'd be together.

I clutch the letter tightly to my chest. Perhaps I should feel guilty that Dottie's bad first day brings me comfort. But it's nice to know I'm not alone. I have no idea what I was expecting in that board meeting. How would I feel if I was in their shoes? Maybe I'd be doubting my own competency as well. But the leadership team is missing the big picture. My only role is loyalty...to Dex. I'll be stellar at that.

There's a firm knock on my office door. Based on the tall silhouette visible through the frosted glass door, I know it's my husband.

"Come in," I call out.

The door handle jiggles. "It's locked," Dex says back.

Oh, right. I uncross my legs and pick myself up from the floor by the coffee table. Once I open the door, Dex's eyes drop to my bare feet. "Is this office now shoes optional?" He smiles his sweetest, sheepish smile. It almost looks apologetic. But what the hell would Dex have to apologize for?

"Only for my friends," I reply.

Moving past me, he makes a big deal out of stepping out of his nice business loafers and kicking them to the side. "No shoes it is." Dex makes a beeline to the cupboard behind the desk. He retrieves a crystal decanter of amber liquid and two matching glasses. Looking over his shoulder, he raises an eyebrow. "No protests? This is brandy."

"After today, I think I'll try a stiff drink."

He sighs heavily as he fills both glasses, one more full than the other. After joining me on the small sofa, he hands me the smaller one. "Take a little swig and let it sit on your tongue for a moment. Once you swallow, immediately exhale."

I follow his instructions, taking a generous sip. As I breathe out, the bitter burn of the liquid seems to dissipate with my breath. "I'd give you crap about mansplaining how to drink bourbon, but that actually helped."

Dex undoes the top two buttons of his shirt and drapes his arm over my shoulder. Tucking in my knees, making myself as small as possible, I curl up against his side. "I've never had somebody hate me like that for simply existing. That sucked."

"I'm so sorry. I...what they asked for..." His jaw tenses. "Inexcusable."

"I mean, it kind of makes sense, though—"

"Lennox," Dex scolds. "Absolutely not."

"Just hear me out... What are you going to do? Fire everyone who is uncomfortable with me as the CEO? Hell, Dex. *I'm* uncomfortable with me as the CEO. What if your team quits on you?"

Dex shrugs. "Let them quit. Or I'll fire them one by one until I have a team who respects where my priorities lie."

Glancing up at his hazel eyes, I ask, "Being?"

"Everything else in my life can break and shatter...except us. You're my priority, Lennox. It's as simple as that. I'll get rid of anyone who threatens my happily ever after."

"Are you thinking with your heart or head?" I ask him, trailing my thumb along his tense jaw. "Because one of us has to be reasonable, and when it comes to you, I'm all heart, Dex."

"Glad to hear it," he says. "Forget about today. Let me handle the board. After I made an example out of Jensen, they are all walking around on eggshells. Clearly, they all would like to keep their jobs."

"Yeah, and it's fantastic to know that the people who report to me hate me." I scoff and take another swig of my drink, but this time, I forget to breathe, and the bitter burn catches me in the back of my throat.

"They don't hate you. They fear you. It's uncomfortable for them to realize I have loyalty to more than Hessler Group now. They are used to leaders who eat, sleep, and breathe the job. Maybe they don't like that, all of a sudden, I'd choose my wife over all of it."

"Really?" I lift my brows. "Because you've worked your whole life for this. And you've loved me for what, the two weeks we've been married?"

My eyes bulge as I realize it's the first time Dex and I have brought up the "L" word. It's obvious, but there's something so sacred about those words. In my mind, there'd be a parade, fireworks, and maybe a bed covered in rose petals the first time he said it.

Dex hooks his finger under my chin and guides my gaze to his. He presses his lips against mine softly, barely a touch. "Lennox, it's been so much longer than two weeks. I think I missed you before I even knew you. If I hadn't met you, I'm convinced I would've ended up alone. You have no idea the hold you have on me. I needed us to start as friends, otherwise, I would've called your power over me straight-up sorcery."

For a moment, I take it in silently. The words I wanted to hear for so long. It almost feels like a dream and I'm so emotional I could cry. In fact, if I tell Dex I feel the same, I might. Instead, I turn my cheek, nuzzling into his hand, and decide to cut the tension with my signature sarcasm.

"Eh, for all you know I cast a spell on you." I wink at him.

"Good. Keep it. I want to stay in love with you forever." When he kisses me again, this time he lingers, his warm, full lips grazing mine as he whispers, "I really do love you. I think I finally understand what that means now."

This is better than a parade. It's honest, raw intimacy. No

dramatic fireworks necessary. "Dex, I love—"

He presses his finger against my lips, stopping me midsentence. "Save it," he says. "I know how you feel. But save it, because I have a feeling one day soon, I'm going to really need to hear 'I love you' from you for the first time. Hold on to it for that moment, okay?"

I nod. "Okay. I will. Can we go home now? I need to leave this awful day behind me."

"Sure. I can cancel the rest of my day."

It's five o'clock in the evening what "rest of his day?" My husband works similarly to the way my dad used to—endlessly... relentlessly.

When he rises, Dex notices the open box of letters on the ground. "Doing some light reading?"

I wouldn't call anything about Dottie's letters light. I cry after every other one I read. I'd call it more along the lines of heart-wrenchingly tragic, laced with scandal. "Your grandma wrote letters to her friends," I say, deciding to ease him in. "Seemed like writing was her outlet." I look around the office. "This place wasn't always so easy for her. Do you want to read them with me?"

Dex sighs. "Does she write about my mom?"

"Sometimes. All wonderful things," I admit. Actually, I want Dex to piece this puzzle together for me. I still don't quite understand. I know Dex is Jacob's grandson, not Harrison's. But, does Dex know that? Did Harrison? The problem is I can't ask outright without feeling like I'm betraying Dottie. If Dex were to read these and find out himself...

"Maybe it can just be something between you and Grandma, then. When it comes to my mom, it's just easier to not reopen that wound."

I nod. "Okay, I understand. But if you ever change your mind. They'll be right here in this office..."

Standing, he holds his hand out to me. "Thank you." Then, he pulls me to my feet. "Are you hungry? Want to grab a bite?"

I grimace. "Yes. But I'm in a takeout kind of mood. No fancy, five-course billionaire meals or anything."

He laughs. "How about we go do some regular people stuff? There's a big hardware store up the way next to one of my favorite little hole-in-the-wall places to get real Cubanos. The chef doesn't speak more than twenty words of English. Completely authentic."

"Mmm," I moan. "That sounds delicious. But why'd you mention the hardware store?"

Dex smiles. "Let's go pick out a washer and dryer. What do you say?"

I flash him a wide smile and scrunch my nose. "I'd say that sounds like a perfect date night to me."

CHAPTER 29

Lennox

I've survived my first month at Hessler Group by making myself scarce. Here and there, I sign paperwork, but I seldom talk to anyone outside of Spencer. She guards my office door like a loyal rottweiler. We fill nine in the morning until one in the afternoon by talking about all the things I wish I could implement at Hessler Group. The numbers are weird. The leadership team all make seven figures when we still have entry-level employees like Spencer who have been here for years, barely making more than minimum wage. They work harder than most of the top dogs from what I've seen.

Hessler Group has two different call centers. One about forty minutes from headquarters and another in the Midwest. Being a customer service survivor myself, I asked Brookes from call center operations if I could do a site visit. He simply told me that he'd pull a fresh set of reporting so I could see the margins.

That's not what I wanted. I don't want to know how much money we're saving and how large our profit margins are. I want to know how morale is. I want to know if Hessler employees are as miserable as the ones at Advantage Insurance. I have some ideas on how we can make their day-to-day more tolerable—like allowing them to hang up on ruthless, foul-mouthed assholes.

But no one wants to hear what I have to say. So, I spend my mornings making plans I'll never implement. Then, Spencer and I have lunch in the cafeteria together. I stretch the clock as long as possible before I can justify us leaving our workday early. I know

I'm not particularly helpful on the business front, but I have to earn the money Dex gave me somehow. I can't stand the idea of being paid simply to be his wife.

After a long week of feeling out of place and useless at the office, on Friday evening I just want to cuddle up with Dex. I want to enjoy my new relationship, hidden away from the world. I thought weekends would be ours, ordering takeout, falling asleep on the couch, watching sitcom re-runs. But instead, we have a fancy charity ball to attend.

By six o'clock, I'm sitting in my enormous bathroom in a salon chair that was specially delivered to prep me for a black-tie affair. The event cost Dex nearly one hundred thousand dollars for a table. That's just the door fee. He's expected to make a much more generous contribution to a cause and he's not even sure what they do. It's something I've witnessed based on the small glimpse I've gotten into his world, from the tail end of his phone conversations that I've caught, or from the very brief complaints he makes here and there before he recomposes himself. It's very clear that Dex may have the money. But he's not really the boss. If anything, my husband is bullied and pushed around by his status. Told what he should want, believe in, and support. Dex is like a shuttlecock, being smacked back and forth over a net, used for everybody else's agenda. This is what he meant by money not necessarily being power. Sometimes, wealth is a prison.

Denny's been an enormous help since she's been back. She's running interference as the stylists ask if they can cut my bangs and re-dye my hair a "sensible color"—their words, not mine. She bats them away like she's protecting me from a hungry pack of scavenging hyenas. Denny's normally domineering personality can be off-putting, but tonight, I'm incredibly grateful.

"What about a little lavender eyeshadow? And then a deep plum at the corners." She runs her fingers through a tendril of my hair. "Let's lean into the purple, not dye over it," Denny says.

I smile at her through the mirror. "Love it. Except red for my fingernails. For Dottie."

Denny nods, holding up her own red manicure. "Couldn't agree more."

The nail tech smiles. "I have the perfect jungle red in my other bag. I'll be right back."

Much to her dismay, the stylist doing my hair and makeup unsubtly rolls her eyes. "Purple...goodness," she grumbles. "I'll see what I have."

Once they both leave the bathroom, Denny and I finally have a moment of privacy. "Dex told me about your mom. I'm so sorry." I reach out to squeeze her hand.

"I told you about my relationship with my mother," Denny replies. Her bright red lips curl into a tight, cool smile. "Nothing to be sorry about."

"Loss is loss," I say. "I don't think you have to be on great terms with someone to miss them when they're gone."

She sighs. "Can I be honest, Lennox?" Denny steps in front of me and leans against the bathroom counter, now facing me, instead of looking at me through the mirror. "When I first met you, I thought Dex was thinking a little more with his dick than his brain, but your resiliency... I would've booked a one-way ticket to Bora Bora after that article Tearney put out. But you were unbothered."

I laugh. "Are you kidding? I cried myself to sleep for three nights straight. But I've seen people come back from so much worse. I figured I'd wait it out."

She lifts her brows. "Your dad?"

I nod. "It got dark for a while."

"You know Harrison made a really big blunder once. He did some business with a corrupt bank. By the time he got to the bottom of the shell accounts he apparently funded, it was too late. The SEC was so far up his ass. The entire legal team was terrified. It looked like Hessler Group was going to have to strip down to pieces and sell off their assets piece by piece. He nearly took down an empire in one drunk bumble."

My eyes pop open wide. "How did he get out of that one?"

Denny smirks. "Bribery. A little blackmail. And a whole lot of lying. That's the Hessler way," she says. "Until Dottie, that is. She was the only one who ever operated like she wasn't afraid to lose her wealth. Every decision she made was for the good of the people, so to speak."

"Dex is like that," I add.

Denny lifts her brows. "You sure? I see more Harrison than Dottie in Dex. He's his spitting image."

Denny's like a snake, I swear. Let your guard down, and she'll strike when you're least expecting it. Triggered at her accusation, I can't stop the word vomit. "That'd be impossible since Dex isn't Harrison's. He's all Dottie, both in looks and heart. I'm really proud of the man he is." I instantly regret the words. *Fuck.* Why did I do that? Me and my big mouth. My heart accelerates to the speed of a hummingbird's wings, and I quickly try to digress. "Quick question about the dinner tonight. I really don't know what to do when there's more than two forks. Dinner fork, salad fork—those make sense. But what's the tiny trident for?" I give her an innocent, toothy smile.

Denny levels her stare, her bright eyes fixed on mine. "Mhm... What do you mean Dex isn't Harrison's? I was there the day he was born. I held him hours after Melody gave birth to him. What are you insinuating about my family, Lennox?"

Shit. That went left, fast. "No, no, Denny. I didn't mean..." I sigh. "Dottie left some letters."

Denny blinks at me silently. I glance toward the opening of the bathroom as the nail tech returns. Denny holds up her hands, her eyes never leaving mine. "Rachel, we need another moment. Would you mind putting two bottles of champagne on ice? Everything you'll need is underneath the bar. Dom will be fine."

"Aren't we running out of time, though?" Rachel asks.

"Dex is the guest of honor." Denny's tone is calm and even but wildly intimidating. "They'll hold the whole damn event for him if necessary." Rachel scuttles back out of the room with a simple head nod.

"Lennox," Denny continues, "if there are three forks to the left of the plate, the outer fork is usually for fish, such as a smoked salmon appetizer. Now, would you care to explain what was in these letters? Or, if easier, may I read them myself?"

No. Hell no. I know Denny was like another daughter to Dottie, but I have the strangest gut feeling Dottie would never want to share these stories with her. She wouldn't understand Dottie's connection to Jacob and how it impacted her entire life.

"I do wonder if Melody was Harrison's by blood. By choice, of course. But I'm not sure if maybe Melody was conceived prior to Dottie meeting Harrison," I explain.

She takes a few controlled inhales and exhales before responding. "That'd make sense. Harrison had some medical issues in early adulthood. He *thought* he was infertile," Denny says. "If Dottie was pregnant prior to meeting him, perhaps that was his way of securing an heir. Not to mention, an unwed mother would have no prospects at the time. It wouldn't be the first scandal the Hessler's covered up."

Now, it's my turn to be inquisitive. "Such as?"

"All this stays between us, right?" Denny asks.

"Absolutely."

Denny's big eyes narrow. She smooths her hair on either side of her part. "Harrison had a bastard child. I'm not sure if Dottie knew."

She knew. But this time, I keep my mouth closed. It's not my secret to share.

"He did everything in his power to cover it up. His parents..." Denny lets out a sharp breath. "He got his drinking from his mother. His father was a very cruel man. They took the poor woman he got pregnant, paid her off, and threatened her. She was so scared and without an ounce of fight or good sense. She could've ruined them. Instead, she took the money and disappeared. The child was a bargaining chip."

Crossing my arms, I cradle my elbows, feeling the goosebumps against my forearms. "How do you know all this?"

Denny's eyes drop to her clean, black Manolo's. "You don't hang around the Hesslers for decades without overhearing some secrets."

Lies. My Nancy Drew instincts kick in, and I'm more certain than ever... All the pieces are clicking together like finding the final part of a 2,000-piece puzzle. Here it is: Dex is not a true Hessler.

But Denny is.

D e x

"Goddamn," is all I can say when I see Lennox fixed up like royalty. She's wearing a strapless, floor-length, sparkling pearl gown. Her makeup matches her hair. Colorful but elegant. I can't really see her shoes, but judging by the way she's walking so carefully across our living room, I know they must be dainty stilettos.

She shows me my favorite sassy smile. "Same to you, *Sir.*" She stumbles as she takes another step. "Dammit."

"Are they too uncomfortable?" I ask, holding out my hands to her.

"No, not bad. I've worn worse. It's just..." She drops her voice to a whisper. "I don't want to mess them up. I googled these shoes. They are custom Stuart Weitzman's, and the internet says they are worth half a million dollars, Dex. The stylist didn't bring me any other options." She teeters and holds up her foot. The thin straps are embedded with small diamonds. "I mean, they're real. There are enough diamonds on here to fill an entire case at Kay Jewelers."

Lennox's hair is slicked back, tucked behind her ears, not a stray hair out of place. Her hairstyle shows off the massive diamond studs in her ears. I touch the stones one by one. "They are indeed real. These too."

"Dex, this is bananas. My shoes are worth more than a diamond engagement ring."

I scoff. "Baby, the ring I put on your finger will be worth way more than these shoes."

She shakes her head. "I don't think I'm ever going to get used to it."

"Good. Don't," I say. "Then I'll have a lifetime full of surprising you. Actually, speaking of which," I say, reaching into my inside coat pocket. I pull out a small plastic bag with my present for Lennox. "It's nothing too fancy. But it's your favorite color," I say as I pour the thin bracelet into my palm. I hold the end clasps in my hands, ready to put it on her. "I think it matches well enough."

"You'd have to check with my stylist. It might ruin the ensemble," Lennox says, rolling her eyes. She eagerly holds out her wrist. "You picked this out for me because it's purple?" she asks, bright-eyed.

"Sort of. I told you me and my mom were born in February, right? This is Amethyst. Her birthstone. It was her favorite bracelet. It's the only piece of jewelry of hers I have. Happy accident that it's your favorite color." I fasten the bracelet around her wrist, a perfect fit. I glance at her eyes, starting to water. "Don't cry on me now, baby. You'll ruin your pretty makeup."

She sniffles and shakes her head. "No, no, it's basically superglued on. I was in the chair for like four hours. I didn't realize how long it takes to get glam." She chuckles as she sniffles again.

I gently dab her cheek with the tip of one finger. "Still... You look so beautiful. And I hate making you cry. You were never a crier until I brought you out here."

"Wrong." She holds up her wrist, examining the little purple stones alternating with small, round diamonds. "I cry a lot, just not in front of people. I don't like when people think I can't handle things. Crying makes me feel vulnerable. But I guess now I'm willing to be vulnerable with you."

I pull her into my chest, hugging her tightly. I breathe in the smell of all the hairspray, perfume, lotion, and makeup as I kiss the top of her head. She smells like a meadow of about five different types of flowers. "Me too, Len."

Pulling away, she asks. "Really?"

"Really."

"Then may I ask... How come you don't like talking about your mom? She seemed like such a wonderful person."

"She was." I feel myself shutting down, the way I always do when Mom gets brought up. I don't avoid the topic because of anything other than human nature. It's still too painful. Isn't it basic instinct to avoid the things that hurt us most?

"It's okay, Dex. You don't have to—"

"I feel robbed," I admit. It's Lennox. If I don't open up to her... then who? This is my wife. My partner. I have to at least try.

"What do you mean?"

"Mom never really bought into the whole heiress mentality. She had such a love-hate relationship with Grandpa. She loved him as her dad but never loved what he stood for or how he treated people. Now, in a way, I think I've turned into him. When I fired Jensen..." I think about Grandpa, red-faced and angry. His cheeks used to puff out when he was about to rip someone a new one. His eyes were always slightly bloodshot from all the bourbon and whiskey. I remember being afraid of him sometimes. "It was exactly how my grandpa would've handled that situation. I don't know if I should be proud of that."

Lennox reaches up to straighten my bow tie. "You start nice and clean up even nicer, Dex. Your mom would be so proud of you."

"Would she?" I ask. "Or did she die, and then I turned into the exact opposite of the man she would've raised me to be? I don't like talking about her because I know I let her down...in most ways." I kiss Lennox gently. The thick, sticky gloss she has on transfers to my lips. "She would've loved you, though. I know it. You bring me back to the man I think both my mom and grandma wanted me to be."

She tilts her head to the side. Lennox keeps opening her mouth, then shutting it, like she's about to say something, then keeps stopping herself. "Who do you want to be?" She goes to work, wiping my lips off with her thumb, cleaning her makeup off of me.

"Right now, exactly who I am. I was always destined for the job, but now I have my girl. I'm happy with you by my side." I smile at her, but she doesn't return it.

"But does the Hessler part really matter? If it was just you and me and none of the glitz and glam? If you could be a scuba dive instructor, and your wife and children didn't care if we were broke, living paycheck to paycheck, would you still be happy? Am I enough for you?"

"Wow, baby. Those are a lot of big questions." I drop to my knee and lift her long dress so her shoes are visible. Running my fingers over the diamond-studded straps, I say, "Don't worry, Len. You'll get used to all this. Maybe one day, you'll even like it." I plant kisses up her leg but stop at her knee. "We're already late. Otherwise, I'd take this dress right off."

She puckers her bottom lip. "Can we stay in next Friday? Just you and me? Movie night. Junky snacks. Turn our phones off?"

I frown. "I'm so sorry. Next week I'm in New York until Sunday. Then the week after that is the dive trip, remember? Last one." I run my thumb across her cheek. "Don't worry. It'll slow down soon. We'll make some time." She mumbles something under her breath in a bitter undertone, so I add, "I promise."

"Okay, fine. Is Joe downstairs?" I nod in reply, and she proceeds to make her way to the elevator. Lennox stops and spins around in place when she notices I'm not following. "What's wrong?"

"Nothing, just enjoying the view."

She laughs and continues to the elevator, exaggerating her walk so her hips swing dramatically side to side. The nerves calm as I hear her sweet laugh. My favorite sound in the entire world. Everything is okay. I can make this work. Keep my company afloat, keep my wife smiling.

Hesslers always find a way.

CHAPTER 30

Lennox

My face hurts from fake smiling. For the past three hours, it's been the same conversation over and over again. By now, my answers are rehearsed. *Yes, Dex and I are very happy. No, I'm not hiding a pregnancy; we just didn't want a big ceremony. Yes, my parents are thrilled. No, we aren't also billionaires. Also, no, I have absolutely no damn clue what I'm doing as the CEO of Hessler Group.* That last part is an exaggeration. I've kept my trap shut about my work assignment to avoid any open-mouth, insert-foot situations.

Still, the invasiveness of this community knows no bounds. Somebody told me their daughter also has purple hair. She's thirteen, of course, so I'm not sure if that was a dig or just a desperate attempt to cover the lull in conversation.

After Dex's short speech, he had to make a few rounds, shaking hands and schmoozing. He left me at our VIP table to rest my feet and fill up on champagne. I'm actually still starving after a five-course meal. The plates were beautiful, but the filet mignon was the size of a shot glass for goodness' sake. I thought wealth made things plentiful, but apparently, rich people don't really eat. Between the hunger and the copious amounts of Dom Perignon, I'm sleepy and slaphappy. All I want is for Joe to pull the limo around and take us home.

As I drain my glass for the umpteenth time, a large man with a white mustache sits down in the chair beside me. I blink, surveying the uninvited stranger, dumbfounded at his shocking resemblance to a walrus.

"Having a good evening?" he asks with a warm smile. His pudgy cheeks bulge into perfect spheres.

"I am. Thank you," I say, trying not to slur. "How about you?"

He laughs. "I hate these things," he grumbles. "As soon as the sorry excuse for dessert is served, I'm finding the nearest drive-through and getting a proper meal."

I drop my jaw. Finally, a normal person here. "What in the world was that green salad thing they served that looked like spaghetti?"

"The seaweed salad?" He barks in laughter. "You were brave enough to try it?"

I nod, smiling. "It did indeed taste like it was from the sea."

He holds out his hand. "I'm Richard Spellman from Royal Bahamas."

The name sounds vaguely familiar. "Lennox Mitch—or, Hessler. Lennox Mitchell for now, but eventually Lennox Hessler."

He nods. "I know who you are, ma'am. You and I have some business to finalize." He laughs again when he sees my eyes widen in terror. "Don't worry, Dex has already explained Hessler Group's current leadership setup. I'm not trying to put you on the spot. I mean, I'm honored that our companies are merging. It's been a deal long in the making. I'm sorry Dottie isn't here to finally see it through."

"Were you and Dottie close?" I ask, blinking to try and focus. I must be a little tipsier than I thought, as his face keeps coming in and out of focus.

"We were what the kids call 'frenemies,' I suppose." His chuckle is hoarse and raspy. He beats his fist against his chest. "My days of smoking Cubans are catching up with me." He clears his throat and continues, "I had a hell of a lot of respect for Dottie. I spent my entire life in her shadow. I think her grandson is going to do a fine job with my company."

I reach out to tap his arm. "Dex cares," I say softly. "About the people, about his team. He would break his back to make things work for everyone."

"I'm sure he would. He has some growing up to do, but I think one day he'll make a fine leader," Richard says, his tone condescending.

My defensiveness rises. I don't think these old grumps realize what a masterpiece Dex already is. "I wouldn't underestimate him. You know Luxe Adventure was a struggling cruise line until Dex came up with a fantastic idea to turn that entire money pit around."

Richard scoots his chair in before sitting up taller at the edge of his seat. Leaning in close, he whispers with a sly smile, "Well, fill me in, Mrs. Hessler. I'd love nothing more than to hear about how our future company is going to annihilate the competition... which, by the way, was me, until recently. Nice to be on the inside, now."

Fully intent on giving Dex all the credit so his new partner has full faith in his brilliance, I fill Richard in on the concert cruise idea. Soup to nuts. I explain in great detail the intricacies of our endeavor. I even name-drop Shaylin and mention our plans to contribute to her favorite charity.

"A concert cruise," Richard repeats, bobbing his head in approval. "That's actually a fantastic idea."

I beam, my cheeks aching from my overextended smile. "All Dex. The cruise line was in trouble, and now it's going to be the most lucrative fleet in the company."

"Hmm," Richard says, "I have no doubt. A billion-dollar idea indeed." I look over Richard's shoulder and see Dex approaching. He's loosening his bow tie, a sleepy smile on his face. Damn, my man is a dream. I'd be drawn to him in any crowd, at any event, in any city. He's a magnet's pull. My heartbeat flutters with excitement as he approaches, knowing that he's mine. *All mine.*

"You ready to go, Trouble? I think I'm talked out for the evening." Dex glances at my empty champagne flute. "Unless you'd both like another round?"

"No, I'm okay."

"I'm about to call it an evening as well." Richard scoots his chair out and rises. Dex is well over six feet, but Richard is

304

taller and nearly double his width. He holds his hand out to Dex. "Hessler, nice to see you. Very nice speech this evening."

Dex shakes Richard's hand, and I can't help but notice the tension. Richard's wearing a cocky smirk and Dex looks uncomfortable. "Nice to see you as well. Have you had any time to look over my counteroffer?" Dex asks.

"I have indeed," Richard replies. "I think your lawyers made a mistake. The offer seems to be missing a digit."

"I'm just going off the numbers, Richard. The actual value of the company versus the perceived value. Please take your time considering it. It's a very generous offer, and you know Hessler Group is the only one in a position to offer anything close to that range."

"Hmm," Richard grumbles out. "I think we have different definitions of generous."

"Richard, come on. It's ten percent more than my grandmother offered. My show of good faith. But I can't double an offer on a company that's nearly bankrupt. You know that. The numbers don't lie."

I'm not sure if I'm imagining it, but Richard flushes—maybe from embarrassment, maybe from anger. "I'll be in touch," Richard huffs. "Ma'am," he says, saluting me with two fingers. "It was a pleasure meeting you in person, finally."

"What was that about?" I ask Dex as soon as Richard is out of earshot. "I thought you guys were acquiring Royal Bahamas. Isn't that why you flew back to Miami early after we got married?"

"Yes. But right before the paperwork was signed, he asked Hessler Group to double down. Greedy old man who wants to retire off of pure pity. Grandma would never fall for his tricks. He clearly thought I was more gullible."

My stomach sinks. I spoke to Richard like he was part of the team, not an outsider looking in. I have no idea the ramifications of what we talked about. "Dex, Richard, and I were chatting and—"

"Baby, don't worry about him. He's been weaseling around for the better part of two decades. I can handle it. Come on," he grabs my hand, and I stumble as I step toward him. Catching my elbow, he braces me. "Is that because your feet hurt? Or because you've had one too many."

"Definitely the latter," I admit. "And I can no longer feel my feet."

Dex laughs. "Come on, sweet wife. I want to take you home, take those shoes off, then that dress." He leans down to whisper in my ear. "You've been a walking cock tease all night, and when we get home, I'm going to do something about it."

Dex

We're barely home and through the elevators before Lennox kicks off her shoes, flinging them across the room like she's angry at them. But then she throws her hand over her mouth and collects the shoes, setting them neatly side by side against the wall. "Sorry," I hear her mutter to her stilettos. I can't help but laugh.

"Did you just apologize to your shoes?" The glass of champagne in the limo tipped her over the edge. My wife is silly, sassy, and sexy, and I'm eating up every second of it. Joy is a feeling. It's warm and heavy. Most people say happiness makes you feel light. I disagree. For me, happiness is thick and heavy, working with gravity to make me feel secure and grounded.

"Well, Mr. Hessler, these shoes are so damn fancy and expensive, it's quite possible they have real feelings."

Following her, I slip out of my coat and toss it on the back of the living room sectional. Next, I loosen my bowtie then pull it over my head. I fling it over my shoulder playfully. "And how are you feeling right now?"

She pivots, waiting for me to catch up to her. Then, she's working furiously at my shirt buttons. When my button-down is on the ground, she runs her hands over my chest and pecs like she's blind and is trying to get a visual with her hands. I let out a low, growly moan, loving the sensation of her hands on my body.

"Does that feel good?" she asks.

"It does," I say. "Try a little lower."

Lennox smirks at me as she unbuttons my pants and pushes them down along with my boxers. She surveys my growing erection, then her eyes snap to mine. "I trust you," she says, a little out of left field.

"Glad to hear it. Turn around."

She lets me unhook her dress and pull the zipper down to the top curve of her ass. Carefully, she steps out of the gown and then drapes it on the back of the couch like it's precious. I reach for her, trying to strip her naked so I can make love to her right on this couch, but she slips right out of my hands.

"Follow me, Mr. Hessler. There's something I want to try."

"Where are we going?" I ask, glancing down at my eager cock that really is not in the mood for any games. I just want to bury it into my sexy wife, then fall asleep with her in my arms.

"Bath," Lennox says over her shoulder. I follow her through the living room, then the bedroom. She sheds her strapless bra as she walks, tossing it over her shoulder and right into my face. I laugh as I toss it aside, just in time for her underwear to hit me square in the chest.

"As much as I'm liking the moving strip show, how about you stand still so I can put my head between your thighs?" I smirk.

"Tempting," she says, now completely naked, her pert nipples look hard as diamonds, begging for attention. I bite the inside of my cheek when she bends over to reach under the bathroom cabinet, flashing me her swollen pussy from behind. It takes every ounce of restraint I have not to pin her against the countertop and have my way. Instead, I'm patient, wondering *what the hell is her game?*

She straightens up with a bottle of bath oil in her hand. It takes me a moment to understand what she's suggesting.

"Really?" I ask, eyes wide. "Tonight?"

"I want to try everything with you, Dex."

"You never have before?" I ask.

She shakes her head in reply, looking at me with eager eyes.

I blow out a deep breath. I don't know about this. "Len, you're drunk," I say.

"I've been drinking. I'm not drunk." She holds her arms out and spins around. "See?"

I chuckle. "Pretty sure a drunk person could do that."

She narrows her light brown eyes. "Stop teasing. You're my husband, and I want to give you this. A first for me. This is me, asking for what I want. Let's just try it. If we hate it, we don't have to do it again."

I can assure her I won't hate it. Unless it hurts her. That'd be more than enough to deter me further. An easy lie would be to tell her I'm not in the mood for anal, but my throbbing, hard cock gives me away. "Turn the water on, then." I point to the tub.

After setting the oil on the ledge of the tub, she turns the hot water knob all the way, then the cold knob one rotation. She plugs the tub, then rises, nothing left to do. Crossing her arms, she covers her tits.

"Nuh-uh. Drop your arms. I want to see you. Every single inch of what's mine."

She does as I say but rubs her toes anxiously against the tile floor. She's shivering, but between the heated floors and the steam coming off the hot running water, she can't be cold. It's all nerves. I quickly cross the room and pull her into my arms. "You don't have to prove anything to me." Reaching between our bodies, I run my finger against her slit, feeling her wetness. "This is more than enough to keep me a happy man forever."

She nuzzles into my bare chest. "I'm not trying to prove anything. I just want you in every single way. I want sex to be our adventure. Likes and dislikes, yesses and no's. We still have so much to learn about what being together means." She grips the tip of my cock, massaging it in her small hand.

"Okay, bend over. Hands on the ledge." She must think I'm going to take her from behind like this because she hunches over and grips the edge of the tub like she's bracing for pain. Instead, I grab the oil, dripping it over her shoulders, down her back, then over her ass. I thoroughly coat between her ass cheeks, ensuring she's drenched in oil, before I push my finger into her tightest hole. She shudders but pushes her hips backward, taking my finger deeper. After pumping my hand a few times, I add another finger. She blows out a deep breath as I grab the bottle of oil, recoating her and my hand.

"Fuck, Len. That's so tight. How do you feel?"

"Full," she groans. "It feels good."

By now, the tub is filled enough. Pulling my fingers away, I climb into the bath, enjoying the feeling of hot water covering my feet and ankles. I help Lennox in. She stands, her back against my chest. Pinching her nipples one by one, I murmur in her ear. "We'll go slow."

"Okay," she murmurs. "I can handle it."

"I know you can, baby, but I want you to like it. So, follow my lead." This time when I grab the oil, I coat my cock. Everything is soaked and warm. When I kneel in the tub, hips submerged underwater, I guide Lennox down on all fours. My tip touches her tight ring of muscle and at first, it seems impossible. I nudge against her, and she winces. Reaching around her hips, I play with her clit, flicking her sensitive spot until she tenses her thighs and her breath grows ragged.

"Good girl," I growl into her ear. "Just like that. Feels good, doesn't it? You're so warm and wet for me baby. Just come. As hard as you want." I flick my finger faster.

As if she knows what I'm trying to do, the moment she climaxes, she pushes her ass backward, sliding over my hard, slippery cock, letting me completely fill her ass. We both freeze when my balls bump against her sex.

Fucking sweet paradise. I have never felt anything like it. I've done this before, but not like this. Not with a woman I loved. Not with a body I reveled in like this. Lust mix with dirty, wanton, need. It's fucking bliss.

"Oh hell, Dex. It's...it's...okay. Better than okay. I..." She slowly pulls away from me, then throws her hips backward once more. Raising up to just her knees, she tries to grasp the sides of the tub for leverage but can't quite get a good grip. Despite her trying to brace herself, she lunges forward every time I push into her. Her ass is so damn tight, it's hard to maneuver.

"You like it?" I ask. She nods fervently, making her long hair jostle in front of my face. I hold her hips steady. "Then relax, baby, let me do it. Stay still. Let me fuck you." I grind my hips, sliding in deeper. In and out, her tight walls massaging me with pressure like I've never felt before. I won't last like this.

"*Yes*. Like that. A little faster, Dex. Fuck, it feels good." Reaching around, I grab her breasts as handles as I push into her with long, slow thrusts.

Goddammit, she feels so good. There's so much pressure, it's borderline painful, but just enough edge to be the most invigorating sensation I've ever felt. "I'm going to fill your ass, baby. Is that what you want?"

"Yes," she rasps out. Plunging her hand in the water, she touches between her thighs, furiously rubbing her clit.

"That's good. One more time. Come for me again before I fill you up. I love it when you take care of yourself. So sexy."

I slow the pace down, curious about how it feels when Lennox comes with me buried balls deep in her ass. After another moment, she's shaking, mewling with pleasure as she cries out loudly. "*Yes, yes, so fucking good*," she whispers. "I love it."

Tension brewing in my balls, I know I don't have long. I come hard, filling her as promised. Breathless and not ready to leave her warmth, I playfully pat her ass. "Such a good girl." When we're both spent, she falls back into my chest, causing me to slip out. I kick my legs out on either side of her, so we're now both seated on our asses, the water level barely rising above our hips.

I cup the warm water in my palm, trying to cover her shoulders. But it's not enough to keep her from shivering. Lennox pokes her foot out of the water, turning the hot water handle with her toe. The warmth envelops us both. We soak for a while, nothing but the sound of our breathing and the occasional movement of the water. It's the most at peace I've ever felt. It's comparable to when I'm thirty meters below in the ocean, lost in a different world. With Lennox, I feel less like escaping. I want to be here. With her.

Lennox must get sleepy because she feels a little heavier as her body relaxes on top of mine. "Hmmm, I'm so tired," she mumbles, "don't let me drown in here."

"Never." I kiss the top of her head. "How do you feel?"

"Probably sore tomorrow," she says with a weak laugh. "But tonight, I'm perfect. How was that for you?"

"Addicting," I admit. "I love you, Lennox. So much."

She lets out a sweet, low hum. "Thank you... I'm still saving mine. Moment's not quite right."

I chuckle softly. "Okay, then. Save it. Come on, let me put you to bed."

She shakes her head, her damp hair dragging across my chest. "No, can't move," she mutters. "Let's sleep here."

"In the tub?"

She gripes and protests as I push her up by the shoulders so I can slip out from behind her. I grab two towels, then quickly dry myself off. Lennox scowls at me, still seated in the tub. "Come on, baby, all you have to do is stand. I'll do the rest." She rises excruciatingly slowly, making me laugh. Once she's upright, I wrap the fresh towel around her, then scoop her up in my arms. She squeals when her feet leave the ground.

I carry my wife over the threshold between the bathroom to our bedroom, laying her gently on her side of the bed. I pull the towel from her body and wrap her in the sheet and comforter instead. Best I can, I dry her hair so her pillow isn't drenched.

"You take such good care of me. You must like me or something." She flashes me a smart smile.

"Yeah, Trouble, you're all right." I kiss the tip of her nose. "I think I'll keep you."

She laughs as I tuck in bed behind her, pulling her against my naked body.

I drift off, not dreaming of the ocean for once but dreaming of me and Lennox. It's an oddly lucid dream, my brain trying to make sense of the context.

Lennox and I are sitting next to each other on a white-washed porch in black rocking chairs. We're gray-haired and wrinkled, enjoying the warm breeze against our faces, staring out at our big family playing in the yard. The skyline in front of us is hazy. A mix of Vegas and Miami.

Lennox holds out her hand. I take it, our arms full of sunspots and discoloration, but our grip still strong. We hold each other tightly.

"I think now's as good a time as any," dream Lennox says. "I've been saving it for so long."

"What's that, dear?" I ask. "A good time for what?"

"I love you, Dex Hessler. There, you old kook, I finally said it."

Our chairs rock in tandem as we laugh, still holding hands.

The rest of the dream goes blurry as I fall into a deeper sleep.

CHAPTER 31

Lennox

On Saturday morning, I'm still in bed, eyes groggy, with a sex hangover.

Dex and I have been doing a lot of exploring. He's had me in every position. Over the past week, it was the same pattern. He'd come home from the office hours after me, and the moment he was through the door, it was shirt-unbuttoned, pants down, his low grumbly growl telling me what a good girl his wife is. We'd fill up on junky snacks for dinner, getting just enough sleep to survive our days at the office. Rinse and repeat. All week. In my opinion, it was our second honeymoon.

I take him wherever he wants it. He's claimed every part of my body time and time again, and I can't help but wonder if this is exactly what our bodies were made for. We're never hiding under the covers, ashamed of our passion. One round is never enough. I'm never left unsatisfied, just stripped and spent, needing recovery. This is exactly what I fantasized about for years. With Dex, sex is an unmarked map. There's still so much to explore and discover.

It's where Alan and I fell short. I wanted the peaceful, safe happily ever after. But I also wanted the adventure of getting there, too.

My phone rings from the nightstand, pulling me from my thoughts.

"Hello," answers the frog in my throat. I quickly cough away from the phone, clearing my voice. "Good morning," I say, this time sounding a little more presentable.

"Mrs. Hessler, we're sorry to bother you so early, but there's a woman in the lobby insisting on seeing you. She says she's been calling, texting, and emailing, but you haven't answered your phone."

Pulling the phone from my face, I check my recent notifications. Dex messaged me letting me know he was in the air safely. Avery sent me a message late last night telling me she misses me and she's so proud of me, and even though Finn claims he's relieved I'm no longer mooching, he has kept my pink throw pillows in the guest bedroom. My dad texted me a picture of a for sale sign on my childhood home. His message was: *Just saying, baby girl. Would love to have you and Dex a little closer.*

But there's nothing from a strange woman. Is this a Dex Hessler fan girl, wanting to murder me, wear my skin as a costume and my hair as a wig, hoping for her shot at Miami's formerly most eligible bachelor?

"What's her name?"

"Katherine...Tearney. Does that ring a bell?" the security guard asks.

I narrow my eyes to the point my vision goes blurry, as if there's anyone here to see my dirty look. "I'm familiar. Try not to let the door hit her on her way out." Of course, I haven't received any messages from Kat. Once a snake bites you, you block them from everything.

"So, you wouldn't like to see her? She's saying it's urgent."

"No, I would not."

"Okay, ma'am, no problem. Sorry for disturbing you."

But I can hear Kat's frantic shouting in the background. *"Lennox, please! It's about Dex! It's serious, and I'm just trying to warn you guys."*

"Have a good morning, Mrs. Hessler. We'll escort her out," the security guard says before hanging up.

Exhaling in annoyance, I place my phone face down on the nightstand. I try to tuck back under the covers, but my mind starts to race.

Dammit... Kat said it was about Dex. That's enough to get my attention. Ruin my life, have at it...but my husband's? *Fuck.*

I grab my phone and find my blocked contacts. Reluctantly, I remove Kat from the list. Instantly, her blocked messages come flooding in.

> **Kat: I got an assignment, and we need to talk.**

> **Kat: I know you're upset. Rightly so, but this one is over my head.**

> **Kat: Believe it or not, I'm trying to protect you. I think BuzzLit is crossing a line.**

> **Kat: Please call me back, Lennox. I promise I'm trying to help.**

Her frantic messages are enough to pique my curiosity. She has some gall, contacting me after the awful things she wrote about me. But it's the part where she mentioned that she's trying to protect me that has me concerned. What line has been crossed that even has a sniveling weasel like Kat all worked up?

> **Me: What is going on?**

> **Kat: Can we please just talk...face to face? I'm still right outside your building.**

> **Me:** You're most definitely not welcome in my home...but there's a coffee shop called Brewley's about two blocks south. I'll meet you there in an hour.

> **Kat:** Okay, I know Brewley's. See you in an hour.

> **Me:** Kat, I'm warning you, if you mess with my family again, I won't save you. I'll let my husband buy your company this time and burn your career to the ground. Clear?

> **Kat:** Yes, I understand. I promise, no funny business.

She must think I'm an idiot to believe that. This time, I'm taking precautions with a witness to the conversation so I can call Kat out on any bullshit with the truth. I phone in reinforcements. The phone barely rings twice before Spencer answers with a sleepy, "Hello?"

"Sorry, did I wake you?" Of course, I did. It's seven o'clock on a Saturday morning.

"No, no," she assures me. "Not at all. I've been up."

"Why are you lying?" I ask with a chuckle.

"It's a knee-jerk response," Spencer admits, succumbing to a big, vocal yawn. "Have you ever seen The Devil Wears Prada? Executive assistants aren't allowed to sleep."

"Are you suggesting I'm as scary as Meryl Streep in that movie?"

"No, I'm suggesting I'm newly loving my job and my boss who wildly overpays me. So, if you need something at the butt crack of dawn on a Saturday, here I am, reporting for duty."

"Fair enough. I'm going to send a car to pick you up shortly. I need you to meet me at Brewley's in about forty-five minutes for a meeting."

"Roger that. Dress pants or yoga pants?" Judging by the ruckus I hear in the background, she's already shuffling through her apartment, turning her shower on.

"Whatever you prefer. It should be brief."

"Who are we meeting?" Spencer asks.

Kat's face pops into the forefront of my mind, and I roll my eyes. "A snake."

CꙨ Ꙩ

When we walk in, it's easy to spot Kat and her red hair in the corner of Brewley's at a small table. She's already ordered two coffees. Her eyes pop in surprise when she sees me approach with Spencer, dressed in a neat business romper. I opted for a sleek, navy dress that went past my knees. My most professional, least revealing dress, just in case Kat would like to corner me and accuse me of being a Las Vegas hussy again.

"I didn't realize you were bringing company," Kat says, rising when she sees us approach.

I point to the lattes on the table. "Well, we'll wait. I'm sure the kitchen has time to poison one more."

She grumbles. "Okay, I suppose I deserve that. Look, Lennox. I'm sorry. It was all in good fun. Just entertainment. No one takes that column seriously. The world has a very short attention span—"

"I read the article. There was nothing entertaining about it," Spencer seethes.

Kat lifts an eyebrow at Spencer. "You brought a guard dog?"

Spencer pulls out her phone from her clutch. "Nope. A videographer. Mess with my boss again, and I will blast your ass all over snaketok, cheatertok, cringeytok, and lemontok."

317

"You're making these up," Kat replies. "Those can't be real TikTok hashtags."

"Try me," Spencer snaps back.

I glance at Spencer with a small, bemused smile. "What is lemontok?"

"It's kind of confusing. You can find shitty people, crappy cars, lemon bread recipes, and all-natural lemon cleaning supplies. Actually, that whole hashtag is kind of a mess," she mumbles.

"Gotta love twenty-one-year-olds and TikTok, right?" I ask Kat. "Talk and talk fast."

"Okay, okay," Kat says, pulling another seat around the small coffee table. "First of all, the article about you wasn't my idea."

"Not your idea, but you certainly executed it with finesse." I sit down and cross my legs, arms folded tightly over my chest. Maybe I look cold and standoffish. In actuality, I think I'm trying to protect my heart.

"I was blackmailed. I often am. When Denise called—"

"She had no idea you were doing the article on BuzzLit," I say, fervently defending Denny.

Kat scoffs. "Are you kidding? Lennox, are you that naïve? She set you up. The article was far from my best writing. I put in what I was told to."

I ignore the pounding in my chest. The hairs on my neck are rising at the idea of Denny's betrayal. But I force myself to ignore the baseless accusation. I make a move to get up. "I'm not interested in the blame game."

"*Wait, please,*" she insists. "I have proof." Kat glances nervously at Spencer, seated right beside me, wearing the same unimpressed expression. "Can she please stop recording? Just for a bit?"

I exhale. "Spencer, let's give her a moment."

Obediently, Spencer puts her phone down and mutters, "Phone's off. My fist is still working, though."

I stifle my chuckle. "What proof?"

Kat sighs and pulls out her own phone. She clicks through a few apps, enters two different passwords, and then proceeds to show me an image of her. She cups her hand around her forehead, her head hung in shame. "That was from three years ago."

After scanning the somewhat pornographic image, I blink at her. "Well, Kat. That was more of your bare ass than I ever wanted to see. Why are you showing me a naked picture of you from behind?"

She shushes me and lowers her tone. "The man I'm on top of...recognize him?"

"No."

"You must not follow politics."

"Accurate. Hey, put that in your next article. A jab at me that'd be justified. I have absolutely no clue what's going on in the political world."

"His name is Scott Ramsie. He's running for the senate..." She licks her lips as a flicker of shame crosses her face. "He's married."

I widen my eyes. "And was three years ago when you slept with him?"

She nods solemnly. "In my defense, he said he was leaving her. I...ate up every line. I loved him. Still do."

"Which is why you're protecting him?" I ask.

She nods again. "I don't know how the hell Denise got ahold of those pictures. Her ex-husband is friends with Scott. But basically, she owns my ass. I write what she wants when she wants. Once upon a time, I was writing serious articles. You know I spent two months in Qatar, doing field research for serious journalism. Now, I'm a gossip columnist joke, thanks to Denise."

"And a homewrecker," Spencer adds, then dramatically coughs into her fist. "Sorry. Subtlety is not my strong suit."

"His wife cheated first," Kat mumbles. "He's been unhappy for a long time."

"Kat, I'm really not interested in your sob story. Or any more nudes of you, for that matter. What did you want to talk about? And what are you trying to insinuate about Denny?" I ask in a hurry.

"She's not a good person, Lennox."

"And you are? There are only two people in Miami I trust. My husband and the young woman next to me who looks like she wants to clock you. I'm tired of all the manipulative games. I don't understand why everyone I encounter seems to have a vendetta against me."

She breathes out heavily. "Which is why I wanted to warn you about the article that's being published next week. I did my best to convince my boss it wasn't a good story idea, but she's already hooked."

"What article?" Spencer asks.

Kat is tapping on her phone again, pulling up an email. She swivels her phone around, and I see the headline:

A legacy in shambles. Dottie Hessler, the devil in disguise. How she stole a family just for her grandson to run the Hessler name straight into the ground.

My stomach sinks as bile bubbles up in my throat. I'm breathless for a while as the sickening realization washes over me. "Kat...you can't publish this. It'll crush him. Dex loved his grandma more than anyone in the world. If he finds out his entire life has been a lie..."

"I have no choice," Kat replies. "If I don't release the article, Denise is going to put my pictures all over the internet. I have to protect myself, Lennox. I'm sorry. I don't even know where Denise got the tip-off to concoct a story like this."

Me. Me and my stupid, big mouth. I clasp my hand over my heart, feeling the heavy thudding. "Please don't do this," I plead to Kat, clasping my hands together.

"It's already done," she says. "I'm just trying to warn you."

"You know something?" Spencer asks, her eyes narrowed at Kat. "You are exactly what's wrong with the world. You run your mouth, never thinking of the ripple effect of your bullshit. Families are breaking apart, kids are hurting themselves, people have become angry and reclusive all because of this *garbage.* You use humiliation as entertainment and never stop to think how badly you're hurting people. You're a poisonous sludge. I hope your nudes flood the internet one day. A little taste of your own medicine. Then let's see if you can let it slide right off your back like it's *no big deal.*"

Spencer's eyes are watering. Her rant is clearly personally motivated. There's a story there, but right now, I don't have time to press. I think I just ruined my husband's life. I have no idea what the implications are if Dex isn't technically a Hessler. *Can they take everything away from him?*

"Spencer, let's go," I say. "I need to call Dex. He needs to hear all of this from me." We both stand, scooting out our chairs with loud screeches against the wooden floor. Kat's face is buried in her hands, and for the briefest moment, I feel bad for her.

I let Spencer get a few paces in front of me, then I double back to address Kat once more. "You know, secrets tend to ruin lives. I'm about to come clean. So should you. Then maybe you can go back to being a journalist who matters." I shrug. "Something to think about. And anyway, the world has a short attention span, right?"

Her eyes glued to the table, she nods. "I'll think about it."

CHAPTER 32

Dex

> **Lennox: Baby, can we please talk? I keep calling and it's going to voicemail.**
>
> **Lennox: It's really important. Not exaggerating.**
>
> **Lennox: Please call me. Please, please call me as soon as you get this.**

Shit. How long have I been tied up on the phone? I missed all of Lennox's messages. Since the moment disaster hit, I've been in crisis mode. I ignored all notifications, my sole mission getting the entire leadership team into one room to figure out this Royal Bahamas explosion that just went off.

Richard Spellman is an arrogant, boisterous son of a bitch, far more concerned with his status than the well-being of his company. I was hardly surprised that he rejected my counteroffer. The major issue is that early this morning, Royal Bahamas released a press statement announcing new investors who had full faith in their new endeavor, 'Once in a Lifetime' cruises to host a one-week feature of celebrity musicians. Their first headliner...

Shaylin, and a quarter of their proceeds were being donated to her favorite charity, Guardian.

And now I have to get to the bottom of this because there's a rat on my team. A rat that just cost me nearly a billion dollars and tens of thousands of people their jobs.

I've never been this livid before about work. Every cell in my body is on fire, inflamed with putrid hate. All I've done is break my back for this company. Years of education prepared me for this position—all the grunt work I did earning my stripes, and now, even after losing my Grandma, going as far as getting married in a hurry just to secure the company's future. My family has been nothing but generous and forgiving, and yet...there's still an ungrateful fucking weasel on the team.

This is why Grandpa had very few friends. *"Kindness is a distraction,"* he'd always tell me. Be a leader who makes no exceptions. Better to be respected and feared than liked.

> **Me: I'm sorry, Len. I'm actually back in Miami now. I'm headed to the office.**

> **Lennox: Why?**

> **Me: Emergency. I'm calling everyone from the leadership team into a mandatory meeting.**

> **Lennox: But it's Saturday. It can't wait?**

> **Me: No, I'm sorry. I'll meet you right after I figure this all out.**

> **Lennox: If it's a meeting with the entire team, should I be there?**

> **Me: Up to you, baby. But I warn you, someone's head is about to roll. I'm livid.**

> **Lennox: Why?**

> **Me: I'll explain soon. Love you.**

Lennox is going to be crushed. Half the reason I pushed for the 'Once in a Lifetime' cruise endeavor to come to fruition is that I wanted to give my wife a big win. I wanted her to see what kind of impact she could have on the company. I've always believed in her.

I wanted her to believe in herself, too.

And now the jackass that ruined everything is going to have literal hell to pay.

ଓ ଜ

"I want to convey the severity of the situation...and how infinitely fucking furious I am," I say between gritted teeth. "The entire server is being searched as we speak. The legal team, PR... everybody is on this, and it'd make the situation so much less complicated if the culprit would just *fess up*. Who the hell spoke to Spellman?" I bury my hands in my face. "The people in this room are the only ones who knew about the endeavor."

"Dex, take a breath," Hank says, sitting right next to me. He clasps his hand on my shoulder. "We'll figure it out. Have you spoken to Spellman?"

Of everyone in this room, Hank might be the only one I trust. "Legal reached out. We're waiting on a response."

There's a soft knock on the meeting room door, and Lennox,

with her hair pulled back and wearing a sleek blue dress, waves at me through the glass doors. Even with my chest tight with fury, the sight of my wife makes me smile. I beckon her in. She flocks to my side, taking a seat on the other side of me. She must sense the tension in the room because once she's seated, she starts rubbing small, soothing circles against my back.

"What's wrong?" she asks softly, eyeing the room before looking me in the eyes.

Hank jumps in to clarify for me. "Lennox, our business plan was leaked for Luxe Adventure. Richard Spellman this morning not only officially declined our merger offer, but also announced that Royal Bahamas intends to launch their 'concert cruise' idea—aka our idea—by the end of next year."

Lennox's eyes grow into wide, unblinking saucers. "I mean... that doesn't stop what we're doing right? All companies do that. One person has an idea, everybody follows suit?"

I close my eyes and pinch the bridge of my nose. "There are certain logistics to piggybacking. Typically, it's frowned upon. Not to mention, they also got our headliner. If it helps, Shaylin was honored by the request and very enthusiastic about the charity idea... Your idea would've worked."

"But...but..." Lennox stammers. "I...wait—Emmett, right? He can ask her to help us instead of Royal Bahamas, can't he?"

"Lennox, he's a label exec. He doesn't own her. I asked Emmett for his help in persuasion. It was his decision to make. Royal Bahamas got to her firs...independently. They must've had some sort of contact on the inside."

She shakes her head, her big brown eyes starting to glisten. "Dex, there has to be a way that we can—"

"We have to shut down Luxe Adventure Cruises in phases to prevent further loss. We'll retire the ships one by one. By the end of next year, nearly twelve thousand people will have lost their jobs." I bang my fist on the table. "And I want to know who's *fucking* responsible. If I have to find out the hard way by searching every single email on the server, I will ruin them. Releasing trade secrets is a breach of contract, a violation of an NDA, and at this magnitude, *illegal*." Everyone squirms in their seat, exchanging nervous glances. "No one wants to speak?" I turn my lips down and nod. "Fine, then we'll all wait here together until legal has answers for me."

I turn to my right to see my wife looking on the brink of hysteria. Her bottom lip is shaking. I can barely make sense of her words. But I hear enough...

"Me," she whispers. "It...it was me. I talked to Richard. Stop yelling at them," she musters out. "I'm the one to blame." She throws her hand over her mouth as she kicks her chair back. "I'm so sorry. So, so sorry," she says between short gasps, then flees the room.

Lennox

I've never seen Dex so angry. What's worse is that he's angry at me. After I confessed in the board room, I practically sprinted to Dottie's office. I kicked off my shoes and tucked myself onto the couch, holding my knees tightly to my chest like a frightened child. An apt description—that's what I am here. A child.

I wrecked my life in Vegas with stupid decisions, and it took me less than a month to destroy Dex's too. The weight of the consequences is so much heavier now. Before, I lost my job, relationship, and apartment and had a few thousand dollars stolen from me. But at least my wrecking ball behavior was localized to my life. Now, tens of thousands of people are going to lose their jobs. How many dads are going to feel like mine did? Lost, scared, and unsure if they can keep feeding their families. All because I can't seem to spot a snake in the grass. Everybody else can. Even my twenty-one-year-old assistant seems to have better character judgment than me.

It wasn't like this back home. There were good people and bad people. But none of this conniving. I didn't want to make mistakes. I made them all innocently. Not that it matters. On purpose or not, somebody is still going to pay the price for my screw-up.

I dig through Dottie's letter box, trying to find something to comfort me. Her letters have been my constant companion. When I feel lost, it helps to dive into her feelings. Yes, she was an amazing leader, but like me, she was also a woman in love—questioning her decisions and her identity just as much as I am.

Maybe this is what Dex needs, to feel close to his Grandma like I do right now. My stomach churns because I have to make matters worse and tell Dex the truth about Kat's article. But maybe... I think Dottie needs to tell him. I just need to find the right letter. The one that conveys how much she loved him and how Dottie isn't some master manipulator. Every choice she made in her life was rooted in love. For her daughter, her family, her husband... The only person she left out was herself. Never finding her happily ever after with the man who held her heart.

I think that's why she did all this. To break the cycle. She wanted Dex to choose love. No matter how difficult it'd make his life.

The various scenarios play through my mind as I try to determine the perfect first letter to show Dex. Nothing is landing quite right. I've pieced together the truth with dozens of letters by now. I don't know how to sum it all up in one perfect introduction to the truth. Where's the best place for Dottie to start? I have to hope it'll come to me in the next few minutes because it's time to face my husband.

Letter box in my hands, deadest on winging it, I leave Dottie's office to find Dex. I tiptoe down the long hallway and bank right. The final twenty feet is the hardest. My footsteps are slow, and my legs feel heavy. Dex has been so wonderful to me, but every person has a breaking point. *I fucked up.* Accident or not. What if he sees me differently now?

Tucking the box under one arm, I knock.

"It's open," he calls out.

He's sitting at his executive desk, face hidden behind his monitor. When he sees me, he smiles. Rolling back in his chair, he loosens his tie.

"There you are," he says softly. "I was going to give you a few more minutes and come find you. Want to sit?" He points to the couch. "Where are your shoes?" he asks, peering at my bare feet.

I wore my most intimidating designer shoes to meet Kat. My poor feet are an angry red. "I left them in my office...if it's even my office anymore." I hang my head as I take a seat on Dex's sofa. His office is set up similarly to Dottie's. Desk area, built-in shelves behind, a sitting area with one sofa and two single chairs. The difference is Dex's office is decorated with dark colors and leather furniture. Sort of a yin and yang situation in comparison to Dottie's office.

"Len," he says softly. He joins me on the couch, wrapping his arm around my shoulders, pulling me in tight.

"I'm sorry," I blubber out. "You have to know it was an accident."

"I know. Thinking back...it was the charity event, wasn't it?"

I nod glumly. "I thought Richard already committed to the merger. I told him everything. He made a comment about you being in charge of Hessler Group and I was just trying to brag on you and your great idea."

Dex looks so tired and worn down. It must've been a long day for him too. He looks like a babysitter who's been put through hell with rebellious toddlers. From what I've learned, it's kind of what this job entails. Babysitting me, his company, and his leadership team. There's always something going wrong, and I don't understand when he'll ever find the time to rest.

"I understand. It's okay. But..." He hooks his finger under my chin and guides my eyes to his. "I made quite a show back there. The leadership team is calling for your removal."

"Rightly so," I reply.

"That's why I'm upset. Now this is out of my hands. I wouldn't fire you. In fact, I can't. But what happened with Spellman...

technically it's considered releasing trade secrets. It's against company policy, and in a way, illegal."

Hot tears coat my cheeks, but I force myself to keep my voice steady. "So, based on a company policy, I'm out and the position goes to you. Problem solved."

"I can try to fight it," Dex adds.

"Why?" I ask. "This is perfect. Happy accident that we stumbled onto a loophole. I'm just sorry I let you down."

He holds my gaze. "You didn't let me down."

"Stop protecting me, Dex. If anybody else had spilled the beans to Richard you'd be coming down on them ruthlessly. I saw how angry you were. This whole situation is ridiculous. Who would be crazy enough to trust me with a company like this?"

He smiles. "My grandma...me. Why is that so crazy? You think people don't make mistakes? I could tell you about some of my blunders my first few years here, and that was after a Harvard Business School education, mind you."

I shake my head. "It's not the same. All the mistakes I've made have been because I'm trying to make friends. I'm never going to have real friends here or a normal life. Being with you means isolating myself. I guess I have to get used to that."

Dex drops his eyes to his lap as he squeezes my shoulder. "Is that really how you feel?"

"Come on. We both know I don't belong here." I roll my wrist, gesturing around the room.

"You don't belong here in this office? Or, in Miami with me?" he asks quietly. His words are barely above a whisper but I know what he's asking, clear as day. "Are you unhappy? Be honest."

I place my hand on his cheek. "I'm so happy when you're here. But, when you're gone, I'm..."

"Not," he finishes for me. "And I'm gone more often than not."

"Exactly," I admit.

He nods his head slowly, like it's heavy. "It's only going to get worse. Especially with Luxe Adventure shutting down." He pinches the bridge of his nose and clamps his eyes shut like whatever thought he has is painful. "Len, I'm going to ask you something and please be honest with me." His eyes are firmly fixed on mine. "Do you want to go home to Vegas?" He grips my shoulder tighter like he's bracing himself for my response.

I don't answer right away. I inhale and exhale, trying to control my sniffling. "I said I'd be here for you."

"That's not what I asked."

I force myself to meet his eyes. "I never imagined a life where my entire purpose is to wait around until you have time for me. It's weird for me not to have to work but still have everything in ridiculous abundance. I don't want to feel like a doll on the shelf, collecting dust. I still want to do something with my life. I thought marrying you would help me find that purpose. But right now, I still feel very lost. And yes...I miss home terribly."

"Doll on the shelf," Dex parrots back in a murmur. "That's something Grandma used to say."

"I read her letters, Dex." I point to the box I placed on the coffee table. "I think that's much how she felt until she took over Hessler Group. She found her calling. I guess I thought I was following in her footsteps in a way. But I think we've established that I don't have the business chops that she did."

"You didn't even give yourself a chance," he says.

"There's no time for chances when people's livelihoods are on the line. I don't want to hurt anyone else. Not the Hessler employees, not you...not myself. I just want—"

"To leave?"

I want to deny it, but it's true. I want to go home. I miss my old life, things as they were. But the look of sadness in his eyes is making my stomach twist. "It's complicated," I say, placing my palm on his cheek.

"Len, I don't want to trap you in a life you hate. I don't want us to have a marriage like my grandparents or their parents before them, where we lead separate lives and grow to secretly resent each other. Is that where we're headed?"

"I don't know," I answer honestly. "But you know what I do

know?"

"What's that?"

I smile at him. "I love you, Dex. With my whole heart. Always have, always will."

He kisses my forehead. "Perfect timing. I needed to hear that right now. I love you too."

"Good, so we'll figure it all out together."

"Why don't you go home tomorrow? Spend some time with your family and friends while I sort things out here with your transition out as CEO. I'll meet you for the dive trip and we can talk about how we can make this work."

I breathe out in relief. "Okay, yes, that sounds good." I'm liberated. I no longer have to play career woman Barbie in this office, but a glaring issue arises in my mind. "But wait...what about my salary, Dex?"

"What about it?" he asks.

"You paid my salary up front, and now I didn't earn it... I already spent a huge chunk of it."

Dex lifts his eyebrows in surprise. "Not that I'm complaining, but on what? Do we own a Bugatti I have yet to see?" He smirks.

"I paid off all my debt. And my dad's. It was...a lot."

"All that money and the first thing you think to do is pay off your parents' debt?" Dex asks.

I shrug. "What else do I really need?"

He scoots closer, pulling me into his embrace. "This is why you hate it here. Your heart is too good. You'll never fit in here in my world," Dex mumbles. "Don't worry about the money."

"I am worried," I say. "I didn't hold up my end of the deal."

"Technically, you did," Dex murmurs against my neck. The familiar swirl of desire brews between my thighs. "It was shorter than a year, but you held the position. Now, the shares are going back to me. It's done. Money's yours. And it's just a drop in the bucket, Len. I'm going to take care of you, your family, and our family forever."

His hand slips between my thighs as he continues to kiss my

neck. "I really missed you," he murmurs. "And fuck, you smell so good." He grabs my hand and lays it across the bulge in his lap, then heads right back up my skirt, trying to wedge my thighs apart.

Glancing around the room nervously, I try to ward off Dex's advances. "Wait, Dex, this is your office."

He takes a brief break from kissing me to flash me a mischievous smirk. "Sure is. My office. My wife. And I want you here. Right now."

"There are people here," I insist, struggling to keep my head from going fuzzy as his lips touch all over my bare skin.

"It's Saturday. We're alone." One of his hands is still maneuvering up my thighs, now spread as far apart as my skirt will allow. Dex's other hand is on the back zipper of my dress, peeling it down.

"What about the executive team? They were *just* here."

"They're gone. They left in a hurry. It's fine." He grazes my clit with his thumb through my thong, and a tremor of desire surges through my body. But I stop myself before I get carried away.

"Wait, Dex, there's something I need to tell you about Denny," I say, clamping my legs shut, squeezing the life out of his hand.

There's a smirk on his face. Like he's thrilled I just denied him. "Did you just close your legs on me?"

I nod slowly, once again glancing at the box on the table. "I hate to pile on, but there's something else you need to know... I don't know how to say it."

"Are you leaving me?"

"No," I assure him with wide, horrified eyes.

"Is it medical? Are you hurt? Is someone else hurt?"

Puzzled, I answer, "No."

"Then I don't care right now. We can talk later."

"Dex...you can't possibly want sex."

He glances down at his crotch, proving me wrong. The obvious thick bulge is my clear answer. "Why wouldn't I want to feel close to you?"

"Because I just fucked your whole company up. You treat me with kid gloves, but admit it, if I were anybody else on the leadership team, you'd be ripping me a new one right now. I messed up. It's okay if you're angry with me."

He scowls at me. "Yeah, so mad," he says sarcastically, but then he pumps his eyebrows at me. "Bad girl."

"Dex."

"What?" he asks with a light laugh. "I'm sorry—you want me to be upset? I can't. Sure, it's an inconvenience, but it's not lost on me that even on my worst days, I'm not alone. Lennox, never forget that all you do is add to my life, not take away. I never needed a business guru of a wife. I just wanted someone who sticks by me even in the worst of times. I wanted a partner... My *best* friend. You've been so patient with me for three years when I was denying how much I actually wanted you. Even more so since we got to Miami and I left you alone. I'm not angry. I'm just grateful you're still here."

I cock my head to the side, staring at his handsome face. His light green-brown eyes look a little hazy at the moment. It's like he's in the eye of the storm, blissfully unbothered by the wreckage I've caused. *Is this love?* Automatic forgiveness? Problems become *our* problems. And there are no real consequences as long as we're together?

"That was a good speech," I say.

He smiles. "No speech. It's honestly how I feel." His hand is back on my breasts, cradling the right, then left side firmly. "Relax. Let me make this bad day better. Okay?"

I roll my eyes. "You're annoyingly kind to me. You shouldn't be trying to fix the bad day *I caused*. If anything, you should be punishing me."

I meant something along the lines of having to figure out a way to give back the salary I didn't earn. But, based on the devilish expression that consumes Dex's face, I know he took that a different way.

"You want a little punishment?" He lifts his brows. "Oh, Mrs.

Hessler, I can most definitely do that."

"I didn't mean..." I trail off, losing my words because I'm transfixed on his sexy smile—dangerously arousing. And now, I'm curious. "What'd you have in mind?"

"Spin around," he commands as he rises and undoes his necktie. He pulls down my zipper all the way and helps me step out of my dress. "Good girl," he says, smoothing out the tie in his hands. "Now, hands together." He makes quick work of binding my wrists securely. I'm barely able to wiggle my hands. "Too tight?" he asks.

I shake my head. "No, I'm okay."

"Good," he says, fisting his hard-on through his pants. "Now go bend over my desk."

CHAPTER 33

Lennox

Smack. I clench my toes when Dex's palm collides with my ass.

I'm going to come just like this—wrists bound, bare breasts smashed against the desk, my panties pulled down around my ankles.

He's torturing me with pleasure. Dex drops to his knees, spreading my ass cheeks so he has room to slide his tongue from my clit to my entrance. My knees buckle when he dips his tongue inside of me. There's something so viscerally delicious about getting eaten out from behind. I can't see what he's doing. Completely at his mercy, all I can do is feel. He flicks the tip of his wet tongue all over me, and right when I'm at the brink, the words spill right out of my mouth. "Oh, fuck...I'm close."

Dex stops what he's doing and spanks me on the other ass cheek. "Not yet," he warns.

I should've kept my mouth shut. "Fuck, Dex. *Enough*," I plead. "I need to come."

We've been playing this game for what seems like hours. My endurance is running out. Every time I'm close to relief, he pulls away and watches me, waiting for me to cool down and my brewing orgasm to completely dissipate. Then, he gets me all worked up again. The man has endless stamina for this.

"I thought you liked being edged."

"I do...for like ten minutes. Now, it's time."

"Oh, ho, ho," he says with a chuckle before smacking my ass again, making me grunt. "I don't think you get to decide when punishment is over, Trouble. That's my call."

"That's what this is? Payback for messing up?" I ask breathlessly. It dawns on me that Dex might actually be working out his aggression on my rear.

He leans over me from behind, one hand wrapping around my throat. He doesn't squeeze hard, just a little pressure as he whispers into my ear. "You messed up. But you're my wife, and you have my loyalty in all things. So, when I punish you, it's not because I'm angry. It's because you love it."

Whack. My ass burns then tingles as I groan in delight when he spanks me again. "*Oh, fuck,*" I wail.

"Let's see. Are you ready for me?" His fingers tiptoe down my lower back and over the curve of my ass before he sinks two fingers in. "So fucking wet. Say it," he growls in my ear.

I may be bound, pinned under him, with a red ass, but I have total control over my husband. I know exactly what he wants to hear. "I'm so wet, Dex. Only for you."

"Mmm," he moans into my ear. "I fucking love you."

"I love you too. Now, fuck me like you're trying to break me."

Already shirtless, he walks around the desk so I'm eye-level with his crotch. "Such a filthy mouth. Let's see if we can clean it out, hm?" He unbuttons his pants before untying my hands.

"Freeing me already?"

"I want your mouth, your hands, your dripping pussy, and your tight ass. I can't get enough. I want every single part of you, Len. Do you understand? *I need every part of you.*"

"Then take it." I open my mouth and grab him by the hips, guiding him to the back of my throat.

I expect him to buck his hips, trying to find his release, but instead, he cradles the back of my head gently, letting me barely wet his hard cock before he pulls away. "Spin around, baby." He taps the edge of the desk.

After kicking off my thong that was dangling by my ankles, I swivel my legs around so I'm seated at the very edge of his desk. His entire demeanor has changed. There's no playful smirk or dangerous smile. His brows aren't pumping as he's teasing me, withholding my relief. He looks drunk on desire, a man with one sole mission.

"You earned this one, baby. I'm going to make you come so hard." Dex grabs my ankles and crosses them before hooking them over one shoulder. He buries into me, balls deep, in one rapid thrust.

The spot he touches feels like a detonation button. Something electric surges through me and I can't even scream like I want to. I can't find my dirty words to egg him on. My brain empties of everything. Dex's eyes roll in the back of his head as he grinds into me in no hurry. Somewhere along the line, our kinky fucking turned into lovemaking. He sweetly kisses my ankles and calves, worshiping my body.

I win the race, trembling around him as I finally find my release. My orgasm is overwhelming and doesn't dissipate. I'm wrapped up in the surge of pleasure for so long that Dex has time to clamp his hands around my thighs, holding them as they shake, feeling the powerful effect of his body on mine.

"How was that, Mrs. Hessler?"

"So good. So, so, good, Dex."

"I want to hold you when I come." He scoops me off the desk, carrying me to the couch. He sets me down before positioning himself with his ass at the edge of the sofa. Then, he guides me onto his lap to straddle him. I slide down on his soaked cock, covered with my orgasm.

"You feel so fucking good," he moans when he buries back inside me. "So wet for me. Like you belong to me."

"I do." I grind my hips against him so he's touching that spot again. I flinch because it's too sensitive. The pleasure is now a little painful too. "Finish, Dex. In me."

He wraps me in a bear hug, pinning me against his chest, our sweaty, naked bodies melting into one. Bucking his hips like a madman, he roars in relief as he fills me. "Fuck, baby." He slumps backward onto the sofa, pulling me backward with him. I try to climb off his lap, but he tightens his grip. "No, stay a minute."

"Okay." I rest my ear against his chest, listening to his rapid heartbeat slowly calm. It's just the sound of us breathing for what feels like hours. Too warm and comfortable we can't move. Our breathing and heartbeats synchronize in silence until the office goes fuzzy and my eyelids grow too heavy.

I'm not sure who dozes off first. But eventually, the office disappears as a sweet, vivid dream replaces it...

I can almost feel the sunshine on my face as I look up at the blue sky. I'm lying in a hazy field of daisies. Dex lies right next to me, his large hand draped over my swollen belly.

"How about we name him Hayes?" Dex asks.

"As in Jacob Hayes?"

"Yeah," he says. "I think Grandpa would've liked that."

"Me too," I murmur, placing my hand over his. "I love that. Baby Hayes."

Dex

After pulling on my briefs and pants, I cover my naked, sleeping wife with my button-down shirt. I try to be gentle, but she stirs, her big brown eyes popping open.

"Time to go?" she asks.

"No, shhh. Rest, baby. I'm going to go grab some snacks from the breakroom and find you a blanket."

She snuggles into my shirt. "Thank you."

"Be right back."

I remember that Grandma kept throws in her office. I leave Lennox behind to relax on the couch while I hunt down supplies. As I turn the corner, it's clear from down the hallway that there's already someone in Grandma's office. *That's odd. Maintenance, maybe?*

I push open the cracked door and am surprised to see Denny sitting behind Grandma's old desk. Her legs are crossed, and she's

338

scowling as she stares out at the Miami skyline. With the sun just beginning to drop, the sunset glowing over the water line is stunning. How can she be looking at a view like that with such a miserable expression on her face?

"Hey, what're you doing here? Meeting Lennox? She's sleeping in my office."

Slowly swiveling in the executive chair to face the door, she looks me up and down. "Since when are shirts optional in this office?"

"It's a Saturday," I say. "No one should be here."

She gestures to herself with both hands. "And yet, here I am." Her tone is very cool and clipped. "How'd the meeting go?"

Denny was one of my first calls after I saw the article with Spellman's announcement. She's the one who suggested an immediate all-hands meeting to hunt down the rat. Except it wasn't a devious rat at all. Just my innocent wife who had no idea how Spellman would use her against the company.

"It was Lennox. An accident. She ran into Richard at the charity event and no doubt he lured her into spilling some secrets. She had no idea—"

"Please, Dex. She's not an idiot. She should know better."

I narrow my eyes. "He alluded to the fact that we finished the merger. She thought she was talking to a team member."

Denny shrugs her shoulders. "Dismiss her from the CEO position. We've dealt with this incompetence long enough. First Tearney, now Richard. Get rid of the weak link."

Now I'm pissed. "The weak link you're referring to *is my wife*."

Denny crosses her arms tightly, her lips pursing. "This whole dedicated husband bit was cute at first... Now I'm over it."

"What the hell are you doing right now?" I ask, shocked at her audacity. "Why are you speaking to me this way?"

Denny holds up two fingers, her long, white acrylic nails filed into what look like daggers. "Two things you need to know, Dex. One, Lennox will be removed. That was an extreme dereliction of duty, and the leadership board will call for her termination."

"Denny, why are you coming down so hard on Lennox? She's been nothing but kind to you."

She grumbles in frustration. "The *second* thing you need to know is that once Lennox is removed, I'm legally challenging you for ownership of the company. Actually, I'm challenging you for ownership of *everything*. We both may be bastards, but at the very least I'm a Hessler. This is my office"—she glances around the room, then narrows her gaze on me—"not your wife's, not yours, and goddamn, am I sick of babysitting your spoiled ass."

Denny picks up a folded piece of paper on the desk and holds it out to me. I take two steps in from the doorway but don't reach for the paperwork. "What's that?"

"DNA test."

The familiar rush of adrenaline fills my veins. The throbbing in my head begins as the familiar signs of a panic attack emerge. I fight it the best I can. This is not a moment to show weakness. I'm feeling a lot of things, mostly shock. This is the woman who all but begged to be my second mother, and now she's trying to take away my company.

"Whose DNA test?" I muster out.

"Yours, of course. I've known who my father was since I was thirteen years old. Why do you think I never left with my mother for Europe? I found out I was a product of Harrison's affair from my mother's drunk ramblings. She wasn't supposed to tell me, but it slipped. And once I knew, I stuck around for so long because I thought..." She shakes her head, not finishing her sentence.

Thinking back on the stories Grandma told me, I begin to fill in the blanks. "You thought you'd win Harrison over if he got to know you? Then he'd give everything to you?"

Denny rolls her eyes. "It's not that wicked. I just wanted a relationship with my father. I wanted one of my parents to give a shit about me. The closest I got was Dottie. But I never really had her, did I? I thought I got close when your mother died."

I take a few steps closer. "Tread lightly when you talk about my mother, Denny," I say between gritted teeth, not knowing where this is headed.

"I could never say anything bad about Melody. She was perfect. So *fucking* perfect that even when she was gone, Harrison would rather drink his grief away, mourning the daughter that wasn't even his. He couldn't be bothered to get to know the one that was still right in front of him. And Dottie..." Denny has to press her trembling lips together. She takes a moment to compose herself. "As soon as Melody was gone, she fixated on you. *Golden Child Dex.* You're all Harrison talked about when he was sober enough to form words. *Fuck,* I was so sick of hearing your name. I was always the help. Never family. And now...well, let's just say payback is a bitch."

It's too much to absorb all at once. Denny has secretly hated me all this time? So, all her affection and attention wasn't love. It was just to keep tabs on me. Like a cobra waiting for her moment to strike. "What do you even want with Hessler Group? Hmm? I thought your passion was spending money, not making it. You really want to inherit and run all this bullshit?"

"No, I don't. I'm going to sell it off in pieces. Then, I'll do the same with Hessler Estate. I'm going to tear down everything that piece of shit worked so hard to keep together."

I shake my head in disbelief. "Spite is a poison, Denny."

"Well, revenge must be the antidote." She taps the desk, her lips curling into a cruel smile. "Because this feels pretty damn good."

I glance at the paper in front of her, wondering if she actually has a claim to any inheritance. I supposed it's possible if Harrison had an affair. And if Denny is a product of that affair and I'm not a Hessler... But wait, how can that be? That would mean Grandma lied to Harrison, to Mom, and me—for my entire life. *Grandma's not a liar.* This...this can't really be, can it? I need more answers. "If I'm not Harrison's, then who?"

"Hell if I know, Dex. This paper just proves you're not a Hessler," Denny says with a snarky tone. "You're a lost puppy. Sucks to be lied to your whole life, huh? Join the club."

She's around so much, I have no doubt she snagged a hair or a used cup for those test results. Denny's my emergency contact. She hires my staff and orders my medication. This woman has had so much access to my life...while hating my guts the whole time. "I didn't agree to that DNA test. It's not legally admissible."

She nods. "You're right. But when I sue you in place of your grandma for fraud and con artistry for impersonation of a family member to steal a fortune that was never yours...well, the court is going to require a legal DNA test that'll give the same results I have right here." She taps the paper in front of her. "Just bow out, Dex. This isn't your fight."

"I'm still Dottie's grandson. That means something."

"You're forgetting," Denny seethes as she rises. "*She's not a Hessler.* I am. I am the only motherfucking person alive with a legitimate claim to *all of it.*" By the end of her sentence, she's shrieking, near deranged, as if years of angst and hatred are bubbling to the surface. "I gave up everything for this family. My marriage. My chance at motherhood. I tried for years to be the mother you lost, and never once could you look me in the eyes and tell me genuinely that you loved me. I was always treated like an outsider. Fuck all of you. Now you can be the one left out, watching everything you ever wanted from outside a glass window. An article is running next week exposing Dottie for the con artist she was. I'm telling the world what the Hesslers did to me. Hiding me, bullying my mother...all of it. It'll ruin you."

I press my lips together as her breathing calms. Her brows finally relax, and her eyes shrink to normal proportions.

"This is the part where you beg me to keep your secrets," Denny snarks.

"I did...Denny."

"What?" she asks, confused.

"I loved you. I have a hard time saying it because the people I love most tend to leave me. Of course, I didn't want another mother. It would've been too painful to lose you, too. Up until about ten minutes ago, you were my friend. Friendship is the base of some of the strongest relationships, even more significant than bloodlines and family." I point right at her. "But thank you for showing me your true colors. I don't need to pity you anymore."

Denny glances over my shoulder. "She makes you weak, boy."

I turn to see Lennox standing in the doorway in just my shirt, clutching tightly to an envelope. She's staring at Denny. If looks could kill, Denny would be a limp body on the ground.

Instead, she keeps talking. "A better man would at least try to defend what's his. You were never cut out to lead this company. There's not an ounce of Harrison in you."

"You sure are obsessed with the man you claim to hate," I say. "Like I said, *poison*."

"Shut up," Denny snaps back. "And by the way, Lennox, *thank you*. I had my suspicions, but your little tip before the charity dinner really helped put things in place. I thought I'd have to get rid of you, but it's been kind of fun watching you ruin your husband. I can always rely on your loose lips to get you in trouble." She winks.

Lennox takes a few angry steps towards Denny and ends up right by my side. Her fists ball up. "You snake. Kat told me you set me up for that article, and you sent Richard over to my table that night at the charity event, too, didn't you? You told him to make me think the merger had gone through so I'd say whatever."

Denny smiles. "And tipped the server an outrageous amount to keep your champagne glass full all night. Too fucking easy. You're all just puppets."

"Get the fuck out, Denny," I roar, finally hearing enough.

"I thought I made it clear when I said this was my office now."

"Get out!" I bellow, making both Denny and Lennox jump. "Call your lawyer. You want a fight? You got one. Good luck to you. But as of right now, you're not the CEO, and you're not an heiress. You're nothing but fired. Get the fuck out of my sight." My clenched fists and throbbing temples must be enough warning because Denny, without another word, brushes past us and exits the office, a sickening smile on her face.

The moment she's gone, I pick up the DNA test she left behind, trying to make sense of the paperwork. Outside of the "no match" at the top of the document, it's just a lot of medical jargon I don't understand.

"This is what you were trying to tell me, isn't it?" I ask, spinning around to face Lennox.

She nods somberly. "I didn't lie to you. I had my suspicions but never proof."

I hold up the paper. "Here's proof."

"I didn't want you to be mad, Dex."

Lennox has never lied to me before. Her honesty is my favorite thing about her, and admittedly, I feel a little betrayed. But at the same time, how could she explain? To walk into all of this as a stranger and have to shatter everything I thought I knew about my family...how could I ask that of her?

"I'm not mad at you, Lennox," I interrupt. "I get it. Some secrets aren't yours to share."

She closes the space between us and weaves her fingers in mine. Squeezing my hand hard, she adds, "Not at me, Dex. I didn't want you to be mad at your grandma. She had her reasons. I asked you to read the letters because they tell her story. She left them in plain sight in her office. Come to think of it, she probably *wanted* someone to find that box of letters. She wanted someone to know her real story."

I'm trying not to be angry. All that time Grandma preached loyalty and love, yet she lied to me. I look at Lennox, her soft brown eyes calming me. "I never knew my father. Now, I don't know my grandfather. All I have is what Grandma told me...except now she's a liar."

"I knew your Grandpa," Lennox says with a small smile.

I blink at her. "You're suggesting Jacob—"

"Not suggesting. *Confirming.*" Lennox pulls me by my hand to the sofa, guiding me to sit. She hands me the letter, now wrinkled where she was clutching it so hard. "I've been reading the letters for over a month now, piecing the story together. Jacob used to write these tragic poems about 'Daisy' and how he missed out on his long-lost love. When I met your grandma, I assumed they were about her." Lennox taps her temple. "It dawned on me tonight that he wasn't writing about your grandma. He was writing about his daughter. The baby he never got to meet."

My chest constricts, the familiar ache anytime someone brings up my mom. I hate this topic. I hate longing for what I can't have. No matter how much money I have, I can't turn back time and save the years with my mother that I was robbed of.

"What're you saying, Len?"

"I was poring over that box, trying to find the perfect Dottie letter to begin to explain everything. But when you left a few moments ago, I found *this*." She points to the letter in my hands. "It's the only letter in the box that was to Dottie, not *from* her. She kept this close because it must've meant a lot to her. This letter has all your answers, Dex. I promise." She tilts her head to the side, studying my expression.

"This is from Jacob, then?"

Lennox shakes her head. "No. From Harrison."

CHAPTER 34

Dottie

Ten Years Earlier

Miami

Heart racing, I pace back and forth on the throw rug in my office, feeling the plush fabric flatten under my feet. I stare at my box of letters set neatly on the coffee table. On top, an envelope with a blue sticky note:

I'm sorry. I read your letters.

– Harrison

Years of being in a leadership position have taught me composure under pressure. I assess the situation in front of me and try to draw all the possible conclusions so I can counteract each with a viable solution.

Obviously, Harrison managed to get himself out of his chair today and make his way to the office. It's been nearly six months since he visited headquarters. Every now and then, he asks questions at home about business logistics. Perhaps just for something to talk about at the dinner table. Now that Dex is away at college, dinners are mostly silent. The sound of ice clinking in glasses and silverware scraping across the dinnerware is the only thing we hear as we hurry through the meal the chef prepared.

After that, we usually retreat to opposite sides of the estate. Harrison drowning himself in liquor. Me, drowning in fantasies of a different life.

I was late to the office today. It's Friday, so I went to lay daisies on Melody's grave. When I got back, my secret box of letters was on the coffee table, topped by a letter from Harrison and the sticky note confession. I know Harrison always suspected I kept in touch with Jacob. He hated the notion, wanting me to be devoted to only him. But more for possession, not love. He's a jealous man, quick to anger.

I'm quite shocked he took the time to write me a letter. He could've told me off much quicker. Harrison lives in a state of delusion. Me writing letters I never intend to send would be the utmost treachery in his eyes. However, the child he fathered, then tried to erase like she was an arithmetic error written in pencil, was merely a speedbump in our marriage. Narcissism at its finest. He was so different from the man who proposed to me all those years ago.

He's also never forgiven me for keeping Denny so close. Yes, I pitied her. Her excuse of a mother couldn't see what a beautiful daughter she had the privilege of bringing into this world. Product of an affair or not, Denny was just an innocent child who deserved love. But also, I wanted Harrison to rise above the circumstances and give this child the life she deserved. If I could move on from his indiscretion...why couldn't he?

After dodging all the legal red tape Harrison and his parents set up to keep her from knowing who she truly was, I found a way to keep Denny. Our guardianship expired on her eighteenth birthday. Keeping her as an assistant was the only way I could take care of her the way she deserved. Once my initial anger subsided, all I wanted was for Harrison to have a real relationship with his daughter. He refused.

And now, here I am. Staring in the face of my own so-called unfaithfulness. But can we really compare a child to unsent letters? I'm sure Harrison could find a way. My hand trembling,

I pick up the letter, ready to face the consequences. If Harrison read every single letter, he knows where my heart has been for our entire marriage.

Deep breath, I tell myself, bracing for the putrid anger I'm sure this letter contains.

Dear Dottie,

I can imagine what's going through your mind at the moment. If you're angry with me for reading your letters, I'm sorry. Perhaps you think I'm angry with you for the contents. I assure you, I'm not.

Actually, I'm thinking of how little I know you after four decades of marriage. How much you like to write, your favorite flower, your worries and fears in the office.

I suppose I never took the time to get to know you all these years together, which is why none of your beautiful, heartbreaking love letters are to me.

I know the man I am. I am a product of my parents and their parents before them. Maybe that's why I was so drawn to you. Somehow, I sensed you could break the cycle.

My original intention was to become more like you. In the end, I fear I changed your heart more than I allowed you to change mine. And for that, I'm sorry.

You deserved better, my sweetheart.

I never thanked you for being loyal when you could've strayed. Where I was weak, you were strong. You gave me a family when I thought I'd never have one. And please know,

Dottie, in my way, to the best of my ability, which I know has been unimpressive, I do love you.

I miss our daughter every day. She may be Jacob's, but she's also mine. We shouldn't have hidden Melody's adoption. It was never a shameful thing. Becoming her father was the pride and joy of my life.

And now, Dex is just as much a piece of me. In a way, the son I always dreamed of having. I am so proud of him. He only has the good parts of all of us. Your intelligence and kindness. My strength. Melody's beauty. And the parts of him I don't recognize in myself...maybe that's Jacob's spirit.

When we're gone, all that'll be left are the pieces. Just a snapshot into the lives we led. The world may never know the full story, but the beautiful parts they'll see I know are all because of you.

Thank you for that, Dottie. And I'm sorry I've taken so much more than I could give.

I'll see you for dinner.

Tonight, I'll bring daisies.

Love,

Harrison

I'm normally not a crier, but the warm tears drench my cheeks as my heartbeat thuds hard in my chest. Completely awestruck, I reread the letter twice more.

It took an entire lifetime, but here's a glimpse of the old Harrison. The man I thought I could love. And I do. In a different way than I expected, but it's still profound. My heart may be with Jacob, but my family is with Harrison.

I tuck Harrison's letter into my box, deciding it's sacred enough to stay.

The remainder of my day is back-to-back meetings—budget approvals and quarterly earnings. But I decide to cancel it all. I can't remember the last time I took a day off. I think I'll cut out early and get my hair touched up and my nails refreshed. Bright red, as always. It's Harrison's favorite color.

I smile to myself. For the first time in as long as I can remember, I'm looking forward to dinner with my husband.

CHAPTER 35

Lennox

Present Day

Las Vegas

On Tuesday morning, I find myself on Avery and Finn's porch, a place that's always felt like a second home. Before heading inside, I pull out my phone, debating if I should call Dex this morning. It's already near eleven o'clock in Miami. No doubt he's awake. He's probably been buried in meetings since the crack of dawn, still dealing with the fray.

After our confrontation with Denny a few days ago, Dex asked for a little time to himself. We had already agreed that I would go home and visit friends and family in Vegas, but after Denny's threat, I didn't want to leave him. Dex was eerily calm and quiet. He didn't say much after reading Harrison's letter. Instead, he asked me to stay in Las Vegas until our dive trip.

When Kat's article hits the media, he knows the reporters and lawyers will be swarming. He wants me far away from the chaos as he handles the shitstorm himself.

Very reluctantly, I agree to his wishes. But I feel like I made the wrong choice. I should be there with him, braving the storm right by his side. I'm not against the whole idea of the damsel in distress. Some call it anti-feminist, but personally, I love when Dex sees me, validates me, and saves me. However, sometimes it's my husband who is in distress. I think in a healthy relationship, I'm supposed to save him, too. That's equality. We're strong for each other, and we're soft for each other. Balance.

I dial his number when the urge to talk to him wins over my logic to give him space.

"Hey you," he answers. "How'd you sleep?"

"Not so great without you. Why'd you send me away again?"

He grumbles. "I did *not* send you away. I wanted you to be with your parents, Finn, and Avery, and not waiting around the penthouse alone while I sort through everything."

I scoff. "Sure, that's why."

"What's that supposed to mean?"

"You didn't want me there messing more stuff up," I tease. It was mostly a playful joke, but when Dex doesn't respond right away, my feelings are hurt. "Sorry...that's probably accurate, isn't it?"

"No, not at all. I just didn't want you to see me like...this."

"Like what, babe?"

He sighs heavily. "The Denny stuff is bothering me more than it should. I'm upset, I guess."

I plant myself on the edge of the concrete porch, crossing my ankles on the step below. "You should be very upset. Talk to me."

"I closed all the bank accounts she had access to. I rescinded my offer to give her Hessler Estate. She's broke and had to leave the property today. She came out swinging, cocky and overconfident, but she overlooked the fact that my mom was *legally* adopted. It just wasn't publicized. Meaning, I'm still Harrison's legitimate heir."

"Isn't that a good thing, Dex? She tried but failed to take everything from you."

"She was so angry, Len. She hated Harrison so much it bled into her relationships with all of us. That's what his absenteeism did to her. He drove her to be this unhinged."

I wiggle my toes inside my shoes, waiting for him to elaborate, but when he doesn't, I bring myself to ask, "What's worrying you?"

"Will I do that to our kids?"

I clear my throat. "Well, I'd very much prefer you don't cheat on me and expect me to raise your love child."

"You should've seen the contract Harrison and his parents made Denny's mom sign, Len. Hank helped me dig it up. He had a lot more information about the whole situation, being one of Harrison's only real friends. Believe me when I say Harrison didn't love Denny's mom. That contract was a prison sentence. Harrison's parents even offered to incentivize her to abort the baby so they wouldn't have to deal with it."

"Oh, God," I murmur. "That's awful of them."

"I read all of Grandma's letters, by the way. In one sitting."

"Oh, for shame," I tease.

"What?" he asks with a chuckle. "You told me to. You read them all."

"Um, no. I savored them. A letter or two a day. It was the only thing I looked forward to at the office."

"You hated it that much?" Dex asks, his tone somber.

"No, I didn't hate it. Actually, I had a lot of ideas that I couldn't really see through. I was there to support you, babe. Not move mountains."

"That's how Grandma started, too. Just there to support Harrison. And look at what she was able to build. Maybe we should hear some of your big ideas."

I roll my eyes at the phone. "I'm no Dottie Hessler. And are we forgetting I got fired?"

"Well, I'm the boss now, and I can offer you whatever job you want...or..." he trails off.

"Or what?"

"With everything that happened...it got me thinking. Maybe it's time for Hessler Group to go public. We can take on investors and hire a board who actually gets to make decisions. The burden wouldn't be all mine anymore. We could walk away and have a normal life if you want. Move back into the Las Vegas house, be neighbors with Finn and Avery. See your parents every weekend. What do you think?"

What do I think? It's my dream come true. But I can't help but wonder if that's what's best for Dex. "Going public means pretty much giving up your company, right? If you have a real board in power, they could fire you as they please."

"Yes, and they most definitely would. Their decisions would be made on the biggest profit margins, not about what's best for the employees and customers."

"Then why would you even consider that?" I ask, gripping the phone tighter in my hand.

"Because I don't want to waste away in an office like Grandma and Harrison. I also don't want to lose you like Jacob lost Grandma. I want to see you every day I'm alive. I want to be there for our future kids and have priorities that matter. After forty years of marriage, I don't want to be writing apology letters to you as you pine for another man. I refuse to let the woman I love live a lonely life."

"Dex, I won't—"

The front door opens behind me, and Avery peeks her head around the door. "Hey, I thought I heard you out here. Am I interrupting?"

"It's Dex," I tell her.

"Oh, okay," she says, stepping out onto the porch. "I put an alert on my phone every time BuzzLit drops a new article. Kat just published something a few minutes ago."

I nod in defeat, then tell Dex, "Kat's article is live on BuzzLit. Do you want to let PR know? I read it over, and if she reported one false thing about Dottie..." I look to Avery. "You said we have a case for defamation, right?"

Avery nods slowly. "If it impacts revenue. We'll figure it out together. Finn's grandpa, Senior, has some friends really high up in the publishing industry. We're all ready to pull some strings and get this taken down." She squeezes my shoulder sweetly, then gives me a quick, silent wave before retreating back into the house. She leaves the door ajar for me.

"Did you hear that, babe? Avery's going to help. Same with

354

Finn and his family. You have me. We're not going to let this pass without a fight. We're all here for you...and Dottie. And no matter what ridiculous bullshit Kat puts out there, and no matter what anyone says in response, don't forget who you are and where you belong."

"And where's that?" Dex asks softly.

"With me. I don't care if you're a scuba diving instructor or the CEO of a billion-dollar conglomerate. It doesn't matter. Don't you see? You sent me home, but I'm not really home, am I?"

"So, Miami feels like home now?" he asks with a small scoff.

"No. But you do."

He exhales long and slow. "I really love you, Len."

"I love you too." I peek through the cracked open door, feeling the itch to face the music and get this over with. "Okay, babe, do you want to read this article together?"

"No, I don't think I can stomach it. I'll let PR know to take a look, but otherwise, let's just move forward together. I have to run to my eleven o'clock meeting. After that, I'll have them warm up the jet. How about I cancel the rest of my week and we head to Cozumel early? I can give you the honeymoon I've been promising."

I smile into the phone. "Sounds perfect, Mr. Hessler."

As soon as I hang up, I head into the house. I'm intercepted in the hallway by Finn who ruffles my hair in the annoying big-brother way he always does. I'm just about to sass off to him for ruining my hair when he pulls me into a tight bear hug. "Hey, Lenny," he says and kisses the top of my head.

"Don't call me that." My voice is muffled with my face smashed against his chest.

"I really missed you being here and mooching. I have so many snacks lying around without you here to devour them." He's teasing me, but his tone is genuine.

"I missed you too," I say.

He finally releases me. "Want some coffee? Avery says this article is a big deal. Are you and Dex going to be okay?"

I nod. "Yeah, we'll figure it out."

I follow him into the kitchen, where Avery's perched on the countertop, legs crossed. Finn squeezes Avery's knee as he passes her to fetch me a mug. Her perplexed expression relaxes into a sweet smile at his touch, then she's right back to scowling at her phone again.

"How bad is it?" I ask, grimacing.

"Are you sure the article about Dex's grandma was going out today?"

"That's what Kat said."

"I don't know, Lennox. This is about an affair, and it's certainly scandalous. This man, Scott Ramsie, is running for a senate seat. But I read the whole thing, and this has nothing to do with the Hesslers." Avery holds out her phone, showing me the title of Kat's article.

Confessions of a Gossip Columnist: One affair, years of blackmail, and the resignation that's been a long time coming.

By Kat Tearney

My jaw falls open in shock. "Oh my God... Kat actually did it," I murmur.

"Did what?" Avery asks, tilting her head to the side.

"She set herself free."

Actually, she set all of us free.

CHAPTER 36

Lennox

Present Day

Cozumel

Dousing my mask with baby-safe soap, I rub little circles into the lens. Leaning over the boat rail, I scoop water into the mask, rinsing it off.

"Want me to defog your mask?" Dex asks, making his way to the front of the boat.

"Just did it," I answer back. I glance at the phone in his hand and very seriously consider snatching it and throwing it overboard. "I was promised a work-free honeymoon, husband. How do you even have service out here?"

The cerulean blue ocean surrounds us on all sides. There's no shore in sight. The water looks like an endless field of aquamarine gems. I've never experienced dive conditions this calm and clear before.

Dex holds up his hands in surrender, then tucks his phone away into the front pouch of his backpack. "I wasn't working. That was my insider at Peak Publication giving me the details on what happened with Kat."

"What happened?" I scoot to the edge of the bench.

"Apparently the article written about the Hesslers magically disappeared from the server the day before it was supposed to post. Her boss was furious and told her to pull an all-nighter to get it rewritten and ready for publication. She did. It went through editing and everything, but somehow, the wrong article was mysteriously uploaded." Dex widens his eyes. "She quit before they could fire her. They were going to pull the article down, but it's getting more click traffic than all of the other articles on their site combined."

"Where's Kat now?" I ask.

"Packed up and left. No one knows," Dex says with a small shrug.

I bet I do. I bet Kat went overseas chasing world news stories. Maybe she'll resurface one day in the *New York Times* or the *Wall Street Journal* with a new pen name, writing the stories she always wanted to.

"I think I'll write her a thank you letter," I say.

"But you don't know where she is."

"I'll pull one from Dottie's playbook. Maybe I'll start my own letterbox. Sometimes things need to be said, even if they can't be heard."

"Grandma used to say that letters were for lost apologies." He smiles. "Maybe they can be for lost 'thank you's' too."

Dex rises and makes his way to the dive equipment. He checks the gauges and synchs something up to his fancy dive watch. Picking up my BCD that he already hooked up to the tank, he says, "I brought another set of weights today. You almost floated away yesterday."

When we got to Cozumel yesterday morning, we hit the water right away. Just a short dive. I had trouble getting my bearings at first. It had been so long since I'd been in the water that I'd forgotten most of my technical skills. For Dex, it was like riding a bike. He patiently paced with me as I blew through my tank in twenty minutes. I got a little nervous as we dipped below thirty meters, unable to keep my breath calm and collected. We had to cut the dive short when I ran out of air.

"I've got my sea legs today. I'm fine."

"Humor me?" he asks with a cute pout. He holds up the weights, asking for my permission. Why fight? He's always right.

"Fine," I mumble.

Dex slips the flat-weighted plates into the pockets of my BCD. It makes me feel like an amateur. Dex can free dive with ease. The more I practice, the faster I'll get there. I'll never move as gracefully as my husband in the water, but I'll spend a lifetime trying.

"It's distracting to dive with you," Dex says as he makes his way over to the bench to sit right next to me.

Instinctively, I turn so he can zip up my wet suit, covering the top half of my bikini. "Why do you say that?"

"I should be appreciating all the marine life down there. Instead, it's impossible to take my eyes off of you."

I laugh. "Only because yesterday, I was a flight risk and kept floating away."

"Partially," he says with a smirk. "But mostly because you're the only thing I think is more beautiful than the ocean."

I smile at him. "Dex, you better stay this sweet and cheesy for the rest of our lives. Promise me."

He laughs. "I promise."

I tap his shoulder. "Okay, now let me zip your suit up."

But instead of turning around obediently, he grabs my hand, bringing it to his lips. He plants sweet kisses across my knuckles. "I did a thing," he says.

I lift my brows. "Care to elaborate?"

"Denny dropped her lawsuit trying to claim Hessler Group."

"I know, babe," I answer absentmindedly.

"But I still gave her the Hessler Estate. Is that okay with you? I mean, she hasn't accepted yet, but my real estate team reoffered. We'll see what she says. The condition is that she leaves us alone. No contact."

My heart thuds for nothing else but confusion. "Why?"

"Because I feel guilty. Denny faced all the same obstacles and pressures that I did growing up, and I think...maybe I could've turned out similarly. Angry and bitter. Feeling empty, alone, and full of regret. Grandma saved me when she sent me away to Vegas. And I met you. *You saved me.*"

I place my hand against his cheek, watching the sun gleam against his face, making his hazel eyes look like a bright, light green. "What does that have to do with the house, though?"

"A peace offering, I suppose. As much as I want to hate her, I just feel bad for her because, somehow, I got out. I'm happy. I have you. She lost her whole family, and I'm just starting mine." Dex places his hand against my stomach.

I squint at him like he's crazy. "I'm not pregnant."

"Yet. That was the other thing I wanted to talk to you about. I asked Hank to step in as an intermediary for a while at Hessler Group."

My eyes nearly pop out of my head. "What? I thought you decided to keep Hessler Group privately owned. What about the employees and—"

"I am. *I am.* I trust Hank. He'll still report to me, and I'll oversee everything. I'll still consult in a similar fashion to what I was doing before Grandma's passing."

"Does that mean..." I bite my bottom lip, not finishing my sentence, a little afraid I'm drawing the wrong conclusion.

"Yeah, if you'd like, we'll move back into the Vegas house. Let's take a few years and put down roots. Let's start a family alongside Avery and Finn. Spend time with your parents while we can. Hank says he can more than handle it for a few years while we live our lives."

"Dex...I..."

"Is that what you want?"

"*Yes,*" I muster out before he can misunderstand my response. I'm struggling to give any other answer because I'm so overly enthused. "I would've gone back with you, you know. I would stand by you through anything."

"Well, one day, we'll go back. But right now, I want to give you these years while I can. Just you and me and all the little people I'm going to put in here." He pats my stomach.

I smile, enjoying the warm sun against my skin. The boat rocks softly on the water, lulling me into a trance of comfort. I'm enjoying paradise. "We'll make some babies soon. But for now, maybe I want a couple more honeymoons."

"Fair enough."

"Hank is really okay with all of this?"

"Of course. I mean, he's about to get a hefty salary bump, but overall, I think he's just happy to help Harrison and Grandma in some way. He did have one condition, though."

"Being?"

"He wants you on his board of advisors."

"What?" I squall.

"Minimal commitment," Dex says. "Just join a few video conferences. Hank likes your ideas, and he wants your help bridging some gaps."

I roll my eyes, pretending like I'm put off. "You're never just going to let me be the trophy wife I am, are you?" I flip my hair as sassily as I can.

"Funny. I can tell him no if you want."

"I can't turn down his only condition. I'll learn. And plus... Hank's right. I have some ideas if anybody cares to listen."

"I'm listening." Dex kisses my forehead, then each of my cheeks. I catch a whiff of his sweet, spicy cologne mixed with the salty ocean spray. If I could bottle up this perfect moment and keep it forever, I would.

"Okay, baby. Time to suit up."

We tug on our BCDs, test our regulators, and the instructor side of Dex even doubles back to check my straps. Force of habit. He'll be doing this all day tomorrow and the rest of the weekend once the dive students arrive.

The radio intercom crackles to life, and our boat captain, who has been quietly ignoring us, answers the call. He speaks in his native language, back and forth with another boat captain. Luckily for me, he's bilingual.

"Señor Hessler," he says when he's wrapped up his conversation. "Great news. We got a report from a few divers just coming up. There are at least two sharks down there."

Shark. My stomach flips as the dread washes over me.

Dex's eyes widen and he shakes his head fervently at the boat captain. He unsubtly nods his head toward me. "Some of us are a little skittish around big marine life."

"Well, this was an almost fun dive trip," I say, flashing Dex a disingenuous smile. I start unbuckling my equipment. "What should we do for lunch? I'm craving shrimp tacos."

"Lennox, we're all the way out here. It's beautiful dive conditions and nurse sharks are bottom feeders. They are harmless unless you swim right up and punch one in the gills. I promise it's okay."

"Oh no, no, no, buddy. Don't even think about it. I'm not going anywhere near a shark."

"They're basically sea puppies," Dex says. "Sweet and peaceful."

"And they're vegetarian!" the boat captain adds with a chuckle.

"Not helpful," I say, unimpressed with his sarcastic joke.

"There are big sea turtles down there. Rays too. So many big, colorful fish. Stunning coral in kaleidoscope colors. It's breathtaking, Len. Don't you want to see?"

I pucker my bottom lip and nod. "A little. But I can't do sharks. Any kind of shark."

Dex stands in front of me, refastening my vest one buckle at a time. "You helped me face my fear. Let me help you face yours. Do you trust me?"

"I do, Dex. But I'm scared."

"I know. But I'll be right there with you. I've got you." Pulling me to the edge of the boat, his hand firmly in mine, he squeezes. Then he steps off the edge with barely a splash. Dex disappears under the water for what seems like an eternity, then resurfaces.

"Water feels amazing, Len."

I shake my head, the anxiety buzzing like electricity all over my body. "I can't do it!" Maybe if the stupid boat captain didn't say anything. But I heard "shark," and now my flippered feet won't move.

Dex holds out his hand. "Come on, baby. You and me. If we're going to be shark bait, we'll be shark bait together."

"That's not as romantic as you think it is," I call back.

He laughs. "Lennox Hessler, get your perfect ass in this water. I won't let anything happen to you. *Please?* I want to share this with you. It's like nothing you've ever seen. I promise."

I blow out a deep breath and keep my eyes fixed on Dex's face. Like I always do around Dex, I push out all logic and reason and trust my gut. I trust the man who holds my heart and has since the very first day I met him. My best friend. My partner. He smiles at me, and I know with my whole heart it's the only smile in the world that could convince me to swim with motherfucking sharks.

I clamp my eyes shut and draw in a deep breath. I hold it as I force my feet forward.

One...two...three...

Splash.

THE END

EPILOGUE

Dex

Two Years Later

Miami

Lennox holds up the old, taped-together Polaroid, lining up the dock in the picture perfectly. Grandma and Jacob are sitting side by side in the photo, a few inches between them. Grandma's hand is planted flat on the dock, and his is draped over hers. Jacob's staring at her, his profile clear while Grandma looks out ahead at the water.

"Right here," she says. "This is exactly where they must've taken the picture." Lennox points to the rickety gazebo behind us. "Whoever took the photo must've been standing there. I bet there are more pictures lost out in the world. No way they would've just taken one. Look at this view."

You can't buy property like this anymore. It's all been snapped up by real estate developers. This might be the last quiet marina in Miami. The water is still, undisturbed by boats. The neighbors are far away, their homes veiled by the thick foliage. This is as close to a private retreat anyone can get.

After some heavy investigative research, we learned that this residence belonged to Jacob's employer long ago—a ship captain from a revered family line. They owned an entire acre right along the marina and let a few of the ship's crew members stay in the guest houses from time to time. This gazebo is apparently where Grandma and Jacob would sneak away to be together. Fifty years later, the property is all but abandoned, the family now living in Europe somewhere, or so our real estate agent tells us.

I stomp my foot against the dock. The unsteady board bends underneath my feet. "Needs some maintenance," I say. "This whole dock has to be rebuilt, and that thing"—I point my thumb over my shoulder—"is a safety hazard. The wood is well beyond rotted. It has to come down."

Lennox's eyes bulge. "Mr. Hessler, have you no magic in your soul? You can't rip this place apart. This is your legacy." She steps out of her sandals and sits down carefully at the edge of the dock, dangling her feet so the very tips of her toes touch the water line.

"Please be careful, Len," I say.

"Sit with me," she instructs, patting beside her. Len seems completely unbothered by the splintering wood. She plants her hands behind her and leans backward. Her flowy tank top catches the breeze, and it melds to the obvious curve of her stomach.

"You're finally starting to show." I sit down next to her so carefully, as if my weight could snap the boards and send my five-month-pregnant wife right into the water below.

Lennox cradles her stomach affectionately with one hand. "He's getting pretty big. But the reason my stomach looks like it's about to pop is that footlong I just wolfed down."

I cackle. "Baby, I think that's my favorite thing about you."

"What is?" She tents her hand over her forehead, protecting her eyes from the sun as she turns to look at me.

"Two years of being a billionaire, and you still ask for Subway every time we're on the road." Lennox craves a sandwich at least three times a week. She's enjoyed her Italian B.M.T.s all throughout the pregnancy thus far. Just these days she has them nuke the deli meat in the microwave first.

She laughs. "Honestly, I've grown to appreciate the fancy shoes, but you will never ever convince me to eat caviar and pâté again."

"Fair enough," I respond with a chuckle.

A dreamy smile on her face, Lennox takes in a panoramic

view of the entire dock. "Hmm," she murmurs.

"What's on your mind?"

"I feel really close to Dottie right now." She picks up the picture she set beside her, then scoots closer to my side. I wrap my arm around her shoulder, and she cuddles in next to me. "We both sat here, pregnant...in love." She hands me the Polaroid.

"You can't know she was pregnant in this picture."

"Yes, I can. See the way he's looking at her? Like it hurts... I bet you this was the night they said goodbye. They must've taken a picture to mark a memory. She was pregnant and walking away from the love of her life. And it broke him to let them go."

I stare at the picture, trying to make sense of the situation. "If they were that in love, he shouldn't have let her go. He should've fought harder to make something of himself and take care of his family."

Lennox turns down her lips and shakes her head. "I guess that's one way to look at it. You were born into privilege. But when you have nothing and your family's wellbeing is at stake...that is love. Wanting what's best for them even if that means saying goodbye."

I put my hand over Lennox's stomach. "That's not my kind of love. There's no goodbye for us, Len. You're stuck with me forever." I wink. "Make your peace with it."

Lennox

I tuck the Polaroid carefully into the back of my jean shorts pocket. For a while, Dex and I sit quietly, enjoying the tranquility as the sun starts to set. We came back to Miami this week for the big annual board meeting. Over the past year, I've been watching and learning for the most part. I never thought I'd have an interest in corporate business. Actually, I still don't. But I am very interested in people.

I like to understand what motivates people. What makes employees loyal and determined, or what makes them give up.

Spencer is my eyes in the corporate office. We offered her a spot on the marketing team, but she really hit her stride as Hank's executive assistant. She's loyal and smart, so Hank is attached. Spencer likes that Hank calls her Ms. Brenner, and never asks her to fetch his coffee. It was a good match. Not to mention, now Spencer gets first dibs on all the juicy office gossip and keeps me well-informed on the morale of the company.

That's my dream for Hessler Group. Dex is busy building a rich empire, while I want to make sure that the people building the empire are never put on visual leadership boards for comparison purposes. They should never have to endure customers calling them profane names as they bite their tongues or face being fired for standing up for themselves. I'm not a numbers girl, but I know this company needs me. It needs a pulse and a heart. I have a voice...a powerful one. I'm learning to use it.

I know Dottie's end goal was to help Dex find love. But even if it's just a hunch, I like to think that she had me in mind for bigger things, too. That I was always a part of the picture. Love, loyalty, and family—all the things Dottie wanted for her grandson and her company. Who knows...maybe I was the key.

"Are you ready to go, baby? It's about a thirty-minute drive back to our hotel," Dex says. He squeezes my shoulders before hoisting himself up and holding his hand out for me.

"What's going to happen to this place?" I grunt as Dex tugs me to my feet.

"I have no idea." He collects my sandals and slips them back on my feet one by one.

A little off balance with my belly getting bigger, I have to brace myself with my hand on his shoulder. Dex rises and then scours my face as I flutter my eyelashes at him.

"Oh, no," he murmurs as if he can read my mind.

I nod. "Oh, yeah."

"Baby...no. The renovations would be worth more than the property itself. We can find a much nicer place closer to the office."

When we first moved back to Las Vegas, I insisted we keep

Dex's old home. Yes, we could've purchased something far more extravagant, but I didn't want luxury. I wanted happiness. We have dinner with Avery and Finn at least twice a week. My parents come over, and Dex fires up the grill almost every single weekend. We conceived our son on the very bed where I tried to kiss Dex for the first time...and he turned me down. I still like to remind him of that from time to time.

"No, Dex, this place. We have to. Yes, the renovations will cost a small fortune, but we have it. They may take years, but that just means it'll be ready when we have to come back. This is where we're going to raise our family. Where Dottie and Jacob started everything." With a pleading look in my eyes, I cradle my sweet baby boy. My son would love this view, I'm sure of it.

Dex looks around, a pained expression on his face. "It's thirty minutes from the office, Len. Maybe an hour with traffic."

"We'll build at-home offices and work from here half the week. We can do everything virtually these days."

He squints one eye. "Being right on the marina isn't safe for the kids."

I point to the edge of the property line. "We can build a fence and a safety rail behind it. We'll install cameras with security notifications anytime someone's on the dock, and most importantly, we will teach our kids to swim early. We might not even need to teach them." I pump my brows at him. "You're half-dolphin, I swear. It's in their DNA."

"The nearest Subway is over half an hour away."

"That's DoorDash's problem," I sass.

He laughs. "You're serious? This'll be a huge undertaking. We're going to have to build our home from the ground up. You want to take on a construction project like this when you're pregnant and then finish it with a newborn? I'm telling you, baby, this stuff always gets more complicated than you originally intend. You never know what you're getting into."

"I'm good with complicated." I wink at him. "And not knowing what I'm getting into."

He laughs, understanding the irony of my statement. "It's a sweet idea, and I hate to say no, but I really don't think it's going to work for us. Just on safety alone."

"Fine," I huff out. He has a point. Everything is rotting and the property is so overgrown it looks like a jungle. It'd take a forest fire to clear out the foliage and make this place livable.

Grabbing Dex's shoulders, I rise to my tiptoes and find his warm lips. I kiss him sweetly...at first. He wraps his arms around me, pulling me tightly against his body. I slide my tongue into his mouth, and almost instantly, I feel the bulge through his jeans growing against my belly. He tries to step away, but I lock my hands around his neck, keeping him close.

"Are you trying to seduce me?" he asks, finally breaking our kiss.

"A little." I smile at him innocently. "Is it working?"

He rubs his hand behind his neck. "Yeah...kind of. It's been a while." He laughs.

I've been toggling from sleepy to nauseous for the past few months, and it hasn't been the sexiest start to my pregnancy. Dex hasn't been pushy in the slightest. Instead, he rubs my back, brings me soup in bed, and presses cool compresses against my forehead.

"We're parked right out front. Can you wait thirty whole minutes, or want to go get into some trouble?"

"Really, Mrs. Hessler?" he asks in surprise. There's a boyish look of glee on his face. "There's my old firecracker of a girl. You sure you're up for car sex?"

"Sure am." I remind myself the third row flattens, making a flatbed to lie on. I am in no condition for bouncy maneuvers with my belly this round.

Feeling the familiar excitement and stirring between my thighs, I grab Dex's hand and try to lead him off the dock, but my hand slips from his. I turn around to see my husband's feet planted, staring at the property, then pivoting to stare out at the water behind him. He pulls out his phone, and I pout.

"What're you doing?" I step back toward him, a little

perturbed that he got me all worked up, and now he's stalling.

"Making a call."

"For what?"

"To buy my wife our dream home."

I drop my jaw. "Just because I offered you car sex?" I chuckle.

He shakes his head. "No, I forgot for a moment. When I couldn't see clearly, you could. The smartest thing I can do is trust you, Lennox Hessler. If you say this is where we should raise our family, then that's what we're going to do." He surveys the land again. "But we'll be building a really big fence, just so you know."

I place my hands against his cheeks. "Dex, thank you. That means more to me than you could ever know. I love you so much."

"I love you too." He pulls my hand from his cheek and kisses my palm.

I smirk at him. "And I'm about to give you the best car blowjob you've ever had in your life."

He bursts out laughing and tucks his phone back into his pocket. Dex weaves his fingers in mine, leading us with haste toward the car. "Okay, Trouble. I'll make the call later. We're not wasting any more time."

ACKNOWLEDGEMENTS

To my hubby who reminded me daily that reorganizing my office for the fifth time in one week was blatant procrastination. Thank you for being a superhero, bringing me endless cups of coffee, and for confiscating my laptop and requiring me to sleep and eat so my brain could function. I started this story while you were away, and I should've known I couldn't finish it until you got home. My forever best friend and the source inspiration for all the best banter.

To Solange, for everything. You metaphorically held my hand when I was in the thick of it and none of it made sense. Thank you for reminding me to trust my voice. You pull out my absolute best work every single time. I am growing right along my stories, thanks to you.

To Meredith, for your keen eye and all of your support, start to finish, as we got the best version of *Snapshot* ready. Thank you for helping me elevate this story in every single way. I am so incredibly grateful for everything you continue to teach me.

To Kristin, I've lost count of how many beautiful books we've worked on together. Or how many times you've saved my tush. Or how many times you've encouraged me to trust my vision. I am so grateful for every pep talk when I was at my lowest and for every inside joke when I needed to laugh the most. Thank you, my friend, for always knowing exactly what I need.

To Trisha and Tatyana, thank you for being Team Kay and supporting me through every pivot and adjustment, and for helping me put out all the little fires. We've come such a long way in such a short time, all because of your genius. Thanks to your tireless work, I was able to focus on bringing Dex and Lennox over the finish line. I would not be able to do any of this without you amazing ladies! I'm so grateful for you both.

To Shaima, for being my emotional support person through every stage of doubt. Every time I can't see the light at the end of the tunnel, you remind me to be true to myself, and I am forever in your debt, my friend.

To Allison and Cathleen, thank you for your fervent enthusiasm, your kindness, and your positive energy every time I need it the most. You guys are absolute superheroes.

To the entire Page & Vine editing and marketing team who has worked so hard to make *Snapshot* a magical experience, thank you so much for your dedication, especially in a pinch.

To my street team, Masterlist, OG readers, and the million other names I've used for my incredible reader support team. You guys are the reason I'm still here and clicking away at my keyboard. I can't thank you enough for all the precious time spent reading my stories. This industry is here because of you. These stories only come alive because of you. Thank you to each and every single one of you.

Last but not least, to my new readers and friends, thank you for taking a chance on me. I hope Lennox and Dex brought you as much joy as they've brought me. In a world full of wonderful stories, I am so honored you chose to go on this adventure with me. I really hope to see you again!

ABOUT THE AUTHOR

Kay Cove is a contemporary romance author, committed to crafting plot focused stories with sassy heroines and dirty-talking MMCs, full of witty banter and situations that force flawed characters to grow. She likes to challenge herself by writing in a variety of sub-genres.

After a successful career in corporate HR, she ultimately decided to pursue her dream of becoming a published author. Her current works include, the *Real Life, Real Love* series, *Camera Shy,* and the *PALADIN* Series.

Born in Colorado, Kay currently resides in Georgia with her husband and two sweet and rambunctious little boys.

ALSO BY KAY COVE

Lessons in Love
Camera Shy
Snapshot
Selfie (Summer 2025)

Real Life, Real Love
Paint Me Perfect
Rewrite the Rules
Owe Me One
Sing Your Secrets
First Comes Forever

Paladin
Whistleblower
Tattletale